P9-AOY-933

ALSO BY SAUL BELLOW

Him with His Foot in His Mouth and Other Stories

The Dean's December

To Jerusalem and Back: A Personal Account

Humboldt's Gift

Mr. Sammler's Planet

Mosby's Memoirs and Other Stories

Herzog

Henderson the Rain King

Seize the Day

The Adventures of Augie March

The Victim

Dangling Man

MORE DIE OF HEART-BREAK

SAUL BELLOW

VIKING

VIKING
Penguin Books Canada Ltd. 2801 John Street,
Markham, Ontario, Canada L3R 1B4
Penguin Books, Harmondsworth, Middlesex, England
Viking Penguin Inc., 40 West 23rd Street, New York,
New York 10010 U.S.A.
Penguin Books Australia Ltd., Ringwood, Victoria,
Australia
Penguin Books (N.Z.) Ltd., 182-190 Wairau Road,
Auckland 10, New Zealand

First published in Canada by Penguin Books Canada
Limited, 1987

Printed and bound in the United States of America

Canadian Cataloguing in Publication Data

Bellow, Saul
More die of heartbreak
ISBN 0-670-81899-2
I. Title
PS3503.E4488M67 1987 813′.52 C87-093580-1

Although portions of this novel are derived from real events, each character in it is fictional, a composite drawn from several individuals and from imagination. No reference to any living person is intended or should be inferred.

Last year while he was passing through a crisis in his life my Uncle Benn (B. Crader, the well-known botanist) showed me a cartoon by Charles Addams. It was an ordinary cartoon, good for a smile, but Uncle was hung up on it and wanted to discuss it elaborately. I didn't feel like analyzing a cartoon. He insisted. He mentioned it in so many connections that I became irritated and considered having the damn thing framed for his birthday. Hang it on the wall and be rid of it, I thought. Benn could get on my nerves now and then as only a person holding a special place in your life can. He did hold a special place, definitely. I loved my uncle.

What was curious and deserves to be noted is that he didn't much care for the rest of Addams's work. To leaf through the big collection, *Monster Rally*, in the end depressed him. The sameness of it, black humor for the sake of blackness, was boring. It was only the one cartoon that struck him. A pair of lovers was its subject—the usual depraved-desolate couple in a typical setting of tombstone and yews. The man was brutal-looking and the long-haired woman (I think the fans call her

Morticia) wore a witch's gown. The two sat on a cemetery bench holding hands. The caption was simple:

"Are you unhappy, darling?"
"Oh yes, *yes!* Completely."

"Why should this get me?" said Uncle.

"Yes, I wonder too."

He apologized. "You're tired of having it dragged into the conversation five times a day. I'm sorry, Kenneth."

"Taking your situation into account, I can sympathize. Other people's obsessions don't turn me on. I can weather this one for a while—but if it's satire or caricature you want, why not Daumier or Goya, one of the masters?"

"You don't always have a choice. And I haven't got your culture. In the Midwest, minds are slower. I can see that Addams isn't in a class with the greats, but he makes a contemporary statement, and I like his meshugah approach to love. He isn't manipulating anybody. Unlike Alfred Hitchcock." Uncle had taken a strong dislike to Hitchcock. "From Hitchcock you get a product. Addams works from his own troubled nature."

"For centuries love has made suckers of us, so it isn't just *his* troubled nature."

Uncle bent his heavy shoulders in silence. He didn't accept my remark, and this was his way of refusing delivery. He said, "I wouldn't have wanted to talk to Hitchcock even for two minutes, whereas with Addams I think I could have a significant conversation."

"I doubt it. He wouldn't respond."

"In spite of being my junior by decades, you've seen more of life than I have," said Uncle. "I grant you that." What he meant was that I had been born and brought up in France. He would introduce me as "my Parisian nephew." He himself liked to disclaim worldliness altogether. Of course he had seen a great deal, but maybe he hadn't looked hard enough. Or not with practical intent.

I said, "You'd have to admit to Addams that it was only this one cartoon that you admired."

"One, yes. But it goes to the fundamentals."

And then Benn began to tell me, as a person in crisis will, about the fundamentals as he saw them. Disoriented by his troubles (his unhappy attempt at marriage), he wasn't altogether clear.

"Every life has its basic, characteristic difficulty," he said. "One theme developed in thousands of variations. Variations, variations, until you wish you were dead. I don't think obsession is quite the word you want. I don't like repetition compulsion either, with all respect for Freud. Even *idée fixe* isn't right. An *idée fixe* can also be a cover-up or feint for something too disgraceful to disclose. Sometimes I wonder whether my theme has any connection with plant morphology. But the occupation is probably irrelevant. If I had been a florist or, as my mother hoped, a pharmacist, I'd still hear the same deadly *Bong bong bong!* . . . Towards the end of your life you have something like a pain schedule to fill out—a long schedule like a federal document, only it's your pain schedule. Endless categories. First, physical causes—like arthritis, gallstones, menstrual cramps. Next category, injured vanity, betrayal, swindle, injustice. But the hardest items of all have to do with love. The question then is: So why does everybody persist? If love cuts them up so much, and you see the ravages everywhere, why not be sensible and sign off early?"

"Because of immortal longings," I said. "Or just hoping for a lucky break."

Uncle was forever proposing to hold heavyweight conversations, and you had to be careful with him. He would only increase his unhappiness by confused speculations. I had to be vigilant with myself too, for I have a similar weakness for setting things straight and I know how futile it is to work at it continually. But during his last crisis, Uncle's attempts at self-examination had to be tolerated. My job—my plain duty—was to hold his head. Where he had gone wrong was so clear that I was able to spell it out to him. Doing this increased my conceit. In ticking off his palpable errors, I saw how greatly I resembled my father—the gestures, the tones, the amiable superiority, the assurance capable of closing all gaps, of filling all of planetary space, for that matter. To discover whom I sounded like shook me up. My father is an excellent man, in his way, but I was determined to go beyond him. Made of finer clay, as they used to put it; smarter; in a different league. Where he outclassed me he outclassed me—tennis, war record (I had no such thing), in sex, in conversation, in looks. But there were spheres (and by this I mean higher spheres) where he had no standing, and I was way ahead of him. And then, in dealing with my uncle, to hear my father's accents, down to the French words he would use in setting you straight (where English wasn't subtle enough), was a deadly setback to my life plan. I had better have another look at the spheres to make sure that they *were* spheres and not bubbles. Anyway, when Uncle fell, I fell with him. It was inevitable that I should go down too. I thought I should be continually on hand. And so I was, in unforeseen ways.

Benn specialized in the anatomy and morphology of plants. The standard position of the specialist is that he knows all there is to know in his own line, without further accountability. Like: "I fix oil gauges, don't bother me with odometers." Or as the wisecrack used to go, "I don't shave people, I only lather. You get shaved across the street." Understandably, some specialties are more exacting and remove you from the world; they carry with them the right to hold aloof. Through Benn I became acquainted with some exact-science types whose eccentricities had the color of prerogatives. Benn never claimed this privilege of human distance. If he had canceled his "outside connections," he wouldn't have had so much grief from the ladies.

I can give an instance of this cancellation phenomenon: We are having lunch at the faculty club with a top scientist. The waiter, who is a student waiter, comes up to take our orders. Benn's colleague says to the young man, "Bring me the chicken à la king." The boy says, "You've eaten chicken à la king for three days running, Dad. Why not try the chili con carne?"

After a lifetime of it, the son took this in stride. The other lunchers smiled. I laughed somewhat. It was one of those sudden-glory moments. And as I was laughing I had a vision of myself in profile as a man-sized monkey wrench, the lower jaw opening. I am subject to such involuntary pictures. This unflattering one may have been suggested by the metallic company I was keeping.

His extreme absentmindedness did the scientist friend no harm with his colleagues. It meant that he was far away, doing his duty on the frontiers of his discipline, so goodbye kith and kin. Top scientists are a princely caste. After all, they are the inmost, foremost intelligences of the two superpowers. The Russians have theirs as we have ours. It's really a pretty high privilege.

Well, the absentmindedness is really not such a big deal. Everybody understands that while mastering nature, you have a clear right to leave humdrum humanity, which isn't going anywhere on its own. We are looking at a posthistorical elite, and so forth. But in this respect as in others, Uncle was different. He didn't ask to be excused from the trials of creaturely existence. He *conspicuously* didn't. In this he might have been considered retarded by fellow specialists. Even I sometimes thought him retarded, humanly more confused than many persons of normal gifts. Nobody ever accused him of being dumb. In his specialty, his brilliance was conceded. Besides which he was observant and he read a lot—looking, as Caesar said of Cassius, "quite through the deeds of men." If I were playing Caesar I would speak these lines sarcastically. To Caesar in his greatness the accomplishments on which ordinary people pride themselves are beneath contempt. Caesar was by far the smarter man. But one thing is certain—Uncle didn't look through the deeds of women. Otherwise, if he applied himself, his judgment wasn't too bad.

So when he began to talk about the complexities of existence it was better (for his own sake) not to encourage him. Genius though he might be in the vegetable kingdom, his high-level seriousness could be harrowing. He sometimes had the effect on me of a bad driver failing to back into a parking space—ten tries and no luck; you wanted to grab the wheel from him. Yet when he stopped being "analytical" and the thought-bosh ended, he could surprise you. He had an uncommon gift of direct self-description. On the simplest level he could tell you in detail what he felt—what effects an aspirin had on him, what it did to the back of his neck or the inside of his mouth. I was curious about this, because for the life of them most people can't describe what goes on inside. Alcoholics or druggies are too confused, hypochondriacs are their own terrorists, and most of us are aware only of a metabolic uproar within. Well, matter is being disintegrated within, in the cyclotron of the organism. But if Uncle took a beta-blocker for his blood pressure, he could give a minute account of the physical reactions and the emotional ones as well—his descent into despondency. And if you bided your time discreetly he would eventually tell you his most secret impressions. It's true that I often had to help him locate them, but once he had grasped them he was only too glad to talk.

Physically he was on the large side. The job nature had done with him was easy to make fun of. My father, who didn't have the gift for humor he thought he had, liked to say that his brother-in-law was built like a Russian church—bulb-domed. Uncle was one of those Russian Jews (by origin) who have the classic Russian face, short-nosed, blue-eyed, with light thinning hair. If his hands had been bigger he might have been a ringer for Sviatoslav Richter, the pianist. The weight of *those* hands, when Richter advances on the piano, drags the arms from the sleeves of his tailcoat so that they hang well below the knees. In Uncle's case it wasn't the hands but the eyes that were conspicuous. Their color was hard to fix; they were blue—marine blue, ultramarine (the pigment is made with powdered lapis lazuli). More striking than the color was his gaze, when he looked at you in earnest. There were times when you felt the power of *looking* turned on you. The eye sockets resembled a figure eight lying on its side and this occasionally had the effect of turning you topsy-turvy and put strange thoughts into your head—like: This is the faculty of seeing; of seeing *itself;* what eyes actually are for. Or: The light pries these organs out of us creatures for purposes of its own. You certainly don't expect a power like the power of light to let you alone. So that when Benn sounded off about the complexities of existence and talked about "social determinants," you didn't take him seriously, since what you saw when he was bearing down on you was not the gaze of a man formed by "social determinants." However, he didn't often bear down. He preferred to come on innocent—innocent and perplexed, and even dumb-looking. That was better for all concerned. This business of deliberate or elected "innocence" is damn curious, but I'm not about to go into it here.

It's clear that I watched him closely. I guarded and monitored him, studied his needs; I fended off threats. As a prodigy, he required special care. Odd persons have their odd necessities, and my assignment was to preserve him in his valuable oddity. I had come all the way from Europe to do this, to be near him. We were doubly, multiply, interlinked. Neither of us by now had other real friends, and I couldn't afford to lose him. He didn't act the prodigy, he disliked the high manner and avoided it, being singularly independent. Not even the "laws" of physics or biology were permitted to inhibit him. The guy never spoke of "the scientific world-view." I never once heard him refer to any such thing. He avoided any show of the "valuable oddity" I attributed to him, and he didn't care for monitoring or supervision, either. He'd say, "I'm not a fugitive freak from a sideshow." A remark like that dated him. Carnival sideshows with their geeks, their bearded ladies and Ubangis with platter lips, disappeared long ago. Sometimes I suspect that they went underground and that they turn up again in private life as "psychological types."

According to one of his colleagues, and colleagues are generally the last to say such things, Benn was a botanist of a "high level of distinction." I don't suppose that this will cut much ice with most people. Why should they care about the histogenesis of the leaf, or adventitious roots? I wouldn't myself, if it hadn't been for Uncle. Scientists? Unless they do cancer research or guide you through the universe on television, like Carl Sagan, what is there to them? The public wants heart transplants, it wants a cure for AIDS, reversals of senility. It doesn't care a hoot for plant structures, and why should it? Sure it can tolerate the people who study them. A powerful society can always afford a few such types. They're relatively inexpensive too. It costs more to keep two convicts in Stateville than one botanist in his chair. But convicts offer much more in the way of excitement—riot and arson in the prisons, garroting a guard, driving a stake through the warden's head.

Being an American academic is quite a thing. You can take my word for this because I'm an academic myself. I don't say that I'm sold on being one, only that I am one—for the time being, marginally—an assistant professor of Russian literature. Exciting to me, but how many are worked up over such studies—compared, say, to Bruce Springsteen or Colonel Qaddafi or the majority leader of the U.S. Senate? I teach at the same university as Uncle Benn. Yes, he did use his influence to get me appointed. But I am not a genuine university type. In the conventional, traditional "ivory tower" sense, there is no such thing now. Yes, there are learned scholars, but they're not very conspicuous. Part of the university is in the "consciousness-raising" business. "Consciousness-raising" implies inertias which it is necessary to dispel. As the old inertias come to an end, people are eligible for a life of fuller consciousness. For instance, the long inertia of the Negroes ended in the civil rights movement and they were drawn into the consciousness community, where it was imperative to develop an "idea language." Without concepts it is impossible to advance or publicize your interests, and the universities have become a major source of the indispensable jargons that flow into public life through such channels as the courts, the pulpit, family counseling, criminology, the television networks, et cetera. This is only part of the picture. Vast powers stream from the universities into government—the Defense Department, the State Department, the Treasury, the Fed, the intelligence services, the White House. Your modern university also is a power base in biotechnology, energy production, electronics. Academics polarize light for copying machines, they get venture capital from Honeywell, General Mills, GT&E, they are corporate entrepreneurs on the grand scale—consultants, big-time pundits, technical witnesses before congressional committees on arms control or foreign policy. Even I, as a Russian expert, occasionally get into the act.

Well, my uncle was remote from all this, one of the learned scholars, almost unaware of the activities of the power players and high rollers, the engineers and the business school types. He represented (*seemed* to represent) the *old* innocence of the days before so many inertias were overcome. Here I need to say no more than that he was devoted to plant studies. To this plant-based fulfillment he wanted to add certain human satisfactions—normal, ordinary satisfactions. So he did. And then items for the pain schedule began to appear. A few simple facts will make it all very plain. After fifteen years as a widower-bachelor he got married again. His second wife was very different; she was more beautiful than the first, more difficult, more of a torment. Naturally *she* never saw herself in such a light, but there you are. She was a beauty. The beauty and the charm were up front. Nobody was invited to go behind them to get a different perspective. Uncle was perfectly willing to see her as she preferred to be seen. All he wanted was to live peacefully. Two human beings bound together in love and kindness, a universal human aim which shouldn't be so hard to accomplish. In the West, anyway, people are still trying to do it, rounding off the multitude of benefits they enjoy. I can't speak here of the rest of mankind, convulsed with its struggles at a lower stage of development.

Carried away by "unreasoning passion or attraction"—the second dictionary definition of "infatuation," the first being "made foolish"—Benn spoke of his bride as if she were a "beloved" in a poem by Edgar Allan Poe: "Thy hyacinth hair, thy classic face." First hearing this from him, I lost my bearings altogether. My response was dead silence. I had been away, visiting my parents abroad, and he had taken advantage of my absence to marry this lady without prior consultation. He damn well knew that he should have discussed it with me. We had that kind of relationship. I never dreamed that he might be so irresponsible, downright flaky. Breaking the news to me, which was like a slap in the face, he moved immediately to disarm me by declaring his love in highfalutin terms—"hyacinth hair" and "classic face"! Christ, what was I supposed to say! I can't bear to have this kind of stuff laid on me, and I was sore as hell. I never hinder people from expressing their emotions. *Let* them! He understood that it was a principle with me to defer to their feelings and make allowances for the awkwardness or vulgarity into which even well-developed people can fall when one of the more powerful sentiments descends on them. Even a four-star general, a man highly respected by his NATO colleagues, will sing a Bing Crosby "Boobooboobooo" refrain in a moment of softening or weakness about love. The best term for this gap between high achievement and personal ineptitude is "barbarism"! My uncle offered me Poe's Helen: "thy beauty is to me/Like those Nicaean barks of yore . . ." Trying to appease me. I would as lief have had Bing Crosby. I couldn't have been more depressed and angry. I happened to know the bride. She was Matilda Layamon. I suppose you would have to concede the classic face, and as a student of plants he would naturally go for hyacinth hair. At this point I remembered Wordsworth's coldhearted scientist who would botanize upon his mother's grave and I thought, Is this what happens when these guys stop botanizing on the grave, and their hearts return to *normal*!

It wasn't exactly fair to put Uncle into this category. He *was* a man of feeling. To keep track in this day and age of the original feelings, the feelings referred to by some Chinese sage as "the first heart," is no easy matter, as any experienced adult can tell you. If the "first heart" hasn't been distorted out of recognition, it's been thrown into the ego furnace to keep your pragmatic necessities warm. But Uncle *was* a man of feeling, especially family feeling, and pious about his parents. On a pretext once, he got me out to the cemetery and he cried a bit at the graveside. He himself had chosen the plant that bordered the two plots: a thumb-shaped dark-green succulent—of no special scientific interest, he said. This was an aside, but it was also a mention. Any plant would draw a comment from him. I even thought that these succulents acted as intermediaries, conveying something or other to him from his dead.

I was forced to wonder whether *I* would ever shed a tear at the graves of my parents, assuming I outlived them. I don't have a robust constitution, whereas my father is biologically very successful, a man of cast-iron good looks who still attracts women in his late sixties. Kidding himself about this, he remarked a couple of years ago that the sentimental old ballad "Will you love me in December as you did in May?" in his case should go: "Will you love me in December as you did in November?" He hasn't got much ironic distance on himself, but he does make a funny remark now and again. As for my mother, she looks her age, and more. Physically, she has lost ground. Not at all robust. About ten years her brother's senior, she doesn't resemble him at all.

Now I have to tell you up front that I approach my uncle with the thought that what everybody today requires is a fresh mode of experience. This is demanded as a right, virtually in the human rights category. "Give me a new mode of experience, or else get lost." This is no minor item of individual psychology. . . . And please don't get me wrong. I take very little pleasure in theories and I'm not going to dump ideas on you. I used to be sold on them, but I discovered that they were nothing but trouble if you entertained them indiscriminately. We are looking at matters for which theorizing brings no remedy. Still, you don't want to miss what's happening under your very eyes, failing to recognize how disappointing the familiar forms of experience have become.

All of this, not to beat around the bush, refers to the fallen state in which our species finds itself. A profusion of made-up events is supposed to divert us from it or to compensate us. The profusion, often passing for "information," is really a disguise for kitsch entertainment. Death also, while you enjoy a viewer's immunity from it, is entertaining, as it was in imperial Rome, or in 1793. As, today, Sadat is murdered, Indira Gandhi is assassinated, the Pope himself is gunned down in St. Peter's Square, while, personally unharmed, *you* live to see more and more and more, until after many deferrals death gets personal even with you. The jumpmaster says, "You bail out next."

Curious, I said to my uncle, "Uncle, how do you picture death—what's your worst-case scenario for death?"

"Well, from the very beginning there have been pictures—inside and outside," he said. "And for me the worst that can happen is that those pictures will stop."

Uncle was not worried about a fresh mode of experience because he had always interpreted experience for himself. He had furnished his *own* pictures.

To get on with this small aside: Events are profuse, but (and this is what "a fallen state" signifies) the personal space for their accommodation is very limited. A good observer who knew General Eisenhower well suggests that the European invasion Ike organized and supervised was to him personally an external event. He had no inner theater corresponding to the European theater of war. Maybe the struggle for Europe was not too much for Churchill personally, and de Gaulle may have *thought* he personally was up to it—he could contain the whole history of civilization, and maybe he was its favorite vessel. Stalin wasn't even interested in such exercises. For him it was enough that he could order anybody at all to be killed.

Now let's cut the theorizing (which is like a small case of leprosy—you lose a toe now and then; none of the main members have to be affected).

I recommend to everybody Admiral Byrd's memoirs as an introduction to this primary modern theme. *Alone* is the book I refer to, an uncanny piece of work. I read it because Uncle Benn, who had been in the Antarctic, insisted. Commenting on people isolated in small groups during the long polar night, Byrd says that under such conditions it didn't take them long to find each other out. And what was it that they so quickly found out? "The time comes when one has nothing to reveal to the other, when even his unformed thoughts can be anticipated, his pet ideas become a meaningless drool." Recall Charlie Chaplin in *The Gold Rush*. When he and his bearded pal are snowbound and starving, Charlie turns into a chicken in the eyes of his hallucinated partner. Here comic fantasy steps in. However, the strict truth is merciless and Byrd puts it to you straight: "There is no escape any where. You are hemmed in on every side by your inadequacies and the crowding pressures of your associates." So in the coldest cold on the face of the earth, X-rays are struck off, showing in gray and white the deformities and diseases of civilized personalities, and your own are at the center. If you had to spend six months in solitude on the dark side of the moon rummaging your bosom, what rich materials do you suppose you would turn up?

Slightly different in emphasis is the Russian version of this, which I found, as a Russian literature nut, in books like Shalamov's *Kolyma*. Kolyma is one of the most northerly of the forced labor camps. There the authorities played a peculiar game with the prisoners, and kept them always at the point of death. A pair of them creep out to the permafrost grave of a recently buried official and steal the stiff's socks and underpants. Beyond rigor mortis, he is solid ice through and through. These garments, traded for bread, might extend life by several days. The policy of the camp administration was to keep you just a few degrees above the survival level. Thus you were challenged to give metaphysical grounds for wishing to exist at all. What for? And sometimes it was not fully clear to you that you really did exist. If a sworn statement were demanded, you might not be able to say confidently that you were indeed alive. But the Soviet system itself contrived this, and as all the evil was done by the authorities, the individual slave laborer had nothing to accuse himself of. It was only his body in outward history that was in exile and enslaved. In the West, sleeping on down pillows and percale sheets, a very different ordeal had to be faced.

I can't say whether it's really worthwhile to read all the Russian stuff I read professionally. That's not for me to judge. What I can tell you is that it sometimes provides curious perspectives. I'm thinking, now, of informal statements made by one of Stalin's pals, Panteleimon Ponomarenko—still an apologist. He tells you that the tasks of government are heaped up on the heirs of the Revolution like a mountain of filth, that the necessary cruelties are so vast, so vile, the crimes so staggering, that the innocence of the masses has to be protected by their leaders. This is why so many operations have to be "closed." The "open" facts with which the populace is supplied keep it in a world of kindly illusion, like Rebecca of Sunnybrook Farm. The sacrifice of the bureaucracy is to assume the whole priestlike burden of secrecy. Thus the masses are shielded in their innocence and can be naively happy. And all governments are more or less like this—Grand Inquisitors who protect the frail multitude. (Not all governments, of course, have massacred their *own* innocents.) So it's "Keep 'em in the dark for their own good," and this explains why the Russians are hermetically sealed off from the rest of the world. Such brutal sentimentalism about the innocence of peoples is a common fiction of politicians everywhere. More than likely nobody is innocent, and the masses really share the cynicism of their rulers. Canny habits of mind are widely distributed. Outer forces inject themselves into us, penetrating the very nervous system. When the individual discovers them inside his own head, their appearance seems to him entirely natural and what these forces say he can truly understand, just as Hitler and the population of Germany spoke a common language. Voices, live or taped, approach from the air and speak to you, or for you. Heard in extreme isolation, they can have a special significance. Depressed, you dial a voice to talk you out of committing suicide, to recite a prayer, or to bring you to a sexual climax. Many papers list the numbers. According to your special sexual need a voice will incite, talk sweet, talk dirty, and work you up until you get your rocks off. Give your Visa or Amex number and you will be charged on your monthly bill, as for any other service. You lie in bed with your instrument, your cordless phone, and it's like a retake of the State of Nature, a second return to beginnings. It reminds you somewhat of Hobbes and Locke, only it never occurred to Hobbes what numbers you might dial in your new solitude.

Almost in relief I take down one of my uncle's books and open it, and I read about the similarities and differences between *Selaginella* and *Lycopodium*, the ligulate leaves or the polystelic stems, or how the female gametophyte nourishes itself on material stored in the megaspore. Now I am in a different world altogether. Pure, pure, pure! But I say no more about this here. I have an urgent project to get on with.

My uncle spent one season in Antarctica and had great respect for Admiral Byrd. Byrd's book changed Uncle's mind about the navy, which formerly he had thought of as high tech on the water. In any case, the Antarctic had a beneficial, calming effect on Uncle because the environment was all but plant-free. Abundant vegetation could excite his imagination so strongly that it affected his judgment. But in Antarctica you had to have your wits about you. If you didn't watch out you might lose your fingers or a piece of your nose, so while the grandeur of the surroundings might be dreamlike, the murderous cold acted against all fantasy. There you saw as nowhere the features of the planet in pure forms and colors. Benn made a helicopter expedition to collect lichens—he said they formed brilliant patches against the snow—on the slopes of Mount Erebus. I have a photo of the landing. In it he is muffled in insulated clothing like a science fiction character or one of the moon astronauts. Too bad the hues of the lichens don't show.

Uncle was a magical person to me when I was a kid, and somehow he remained one. To my father he was the goofy scientist. Dad broke us up when he happened to be at home for dinner, with ludicrous imitations of Uncle's gestures, showing how Benn would shoot away an objection with his thumb, or check under his jacket to be sure that his shirt was tucked in. Dad was a clumsy mimic; it was just fun in the family circle. I'd laugh, of course, and then I'd go to my room and paint a bar in india ink, indicating betrayal, in the private diary I kept when I was at the *lycée*. Sometimes Mother objected: "Not fair. You make him too quirky. That's not the way his feet point out." Yet she enjoyed the fun too, and her protests weren't very strong. Daddy's parodies only increased my loyalty to Uncle. Uncle had whatchamacallit for me—charisma. I don't really trust that word. It sounds like some disease. "What did the fellow die of?" "I think it was charisma that killed him." As sinister as AIDS—and incidentally, Uncle made it his business in his steady scientific fashion to inform himself about herpes, AIDS and other venereal diseases. Assuming a purely clinical tone, he made horrific conversation about rectal and pharyngeal gonorrhea, cytomegalovirus, enterically transmitted protozoal infections, the insertion of a fist into the partner's anus common in the homosexual act. He sometimes added that you might appraise an age by the nature of its sicknesses—that a death from AIDS was analogous to the judgment of human inadequacy reported by Byrd, an elaborate terrifying organic figure for the same. I mention this clinical interest because it foreshadows Uncle's later preoccupation with the demon of sexuality. He tried to take refuge from that in marriage.

Sizing up the people I knew to see which of them might be capable of love in a classic form, I decided that Uncle Benn was a front-runner. He was born with that increasingly rare capacity. He actually could fall in love, I thought. For me he had the "magics." This is the term I've substituted for "charisma." Henry James was fond of "magics." Like the word "numerosity," used by no other writer that I know of. For me Uncle had the magics, and his glamour only increased when Papa put him down.

Papa was, he still is, such a dude. And I resemble him, inevitably. Sons are bound to pick up the graces and gestures of their daddies. I was using his conversational tricks and mannerisms before I could know what I was doing. In what follows I may appear to poke fun at him. Disavowal is useless. One is forever finding pockets of venom beside one's best feelings, so let's not ask for the moon. My father was an American Francophile, originally from Valparaiso, Indiana, determined to be a Parisian. The Second World War delayed his arrival, but he was there as soon as possible immediately after. When the navy discharged him and the Germans were driven out, there he was—a Parisian. My mother, too, was happy in Paris, as long as you could still hire servants. From my side, I can see nothing wrong in any of that. Parisians are just as free to become New Yorkers, or Bostonians, as are Koreans and Cambodians; so to opt for France seems a reasonable turnabout for an American. Eighty thousand U.S. citizens are said to have settled in Rome alone. Some Parisians will tell you that to leave Paris is exile, if not death, yet lots of them do fine in New York. My father's motives were romantic or impulsive. As a student of French literature and politics, he might have taken to heart the psychotic anti-Semitism of the French, or recalled the riots set off at the time of the Dreyfus case by Drumont of *La Libre Parole* against the "Yids who poison France." To be fair, it wasn't Drumont who drew him but Stendhal and Proust. Also the Seine, the restaurants, the women.

While Uncle had certain magics yet to be described, my dad had magics of his own, and if I elected to follow Benn's way it was not a choice entirely of strength. Physically, I resemble my father. I'm one of those slender Trachtenbergs; my face is narrow, my hair black, and I am a dolichocephalic. Benn has a round face, a wider figure. Papa in his heyday was a strutter. He put on the kind of sex display you see in nature films, the courting behavior of turkey cocks or any of the leggier birds. (Storks clatter their beaks to attract the females.)

Dad was a hit with women. I, who wasn't, nevertheless went through the same motions. I shared his keen taste for classy shirts and sumptuous neckties, especially the red raw silks. I can wear a fine tie by reason of my height. In a shorter man, either the knot is too fat or half the tie hangs below the belt. The average figure has become bigger than it used to be. But I'm somewhat too tall for my character; I haven't got the sort of character that requires so much height, and this discrepancy has made me a diffident person. Earlier I compared myself to a man-sized monkey wrench—I put up little resistance to fantasy. But very often I've been told that I look a lot like the actor John Carradine. In the Westerns, he used to play a consumptive man of breeding. It was believed, in the good old days, that the air of Wyoming or Arizona, if you were from the East, would cure your asthma or TB and make you fit to become President. But skinny Carradine wasn't meant to live, he was part skeleton anyway, and always died in a gunfight. He was an extreme asthenic. A close comparison would not discover too many similarities. I do have the longish center-parted hair falling heavily to each side, like his, and the same gaunt stoop. One additional difference: French, my first language, develops your mouth muscles because of the demanding labial sounds. So just picture John Carradine in a French version. And I might have had a more suitable appearance for a man with my inclinations, which are more like the inclinations of Uncle Benn. Besides, I am no actor. Benn has a build more suitable to his temperament.

I've already said that there was a Russian flavor to Uncle as there is to many Russian Jews. Somebody ought to do a monograph on the Jewish responses to the various lands of their exile, those in which their hearts expanded and those which were most forbidding. The more Germany rebuffed them, the more eager they were to Germanize themselves. Russia was peculiarly nasty, but Jews nevertheless were strongly drawn to the Russians. The Slavic idea somehow suited Uncle. He even had the broad rounded back oftenest noted among Russians, and it wasn't the scholarly habit that gave him this interesting curvature. I've observed it among Slavs who never cracked a book. They look as if they carried a wing case under their clothing. And then there's the diffident air, which is an adaptive disguise of people who have potent essences and don't want you to know about them. As a boy in Paris I was attracted to Russians and I sought them out. Making use of my father's connections, I used to visit Boris Souvarine, the great biographer of Stalin. The quickest way to learn any subject is to make private contacts with those who know it best and get them talking. Alexandre Kojève, the Russian Hegel expert, also came to the house. The conversation of great men gave me such education as I have, and I wasn't aware that I was being educated, I was simply pursuing my Russian interests. I learned the language early and grew up to be a specialist. My parents were annoyed when I took a job at Uncle's university and moved to the Middle West, which they had been so eager to leave. It seemed perverse of me, as if their only child was repudiating their worship of Europe. My mother and my uncle were natives of this city, my immigrant grandparents are buried here, my great-uncle Vilitzer was a top operator in the Democratic machine. Such an American place. Arriving, I felt conspicuously foreign. But in fact Iranians are driving the taxis, Koreans and Syrians own the vegetable markets, Mexicans wait on tables, an Egyptian services my television set, Japanese students take my Russian courses. Italians? Well, they've been here for five generations. Henry James, who was moved to ecstasies when he saw Italians in Italy, was depressed to meet them in Connecticut. America has turned all that around and given a new sense to foreignness. Of which the ultimate form perhaps is death.

Anyway, my Uncle Benn had become my closest friend, none closer, virtually the only one. In my generation such intimacies within the family are unusual. Uncles, aunts—parents, for that matter—collect dust on the mantelpiece like old Christmas cards. Noticing them in July, you say to yourself that it's time to throw them out, but you don't get around to it. Eventually they wilt and turn yellow, they die and go into the incinerator. With Uncle and me, for reasons yet to be ascertained, the case was different. Ours was a genuine, I'd say a devouring, friendship.

"Professor Chlorophyll," I called him when I was a kid, and I took his profession for granted. Now I puzzle over it, realizing that he was a genuine botanist, realizing also that plants are very strange beings (this recognition I also owe to him). There must have been upwards of a million children of greenhorns delivered in this town around the time of his birth, and of them all, only he became a professor of plant morphology. Others went into the liquor business, or used cars, or household appliances, or the Bureau of Streets and Sewers. In a better sense of the term he was a deviant, and his deviation had its effect on me. Everything he had he put on the plants. Let's not speak of uncles now—let's put it that my most intimate companion, coinhabitant of my bosom, my friend, was a Jewish botanist. "Applied science" was not his field—no agronomy, no genetics. Out in the Negev there are experimenters working with high-protein algae. What looks like puddle-grown slime may save the famished populations of Chad or rural India. Uncle had no such useful orientation. The position he took up amongst the plants can't be seen for what it was if you leave out his imaginative activities. What you have to consider is a Jew who moves into the vegetable kingdom, studying leaves, bark, roots, heartwood, sapwood, flowers, for their own sake. There was something Druidical about this. Of course he didn't worship the plants, he only contemplated them. Contemplation also needs to be qualified—he saw into or looked through plants. He took them as his arcana. An arcanum is more than a mere secret; it's what you have to know in order to be fertile in a creative pursuit, to make discoveries, to prepare for the communication of a spiritual mystery. (Excuse the language; I'm in a hurry and I can't stop to pick and choose among the available terms.) If I were a painter—I would have had to be a primitivist on the order of the Douanier Rousseau—I should picture Uncle together with a tree, as a pair, as associates or buddies. A silent green circle, an opening in a forest, and against a background of waist-high ferns you have a stout man (the image of stability, though in fact extremely jumpy) in communion with a huge tree, a maple, say—old, arthritic, corpulent, swelling towards the crown like a mammoth tuba, an ancient and noble being about to break under its own weight but still capable of putting forth millions of leaves. This modern-dress Eden of my painting would combine peace, permanence or consummation with twentieth-century instability—impulses from the fallen world surrounding this green seclusion.

In a worldly perspective this "fallenness" is the bunk, religious stuff towards which strong personalities might now and then be tolerant. A full-blooded man would be engaged with government, with markets, with computers, with law, with war, with virile action—above all with public life and politics: the armed might of the superpowers, the ambitions of Stalin's heirs, the Middle East, the CIA, the Supreme Court. Or money equivalents of the same. Or sexual ones, an eroticism matching superpower politics. A mature mind would note also that the Edenic picture I have just projected contains no woman, only my contemplative uncle, whereas Rousseau's famous painting of a forest clearing has a nude at the center, lying on a recamier sofa with the tigers of desire glaring at her. This is an arcane vision, but more like the real thing.

And that's exactly it. That's my subject.

Now let's return to Uncle: A while back I spoke of an influential irregularity, and I'll explain this now. Let's start with childhood. You're a kid in a poor neighborhood, your parents are immigrants, you have to play with milk bottles on the back porch, you study the esthetics of dust motes, you sit on the curb. And by and by you make your decision to become this or that when you grow up. I don't speak now of doctoring or electrical engineering, or even Streets and Sewers, but of singular choices. You decide upon something singular and then you *become* it. Just like that? How do you know that there's a future in it? You don't. But this is what Professor Popper calls an Open Society, and in an Open Society what's to stop you? Nothing except ideas of regularity, which gain ascendancy over you as you grow older and more cagey. How can you trust a small child of a singular bent? Not even little Samuel in the Temple recognized that God was calling to him; he thought it was the High Priest, needing a drink in the night. Well, prophets are secured to God. Our times are riskier. The venturesome child is like a space walker whose lines may tear loose from the mother ship. If they do, he'll be sucked away into outer space. But three decades pass. The earnest student is immersed in the Psilophyta, the Arthrophyta, the Pterophyta, and instead of being blasted away beyond the moon, he holds a university chair. He may not have deserved to survive. Dumb luck perhaps saved him.

There are crackpot ideologists who will argue that this was an achievement of capitalism. But that's like saying that Athens made Alcibiades. Alcibiades cared about Athens, sure enough. To get what he wanted, however, he would have swapped it in a minute for Sparta or Persia.

But let me not be sidetracked again. My move to the Midwest was interpreted by my father as a rejection (excuse the jargon; so misleading). It became a double rejection since my mother also left, after years of threatening. "Ditched me," was what Father said. And he had never been a complainer. So he was alone on the Rue Bonaparte, such an enviable location. Mother moved out in protest against the life he had led her. But to say that he was alone misstates the case. He had a nice UNESCO pension, plus stock in the Pittsburgh firm that had hired him in the early years to represent it in the French-speaking parts of the Third World, where government officials educated in France were longing to have a good talk about Camus's latest play or Queneau's *Zazie*. God, they were dying for civilized gossip, and he did well at it, being clever and urbane, never cynical. Princes and military dictators were his chums all over Africa and Southeast Asia. These exotic connections made him happy. Being pleased, he pleased most of the people he met. I can't say he had no detractors, and he was often bad-mouthed as a womanizer and a frivolous character. He was not, however, a superficial person. Old categories like "libertine" simply don't apply to him. Many excellent men have made out with large numbers of women. Anyway, he has his pension and lives well. You can't budge Rudi Trachtenberg from Paris and its companionable streets. He has a circle of pals, and then there are the women, four decades of women—a benevolent society, a fan club, a veterans' organization.

Mother joined a group of medical volunteers stationed near Djibouti, where the famine victims died by the thousands, daily. She wore chino skirts, cheap cotton twill, as close to sackcloth as she could get. No more high-fashion cashmeres and silks, no more couturieres, an end to tea dates, according to the Paris convention, with Papa's girlfriends. In her letters from Somalia she asked to be remembered to her brother but avoided asking for details of his life—sunk in botany, or dredged in floury relationships by ladies who could fry him like a fish if they had a mind to. Papa also wrote, trying continually to lure me back to France with news of the Russian dissidents in Paris, and collecting names of old residents who were probably mines of research material if I was still planning to study Blok, Bely and Tsvetaeva. He could direct me to the agent who had forced Tsvetaeva's husband to work for the GPU. The man was dying of old age on a street behind the Boulevard de Sébastopol. Hurry, if you want to interview him. (I could see myself grilling this moribund old spy, laying my head on his chest to catch his dying words.) Father didn't care for these Russkis himself, but he would have had appointments set up for me. Maybe a foundation grant could be wangled to give me a year abroad. Why did I want to live in the Midwest anyway? Such a cultural throwback, unconscious of its own philistinism. "Out there they can't even spell the name of Mammon, which is just the way Mammon likes it." I answered him that I could return to Paris overnight when the philistinism became too oppressive. Travel was no problem, if the metal fatigue of Pratt Whitney engines didn't kill you, if Arab terrorists didn't shoot you down on the tarmac or a Sikh bomb plunge you into the Irish Sea.

Being busy, fully booked, having a flooded mental switchboard night and day, seems necessary for self-respect in certain circles. I have so many irons in the fire that if I had a hundred fingers I'd burn them all. Like my father before me, I do lots of traveling. Less than Uncle Benn, who is a demon traveler himself, but far too much. Knowledge of Russian will get you into politics (on the dark side) if you have a taste for thinking you're behind the scenes. So many institutes, intelligence agencies, consultantships. I could do a conference a week if I wanted to. It doesn't hurt to have known the great Souvarine in my boyhood and others, like Manes Sperber. Without being a Kremlinologist or anything like it, I have naturally followed the politics of Stalin's succession, and so forth. Familiar with dissident groups, I'm asked from time to time to give background papers. I keep up with *Kontinent* and *Syntaxis* and with the activities of Solzhenitsyn, Maximov,

Sinyavsky and Lev Navrozov—commanding figures, men of genius, some of them. I keep track also of the Russian right—fanatics, fascists, the occasional double agent (faithful to whom? unfaithful to whom?). None of the above is a basic concern, only second-order "professional activity," keeping me on the move. Meantime Uncle Benn goes on trips too, much longer ones. He flies around, but his thought lag is such—I refer to the gap between his personal interests and the passions of contemporary life—that he might as well be circling the Dead Sea on a donkey. If *he* hadn't traveled so much, I would have spent more time at home. (So many things of a serious nature to discuss with him!) Mine were mostly overnight trips to Washington or New York, whereas he made lengthy expeditions. And it was to be near him that I had emigrated, pulled out of Europe, chosen the U.S. Heartland (the spacy continent between Pennsylvania and the Pacific). Occasionally I was hurt. My sacrifice was slighted. Time was escaping through hundreds of gaps. Why wouldn't he stay put?

Well, he had his reasons. When Lena, his first wife, died fifteen years ago he began to circle the world (as if it was an electrostatic field, a cyclotron to energize his particles).

Therefore, at lunch, as he reached across the table for a roll you would see an Air-India ticket folder sticking out of his pocket.

"Another junket, Uncle? Where the hell are you going now!"

Above his ultra-blue eyes, explanatory wrinkles began to rise. He was preparing to put me off with a dignified answer. "Oh . . . Absentmindedly, last fall, not thinking, I accepted an invitation and forgot it until this prepaid ticket arrived."

He was wanted, he was flattered. There wasn't much scientific justification for these junkets. Other specialists were better suited to the specific purposes, and he admitted it. Third World colleagues must have invited him as a "Believe It or Not" memory freak. Upon request, by shutting his eyes, he could name you all the parts of the storage organ of a given plant down to the hairlets. He did this at lunch around the globe, in the Celebes or Bogotá, while a textbook was handed back and forth across the table. He was more complete than the text! His own department frowned on his traveling show. Bad business. He would have done better to stick to the classroom and the lab. But he had written lots of books and articles, some of them solid enough, others fairly mysterious, so he had a big reputation. He corresponded with cranks the world over who believed that he sympathized with their theories. All this jetting to Australia or the Antarctic (although he did know a great deal about the lichens—that was genuine: lichens, algae, fungi) had become part of his life plan.

My only aim was to protect his goddam life. He was on a dangerous course. Whenever a 747 went down I checked the passenger list. My expectations, my hopes for significant closure, were threatened. He and I had a crucial project going. His absences were a double privation for me: one, neglect of the enterprise, and two, personal. He missed me too. He'd telephone from the Celebes, from Patagonia, even. Yes, he reached me from Patagonia once, and I said, "When do you get back? You're needed here. I'm *waiting*!"

Not good, to be a man in his thirties betraying such dependency. Maybe Uncle was crisscrossing the intercontinental skies and pacing the great airports of the world in order to do the thinking he couldn't do sitting still. Maybe he was also running away from me. That, too, I should have been able to bear. I ought to concentrate on greater self-sufficiency. I said to myself, "Why was Coleridge's albatross following that goddam ship anyway? It should have been satisfied with stormy solitude. Why didn't it stick to seafood? Those sailors with their lousy English biscuits were the death of it. Also, longing for human company can be a fatal mistake." It's evident from this that I worried not only about the dangers of travel but about Uncle's basic judgment. I was afraid he would make a bad move, something "ill-advised," "rash." To be more downright, that he might do himself in when I wasn't there to stop him.

He'd yell back from Patagonia—you could hear the raging of the intervening oceans, so it seemed—"Hang in there, Kenneth. Plane on Saturday."

There was always a grand reunion. We would go to his favorite Italian restaurants, drink late, and resume conversation on the telephone first thing in the morning, then we'd have a long lunch. So much to discuss! These talks were my holidays and also the heart of my mental life.

Benn, childless, was free on weekends. I have a small daughter, with whom I used to spend Saturday afternoons until her mother took it into her head to move away to Seattle. After which I had the expenses of a kid without the duties and pleasures—which I admit were mixed pleasures. No small girl to take to the zoo to see the bears and tigers. There's no way that zoo animals can ever know it, but they're part of the divorce world.

Not that a divorce had occurred. Treckie and I never married. She talked about going downtown to get a license, but never brought herself to do it. And by and by she began to beef about the city, preparing her move by making a case against it. It was deteriorating fast, they played too rough here. You couldn't open a paper without reading that a young woman had been kidnapped, raped, pistol-whipped, doused in gasoline and set afire. Life in Seattle was bound to be pleasanter.

So in the Midwest, except for Uncle Vilitzer and his family, who held aloof, Benn and I were nearest of kin.

We were more than that. The "crucial project" in which Benn figured was so queerly special and singular that no simple statement will get it across. I thought, Would it be possible to bring to the human world what Uncle brought to plant life? He himself suggested it. He used to say, "Suppose I were to have the same ability with people that I have in the field of botany?" Well, he didn't. "I'd be one confused man," he said. A certain confusion already was evident, so that if he acted as if he had had a narrow escape, his relief was understandable. Then how did he figure in this? Well, he had a gift for one kingdom, so somebody else might have it for another. Abolish the claustrophobia of consciousness (the thing that Admiral Byrd's companions suffered from): the classic modern challenge. If you conceived of it, you were already in the running. The very imagination of it made you a possible candidate for this achievement. It would have to be done by a power of life. Calculation, deliberate measures, couldn't do it. That power of life I saw in Uncle every day, and I hoped to work my way towards it under his influence. That's what I was here for.

In some sense he had become my father. My mother had taken vows of poverty, as it were. My dad used to dress her gorgeously to compensate for his neglect. She wasn't at all busty, but she wore beautiful apparel with style—was glad to have rich silks and woolens. Becoming too old for this, she turned into a Mother Teresa. I haven't the heart to criticize her. I can recall as a small boy being taken to the dressmaker on the Rue Marbeuf. That day my father had received news of the death of *his* father. Grandfather Trachtenberg's funeral was taking place at eleven o'clock central standard time and Mother said, "We must cheer Rudi up. We'll take him to a good restaurant." She gave him a big lunch—his favorite oysters, *fines Bélons,* with a good wine. Then we went to the couturiere for a fitting. It was here, behaving like an authority on women's fashions, *à la* Proust, that he took charge. He mentioned the problem of Mama's *poitrine,* like a real Frenchman, and also made time with the girls. He was an *homme à femmes,* a chaser. A man of staggering charm, he was able to make good on his *là ci darem* promises. The lady who gave him her hand wouldn't be sorry. She wouldn't even regret going back to her husband, since a sensible person would understand that my father was a one-time event, like the Fall, or Noah's Ark. As a conversationalist he was limited, but his repertory was terrific for his purposes. He had served as a Ninety Day Wonder on a destroyer and he had seen FDR, Harry Hopkins, Churchill and Montgomery close up. In the Red Sea, Ibn Saud and his court had come aboard and camped on the fantail under an awning, roasting their own sheep there and turning their cups over to spill coffee grounds on their fine carpets. Dad had once chatted with the Grand Mufti, who even hinted at a visit in disguise to Auschwitz, where he inspected the gas chambers. In Paris, Dad had met Malraux on many occasions. Sartre had accused my father of being an American spy because he spoke French *too* well. I don't want to get started on my father, but he is indispensable for any understanding of my attachment to my mother's brother. Sometimes even Benn talked about Dad in a tone of envy because of his success with women. Benn liked to describe or imitate the way my father entered a restaurant (they did equally bad imitations of each other), the interview he subjected the *sommelier* to, the messages he sent the chef. If he had taken Proust to dinner, Father would have given him memorable entertainment.

My father, damn his eyes, was an accomplished dancer, master of all the steps back to the fox-trot and the Charleston. Waltz, rumba, conga, tango—when he opened his arms to a woman she could feel that she had come home. He presented himself with a poise that made a body who had spent years in the erotic wilderness looking for a sign exhale until she stopped breathing. To men, Papa's conduct, the style of his approach, was in bad taste. But women were less bothered by the art question. Apparently he was in a class by himself. I couldn't even come close. Couldn't form myself on his pattern. Not cut out for a ladies' man. Well before I was thirty, I had given it my best try. Failed to persuade the girls to adopt my sexual twelve-tone scale (that was how my father put it). And by the way, his conversation was chaste, clean, no offensive words, no detailed descriptions of the act. Yes, once in a while screwers' platitudes slipped out: *Elle s'exclamait à mon sujet*"; "It was like a religious experience." Balls like that. His genius was not for expression. Yet ladies were never the same after they had met Rudi Trachtenberg, whereas when they parted with me they were completely themselves, as before. . . . Why wouldn't the mother of my daughter marry me? Would she have refused my father?

I've mentioned that I had picked up many of his gestures, which were elaborate. I could begin them, but I couldn't complete them properly. With me they had a different meaning. As if I wasn't beckoning girls to come with me but asking them to take me along.

Papa didn't end a ruined *débauché*—as Casanova is described, puffy and decayed, with bad breath and venereal damages. My father is simply fine. I'm the one with the damages.

It never dawned on my old man that he had lived for women primarily. He viewed himself as a person normally interested in girls. He didn't *talk* girls. He was a wide reader and discussed all the principal modern questions. Outstanding people took him seriously. Years back, Queneau used to come to the house. We had bourbon whiskey from the PX in the days when it was hard to come by. Queneau did like bourbon, but he wouldn't have come only to get drunk. Then there was our frequent guest Alexandre Kojève, and he wouldn't have dined with dummies. I mention Kojève because of his description of Hegel completing the *Phenomenology* at *the* appropriate historical moment, within earshot of the cannon at the Battle of Jena—an epoch culminating in the victory of Napoleon and completing an edifice of universal history from which absolute knowledge, *only now possible*, might view all Being.

This is a sample of the topics discussed in our dining room: whether Man at the end of History remains alive simply as an animal; whether it is time for him to become "merely natural." This would curve about with other windings through the labyrinth of events. I grew up hearing about the partition of Europe by Hitler and Stalin, and then by Stalin and the Western powers; about the Warsaw Ghetto and the Umschlagplatz; also, the genocides, "the Gypsies of Europe roasted like coffee beans by the Nazis"; about Treblinka and the Gulag, among other terrifying place names. Whether the end of Human Time, the creation of the free Historical Individual, was at hand was a frequent topic. Nothing but high-serious stuff. No porno, sadomasochistic or pederastic lewdness for table talk. And unless your thinking is deduced from a correct conception of history, unless you live in your time, thinking will only confuse you—it will drive you nuts. The terrible result of hyperactive but unfocused consciousness is a cause of our decline.

You have to see it like this: The illuminated man is a microcosm incorporating universal Being in himself, with the proviso that he be on top of the edifice of universal knowledge. It goes without saying that I can't do this myself. However, you'll never be able in the slightest degree to judge these aberrant times if you don't know that there is such a thing as the great Hegelian overview.

Now suppose that instead of Napoleonic armies you have women, instead of Jena you have bedrooms, instead of cannon you have you-know-what—then you begin to see Papa's life in a truer light. The historical thing which millions of sex-intoxicated men were trying to do and botching, he did with the ease of a natural winner. You're lost without accurate reading of the historical compass. And Eros is the fixed pole. Papa's gift was to represent Eros. Mother was terribly upset by this, but she understood that marriage and family life couldn't be neat and tidy, with a husband like Papa. He was never rough and abusive, he was personally generous and considerate, he had warmth, he was an affectionate father. But I think you can see why I had to pull out of Paris. Because he was out of the ordinary, a special case. He didn't have to "make his soul," like other people. His was made for him by special forces. I, with my "soul in the making," had to go to America for the purpose. This can't be very clear as yet, but it will be, I promise.

Meantime we had M. Kojève in our dining room, expounding his theory that the Soviet Union, China and the associated Communist nations were faint carbons of the U.S.A., where the materialist aspirations of modern man were being gratified beyond the wildest dreams of Marx or the philosophers of the Enlightenment. The winners of October had bungled the job. I think Kojève sensed that my father's real interests, intelligent and well-read though he was, lay in a different direction. Also, my mother set a good table. There was a kind of culinary High Mass, with *rognon de veau* on the altar. I couldn't bear the urine fumes, and I have only a mild taste for wine. M. Kojève's palate was as fine as everything else about him. He ate well at the Trachtenbergs'. Naturally he would have been welcome anywhere. We're talking about Paris, after all, where a man of genius still counts for something. Paris, even though the action is no longer there, is set up to evaluate what happens everywhere else. Paris has the language for it. Together with London and Rome, it's in the phase of Tintagel, waiting for King Arthur to come again. For the Age of Gold to get its third wind.

I was in France last Christmas—Rue Bonaparte again, unchanged for some centuries—and Dad was striding up and down, talking, using both arms for emphasis. He's not stout, he's big, and as a talker he's got class. You hesitate to interrupt him. He said, "I don't challenge your affection for your uncle. I suppose he *is* a distinguished person in his field, but in other respects he's a provincial. However, I've tried never to interfere in your life."

True, in a way. Except that as a force of nature, or what have you, Dad couldn't help jamming the broadcasts from other sources.

Here he stopped and took a long look, examining me. I may have seemed inexplicably dim to him, for a son. Like the picture of a long-haired native of central China taken by a tourist. In what way was such a person his "son"? And just look how I proceed—first I'm a man-sized monkey wrench; then I'm one of the billion-plus Chinese population. Dad had all the definition, the finish, of a personage; I was still in metamorphosis. "I can't see why you want to bury yourself in the Midwest. Paris even in the doldrums still is Paris. Once in a while we have an explosion, and there are problems with the Arabs. But where you are it's barbarous. Anarchy. One of my cousins—our cousins—was shot point-blank by a mugger. A very pretty young girl too. Just a cheek wound, luckily, though she had powder burns. The adolescent rat who mugged her didn't care what he did to her looks. They do pick on girls alone in the streets. This happens daily."

"Yes, Dad, that's true."

Never mind the wavering gaunt image of a son he sees, a bad reproduction of himself; he still would like me by his side. Abandoned by my mother, whom he was devoted to in his way. That's not altogether a delusion, either. Her welfare was always one of his concerns. It's not that in old age he'd have nobody to look after him in case of a stroke. He's not the man to have a stroke. And he still has his ladies by the troop. They'd nurse him if he needed nursing. They'd never let him go to an institution, even with Alzheimer's disease. Still, they weren't his family. I can see how Papa thought of this, I can imagine in affectionate pictures how he must have looked while brooding over it. In his declining years (not that he felt much decline), his wife and son should compose the golden center of his life, instead of which they were its lunatic fringe. But that's the way it is with people, Father. The greater your achievements, the less satisfactory your personal and domestic life will be. The wives, children, brothers and other kin and assistants of our very Presidents are drunks, druggies, inverts, liars and psychopaths. I say little about secret relationships that sometimes come tragically to light and about what happens in the weeds behind the billboards . . . senators and other high officials who never can live down their Chappaquiddicks. The personal facts often are base. The scientist who didn't recognize his own son, the student waiting on tables, has set up housekeeping with one of his male graduate students. Never mind his sexual preferences (one of the blessings of the new indifference), but the private life is almost always a bouquet of sores with a garnish of trivialities or downright trash. So Papa with his old girlfriends, his son in Middle America and his wife engaged in relief work in East Africa isn't doing badly after all. Somalia, to Dad, rated higher than the Midwest because it was at least "world political"—that is, hundreds of thousands of Ethiopian tribesmen were being marched to death or trucked away for "resettlement" in trucks donated by the West for food distribution. This was preferable to whatever it was that Uncle and I thought we were up to on native soil.

To Dad, Benn was a schlump, an incompetent. His list of failings, his confused relations with women, made him on a charitable view a fun figure. What was he up to? Supposedly on botanical business, he was circling the globe, said Dad, and while in the air he met ladies who couldn't really explain what *they* were doing at an altitude of 35,000 feet and a ground speed of 650 mph. It had its funny side, as Dad described it; and Benn was funny, certainly. He also was remarkable, and this was what my father couldn't see. He missed out on Benn's largeness of mind. Large-mindedness and strength of body were the big things in Greek antiquity. As measures of the mind we now have IQ and Scholastic Aptitude Tests. The admirable body is bigger than ever in the health clubs, in aerobic exercises, jogging, Pritikin diets. The Sharper Image catalogue that comes in the mail is filled with sophisticated thousand-dollar devices for building up thighs, bellies, biceps and chests—creating a physique to swoon over. On tour, the great Schwarzenegger is accompanied by a ton and a half of steel equipment on which he works out in his hotel suite. In short, the beauty of supernatural beings, but now without wings, in a materialist interpretation.

It galls my father that my perfect French is wasted in the U.S.A. Who was there to talk to in any language, and whom did I see—the family? Uncle Vilitzer? I only read about Great-uncle Harold in the papers, I seldom saw him or his family. This old-time pol and ward boss, a machine alderman, was as crooked as they came. Grand juries couldn't nail him, though they often tried. No exaggeration to say that he could fill the bleachers of a major league ballpark with the officials he owned, and thinking it might entertain Daddy, I tried to explain some of Vilitzer's operations. He took my offering coldly. Compared to a Jacques Chirac, what was a Vilitzer? A crude American *Youpin*.

But then, the family had fought with Vilitzer. Mother had filed a lawsuit against him, and although Uncle Benn was also a plaintiff he was away in Assam, never attended the trial, and had taken no interest in the case. Vilitzer, that wild bull, was the younger brother of Grandma Crader. In her will she had named him as her executor and he made off with a part of the property, which turned out to be very valuable. So to ask whether I saw Vilitzer was a heavy irony. Back in the Rustbelt, Dad suggested, I could choose between intellectual woolgathering with Uncle Benn and the illiteracy of that animal who had given his own flesh and blood such a screwing.

There is affection between Father and me, even though I sadden him. The natural desire is for a son who will take up where you left off and advance along the same front. He wouldn't say it in so many words, but I suspect that sexually he considered me a kind of wraith. If we were to take off our clothes (I try it mentally), the comparison would be humiliating. To right the balance, I try to give myself more mental weight, develop feelings which he's deficient in. This shows how far we've fallen below the classical Greek standard. We've split things in two, dividing the physique from the mind. In Paris a father with a world-historical cock, in America an uncle with large mental gifts. Dad always asks about the little daughter I had by Treckie. He's sentimental about his only grandchild. Maybe he'd like to figure out how I came by her. He asks why Treckie and I don't get married. "She doesn't want it," I tell him. He shakes his head, unwilling to ask the direct question about how lively I am in bed. To a worldly person a bastard is no big deal. I'd be surprised if he didn't have one or two of his own, considering what aristocratic France (the *ancien régime*) has meant to him. He asks to see Treckie's letters. In that respect she doesn't neglect me; she often writes. "If I read her letters I might be able to tell you quite a lot about her," he said. Papa's motive, as I made it out, was to draw me away from Uncle. Being a husband and a father would have reduced my need for an uncle.

Mother didn't like to discuss my attachment to Benn, whereas Father was forever digging up my motives. He said, "Kenneth, you're one of those continuing-education types and you think Benn still has something to teach you. In return, you have to take care of him because, as Aristophanes would say, he's got his head up his ass." (Dad disliked vulgar expressions and always found a respectable sponsor for them.) "What you do for him, you should be doing for a wife and for your little girl."

This was for the birds. If my father had had so much family feeling he wouldn't have been such a screwer of other men's wives. And didn't the wives adopt a similar outlook? The world crisis was everybody's cover for lasciviousness and libertinage (two little words you seldom see).

Family feeling is pretty thin by the time you get to the collateral relatives. It didn't carry much weight with Vilitzer, either. He was often on our campus, invited to address Municipal Government seminars on corruption. He told students that corruption was a thing of the past. So many taxpayers fleeing to the suburbs. So much money coming from the federal government being heavily supervised that stealing became more difficult and dangerous. The machine had lost its patronage clout. I went to one of his talks and hid in a corner. His own sister's grandson, and he would never have known I was there, nor cared much. I was tempted to ask how come the FBI was running so many sting operations and filming the bribe-taking aldermen and other officials. Nowadays the Justice Department is chasing the Vilitzers with harpoons. There's a certain charm in that. In a Republican administration the Democratic mammals (all sizes) are fair game. As for the students, they loved Vilitzer's hokum, he was such a delicious tough guy. Deeply tanned, he had clever lumps in his face and his white hair was combed straight forward to the edge of the forehead, where it was curled under in the style of imperial Rome. Built like a coal-heaver in his youth, he remained chunky. What he lost in height went into his spread, and although he was said to be weakened by heart trouble, his blue eyes still had force enough to fix you with menace. Before he was drafted in World War II he had had minor mob connections and was a strong-arm guy. His family nickname was "the Big Heat." A legend had it that he had led some guy down into a cellar woodshop and put his head in a vise, and when the guy heard the bones of his skull cracking he decided to give the Big Heat the information he was requesting.

When he came to campus he didn't look up his nephew and grandnephew. Mother's lawsuit had offended him violently. Benn ran into him once as Vilitzer was about to enter his stretch limousine with the purple-brown windows. Benn greeted him and the Big Heat said, "I wash my hands of you." Vilitzer's upper lip was curled under, like his bangs.

"And what did you answer?"

"Nothing. You're the one with the ready wit—what would you have said?"

"I would have sent him a box of Lady Macbeth Hand Soap."

Uncle repeated my jokes to his acquaintances. He admired my wisecracks too much. Anyway, Vilitzer would never have heard of Lady Macbeth.

"Was he telling you that you wouldn't inherit one single penny from him?"

"Oh, come. How would I? He has a family of his own."

"The eldest son is out."

"That's right, Fishl was disinherited. Fishl is too smart and his dad associates him mentally with me. But there are more children. They do vending machines and municipal insurance. The good old spoils system. Children are apologies for stealing. Politicians would explain—if it was necessary—'Why do I steal? There's a dumb question. I do it for my kids.'"

"He did a number on you and Mother," I said.

"A niece or nephew is different. If a nephew asks to be a

precinct captain or for a sinecure in the public parks, that's legitimate. But cash dollars are for your own flesh and blood. He got sore at us because we questioned the sale of the property we inherited from your grandmother. Hilda and I turned a nice profit and should have been grateful. The suit we filed threw him into a rage. He called me up and said, 'I'll make you piss purple!'"

I said, "With such family experiences behind you, I don't blame you for preferring the plants."

"Wait a minute. I never said I did. I can still tell sap from blood," said Uncle.

Poor guy, he sure was high on consanguinity. At times it looked like a foolish weakness. I'm sure he married Matilda Layamon partly to obtain a family. And he intended me to be drawn into it too, which was unthinkable. Besides, the Layamons wouldn't have had me on a bet. Matilda told Uncle that I was a sly person. Basically that's wrong. Basically I see myself as a frank individual. Yet to be perfectly fair, there's something about the slenderness of my face and my glance suggesting slyness. Some people don't feel at ease with me and sense that I am watching them. They suspect me of suspicion. To smooth matters over for Benn's sake, I said, "She's not the first to accuse me, and I've often wondered about it myself. I'm a 'sly-frank,' or have some such oxymoron look in the face."

Benn was emotionally earnest *au fond*. Plenty of people will reject this as a symptom of faulty personal development ("What a *time* the fellow picks to be so emotionally earnest!") and I resist it myself, but in the end I admit that such earnestness appeals to me. Through the high connections of my parents I might have written my own ticket in Paris, and Paris *is* improving these days—there's a return of sanity, they've junked all the postwar Marxism and the curse has been lifted from the barbarous U.S.A. But I gave it all up to live near Uncle Benn. He was family to me. From the same motives I still fly to Seattle once a month to see my little daughter, Nancy.

But I grant you the difficulty of making a case for enduring human bonds. Everybody fears being suckered through the affections, although cynical people still adopt a lip-service attitude towards them, just as Stalin's toady Ponomarenko bowed in the direction of the "innocent masses." In this regard literature tries to hold its old positions. Philip Larkin, a poet much admired, writes, "In everyone there sleeps a sense of life according to love." But the sense *is* sleeping. He also says that people dream "of all they might have done had they been loved. Nothing cures that." And this *seems* true too, although there may be an analogy with Ike—they have no inner theater corresponding to the European theater of war. Where's the space for love to perform in? And it's not too heartening to set these Larkin statements against the opposite propositions, upheld by a prodigious number of people who renounce love and go it alone—strong, healthy, rational, rationally wicked or at least "unsentimental" people, who are generally more wide awake than others. Except in a melancholy connection, you seldom hear about love anymore. As in a recent eulogy of the blues singer Billie Holiday, the speaker said, "She was born out of love, and she suffered for lack of love. All her music was about love." Dying of drug abuse and alcoholism, Billie was under arrest on her deathbed. There were cops in the hospital room.

Vilitzer, to get back to him, was the executor of Grandma Crader's estate. He bought her property from Benn and Mother through a dummy corporation and later sold it to Ecliptic Circle Electronics, which built the tallest skyscraper in the city on that site, almost as big as the Sears Tower in Chicago. From this deal he made an unguessable pile. Mother and Uncle Benn together got $300,000 out of it. "Harold gave us a good bath," said Mother. She had hoped to buy a house on the Île Saint-Louis with her share. When Uncle Vilitzer came to Paris years back, before the troubles, she took him to see that house. He said, "What do you want an old dump like this for? You can get something modern and clean for half the dough. I wouldn't live in a joint as creepy as this. At least buy a building where the turds don't come back after you flush, or where they have a window in the kitchen."

So to sue Harold was mad. There's no saying how many judges he owned. He played golf with the bagmen of those he didn't actually own.

I said to Uncle, "Tangling with him was moronic."

"You have a sharp sense of these things," said Uncle. "And I suppose it was a dumb thing to do."

"I'll tell you what's curious: Because he's family you're still sentimental even about him."

"I *used* to love him."

As I heard him say this, a shadow passed over me. One of those versatile damn shadows that slip in and speed away. If he could still love Harold Vilitzer, his love for me (or for anybody) dropped somewhat in value.

Benn went on to say, "In 1946 Harold got back from the war. He was an overage volunteer and enlisted because he got so worked up over Hitler. When Hitler blew himself away in the bunker, Harold was down in Italy and actually made some dough in Naples before demobilization. *Naples,* where people are really good at those games. He was selling army surplus stuff. It became surplus as soon as he got his hands on it. Well, he came back and sat in the kitchen in his uniform. He was loads of fun. By and by he went on the street, right here in town, taking bets, paying off the police. As a bookie, he was such a success out in the fresh air that when he had a big loss the cops collected fifty thousand bucks among themselves to keep him in business. It was worth it to them. Next thing we knew, he was in politics."

"All the affection you tell me about seems to have been from your side only. What about the others?"

"I wouldn't say that Harold was an indifferent uncle in those days. He taught me that mulberries were edible. This was when we had the two trees in the backyard. I think I've told you. . . ."

"More than once."

"Where the Ecliptic Circle Electronic Tower is located now."

"Yes, sure," I said. The part of me that was philosophic didn't have much use for Uncle's details. I was occasionally impatient with his emphasis on particulars. Yet even then I often suspected that my abstracts were more treacherous than his specifics.

"Those mulberries were delicious. Uncle and I spent afternoons picking them. We shooed away the grackles. He also stood me treats downtown. We still had vaudeville—Jimmy

Savo, Sophie Tucker, jugglers, magicians, trained dogs. From time to time, burlesque. Billiards and boxing too. He was fond of both. I think he wanted to make a regular fellow of me, break me in. We went to bookie joints also. Crap games. Movies. Of course I didn't have a penny. It was all Uncle's treat. Once we saw a wonderful specialty film—a surrealist put-on about a crazy Burbank type who extracted real hard-boiled eggs from eggplants. During the war, Harold's wife had moved out to California with the kids to be near her own parents. While waiting for them to come home, he was paternal towards me."

"So for a few weeks you developed an affectionate attachment . . . ?"

"Of course. And even earlier—loved the parents, loved my sister, always trying to talk to them. At the age of eight, I got into bed with Hilda one morning because I loved her. Your mother was becoming a young woman then. She whacked me about twenty times across the face to teach me about incest, although this was the first I ever heard about it."

He was smiling as he recalled this.

"It was all so wonderful," I said. "Even when Mother was bitchy to you. You've told me, Uncle, that as a kid you read fairy tales—all the Andrew Lang collections: the Green, the Yellow and the Blue. And I'll tell you what I think you've done—what those fairy tales were to you in childhood, your family in the good old days are to you now. All the princes, Cinderellas, Sleeping Beauties and wicked stepmothers. Shouldn't you rethink all that before you become a senior citizen?"

I wasn't taunting him; my look was sympathetic and I hardly raised my voice, my view being that he had somehow escaped being possessed by the world most of us experience. Uncle omitted (or disdained) to protect himself, to a degree which was scarcely compatible with the actual conditions (or outrages) of contemporary life. When his sister slapped him, he hadn't tried to defend himself. I mention this because the man was later the object of so much attention from women, and at the point where their interest took a literal, physical form, he didn't always know what to make of it. Sometimes I thought that they engaged his curiosity on a dangerously naive level. His responses to them made me think of the old rhyme:

> When a man takes a wife he soon finds out whether
> Her arms and legs are only glued together.

But of course he wasn't innocent in the sense that is so hateful to worldly people. As if "worldly experience" weren't one set of delusions after another, changed like costumes in the process of "growth."

But I wasn't altogether wrong about the fairy tale of family affections. He went back often—too often, if you ask me—to his earliest years. "When I was seven or eight, I'd come in from the street dying to tell my folks what wonders I'd been seeing. I had such terrific things to report, and I was hyper. But at our house everybody was busy. Meat and potatoes had to be put on the table, so they shut me up. They usually were kind to me; they just didn't have the time. At last I figured that what I saw outside was old hat to them, so I stopped trying. My mother thought that as a kid I was a dreadful liar. She told me so later."

"And that's why you turned to plants?"

"I wouldn't put it that way. We didn't speak the same language in the family. We had endearments, kisses, warm looks. Even my high-strung sister usually was kind. What was missing was the words."

Benn believed I was the only member of the family with whom he could communicate at an advanced level. Maybe my partial deafness made it seem so. I wear my hair long to hide the hearing aid. The hard of hearing have to be twice as attentive; many read lips while listening, and such unusual concentration may be taken for agreement. On the whole I did grasp what he meant. We had read the same basic books. Until the steamship lines went out of business, Uncle Benn and Aunt Lena made annual Atlantic crossings, always bringing books for me in a footlocker—at first, fairy tales, Leatherstocking, Mark Twain and Dickens. Then, as soon as I was old enough, they started me on Balzac. Aunt Lena, so plump and ingenuous-looking, an elusively perfumed darkness over a pale skin, was a Balzac buff. She liked Balzac best when he was most somber, when he was banging on the bars of virtue-and-vice against a background of universal snaredrums and tom-toms: the burial of Père Goriot; the tigress concierge robbing the dying musician, Pons, while her own husband in the lodge downstairs is being poisoned by the terrible Auvergnat, Remonencq, who lusts after her. Who would have thought that a dumpling like Lena would thirst for such strong mixtures? But she would say, "You can't know life or human relations, you don't understand society, if you haven't read Balzac." Towards the end she added, "To understand Balzac you have to go back to Swedenborg. Start with Balzac's *Séraphita*. Then read *Conjugial Love.*"

Benn obviously didn't read Swedenborg on love. He gave me that volume as a memento. (I read it.) He agreed with Lena about Balzac, however, and he said, "If she hadn't put me onto those books, I never would have known where I was at. As for people who haven't read *Cousin Pons* and *Cousine Bette,* I don't see what kind of guidance system they can have. When somebody gives them the business, they can't interpret how they've been shafted. Without *Cousine Bette* I'd have been lost."

Often he was lost anyway. If he had read *Pons* more closely he wouldn't have married Matilda Layamon. She was the only child of rich parents, and Balzac very specifically tells you that only children born to wealth make dangerous wives. Texts are tricky that way. Because you've *read* about philistines you may conclude that you can't be a philistine yourself. That's cockeyed. You may also, unaware, be swollen with a secret fever while reading a book, poisoned by toxic wastes, or be unconscious of the storms of feeling within yourself from which the book is screening you. That Uncle was a susceptible and sometimes hallucinated reader is proven by his enthusiasm for the books he urged on me. In the case of Admiral Byrd's *Alone,* he was dead right; but he also got me to read *The Autobiography of a Yogi*. There was a certain charm to that one, but you had to overcome your incredulity about levitation and out-of-body experiences. As when the yogi's wife, entering his room, finds him lying not on the mattress where she had left him but in the air, floating just under the ceiling.

To such literature Uncle brought an agnostic, that is, a dilettante attitude that I didn't much like.

But seeing what Uncle's tastes were, I was able to interest him in mystical, gnostic, hermetic writers, or people like Soloviev and Fyodorov, in whom I did background work for my studies in Russian symbolism. Uncle was so solid to look at that I trusted him to vet some of my more fragile opinions. When I was very young I compared him to the corner of an old-style fortress. Like my dad, who said he was built like a Russian church, I too went for the architectural simile. Such old masonry is useless against modern explosives, or missile systems. (It wasn't much of a challenge to the Layamon family he married into.) Anyway, Uncle took to Fyodorov, whose position was that death lies behind all human problems. The earth is a graveyard and the one and only project of humanity is to reclaim it for life. That people dear to us should disappear into eternity is intolerable, and we can't accept it without cowardice. A beginning must be made with the immediate family. Sons and daughters must restore life to those who gave it to them. Even if it means going to the moon, we must retrieve every particle of our dead. The dead and the living form a single community. I didn't like this literal struggle of physical restoration. Yet I led Uncle on to see what he would make of it. He read with glee, he ate it up. There were times when he himself, figuratively speaking, rose towards the ceiling. I shouldn't have put him up to this. I did it because on any topic which interested me I could count on him to supply curious commentaries.

A charming uncle is a big asset. Note that I don't say a charming *old* uncle. Unfortunately he wasn't too old for female entanglements. With Aunt Lena he had been perfectly straight—no cheating. While she lived he didn't even look at the girls—well, he did *look*, but he didn't go prospecting. After years of fidelity there were certain doubts about his powers. He referred me to Darwin's *Autobiography* (he never hesitated to keep mental company with the best), to those passages in which Darwin confessed that in his youth he had been moved by poetry and music while in later years these things nauseated him, and this he explained by the neglect of his responsive faculties, disused and rusting. Scientific work, immersion in insignificant detail, the noting of very small differences in organisms, ruined him for the bigger emotions. (My guess is that Darwin's ruin had already begun and he had turned to research because he had sensed this.) Aunt Lena was gentle, softly overweight in the hips and thighs, dark, an elusive perfume about her, black eyes hung, so to speak, in her face, and I had prying thoughts (a widespread masculine peculiarity) about how Benn had made out with her. He was extremely protective of her, no deceit. Also, there were Swedenborgian influences. She couldn't persuade Benn to read that great visionary; nevertheless his views on love between the sexes were familiar to Uncle. Woman is endowed with greater powers of volition, by which Swedenborg means affection. Man's tendency is more abstract. An exchange occurs between man and woman. Love and thought complete each other in the human pair, and something like an exchange of souls takes place, according to the divine plan. Still, Benn worried about Darwinian disuse, and what it was doing to his capacity to catch fire erotically. It bothered him enough to lead to oblique discussions with Lena. She didn't mind talking about it.

Benn the widower-bachelor didn't look like cutting a romantic figure with women, being cumbersome in build. Yet in the years before his second marriage he had his hands full, dealing with ladies: flirtations, courtships, longings, obsessions, desertions, insults, lacerations, sexual bondage—the whole bit from bliss to breakdown. Getting married was supposed to conclude these torments.

"At least I can stop bumming over the face of the earth," he said, justifying his deception to me—I didn't take his marriage well; he should have given me advance notice.

But why did he run around so much? Indian forests, Chinese mountains, Brazilian jungles, the Antarctic. He admitted that his restlessness had an erotic cause, but never could determine how to interpret this. There were contradictory desires in play. In an age when you have Eros on one side and Thanatos on the other in a jurisdictional dispute, you may as well pack up and head for the airport rather than stand and wait for the outcome. Better to be in motion? Running to keep the libido active? This would never occur to a true tomcat. Think of Balzac's Baron Hulot, eighty years old, who propositions a servant girl while his saintly wife on her deathbed can still hear him. Equally curious was the case of Stravinsky's grandfather: One hundred and ten years of age, he broke his neck climbing a fence on his way to a midnight assignation. Uncle wasn't even in it with men of this stamp—the raging old Yeatses, fellows who used to go to Switzerland for monkey gland transplants in the twenties. No, fifteen years a faithful husband, that was his ilk. And he couldn't deal with women who were lavish and oppressive in their demands.

Yes, he had genuine sexual problems, not incapacitating ones—deposits of undiscovered libido which would have made the fortune, sexually speaking, of a smart woman who had the insight and sympathy to bring order (also pleasure) out of these mixed idiosyncrasies. And I can't tell you why he was driven to take the marriage gamble with Matilda Layamon. It still stumps me. If the British Empire according to Macaulay and Winston Churchill was acquired in a fit of absentmindedness, the same applies to Uncle Benn's second wife. Only in the major case an imperial will was gradually taking form, while in the lesser a man's opinion of himself, a self-judgment, was expressed. But I'm not about to get deep about his motives. I trust psychology less and less. I see it as one of the lower by-products of the restlessness or oscillation of modern consciousness, a terrible agitation which we prize as "insight." Let's just say that Uncle himself understood the irrationality of putting a ring on Matilda's finger and saying, "I do." Weren't there enough derelict marriages around him, the wreckage of loves like Boeings that couldn't clear the peaks? When it came time for the two of us to have it out, he was plain enough with me about the "sexual scene." All those mad men and mad women sharing beds. Two psychopaths under one quilt. Do you ever know who is lying beside you, the thoughts behind the screen of "consideration"? A flick of the thermostat and the warmth of love explodes, a bomb of flame that cremates you. As you float away from your ashes into the etheric world, don't be surprised to hear sobs of grief from your destroyer.

But I'd better tone this down, not give in to my great weakness.

To resume more soberly: I can see why marriage should have been an inviting proposition. Most of Benn was taken up by plants—the histogenesis of leaves, or whatever; actually I thought of him as a sort of plant mystic—but the remainder was affectionate. People in his trade, as I have already observed, were frequently affectively bald and no one thought the worse of them for it. He was not ready to follow the Darwinian example, accept total atrophy. He would say, "I'm becoming too self-sufficient." You might have persuaded me that he was tired of taking care of himself, although housekeeping was no burden to him. He rather liked it. He poured blue Vanish into his toilet. He preferred 409 to all other kitchen cleaners. He did his socks with Woolite. Jobs that drove other men wild, like peeling spuds, cleaning out the cheese grater, scrubbing scorched saucepans, doing the floors on his knees, didn't bother him at all. It never occurred to him that it was infra dig, unsuitable for a man who had revised some of the basic concepts of plant morphology. To my dad this willingness to be the maid-of-all-work was a sign of underlying natural dullness—Dad was slightly spoiled, in that he had had one hell of a good time as an American in Europe. No European could possibly have made such a success of European life. Post-Hitler Europe was in disgrace with itself. What was left of traditional privileges was evaporating. In the days of maids, the kitchens were nasty. When the lady of the house had to do household chores herself, modern American-style or West German conveniences were installed. The Trachtenbergs, however, always had a maid. Intellectuals didn't scrub floors. But Uncle didn't mind laundering, ironing, sewing buttons, scrubbing. He also kept his lab clean. Dad said, "Under all those airs of his, he's an old lady." Wrong. It was Uncle's way of saying, "I'm not one of your betters." He went out of his way to proclaim equality. In my opinion, he overdid it. This attitude is somewhat, as a Parisian friend suggested, an excess of politeness. He told me that Marcel Proust, whom he was studying, would bend over backwards to answer the question of a lady making small talk at dinner. He would reply at length and with paralyzing completeness when no such answer was required or expected. People were flooded with unwanted information by this handsome, wearisome, yogurt-faced table companion. You could die of it. Under it all was the gallantry of equality, or presumed equality.

Giving credit from egalitarian motives where it wasn't due (i.e., to parties whose mental processes were totally unlike your own), honoring another soul for forces it might or might not have—like the appeasement of the god of a volcano extinct for hundreds of years. He isn't even there. He manages a chain of volcanoes (like Hyatt Houses), and he's busy with those, the live ones.

It's well to bear in mind also that Uncle was tuned very high and would play on himself because he *was* tuned; on such tense strings, performance was inevitable. Super-politeness mitigated the imposition on others, his hearers. Ingenuity and high energy like his were compulsive. For instance, he is opening a packet of vitamin pills and a dinner companion asks what they are. He begins to describe the advanced cancer research conducted at Valhalla, New York, and the theory of "free radicals"—dangerous neutrons detached in the metabolic process, possibly causing malignant tumors. These wonder-working vitamins dilate the capillaries of the prostate gland and keep it from swelling. They had healed a fingernail cracked for years. (He tries to show it to her; the candlelight is too weak.) One curious side effect, he goes on, is that the vitamins stimulate the growth of intestinal bacteria, causing a certain amount of bloat. The remedy for this is to follow the example of the higher primates, whose digestive tract is wonderfully like our own and whose fiber diet keeps the bowels clean. . . . Sorry she asked, the lady waits for this excitable bore to end his lecture. Yet another unwanted offering.

So Uncle, to get back to that, didn't mind doing for himself. For a change, however, it would be nice to have someone else out of kindness wash the dinner plates. Why, then, did he marry Matilda Layamon? The classic face, the hyacinth hair—she wasn't going to do the dishes. Under it all is the master-slave relationship. The master *is* master because he is prepared to face death to maintain the privileges of a master. The slave is unwilling to stake his life. . . . We don't need to go into this here, explaining why Uncle Benn was not ashamed to do the dishes. But I can't help remembering that in Moscow in the early twenties the symbolist poet Andrei Bely lost his temper at a public meeting because he had had to stand in line to get a piece of fish. A poet's herring should be served to him, on a clean plate! He also said towards the end of his life, speaking of the women he had known, "Not a single one of them deserved me." I can't imagine Benn saying that. Those words, in his voice, would be impossible. And yet he might have been justified in saying it. So many modern thinkers agree that "overvaluation" is the secret of love. For Rousseau, too, it was an illusion free societies couldn't do without. Under all this, again, is the discovery made at the South Pole by Admiral Byrd. There people found one another *out*. It's enough to mention this now, without overstressing it.

If there was a self-deception involved, Uncle would be aware of it. He was no wimp. He was a man widely admired for his knowledge, for the exactness, retentiveness and capacity of his memory. If you ask me, a power of that kind is founded from above, from on high. The "scientific worldview" will turn up its nose at this. That can't be helped. And this is not an argument but a confession from a heart laid bare. Ordinary explanations originating in the commonsense here-below world will never be satisfactory to me. To me the man was a prodigy, he had the "magics." Such unsought gifts grope for human completion. But how much completion do they need? Does it have to be elaborate—won't a sketchy completion do? Yes, for those who are affectively bald. Emotional types, loving hearts like my uncle, exuberant high-energy characters, easily agitated, needy, greedy—they can't see why one high gift should not be followed by another, by a succession of gifts. The demand then was for a sharer, a charming woman, such a woman as Swedenborg describes—made by God to instruct a man, to lead him to the exchange of souls. Maybe to teach him, as Diotima taught Socrates about love.

On balance, reviewing all the facts, Uncle had taken a bad beating. At this time he was feeling, to go back to the damn Poe poem, that he was a weary, way-worn wanderer. In my opinion he was a sex-abused man. In the papers, this term is reserved for little kids, and it may sound like an impropriety to push a man in his fifties into such a category. A famous middle-aged botanist in the kindergarten—what are you giving us here? Still, there are battered men. They, too, are worked over. And in my book Uncle Benn was a woman-battered man. You'll say, "A man of his stature?" I'll join you there. That's exactly it. He was looking for protection, and in any word-association test the American response to "protection" would be "blackmail": "a racket."

What isn't absolutely clear is why Uncle Benn, if indeed he did know better, was so passive under abuse. There's your whole mystery. And when I inspect it as one would inspect an abstract painting for clues to the real world (is that a vase? is it an old artillery piece? a pastry tube?), I see Benn himself in the background, the actual man, a big fellow, overweight, pale, with a Russian curvature of the back. He walks with a heavy poise. Above the midriff he is sedate. Then the round head, a full face, a pair of eyes in a curve resembling a figure eight laid on its side. One of my Russian philosophers says that human eyes fall into one of two categories, the receptive and the will-emanating. Some are wide open to reflect the light and some scrutinize everything, on the watch for prey; eyes for which the earth is a Garden of Eden, an eternal *now*, or else eyes from which there pours an electrifying flood of will. The first was Uncle's category, of course. Man is what he sees. (Not what he eats, as that literalist German maniac Feuerbach insisted.) No; as you see, so you are. What else could those eyes of his signify? His head, shaped for his occupation, was a plant observatory. He might therefore be taken humanly for a dupe, a mark, by the electrifying-will types, the hustlers and go-getters whom the light-reflectors are predestined to serve. (Their servants, their prey, their lunch.)

But somewhere down in the windings of his character, Uncle was also shrewd. After the fact, he *was* shrewd, capable of seeing where he had gone wrong, how he had been had, how he had collaborated with shrewdies and predators. But only after the fact. He looked stable, but it was only a look. He was, however, the real thing, a real exception. For fear of elitism—what a dreary superstition!—we call upon ourselves to disregard the exceptions.

Imagine! Our only hope of liberation, and we're supposed not even to look.

I would ask Uncle how a kid from the sidewalks of Jefferson Street became mad for botany. If you don't count burdocks and ragweed, dwarf ailanthus and the other stuff that grows in the freight yards, there were no plants in that slum. Grandpa Crader wouldn't even eat lettuce. He was offended when Grandma served it. He raised that intelligent face of his, demented by prejudices and harrowing ironies, and said, "Give this to the *behemah*." Although the old man taught Hebrew he was not an observant Jew. He did, nonetheless, take an interest in the mystical tradition and liked to talk about the Tree of Life and the Tree of Knowledge. Curiously, it was the gentiles who possessed the Tree of Knowledge (in the form of Science), while the Tree of Life was a one-hundred-percent Jewish property. Eventually Science and Life would unite. I wondered whether those trees had influenced Uncle's choice of a profession. Not that he knew of, he said.

Now, Uncle didn't like to appear mysterious. He didn't want to discuss his gifts or to think about them. He accepted them with thanks and for the rest he preferred to keep his mouth shut. For my part, I had to think about these mysteries because they affected me so much. When I pumped him about the Tree of Life, all he was able to tell me was that his father had owned a cabalistic book on the subject by the sixteenth-century mystic Haym Vital. I had no time then to go into this—too many irons in the fire—but I had to reckon with it because in the last analysis it influenced my decision to come to the Midwest. I wasn't about to throw my life away. I might *give* it away, but I wouldn't simply junk it. So I've often wondered why I didn't follow in the footsteps of M. Kojève. While listening to his conversation in the dining room in Paris I sometimes imagined that I saw spokes of light coming straight out of Kojève's head. He made me feel like a mental bobby-soxer. He dealt with spirit and nature, he shuffled History like a deck of cards. I was ecstatic. What a fellow! Still, I noticed also that I was filling up with growling suspicions. Very young, just working my way towards my *bachot*, my admiration of his mastery of thought more and more darkened by suspicion, I compared him mentally to my Russian-conversation teacher on the Rue du Dragon—his freezing room with icons and scraps of Bokhara carpet, the raw baldness of his head, the thinness of his voice. He warned me in mind-boggling Russian against the glamour of thought, the calculating intellect and its constructions, its fabrications alien to the power of life. There were two varieties of truth, one symbolized by the Tree of Knowledge, the other by the Tree of Life, one the truth of striving and the other the truth of receptivity. Knowledge divorced from life equals sickness. Uncle knew masses of stuff about plants, but his knowledge was somehow involuntary.

"So, Uncle? Where is that book?"

"About the Tree of Life? Search me. It must have been buried when they razed the building. The old man would read it to me, with commentary. I never studied it myself."

"What did you read yourself?"

"I bought a book from the junkman, for a nickel. It was *Great Mother Forest* by Attilio Gatti. It must have been fished out of the bathtub and dried in the sun, because it was swollen and stained. I was knocked over by it. Also I loved Bartram's book—wandering in unspoiled Georgia and Florida two centuries ago, all alone, collecting rare plants and sleeping in the wilds."

In Paris I've heard the clever opinion advanced that the ghetto is a replica of the Judean desert and that the Jews escape decadence because they lack vegetal elements. They don't depend on sap and therefore they don't wither, either. The ghetto is not so sterile as the minds of French intellectuals who come up with formulations like this one, ostensibly sympathetic. It's one of the things that drove me out of Paris. For centuries, in crumbling slum synagogues, Jews have recited prayers for dew *(tal)*. But this is of interest only in connection with Uncle's vocation.

"So did those exotic books make a globe-trotter of you?"

"I wouldn't say so. There are all those 747 jets waiting to carry everybody away. You can always take a short leave. And funds for special purposes, plus favorable rates of exchange. The weather gets bad—ten straight days of sleet—you're disgruntled, depressed, it's foolish to sit still, even damaging to your mental structure. So you start looking through your desk and find a bundle of unanswered invitations. Then you think, Why not India? This would be the best season for it. There's that big dark accommodating lady in Madras who is always so happy to see you. She's such great company."

He meant Rajashwari. She was a librarian and a notable performer on the deep-toned big-bellied Indian guitar. Nearby was the University of Annamalai, with its famous department of botany, where Dr. Singh experimentally serenaded the mimosas and increased the number of their stomata—Uncle was far from persuaded by Singh's data.

"But to return to the kid from Jefferson Street," he said. "It wasn't *Great Mother Forest* and it wasn't the charm of Bartram, those perfumed subtropical nights. There seems to have been a second person inside me who stepped in and acted for me. *He* told me to give the junkman my nickel. That person I believe was waiting and when botany came along he sprang out and swallowed it whole. My normal self would have deliberated and shillyshallied, like a Nervous Nellie. Certain decisions just kill me. . . ."

"The question, then, is which of the two or more persons makes your decisions. Or wouldn't it be better to say a demon, or daemon—an inner spirit?"

I didn't expect him to answer this.

Uncle and I made one long trip together. Last spring he took me with him to Japan.

It so happened that I had gone to Seattle once more to see my little daughter and to try again to persuade her mother to marry me. Uncle was particularly worried by this. He telephoned me at the hotel, one of those ultramodern places. The rooms were very glassy there. I spent hours reading the *Times,* while the Seattle rains streamed over the glass, streamed and streamed. They wouldn't stop.

It wasn't solely on my account that he was calling. He said, "I'm flying to Tokyo tomorrow, and if you'd like to come along I'll pay your fare."

"What is it—the weather? Is there sleet back home?"

"You bet, and more to come."

"This is the first I hear about Japan."

"Well, I'm expected in Kyoto two days from now."

"We had dinner before I left and you didn't say a single word about it."

"Something has come up. If you'll tell me where your passport is I can bring it with me, Kenneth."

"It's in my briefcase, right here. I can come with you."

"How is it in Seattle? I've been concerned."

"Getting nowhere. What else?"

"As I figured. Taking the usual beating from that dainty little woman. Bears you a child, and then bears you a grudge. You don't need to be such a superconscientious father. You never refused child support. . . ." At the worst of times your friends when their own flies are open will tell you to zip up. They manage somehow to slip away and for a moment take the high ground.

I said, "It's okay, Uncle Benn. We're both up against it with the ladies—both pretty stupid. I'll be glad to come with you and we won't call it escaping. Okay? It'll be a holiday."

He answered awkwardly. He didn't put on false dignities with me. That, never. But there was something squalid about it—running away from a woman, and *such* a woman. True, she had picked *him*. But hadn't he agreed to be picked?

"Let me give you the JAL flight number. I made a reservation for you and you can get the ticket at the counter. Seattle–Tokyo–Seattle."

I said, "So Caroline is in the fast lane and about to catch up with you?"

"She's due here tomorrow."

"And you haven't said no to her. She put the moves on you from the first."

"We can discuss that on the plane. You'll love ancient Kyoto, and their botany is first-class. I've talked on the phone with old Professor Komatsu. He's emeritus now, but they all defer to him in the department." He began to describe the department and the lectures he would give, but I told him I had to leave pronto to take Nancy to the movies (for which she was far too young).

Caroline Bunge was a department store heiress from Cleveland whom Uncle had met on the seafront in Puerto Rico—a setting suitable to promiscuity. Closer to his age than most of the women he took up with, she was a large and handsome lady, on the whole amiable, and tastefully dressed, although strongly perfumed. A vertical crease between the eyes gave her a thoughtful air, but in fact her mind spiraled too high to think and when she opened her mouth you were aware that she had been in hot, reckless pursuit of things no one should name. However, she had the appearance of dignity, the composure and the accent of a woman who had been educated abroad in good schools, French and English. She talked Irish horses, jumping, fox hunting, whiskey. Hearing that I had grown up in Paris, she described her friendships with Jean Genet and Marguerite Duras. She couldn't say worse about them than what they themselves had written. And is there anything in her circles that *can't* be said? As to her composure, I guess it was sustained by the lithium or Valium she dosed herself with. Also, she hit the bottle pretty hard. She was very fluent, rarely silent. But she was not too stoned to identify Uncle as a remarkable man, and as she had long been ready for a permanent connection, she immediately told him that he would make a super husband. She said, "Women in my bracket are frightened to death of a von Bülow–type match."

He was not only a safe man but desirable on other grounds too.

Under present conditions, such decisions are increasingly problematic. Personal freedom is beset by choice-torments. At a lower level this is easier to see. Any catalogue of household goods can be, to certain temperaments, an ordeal by fire. Steam irons, fitted sheets, ovenware, lighting fixtures, kitchen cabinets, upholstery fabrics. It may take a nervous woman a full year to select a wallpaper for the guest bathroom. In a good shop she will find a ten-foot shelf of sample books. As for deciding on a man, think what an effort it is to sift through the eligibles and select a husband. What a torment! And then to persuade the guy you've selected! Money *should* make it easier. It doesn't, though, because where there's money there's business, and business means contractual agreements. You no sooner begin to read a contract than you're thinking of ways to weasel out of it. Even before you've signed, you've laid out your escape routes. It's all private reckonings, every man on his separate system. In France it's called *le petit système à part*. This militates against permanence in human connections. It's a real labor to get a feeling of necessity or inevitability into any of your choices. Love ("strong as death" love) can't be put on a contractual basis, since the challenge is to shatter the contract. The *système à part* cries out for shattering. Contractual terms are merely human, whereas self-love is godlike.

Uncle didn't *have* to get into this. He had his science. The trouble was that he was ambitious. Asked too much. The happiness of a recluse wasn't enough for him, nor were his telepathic powers with plants. I may myself have been to blame, by stirring up his affects continually.

Anyway, out of the troubled landscape there appears, takes shape, materializes, the somnambulistic form of Caroline Bunge. Encountering Uncle, she begins to make plans to marry him. What could be more natural? She's handsome and rich; he is a learned widower and a gentleman, albeit a Jewish one. She talks about Jews as husbands. She tells *me* once (in a bar while we are waiting for Benn to arrive) that a good match *can* be made with a Jew. She says that Mary Logan Smith did very well with Bernard Berenson, even though Berenson was a little swindler and an art racketeer. Of course, those were Edwardian days of wild eccentricity. In that circle, there was an English lady who carried a huge pocketbook in which there were frogs, and those frogs had been trained to jump into her open mouth and back again into her bag. Maybe she lured them with dead flies. The English and the Jews had always got on well together—didn't I think?—because they both practiced usury, Caroline says. As for the situation here, this is one host country the Jews haven't harmed and that's because the Invisible Hand of Capitalism cherishes America. America is the darling of the Invisible Hand. I realize that Caroline is simply repeating conversations overheard at cocktail parties, or fitting rooms at Bergdorf Goodman's.

In any case, she was tired of tough guys. Her desire was to settle. She told Benn that he was good for her. She would be good for him. Out of politeness, he agreed. He wouldn't have known how to frame a disagreement. She announced that she was arriving and asked him to pick her up at the airport. She was bringing a prenuptial agreement her lawyer had drawn. There was going to be a limousine to City Hall. A navy chaplain would perform the ceremony.

As soon as she rang off, Uncle telephoned Kyoto.

In half an hour he had closed up shop, left a note for his departmental chairman, packed his bag, reserved the tickets.

He locked his apartment and spent the night in my rooms at the dormitory. So at the moment when Caroline was landing on the domestic side of the airport, Uncle entered the international terminal and hurried to the Japan Air Lines counter.

I ask you briefly now to consider my own problems with Treckie, in Seattle.

A serious man when he meets an attractive woman will ask, What can she and I put together of a permanent nature?

Anyone would say that he deserves ethical high marks for such a question. Nine hundred and ninety-nine times out of a thousand, this is a preface to self-injury.

I have sometimes stated the case of Treckie in subatomic terms: Particle A carries the charge specifically needed by particle B. True affinity. Also, this eliminates the contractual danger. Although a marriage *begins* with a contract, it has to move into a higher sphere. Anyhow, to this day I haven't shaken off the conviction that Treckie and I had matching particles. Ideally suited for a lifetime of intimacy.

This Treckie, a round young woman, is so receptive, so pleasing. Her dark hair, in curls, usually circles her head but sometimes comes down on one side. I was particularly taken with her shape, short and firm. I can admire long-legged girls, but they aren't my real preference. The fashion word *petite*, referring to height only, is inadequate since it doesn't tell you whether the figure is flat or full. Treckie has exactly the bosom—top of its class—that I prefer. From the first, I especially resonated to the swell of her shape because of what seemed to me its connection with the physical . . . and by physical I mean planetary or, more broadly, gravitational forces—strength for strength. Feeling myself to be lean and random, I react to compact forces. Treckie is a small woman, tiny really, and I have this appreciation for condensation in combination with female maturity. This sexual kid, I went for her, her small face and miniature smiles together with the full figure, her well-developed bosom. She was like a pale girl-aborigine. I may be fixated on child-women—the same as Edgar Allan Poe and the retarded girl he married. By arrangement with her mother, Mrs. Clemm, who bestowed this mental eight-year-old on him. In my case, no such luck.

Treckie is a smart girl with a degree in biology. When I met her she was employed by the Veterans Administration Hospital and lived in our neighborhood.

Poe's wife seemed to be truly simple, whereas Treckie was clever—either very clever or playing by clever rules, those different rules based on the, to me, foreign assumptions of a new generation of young women. I'll be more specific. The first undressing of two lovers is a most special event. The *prise de possession.* Here I still have significant residual sentiments about what a man is and what a woman is. Well, Treckie was no disappointment to me (whatever *I* was to her—skinny, bony, the long-haired Chinese snapped by a tourist allowed to wander in the interior of the country). She was everything I had expected, except that her legs were disfigured by bruises. Her shins were all black and blue. No, blue and green circles like the markings of peacock feathers—that's more accurate. I couldn't ask the natural question, "My God, how did you get those—who did that to you?" Under the circumstances, I couldn't say, "Who did it!" There are rules of conduct even today between consenting etceteras. When she saw me staring at her she shrugged her bare shoulders, she laid her head to one side, and her underlip swelled softly towards me. There being a challenge in this, a "What are you going to do about it?" She seemed to take pride in these injuries. Well, they weren't really damaging, no worse than love bites, except that they would have been another man's bites. And who would be so rough with such a tiny woman—a telephone lineman or another type of hard hat? Some enthusiast or ecstatic who had climbed all over Treckie in his boots? Well, she seemed to be asking how I meant to proceed. Would I keep my mouth shut? Consent by silence to her "way of doing things"? If I treated her kindly, she might not care for it. All I could do in the circumstances was what I knew how to do, and I can't say how satisfactory this was. There are women who like to keep you in the dark.

When I was last in Paris I talked to my father about this and he was very responsive, pleased to be consulted as the expert. Drawing on a lifetime of experience, and paternally solicitous, he went into the subject minutely. What have we here: grown women in the child class? He understood immediately. Girls of this type, tiny creatures, got a special kick out of showing that they were sexually full women. They could make bruisers and giants obey them. Afraid of no man, as hot-blooded and capable as any six-foot Swede or African. "Domineering diminutives," Dad called them. "Let's see who's boss here." He asked, had I been rough with her? And he himself immediately gave the answer: "You're not the type. . . . And there are people who enjoy sex only when it leaves marks on them. I knew a little person once, from a small town in Ohio, a curious little lady. One of her boyfriends had given her a black eye. She told me this with special pride. What a sweet little piece she was! Well, with this black eye she went into a truck stop for her morning coffee and, if you could believe her, the truckers all stopped eating to stare at her. She said she walked in wearing a simple beige linen suit and her hair piled on top of her head, schoolmarm fashion. But this sensational black eye! Those guys were dying of envy and admiration. She turned on a whole dinerful of strong men! All right, Ken, how do we interpret this? One session of lovemaking is converted into a proclamation. Other men, by the dozen, hear the message, are affected by her erotic power. . . . We don't know women, son. Not even after a lifetime of observation, practically research. Science itself is ignorant in this branch of knowledge."

He was now playing the wise man with me, in the French manner. Being an outstanding cocksman wasn't enough; he needed to rise to the theoretical level. This Hegelian what shall I call him—Master Spirit?—who had moved from Napoleonic assault troops to regiments of sexual women, *was* nevertheless instructive in this department. I will say also that he has been a good father to me, warmhearted. No monogamous parent could have been more attentive. I love my father. He was and also was not there—no different from other parents when you come right down to it. I didn't tell him that I adored Treckie; he would have tried to talk me out of it. He would have called me a masochist and theorized at me—from *l'amour propre* to *l'amour passion*. *Amour* this and *amour* that. He was as far from love, as I understood it, as I was from beekeeping. And the truth is that I am a much tougher guy than my father and play for much higher stakes. I emigrated to the U.S.A. because that's where the action is now—the real modern action. What I needed to understand, he couldn't teach me on his Parisian turf.

It's true that in the field of sex I had a lot of catching up to do, and in that department Uncle would have been no great help on either shore of the Atlantic. He wasn't exactly exemplary with Matilda Layamon or her predecessors.

One of these days Treckie might be ready to listen, and then she would come to know the real Kenneth Trachtenberg.

Meanwhile I could do nothing but go along. She had nothing against me, she liked me just fine, she had a child by me. She didn't accept my marriage offer, and that may have been just as well, since she didn't understand what I was all about. Love the magician, *el amor brujo*, would eventually get to her when the foolishness and vanity of being a "new type" became clear, so I settled down to a wait. All through her pregnancy she kept her job at the VA Hospital. In the seventh month I moved in with her. She was glad to have me living there, with the understanding that it was temporary (not a husband but a heavy boarder). It made her cheerful, and being cheerful, she diverted me with daily anecdotes from the hospital, which she considered a fun place. The poor veterans were mainly incompetent and goofy. Lavishly funded, the hospital had beautiful grounds and its own golf course. The ninny patients could look down from their windows at the physicians riding by in golf carts, living it up on fat federal salaries. Against a nightmare background of poor dummies, the doctors led a dreamy life, nine tenths of it recreational.

The birth of the baby, a little girl, put a super edge on Treckie's good humor, but few important changes resulted. She went on living in the same apartment, a graduate-student slum in an English basement (i.e., windows at street level) behind a screen of evergreen shrubs. It was equipped with a deep-freeze, a microwave oven, a toilet tank with the porcelain cover removed so you could dip your hand into the water to flush. The pullman kitchen was nothing but a closet. And yet she got dividend checks in the mail; she owned AT&T and other blue-chip stocks. Statements from Merrill Lynch also arrived. Tactful and oblique, in my sly-frank way, I learned that she had a rich mother, with whom she was on bad terms and who was not informed of Nancy's birth. Stocks and brokerage accounts were the gift of her late grandfather. "Just enough to give me a cushion." Childlike, with a face that looked as if her second teeth had just been cut, she was nevertheless the owner and sole operator of a prodigious will engine. To eat her dinner, she had to sit on telephone books, but she brought back raunchy stories from the hospital. One technician in the hematology lab worked in the dead of night, and while his cultures were cooking or spinning he took off his clothing and put on roller skates. The empty corridors were ideal for skating. Another brought carpets from home and steamed them clean. On the payroll for eighty thousand dollars, the gynecologist had three patients, who were sick old WACs, and a few servicemen from the Korean War stuffed themselves with pillows and came to him shrieking that they were pregnant. Everybody played eccentric, inventing pranks and gags as so much of the country does—novelties, capers, quirks. "And do you know what happened day before yesterday!" The employees do it everywhere. The elevator door opened and it was pitch dark, so Treckie reached for the switch. These two who were spread out on the floor began to curse. "White bitch, don't touch that light!" But she did, and saw that there were several frightened old veterans crowded into a corner of the cab.

"Don't think those people didn't complain to my boss."

"The Iranian?"

"He bawled me out. 'What the hell did you bother them for? How'm I supposed to protect you if you go around doing such things?'"

"They have so much clout?"

"Don't be silly, Kenneth. It's all civil service, with a strong union. A giant bureaucracy like that."

"Also a bazaar," I said.

Treckie said, "The premise is that at the very top of the power structure, in D.C., people are getting away with murder, making themselves government gifts worth hundreds of millions, so why shouldn't the rest of us fool around, play at work." Grownups in play school. Treckie said many clever things. She had the instincts of a champion and was ahead of everybody else. She could win the race without having to break the tape at the finish line, because she was diminutive enough to pass under it. But she wasn't ready for marriage, not quite yet, although she welcomed the child. Like the teenage girls who have an illegitimacy rate of ninety percent in this town, she could see no need for a license.

Telling her hospital tales, Treckie gave cries of laughter with all the force of her little body, swelling her throat and bringing out the fullness of her breasts, being freely sexual with me even while seated on the telephone books. She didn't deny me much. However, it was so far and no farther. "Not ready for a total commitment," she said. And she took a transfer to Seattle.

I pointed out that she was moving into the territory chosen by the neo-Nazis for their separate all-white republic. All she said to this, putting her curls in order with her provoking fingers, was: "This is the kind of information you *always* seem to have."

"I'm only saying—"

"I understand; you're saying our child is half Jewish. Well, you're always welcome in Seattle, for Nancy's sake. The kid needs male parenting and you're very good about it. Being so close to your uncle Benn, you won't miss us all that much."

"Oh, yes I will."

"You're a very self-sufficient person, with a life plan of his own."

There she was right on the nail. Particularly in this day and age, you have no reason to exist unless you believe you can make your life a turning point. A turning point for everybody—for humankind. This takes a certain amount of gall. One would call it ambition, another effrontery. Explain it in a hall to the employees of the VA and they would vote me a straitjacket. Still, if you think that historical forces are sending everybody straight to hell you can either go resignedly with the procession or hold out, and hold out not from pride or other personal motives but from admiration and love for human abilities and powers to which, without exaggeration, the words "miracle" and "sublimity" can be applied. Unconsciously, my interests had developed along lines which, with maturity, revealed a design whose elements can be listed in the following résumé: *(a)* what Americans are; *(b)* what Russians are; *(c)* what Jews—since I am one of them—are; *(d)* what it signifies to say that one is (or is not!) a Citizen of Eternity. To name at random a number of such Citizens will reveal what the word "Eternity" signifies: Moses, Achilles, Odysseus, the Prophets, Socrates, Edgar in *King Lear*, Prospero, Pascal, Mozart, Pushkin, William Blake. These we think about and, if possible, make our souls by. With this object I studied Russian in France, I emigrated to the U.S.A. and I formed a relationship with my uncle Benn. If Benn was not yet a Citizen, if Eternity was not ready to give him his second papers, he was as close to it as I had ever been able to come. As for my dad, despite his wonderful sexual gifts he wasn't really in the running. What he had was a special blessing. In this age of desire he enjoyed the erotic gratification everybody—but everybody!—was seeking. This was enviable, it was heartening; everybody (almost) loved him for it. I might have been happy to inherit this happiness from him. But I didn't. Thus I had my own way to make, which would lead far beyond my father. The premise of his eroticism was mortality. The sex embrace was death-flavored. He translated Eternity as Death. I checked repeatedly with my soul, which always answered, "Your father is not *it*, and if you resembled him exactly you'd go no farther than he has gone."

By now, to report him accurately, Dad was slipping. He told me a couple of months ago that after being with a Danish lady at the Meurice, he got behind the wheel of his car and discovered that he couldn't recognize his surroundings anymore. The Place de la Concorde was very beautiful, it was heavenly to see, but he had no idea how to get out of it, or *why* he should turn right or left. He was lost at the very center of Paris, and had no idea where home was. "While I was with this lovely girl I knew exactly what I was doing, but as soon as I left her, all other sense of purpose went numb on me. But I couldn't go back to the Meurice, either. I had forgotten her name also, and the room number."

"You must have been frightened. Poor Dad."

"I'm sure I turned very pale. But towards evening I remembered where I lived. I didn't feel frightened. I only thought it was time to change my habits. But Paris is noble to look at even with a part of your consciousness missing."

For me this was a first. My father had never before spoken to me about the afternoons he spent with ladies. He now wanted to notify me that his decline had begun. It's significant also that, changing the subject, he asked about his granddaughter.

I've often got the kid in my mind's eye. She's a dolichocephalic Trachtenberg, with her daddy's narrow face and Jesusy look. I have some notions about her future, but she's not quite three and it's too early to prophesy.

With this clarification, the motives for my trip to Seattle are fuller. I came to learn whether Treckie had been missing me. Maybe my chances had improved with separation. No, they hadn't. Once more her shins were bruised, and that wasn't easy to take. Complacently she sat with her pretty legs set forward so that I could see for myself (I, the man who loved her) what somebody had been doing to her. She wanted to make sure that I didn't miss those iridescent peacock markings. My heart sank. To conceal which, I put on a look of composure originating with my father. Possibly the look he wore when he was lost on the Place de la Concorde. Maybe she told herself that she was doing this for my own good—truth is such a wonderful tonic. She wasn't ready for me. I didn't as yet engage her full interest. I hadn't gotten mean with her, and wasn't about to. There just aren't enough first-class sadists to go around. Maybe she tried to respect me, look up to me, and she simply couldn't manage it. Apparently I had filed secretly an application to be respected, based on my tacit ambition to make a life that would be a turning point. I believe this repelled her. I can see why it would. And she tacitly retorted by engaging in sexual roughhouse with abusive men (of after all simple outlooks). Telephone linemen, lumberjacks maybe. I had a fantasy even about the climber back home who had scaled the Ecliptic Circle Electronic Tower, a daring intrepid who used suction cups or plastic adhesives on his hands and feet. Cops and TV crews were waiting at the top of the skyscraper for him. It might have been a man like that whom she preferred to me. I was a man weighed down with sexual infatuations and life aims (like my turning point) too hard to interpret. What should she care—and *why* should she?—for the imaginations, the sexual pictures I carried in my head of her female wealth, the fallopian tubes like the twin serpents of the caduceus; or like the ornate clips for sheet music springing up on the trombones and cornets of marching bands. I'm afraid that such preoccupations identify a genuinely modern individual. (Can you say worse of anybody?) And the more guileless such an individual is, the more kinky the women who will attract him. He pursues lustful girls who may have the cure for his intricately decorative naïveté. I suppose she knew that the more difficult she was, the more I would yearn towards her. And to her, as to my dad, I may have been a sexual wraith.

In discussing Treckie with my father in Paris, in the old flat on the Rue Bonaparte, I said, "A woman is supposed to want a child by the man she loves. So since she had the kid, I figure that she somehow, somewhere, loves me."

"How can you let yourself have such ideas!"

"I'm ready to bet, or even swear, that women who have such emotions can still be found."

Dad answered impatiently, "Go look for one, then." And then he took me by surprise. Being a Ninety Day Wonder in the navy (lieutenant j.g.) had made a gentleman of him, but now he expressed himself like a GI. "As I told you before, you've got your head up your ass, as Aristophanes would say."

I laughed at this, and so did he, but we were laughing at cross-purposes. This was not the moment to explain what I was laughing at. But here I can mention it in passing: At the Faculty Club half a year ago, I had lunch with the university's chief of urology and he asked me whether I would sign up for a survey he was making, using the latest technology. In the control group, he needed a man of my age and wanted to know if I would volunteer, so I did. Then I had the experience in his lab of sitting on an endoscopic device (electromagnetic resonance, or some such *truc*). Inside me a balloon was inflated with water; a TV screen was turned towards me and there I saw my own prostate gland, my own seminal vesicles, my own bladder, with the fluid in it resembling a little pond with a still surface. The prostate entered the picture like the top half of an egg. All this was in grayish and whitish tones. You could make an expedition to the Kalahari Desert or to

Death Valley, but the landscapes of his own interior no traveler ever sees.

So when my father said I had my head up my ass, this was the vision that made me laugh. What would one see there? Was this what Atlantis would look like—this calm, still landscape (courtesy of electromagnetic resonance)? This was where magical technology led. By pushing to the very borders of literalness you got into visionary areas which science wanted nothing to do with.

I should have liked to talk to M. Yermelov about it. In the old days, I would have gone over to the Rue du Dragon and knocked at his door, but he had been dead for a decade. This Yermelov was the first of my Russian teachers. An elderly exile (since the twenties), he was familiar with the mystical tradition. My maternal grandfather Crader had dabbled in it (the Trees of Life and of Knowledge). But Yermelov studied Trismegistus, the Zohar, Eliphas Levi, Giordano Bruno, Paracelsus. Along the Boulevard Saint-Germain there were shops specializing in such literature. Yermelov tried to instruct me somewhat. I was willing and receptive but much too young. However, the old man apparently made a lifelong impression on my mind, for I still remember what he said. He told me that each of us had his angel, a being charged with preparing us for a higher evolution of the spirit. At present we were essentially alone, first in the sense that the recognition of angels was forbidden us by the prevailing worldview, and secondly in our shadowy realization of the existence of others, and consequently of our own existence. In the solitude this enforced upon us, we were aware, each of us, of a small glacier in the breast. (As when Matthew Arnold wrote that he was thirty years old and his heart was three parts iced over.) This glacier must be thawed, and the necessary warmth for that must, to begin with, be willed. Thinking begins with willing, and thinking must be warmed and colored with feeling. The task of the angels is to instill warmth into our souls. Well, the room on the Rue du Dragon was freezing; the old man wore layers of sweaters during lessons, and wrapped himself also in blankets. You could understand that warmth would be a concern to him. We must assist the angels by making the necessary preparations. Here the difficulty is that waking consciousness is nowadays very meager. The noise of the world is so terrible that we can endure it only by being coated with sleep. We can give the angels little help from within when they try to instill warmth into us—the warmth of love. And the angels also are fallible. They were human themselves once; that's why they are subject to confusion. And, said Yermelov, they goof. Our waking consciousness louses up their efforts, and since they have orders to transmit their impulse at all costs, they send it when we're sleeping. What happens then is terrible. (Yermelov, horrified, raises gloved hands towards the ceiling.) Denied access to the soul, the angels work directly on the sleeping body. In the physical body this angelic love is corrupted into human carnality. Such is the source of all the disturbed sexuality of the present age. "Animalized!" Yermelov said. The *prise de courant* led directly into the flesh and the instincts, whereas the current should have gone into the sentient soul. Instead, planetary demons of electricity were entering us from beneath, coming from the interior of the earth. They filled the spinal fluid with their currents of lust. As the millennium approached its end, this was the true picture of human sexuality. Eros himself was assailed by electricity and at the same time by sclerosis. Pure love is overcome by perversity. We become fixated on the sexual members. The angels failing, the physicians take over, as Plato foretold in the *Symposium*. Love is replaced by Health, and Health is obtained by anatomical means. Freud himself writes the prescription, *penis normalis, dosim*. Then, as pharmacology follows medicine, we shoot ourselves full of drugs, hormones, narcotics, our souls are brutalized, human beings become impervious to all higher impulses. Erotic obsessions, concupiscence, lewdness—the sexual furies—are streaming after us. You have to pity the angels too. By their failure to penetrate our sodden sleep they also degenerate. M. Yermelov would insist on this.

And that was how I got my early Russian lessons. There were topics other than sex, of course. Old Yermelov was the great-uncle of Ilya, my pal at the *lycée*. I often visited Ilya's home to practice my Russian on his family, and this was the bonus I was given.

All this may appear to be about *me*. It really isn't; it's about

Uncle Benn, the circumstances of his marriage to Matilda Layamon, the struggle with Harold Vilitzer that resulted from it. I bring it forward *only* as it relates to him. But of course I was affected by these thoughts on the sexual problem and I took part in all of this. Benn confided in me and he was familiar with my way of thinking.

Uncle stopped for me in Seattle and we were off to Tokyo and Kyoto.

Fairly careful with a buck, he was paying my way. I was broke, since I acknowledged paternity, of course, and was shelling out for child support. I couldn't afford a junket like this. Uncle took me along because he was having an extra-hard time. He was humiliated by his undignified escape from Caroline (at his time of life, a man of such distinction). It was only me that he could talk to. I was doing so badly with Treckie that he needn't be ashamed to talk. We were a pair of dubs. Also, I was a more than willing listener, and a fervent consultant. I think I would have made a good priest. You could come to me with your troubles. Many did. I seldom refused to listen, and never refused to counsel. Either I was very nosy or I was cut out for the cure of souls.

I had warned Uncle against Caroline Bunge. Who wouldn't have? She was very handsome, but she spelled trouble. She was a big, graceful (old-style) lady, vampy, rich, ornate, slow-moving, a center-stage personality. Middle-aged, she still stood out like a goddess from a Ziegfeld extravaganza, the Venus de Oro type, one of those figures that would rise through the stage floor while the musicians whipped away with their bows. She would wear egret feathers, pearls on her throat, diamonds on her breasts, and stand in a scallop shell. The note of the past, of the twenties and thirties, was one of the strange nice things about Caroline. She spoke through the nose in a way which used to be glamorous—the Jean Arthur style. But I enjoyed Caroline's company, I have to admit. When you examined it, her air of belonging to the past was caused primarily by her remoteness from the present. It may have been the lithium that made her remote. Being on mood pills was one hundred percent contemporary. If you aren't up-to-the-moment you aren't altogether real. But crazies are always contemporary, as sandpipers always run ahead of the foam line on the beaches.

Now, why hadn't Benn recognized that the poor lady was *détraquée*?

He had met her in Puerto Rico at a seafront high-rise gambling hotel. Colleagues from Río Piedras, where he was a guest lecturer, had brought him to see the sights. As he was not interested in dice tables or blackjack, they parked him near the swimming pool while they went off to try their own luck in the casino.

Uncle said that the hotel pool was an 007 setting for criminal and sexual intrigue. . . . He walked about, trying to place himself in a spot of shade where he could catch a breath of sea air. One of his strongest impressions was that the pool smell of chlorine, combined with the odor of sodden newspapers drying on chair seats, gave off the kind of vapor that you smell near a distillery. Just beyond the crazy clamor, rock music pounding, kids screaming, planes overhead trailing banner advertisements, away from the high rollers and sun idolators, there were quiet palm groves. The beauty of the Caribbean had withdrawn some hundreds of yards up the beach.

Caroline Bunge happened to be lying in the sun near the spot of shade he found. Was it the cool place, the available seat, that determined his choice? Not the Ziegfeld figure? She was stacked, and Uncle was not the man to miss that. Among the children in the pool were several of her own. These never were identified. At no time did they approach their mother.

Benn sat in the white latticed plastic chair and a conversation began. He remembered that the grass underfoot looked papery, all but artificial. He plucked a blade and examined it. The venation was striate, not factory made. "They bring rolls of turf and lay them down like carpeting. I don't like that uneasy feeling of uncertainty at the border between nature and manufacture," he said to me. He commented next on the heaviness of Caroline's makeup. For rouge, eye shadow and lipstick, I prefer the French word *fard* with its connotations—an embellishment but also a burden.

She opened the conversation by asking what Uncle was doing in northern city clothes on a tropical beach. He told her he was a visitor on a quick trip. "The botany interested her," he said. "She even had some notion what it was about. She was remote but not dumb." Her manner of speech was deliberate. Her sentences were composed in advance. You could see preparations being made before each utterance. As she was putting her thoughts in order her eyes moved to one side, and there was a kind of charm in it. She said that Benn's winter tweeds "made a statement" in this climate. Somebody had told her that the Expressionist painter Beckmann would come to the beach in formal attire. Powerful personalities may assert themselves in that way. Benn simply said he hadn't thought to bring other clothing. She was curious about the motives of advanced minds. She always had been drawn to philosophy, she said, and she assumed that as a university professor he must be in earnest about metaphysics. For some time she had been puzzling over an important remark made by Buckminster Fuller. She was in the audience and had heard it herself. Fuller said, "God is a verb." She had taken this as a mantra for meditation. The Word was with God. The Word *was* God. Fuller insisted that *Logos* couldn't be a noun. He mentioned that in *Faust* it was said, "In the beginning was the Deed."

Uncle said, "Very good, provided that you know what you're doing."

In the retelling he made more sense perhaps than she had made. This apparently stimulating talk must in reality have been numbing to the mind. Again, his uncommon gift of self-description, possibly rooted in habitual truthfulness: "I began to be sexually motivated," he said. "While at the same time a yawning paralysis closed in on me as she was talking. It wasn't unpleasant. It was like the Greek drug nepenthe. She talked on." For some reason he always saw more in people than others were willing to see. I myself was one of these unwilling others, so I was intrigued by this special talent.

Caroline told Benn that she had been divorced for several years. She mentioned that she owned a flat in London and a house in East Hampton as well. She spoke of the levels of social life on Long Island—the painters who also were multimillionaires, the multimillionaires who preferred to be among painters. On Sundays painters and millionaires would play softball together. Crowds drove out from Manhattan to watch these famous persons at their ball game. The city visitors lunched on a quick slice of pizza or quiche and then drove home. Five hours on the road simply to have a look-see. She went on to speak of intrigues between art dealers, critics and tax lawyers, describing the scandal of the Rothko estate, of which Uncle had never heard. Dealers always had been shady. Nobody knew how many forgeries had been put over by the Duveens, Berensons and other tricksters. The Mellons, the Morgans, the Altmans, the Fricks, the Gardners and many more had been taken to the cleaners and so had the museum experts. Yerkes the transit magnate and Thompson the Chicago restaurateur had bought phony pieces. At some length then she went into hostile corporate takeovers, the money being made by her friends in greenmail and arbitrage. She listed the U.N. big shots, the gurus, Jesuits, movie stars and rock musicians who came to the Hamptons, their parties, their drug habits, their sexual practices, their diseases (AIDS, herpes and the rest). Some of her stockbroker friends were activists funding revolutionists in Central America. They were "into politics," she said.

Caroline had been a bosom friend of Libby Holman Reynolds, the deceased torch singer, who had once been acquitted of the charge of murdering her husband, heir to the Camel cigarette fortune. This pretty lady had been a vivid heroine of the Jazz Age. Caroline had been her confidante and also a good friend of Shanker, her husband. He was famous for his wall-sized woodcuts. You almost always saw him with a knife in his hand. However, he was very kind and he tolerated Libby's weakness for handsome young guys. She had to have those to keep being the dramatic beauty into old age. Caroline admired Libby, not taking her for a role model, she said, but speaking of her brave attitude to life and of the ducal establishment she ran—great houses, Rolls-Royces, chartered planes, a staff of servants; and again and again (indicating deep feeling) she referred to her erotic extravagances, her tragedies, the death of a child, her abandonment by a lover truly dear to her.

I observed that Caroline had put herself out for Uncle, and had in part portrayed herself by describing Libby. "She was singing like a siren. It worked. You were enchanted," I said. I didn't say that it would be a strange siren who took lithium or Elavil.

Uncle said that she must have borrowed Libby's manner, the manner of a nightclub star who was a credible murder suspect. Dramatically vindicated but marked for life by scandal. Only Caroline, as Uncle described her, occupied her beach chair with a kind of laid-back slackness, speaking obscurely, and frequently incomprehensibly. What did Uncle see in her? Well, all kinds of human matters, as James Joyce said, will not bear being written about in black and white, and she appealed to him by reason of her challenging remoteness.

He himself came back to a present moment from very remote places—from his botanical broodings. Sex drew him back. As he couldn't really discuss science with me, he often wanted to talk about ladies.

"She told me to buy tropical-weight trousers. I was pouring sweat. She said how nice it would be for me to bathe in the ocean. I could rent swimming trunks from the attendant. And did I have to go back to winter so soon?"

On the plane to Japan I had to allow him to sort out his feelings about her.

"Picking you up!" I said. "She lost no time."

"That's not accurate. . . . What was *I* doing wandering around the hotel grounds? I was looking for a Caroline like this, a suitable woman—handsome, responsive, mature."

"Tell me about the mature part."

"She was old enough to appreciate a man like me. She could forgive my inadequacies, and accept me all in all."

"Love is a harder subject than lichens. But what did age have to do with it?"

"Sense is beaten into people by unhappiness, and that takes time, and time disfigures you. She had had beautiful legs, once. Caroline is no youngster. When a man looks at a woman he tends to forget that he's no kid himself. I can't help taking the viewpoint of age eighteen or thereabouts."

He had a special weakness for beautiful women, and in Caroline he found one who *had been* beautiful. He thought he might settle for that.

Anyway, she did most of the talking and she said many curious things. Occasionally, Uncle told me, her conversation was like the fluttering of one of those cartoon books that kids used to animate with the thumb so that the pictures skittered and funny actions were performed. Yet he was drawn to Caroline, although he couldn't quite define the attraction. One seldom can, of course. In this case, perhaps Uncle reckoned that a woman who didn't know what she was doing would be less critical of a man unsure of himself. A woman who was mentally AWOL might be just the thing. Well, I thought he was abasing himself and selling himself too short. But I revised this with another thought: Idiotic women turn some men on passionately. There are examples of this in Russian literature. Tolstoy's would-be saint, Father Sergius, who could resist the seductions of a society woman, succumbed later to a feebleminded girl. Old Karamazov took advantage of a moronic woman and made her pregnant. Was this because he was drunk or because a witless creature had a peculiar power to excite him?

I was going too far in my speculation, as usual. Caroline was no moron. Often she acted stoned. She told me that in the sixties she had been on LSD. There may have been wild experiments—she wanted you to think so when chatting about the Manson cult and the Jonestown murders and suicides. But up to a point she was agreeable company. At any time of day she was gotten up elaborately, and she looked and smelled like a collection of attractions from the finest shops, from Bonwit's, Gucci's, Tiffany's (sophisticated people will know more fashionable names and smile at my ignorance).

I said, "Uncle, by now you've seen her house in the Hamptons and her dinner parties in the East Seventies. Do you really want to make the Caroline scene?"

"She only wanted to show me what she needed to be rescued from, how little there is in such an existence to take seriously. She's had enough of it. She plans to sell the East Hampton property and move across the Sound to new surroundings. Mystic, Connecticut, maybe. She'll buy two Mercedes-Benzes."

"One for each of you? What about your university connection?"

"I could cut it back to half time."

"You're not ready to withdraw from botany and live at Mystic or Old Lyme!"

"Her lawyers would set up a small private research foundation so I could pursue my Arctic lichen studies. I'm on the track of certain cytological details. . . . I won't burden you with that." (He didn't like to get technical with me.) "And then the department couldn't crab about my being away so much. They'd save money."

By this time he and Caroline were intimate. She had come to the Hotel Westbury, where he stayed when he visited New York. He told me that as he approached the bed where she was lying, she switched on the lamp so that she could look him over, and she said, "I'll buy that." It amused him. In fact he was childishly pleased and couldn't conceal it. Having known such a variety of men, she found *him* acceptable. "So I'm not so bad."

"The Bengali lady told you that," I said.

"Rajashwari, yes. But Oriental women don't judge by Western standards."

"Who says you have to meet Western standards? I'd sooner make my deal with the Indian lady than with Caroline."

"No. A Western sense of humor is important to me."

"You have to consider what it is you're taking for humor—whether it's Xanax, Elavil, lithium, plus alcohol and possibly cocaine. Doses big enough to calm the Indian Ocean."

Never mind the sense of humor. When she turned on the bedside lamp she may have seen not one but three men in the buff. Glad to buy them all.

"You worry that she may come between us, that she'll bury me in Old Lyme and I'd never be seen again. That never could happen, Kenneth."

"It sounds as though you were considering marriage. I can't blame you. Nor do I expect you to hang around here because of me. Something central is missing, I realize. Even Adam, who had God Himself to talk to, asked for a human companion. I'd marry Treckie if I could. And at your age you'd like a domestic life. We've been over this ground many times, pro and con: Chekhov saying, 'If you're afraid of loneliness don't marry,' and Akim Tamiroff in *The Great McGinty*, arguing, 'A man without a wife is like a coat without the pants, like a pig without a poke.' Then you say, 'I'm becoming too self-sufficient. Don't need anybody. It makes my blood run cold to recognize how little this or that individual matters to me.' Then why pick Caroline as the individual that will matter? You'll have to be twice as self-sufficient if you marry her. Now, which do you want? Two human beings bound together in love and kindness, or double self-sufficiency with a freaked-out wife?"

He listened, yes, and he understood well enough what I was saying. However, he allowed Caroline to proceed with her plans. She gave him, in installments, a full description of the life they would lead together. He was to have his own lab. She would accompany him on his expeditions—in my pictorial irresponsibility, I saw Caroline with four litter bearers traveling over vast snowfields. Benn once told me that when he landed by helicopter on the slope of Mount Erebus to collect samples, he had felt that he was very near the end of the earth, the boundary of boundaries. "Of course, there's no such thing," he said, "but there is such a feeling." Well, from Caroline herself there came a sense of this boundary of boundaries.

From the angle of divine pity there was plenty of pity in it, let me tell you. And how long can we weak variable creatures hold such an angle? Fantasy helps—in fact we lend ourselves to fantasy because what we call the commonsense, humdrum world makes us flow in that direction by the preposterous tides that have entered it. Free and liberal sexual contacts have now become conventional, and then, falling in love with a girl like Treckie, I find myself involved in the sadomasochistic question. Behaviors that would once have been wild are now no more exceptional than setting the table for a family supper. Uncle told me, for instance (and he didn't often refer to his private contacts, remembering me as a small boy and censoring himself), Uncle told me that Caroline didn't use the pill for birth prevention. Instead, she filled herself with tufts of paper—facial tissues or torn pieces of paper table napkins. This began towards the end of dinner. As she sat at the other end of the table, she would almost absentmindedly begin to pick at the napkins.

Telling me this had been hard for him.

"Any hint that she's doing something unusual?"

"No," said Benn.

"Not what the sex experts call foreplay?"

"She might as well have been brushing her teeth," he said.

I said something about a Western sense of humor. Uncle just shrugged.

I won't pretend that Uncle was an innocent—wouldn't even try. I am convinced, however, that he kept, as in an inner shrine, a vision of an abiding intimacy. Those promises of love and kindness. Only he looked for them in the oddest places. It wasn't just that he fancied big, handsome broads (in contrast to the compactness and brevity I preferred); to beauty in the formal sense there had to be some difficulty added. This is one of the knottiest questions there are, defying the most persistent efforts of the most cunning fingers.

Anyway, Caroline, for all her airs of not being with it *(dans la lune)*, was closing in on the man of her choice. She had bought herself an outfit to be married in. Her "people" had arranged for the marriage license. She asked what he had done with Lena's wedding band. It was in the box at the bank, together with his gold cuff links, his mother's locket, his father's fountain pen. "Come to think of it, perhaps a new ring would be better," she said. She gave him her flight number and arrival time. She laid out the entire program—she had program fever. A suite was reserved at the Hilton. There was no expression of love, not so much as a small-time endearment. As soon as he rang off, it seemed to him an eternity before he could get a dial tone and obtain the code for a direct call to Kyoto.

At the Seattle airport he said, "Do you think I did right?"

"I don't think you had any alternative."

He studied me. The horizontal figure eight eye frame this time conveyed a thought I believed I could interpret: Now that he had given up Caroline Bunge, I, Kenneth Trachtenberg, was once more his only human resource. That was not so good, and I moved immediately to support him. "It may have been that second person inside you," I said. "The one that decided you must become a botanist."

"Possibly. I can't be sure that that person is benevolent. I might have told her on the telephone not to come."

"Farcical escape from a pursuing woman. It isn't so rare, after all."

"That second person of mine sometimes acts like a demon."

"There's a little play by Gogol, *The Wedding*, in which the bridegroom climbs out the window just after deciding to marry. He works it out rationally, and then he flees. All right, what if there should be a demon in you. Would you rather have a baby-sitter? A baby-sitter is all you would rate if you were the innocent botanist these ladies take you for. They turn to Professor Chlorophyll. There's no harm in him. You could trust *him* with a baby. He's not like all the bad men who gave them such a rough time."

"I *am* like them. What about the case of Della Bedell?"

"You aren't going to bring that up! Uncle! It was unfortunate, but it wasn't your fault. She also took the initiative."

"But I went along. There was no excuse for me."

Mrs. Bedell, the lady upstairs, from the apartment directly above Benn's, came down and rang his kitchen buzzer. She hadn't used the front door; she didn't want the neighbors on his landing to see her. She came by the back stairs. One could be sorry for Della Bedell. The divorced wife of an alcoholic, she drank a bit too. A decent unhappy lady, she was nevertheless capable, and downtown she held a responsible position—head of personnel for a big firm. Tightly pulled together on the job, she allowed herself to fall apart on weekends, sometimes evenings. In some respects an attractive woman, she had let herself become too stout for her own good, and wore her hair cropped—stylish but unbecoming, modified punk.

She buzzed Uncle out of his chair. It was 10 P.M. She must have been struggling with herself for some time. But it was no longer an impropriety, according to the women's magazines and TV, to take the initiative.

And what is Mrs. Bedell's pretext? The light has gone out in her kitchen and she can't remove the ceiling fixture. She needs the assistance of a man to change the bulb. Can't she call the superintendent? Uncle asks. His shirt is hanging out. He has been updating his research material. She doesn't like to annoy the super at this hour of the night. He'll tell her to wait till morning anyway. And there is a man downstairs. Single, like herself. No family circle to disturb. Uncle doesn't suggest that she bring a lamp from the next room if she wants to boil water for her tea. It isn't tea she's been drinking. So in his simplicity (maybe), he puts on his shoes and follows her upstairs. She has no stepladder. He has to stand on an upholstered dining room chair. She suggests that he remove his shoes. In the end, everything is removed.

She turns out to be a fat little person. Physically unsuitable for such desires. He is embarrassed to make love to her. Talk about slavery and freedom—he *has* to! He has no position prepared that would enable him to withdraw courteously on the strength of his principles. He may well be a Citizen of Eternity. And my hunch is that he will turn out to be one. He has imaginative powers that let him see things others don't see, and the gauge of a man is the *grade* of what he can see. If he can muster his forces, then Earth becomes his Paradise. But even this does not prevent his being a fool. The firm surface Benn presents to the world is mined every which way by desires, longings, crying needs, hungers. In this respect he does not differ greatly from Della Bedell. She, too, has been mined within to a dangerous degree. Anyway, he is unable to tell her, "You're a very attractive lady, but I don't feel right in the bed of a comparative stranger"; or: "Just because I am a contemporary man and you are a contemporary woman . . ." Or: "The accident of being neighbors is not reason enough for this. Unless we have more in common than this carnal moment, this will be one more dead end." But he's like one of those old-time Kansas banks that any punk robber could knock over. Needy ladies hold him up. She clasps him like a sixteen-year-old girl, making herself drunker than she is and being belligerent about her biological rights. Technical difficulties arise. Finding the right place is a problem. Finally the act gets itself performed. Uncle is able to leave—returning to his own bed and forgetting the whole thing, if he can. But of course he can't. Sleep, that night, is out of the question.

She expects him now to ring *her* bell. He doesn't do that. He doesn't send a gracious note, which is clumsy of him, and also insulting. A few nights later, she comes down and buzzes his kitchen bell again, demanding and angry. She puts messages in his mailbox: "You're pretending to be out. When do *I* get my chance to live!" And: "What am I supposed to do with my sexuality?"

Now Benn is deeply depressed. "What did I do it for!" he says.

Della Bedell had the excuse of intoxication and desperation. He had no excuse. He says again and again, "It was unsuitable for both parties."

I try to make clear to him the latest motives at work, and console him with insights more available to members of my generation. I say, "Whatever troubles people run into, they look for the sexual remedy. Whether it's business, a career problem, character difficulties, doubts about one's body, even metaphysics, they turn to sex as the analgesic."

"No, no, Kenneth, not an aspirin, no. That makes it too trivial."

"All right, then; they do the act by which love would be transmitted if there *were* any."

"That's more like it."

"Furthermore, women are allowed to be more aggressive now. But when they're rebuffed it's terrible for them. It used to go the other way, women saying no to men. The men became accustomed to it."

"I should have rebuffed her right away, without sampling. What hurt her was that I sampled."

"She's set up to be made a fool of—the way she dresses,

wears her hair, the way she speaks. Not like a woman taking herself seriously. How *could* you take her seriously?"

Theoretical considerations don't go far with Uncle in this case. I say to him, "We're in trouble if we don't keep these minor absurdities minor."

"*I* was absurd," Uncle says.

He's in the dumps, blames himself, pities Della Bedell. She now comes to his front door and bangs the knocker. Uncle's building is a decorous place, not one of those swinging condominiums where women live with two husbands and the tenants deal in dope and fire guns at one another—the downtown scene. So Uncle does what he's in the habit of doing. He escapes to Brazil, where he lectures on morphology.

Then the worst happens. While he is gone, Mrs. Bedell dies of a cardiac arrest. He can't get over it. "The life in her already was flickering," he says, "when I opened the door and saw her holding a light bulb. After that, sure it sounded preposterous when she said, 'What am I supposed to do with my sexuality?' But wasn't that the voice of a single life saying something terrible? A single creature speaking of her fate?"

"Watch out, Uncle. Don't exaggerate."

"*I* had the sex with her. I know what I know."

"It was more hysteria than lovemaking. And when you first told me about it, *you* were the one who made it sound preposterous."

"Well, yes. Maybe I did. If I didn't treat it as a joke it would be too awful to face. . . . But now she's dead. It gets me, Kenneth. I see her suffocated by swollen longings. Poor thing, her heart gave out."

"You didn't cause it."

"I might have prevented it, but it probably does no good to harp on it, either. A newspaperman had me on the phone a few days ago. Vulliam, my chairman, got rid of him by putting him onto me, and he wanted a statement about plant life and the radiation level increasing. Also dioxin and other harmful wastes. He was challenging about it. Well—I agreed it was bad. But in the end I said, 'It's terribly serious, of course, but I think more people die of heartbreak than of radiation.'"

"He must have thought you were a flake. I suppose you had Della Bedell in mind."

"Not just . . . No, no."

I went on being helpful. It's terrible how we pester each other from this motive, saying all the right things. I said to him, "You have to set up a principle of proportion. You can't be feeling furiously for everybody that crosses your path. She was a fat little lady who hit the bottle. Why not look at it that way? Why make it the act of darkness; why not consider it a vaudeville turn? You were the handyman who changed the bulb. In the bedroom she put out the light. Didn't want to be seen."

He continued nevertheless to suffer over her.

We didn't discuss Della Bedell after the plane took off. We rose above Seattle's vast rain cloud and entered pure sunlight. I had the sun right in my face as we climbed, which caused me to picture myself, the Kenneth Uncle might see with his dark blue eyes. Owing to its length, my hair tends to fall forward in two curves on the temples. My eyes are set high in the face.

"I wonder what it is that causes these troubles," I said. "A different time frame maybe, assumptions from a different epoch that you make? As if you were still farming with a bullock. Picture it in a state like Nebraska, you and your bullock plow, with your neighbors sitting on their hundred-disk machines, laughing their heads off at your out-of-date effort."

"For what I need, their advanced technology is no more help than my ox."

If Uncle had been insignificant, there wouldn't have been such problems. If Della Bedell had been a beauty, if Caroline had been playing with a full deck, Uncle wouldn't have made his getaway out the window like Gogol's Podkolyossin. There are women who are driven to daring invention, and come on with dazzling initiatives. Others, fearing to be left behind to sink and drown, make desperate but senseless moves. Sometimes people who are managing badly look through their window at Nature. There they see growth, balance, beauty, all the results of billions of years of gradual development, and they are shamed by it, it all makes them seem shabby. They sit and stare like clumsy, hollow dummies. But it then occurs to them, "It's *my* mind that perceives this order, beauty, et cetera. It may even be *my* mind that created it. It's possible that Nature doesn't even exist. I made it up, just to fill up space. Well, if I'm gifted with such a mind, why am I lying here with a quaking heart, like a baby porcupine being ragged by dogs?"

The pilot announced that we had reached our cruising altitude. I think he said that we were at 38,000 feet. We might imagine that we had left the earth behind. We were still, however, within the mundane egg where all creatures, all beings, lived on death, infected by death in the very desire for love, the only force that held out a hope against being devoured altogether. Mere Nature is Hell, as Swedenborg wrote (I ask you to remember that Aunt Lena had left her collection of Swedenborg books to me). Insofar as sex is identified with Nature, the Euclidian logic is simple. In sexual pleasure (or what people are ready to settle for in that department) much pain is incorporated. And the bigger the block of shares assigned to "mere Nature," the more Hell there is in it. In short, as you can tell from these reflections, I felt great pity for Uncle and, insofar as I had taken him as a forerunner, my personal *avant garde*, a certain regret also for myself. I know that self-interest is the very heart of capitalist ethics, but simple experience shows that people are often harder on themselves than on anybody else.

Trying to relieve Uncle of the humiliation of fleeing to the Orient, I talked to him about Treckie and, using skinny Gallic gestures to enlarge the horizon (in my father's style), I pointed out how troubled the whole business was and asked whether Eros could cope with the powers of darkness, arguing that people who were well-balanced and practical had given up on all that long ago. No use pitting yourself against impossibilities on a world scale. Why did Swedenborg say that *mere* Nature was Hell? He meant Nature in a literal view, in a mechanistic interpretation. I didn't want to intrude on his sensitive feelings, but when Della turned the light off it was because she feared to be seen with a literal eye. To be seen literally dries out one's humanity. Still, when a woman puts out the light, should you set yourself the task of interpreting the world as a whole? This implies that you are a microcosm forever responsible to a macrocosm. You're really asking for it then. The macrocosm will beat you to a pulp. It makes far more sense to concentrate on which mutual fund to put your savings into. Don't try to beat the market on your own. The giant investors have shoals of computers. Those electronic sibyls are infallible. There, lower on the scale, is still another macrocosm (the New York Stock Exchange). Stay away from all that. . . . I felt slightly confused myself. What I mainly meant was that the interest of human beings is quickly exhausted by literalness. What was deadly about Admiral Byrd's observation of his companions in the Antarctic was that it was so literal. This literalness, from a sexual standpoint, is lethal. When it becomes a matter of limbs, members and organs, Eros faces annihilation.

"Hey, look, Kenneth—a moratorium on heaviness. We're going to Kyoto for a holiday."

"Sorry about that. Let's go back to Treckie."

"She liked you well enough to have a baby by you."

"Proves nothing. She wanted to have a baby. And a short woman gave birth to this long child of ours. You'll say she chose me. Well, I was welcome briefly. I compare it to being a bum on Thanksgiving Day. Do-gooders invite you to the shelter and give you a beautiful turkey dinner. But it's a Thursday-only deal. Don't come back on Friday."

Others might have smiled. Uncle nodded seriously. "She may be waiting for you to initiate something."

"What should I initiate?"

"Oh . . . something she considers important."

"I have no clue to what Treckie is waiting for. We don't talk about me. These last few days we talked mostly about her. She wanted to tell me about her progress in self-realization, the mistakes she's correcting, her new insights into her former insights and the decisions she's taken as a result. How much better she is now. . . ."

"Difficult to listen to such stuff."

"The way to change for the better is to begin by telling everybody about it. You make an announcement. You repeat your intentions until others begin to repeat them to you. When you hear them from others you can say, 'Yes, that's what I think too.' The more often your intention is repeated, the truer it becomes. The key is fluency. It's fluency of formulation that matters most. Still, she's such a charmer, such a dear person, such a darling."

"But what about the bruises?"

"Maybe that's just a phase. People have their phases. They often sober up."

"She may yet go into a mother phase."

I said without conviction, "Perhaps." Then I added, "I worry about the child. What will she grow up to be? I'm especially sorry for her because she resembles me in character. I think she inherits certain basic assumptions from my side."

"Which makes you pity her?"

"I'm afraid so. And I think I must have an instinct for fathering."

"You might persuade Treckie, if you worked more at it. If she could see you as you are really, she'd feel differently."

"It's her trendy psychology that's the obstacle. It's not as if we were speaking the same language."

"People aren't willing to let you conclude, to reach your objectives. It seems to be a law that they're bound to withhold what you want. Ultimately it may be in our best interests—the withholding—because we don't want what we should. Physically, anyway, you're mad for her. How nice that is! Suppose Caroline had felt that way about me."

"You ought to know something about that. Only, about six weeks ago, you'll remember, you came to meet her at the airport, waiting at the gate, and she passed you right by."

"One can be absorbed in thoughts. It happens often."

"Absorbed, yes. She was zonked out. There's one bride who, if she did have a hope chest, it would be full of cocaine. Say, Uncle, do you remember Hawthorne's 'Rappaccini's Daughter'? About the beautiful girl immune to deadly plants because she grew up among them? But she was death to her lover. All she had to do was breathe on him, and he was a goner. I can't recall—did she kiss him? Anyway, he died of it."

"Deadly plants, eh? Pretty extreme case."

It wouldn't have mattered what our topic was. He felt rotten about having stiffed Caroline on what should have been her wedding day, and he was slow to respond to my attempts to raise his spirits. I had come to America to complete my education, to absorb certain essential powers from Uncle, and I learned presently that he was looking to *me* for assistance. In those departments where he was master he needed nobody, of course. He was one of those special types who are all right until they get into the common life. Once in the mainstream, however, they can't make it without protection.

Well, I loved my uncle, and I didn't expect perfection. He had the magics, but as a mainstream manager he was nowhere. There may have been, broadly speaking, a policy decision in this, a deliberate sacrifice of shrewdness. I suspect that he was innately as shrewd as the next man. You'd never get intensely shrewd people to accept this. They wouldn't believe it. They'd say the man was faking and they would ascribe diabolical motives to him. They'd say he was operating behind a screen of guilelessness and was a superhypocrite. How can you expect such people to accept magics and include them in their reckonings? On the other hand, Uncle shouldn't have disarmed himself unilaterally and let the shrewdies keep the initiative. His policy was wrong. He needed more political fiber in his constitution.

This will become clear in due course. Meantime I found myself in an advisory position, and there I discovered that I was temperamentally "advisory" to a fanatical degree, opinionated to the point of fussiness: There was only one way to set a table, remove staples from parcels, reheat the coffee. Maybe a hereditary passion for meddling came down to me from my ancestors, who for thousands of years prescribed for everything—benedictions for breaking bread, for going to the toilet, for returning from a funeral. A minor vice, true, but it may have hurt me with Treckie. She pulled off the shelf paper I lined her kitchen cupboards with. "You always know the way a thing should be done." She rejected my esthetics. In Somalia, Mother said the affair would have burnt itself out if Treckie hadn't made herself pregnant. "She has everything done as *she* wants it."

"Useful elucidation" was another weakness of mine. Often I might as well have been lecturing myself. On the plane, for instance, I talked to Benn about the characteristics of the women who were giving us such trouble. "A woman will look at a fellow like you," I said, "and she'll sense that there's a certain value in you. She'll probably say to herself, 'There's a man who's up to something special.' That goes with 'making your soul,' a course of life followed by very few. It produces emanations, and educated women will be especially affected by these emanations. That's why so many Romantics favored peasant women and prostitutes over refined ladies. Well, the peasantry is disappearing and there are very few whores who haven't had a couple of years of college. One more inertia broken up, and the pieces tossed into the cauldron of modern consciousness. What you face, then, is modern women who are proud of their education and their developed minds but who secretly fear that they haven't got what it takes to hold the interest of a man who is powerfully energized by an important task. . . . They don't need to worry so much—there aren't too many people doing important things, directed towards a higher life. But they *do* worry. And what they're afraid of is that such a man will be bored by them. He'll find them out. So they dress, they talk, and they put their moves on you. They act light but they feel heavy. Mortally depressed and gloomy. So much was predicted for them by their parents, especially by their mothers: These girls were so gorgeous, graceful, gifted, trained to expect high results. But where are they? In outer darkness, where their poor hearts are breaking. And this feminine disappointment and sorrow is very hard on men. They often feel called upon to restore the self-esteem that's been lost."

Uncle couldn't have been listening closely, because he came up with a non sequitur. "Did you say anything to Treckie about the bruises on her legs?"

"I told her it made me think of child abuse, and I thought she had a talent for picking out child-abusers."

"You never said anything like that. I don't think she'd care for that kind of joke."

I was somewhat disappointed in Benn. I had tried to tell him something most fundamental and he hadn't followed me. But people have to be ready to hear, and you have to bide your time. Anyway, simply the sound of my voice had cheered him up, even if he disregarded my remarks.

As we approached Japan, I didn't like *his* joke about going astray over Korean waters and being shot down. "By your Russian friends," was how he put it.

Landing in Tokyo, he bowed to the bowing people who had been sent to meet us. We immediately went to Kyoto on the bullet train, and booked into the Tawaraya Inn. Quite a place. There you wore a kimono and slept on the floor; you took scalding baths in a wooden tub. The surroundings gave pleasure by their bareness—neither chairs nor tables nor papers nor books: that in itself was a holiday.

Breakfast was brought by an elderly lady. In the morning there was a rustling at the paper door. On her knees, a maid bowed over your tray, waiting for permission to enter. Her hair was pulled back with a tautness that suggested penance or punishment. Her steps were rapid and minute. My room looked into a tiny garden. This, in another country, should have been waste space—an air shaft into which guests threw whiskey bottles and milk containers. It contained a mossy urn, a dwarf tree. White pebbles covered the ground. The effect was curiously continuous—the garden was not genuinely *outside*, nor my room altogether *inside*. There was nothing except the floor to sit on. If you wanted to look at the *Times* you took it to the bathroom.

For Uncle all this was ancient culture and it put him in good spirits. As a morphologist he preferred abiding structures, which was what they had here in abundance. Also, his conscience no longer reproached him. I was able to relieve him of some of his guilt over Caroline. He had fled Caroline and her Bucky Fuller mantras as David had fled from Saul. In my mind she was like the shape above a burning building—flames of sex shooting through the roof and a cloud of smoke resembling a woman lying passively above it. I was prepared to tell him that he might have had to put her in an institution at the last, and then fight her family, perhaps, because there was no telling how big her estate was, nor how much litigation he might get into—being accused in the end of trying to murder her, as in the von Bülow case. However, there was no occasion for this, because after we arrived in Japan, Uncle almost never spoke about Caroline.

He insisted that sleeping on a mat agreed with you. A

change of perspective brought you into a different mental world, and on the floor you had more interesting dreams.

The private diary kept by Swedenborg during the years of his crisis records dreams that go from "angelic sexuality" to erotic earthiness. I wondered whether this was what Uncle was talking about when he spoke of interesting dreams. I suspected that he was, or once had been, a sensualist. Foolish to say "once had been." If you were that, you continued for life to be it in some degree—no, exaggeratedly, like Balzac's Baron Hulot or Stravinsky's centenarian grandfather. Benn wouldn't have been sexually abused by women if he hadn't had the carnal strength to attract abusive types or to endure (perhaps to invite?) the abuses.

Later in the year, when I visited Mother in East Africa, I tried to get her to tell me what she knew about her brother. She denied beating him on the face many years ago, admitting, however, that "he was a sexy little bastard," and that mothers on Jefferson Street wouldn't let their little girls play with him. But a change came over him in adolescence, she said. She wasn't willing to discuss this with me. She thought it strange, in these surroundings of famine and death, to talk about Uncle's sexual history. Was this the place for it? Given her own history with my father, which had brought her to this refugee camp, I couldn't really blame her. I did mention, intending to be circumspect and objective, that these afflicted multitudes even now were conceiving and giving birth. "Well, that's not lust," she said. "That's procreation, or resisting extinction. Not like the West, where they do it because they're spoiled rotten."

She was elderly and frail, risking her life in the relief camp, and she thought it was "unserious" of me to talk about Uncle in her little room. Still, she did tell me, when I unpacked the box of treats I had brought from Fauchon's and she drank a couple of glasses of eau-de-vie or calvados, that at the age of seventeen Uncle had had a crack-up—maybe even a schizophrenic episode. It had been impossible to make him stay in bed. He would keep getting out and lying on the floor. The family GP couldn't explain it. "It might have been schizophrenia," said Mother. "Dr. Clurman mentioned that, but on Jefferson Street in those days, what did anybody know? The doctor might as well have talked about the Great Wall of China." Love was apparently the cause. Benn had fallen for the daughter of Cohen the tailor. She was slight, pale, pretty, said Mother. "Only malnutrition can give you that wonderful look. After a few months here I can tell you that. The Cohen girl had a thyroid surplus and an iron deficiency. You have to live in the back of the tailor shop and sleep in a room without a window to have that kind of charm."

"So!" I said. "He loved her. Didn't she love him?"

"She was a hot little number," said Mother. "And I think he hesitated to do what she wanted done. Somebody less idealistic was more obliging. She began to date the new fellow. Your uncle was out of his head with grief—with sex misery. Benn was backward with girls, didn't understand how to conduct himself." Mother said this with more impatience than sympathy. She's one of your wiry, challenging, sharp women. Meet her requirements, and she'll love you a lot. However, she sets you a stiff test. You have to overcome some hard trials, just as she did and is doing now. As hostess to two or three generations of high-powered French intellectuals, observing how they dined and drank, their tastes in wine and sex, their bold ideas, their cowardly tactics with love objects, male or female, she lost her feminine midwestern timidity about "Ideas." She was used to hearing nations and epochs discussed. World history, existential categories—none of that fazed her. She was past being impressed with your thoughts.

I'm afraid I often tried to do just that. As though she would let her own son come flying in over the heads of so many pundits, academicians, the authors of books on *Existenz* and geopolitics. Your mother is the one goalkeeper you never can score with.

Mother and I were sitting in the small prefab room. Outside, people were dying every minute. The food that might have saved them was being stolen by officials, flogged in faraway places (Aspremont, Montalban, Bizerte, Cathay and who knows where else). Much of it was eaten by rats and birds, or carried away by insects, or simply rotted.

Many of the Ethiopians I found to be persons of singular beauty. I couldn't get over the elegant shapes of their heads, the rich dark eyes. I had in my mind by now the Swedenborgian idea of correspondences, that the Creation was one of the languages in which God communicated with man. Some of my Russian symbolists had inherited this from their French forerunners like Baudelaire and Rimbaud, or got it directly from Aksakov, Swedenborg's Russian translator. So the camp was in part dreamlike, as was the presence of my mother, looking like Mother Teresa, doing her best to minister to the sick and starving.

But with all this, I kept talking about Uncle Benn and pumping Mother for information. Presently she got (rightly!) sore at me. She said, "Darling, you must be out of your mind. My brother and his girlfriends! Your Father—okay. But he had some taste. Your uncle doesn't know which side is up. He was lucky enough, as much as he deserved, with Lena. She was a decent woman, but by any real standard she was a frump. When she died he made such a fuss, you would have thought she was some kind of saint. He should stick to his leaves. Or sap, or whatever his business is."

Naturally I disagreed. When she's angry she gives short shrift to everybody. You can't blame a man for hoping to hear something instructive at last about the female sex from his own mother. Some glowing jewel of wisdom, the only legacy that could possibly interest me. But she didn't mean to give me a damn thing. She was disappointed in me, even angry. She had wanted me to be a big shot. I should have been the *Times*'s number one man in Paris, or *chef de bureau* for *Le Monde* in Washington, or NBC's head for Western Europe with thirty people under me, or *porte-parole* at the Moscow embassy. Would I have felt more for the refugees if I had been a top newsman? I'd be thinking entirely of photos and telexes, or how to beat out the competition.

She didn't have a clue to her brother's real meaning, that he was a Citizen of Eternity, lower in the hierarchy than the Greats I listed earlier, but a person of the first importance just the same.

She blamed Uncle for misleading me. Why couldn't he let me alone? She didn't want me to be like my father, either—although she understood that better: courtship, natural-history sex dances, a pair of naked strutters doing their thing around a bed in Paris. At least Rudi Trachtenberg was responding to a talent, and a talent will cause your death if you try to hide it. Therefore my mother went along, she submitted, she even abetted and, possibly with a certain pride in his gift, she collaborated with him. With a force of Nature, what else could she do? But her brother, as she saw him, wasn't in the same class. His botanical talent didn't mean a thing to her. She blamed Uncle for leading me astray. What was this academic stuff? Why should I become a lousy professor? I was sharing a dormitory shower with undergraduates whose rock music drove me crazy. My meekness with Treckie disgusted her. A man like my father would never have put up with a girl like that. She didn't want me to be an *homme à femmes* like Dad, but did I have to be the direct opposite? My obsession with Uncle was going to set me back a decade or two. A bitter vexation to a spirited mother who had suffered so much for my sake, I amounted, so far, to nothing.

I made the mistake in Somalia of trying to discuss my views with her. I gave in to that besetting weakness of wanting her to know what her child was thinking. I didn't pretend to be a Kojève, or even a Georges Bataille, but my purpose was to take her behind the appearance of tomfoolery and being victimized by a stupid girl, and give her a fleeting sketch or general outline of my project. No reason for existing unless your life is a turning point. No use joining the general march of declining humankind. I had sent her an offprint of my article (from *The Russian Review*) "The Morning of Acmeism, from Gumilyov and Gorodetsky to Mandelstam," underlining the quotation: "To be—that is the artist's greatest pride. He desires no other paradise than existence . . ." and so forth. I discuss in my essay the similarities between this and the nearly identical outlook of Paracelsus, Swedenborg and Blake. Since she is a clever woman, I gave her an opportunity to develop for herself the intimation that I was attached to my uncle because (and this you could see for yourself if you had ever watched him among his plants) he clearly desired no other paradise. And it should be possible to do elsewhere what he did with the stigmatic conduplicate carpel—I refer to a piece of research that made his reputation decades ago. He gave me some reasonable expectation of a high-energy life of my own. Naturally I didn't want to be like anybody but myself. But it was foolish of me to expect her to enlarge on an intimation contained in a scholarly paper. See her, rather, this frail person in her sixties, waiting at a whistle-stop to flip a ride on an express train as it rushes past at 100 mph.

Nevertheless, if you do have an intelligent mother, you don't easily give up the hope of an essential communication.

It was night, the refugees were camped under their thorn bushes, you couldn't see their suffering. Conditions were favorable for a talk on larger topics. We didn't have to eat in the camp mess that evening. I opened some tins of Fauchon *charcuterie* and we finished up with a first-rate calvados. I forgot myself, I suppose, and tried out some of my East-West ideas on her. The combination of famine and *pâté* got me started. But after all, Boccaccio had young ladies and gentlemen entertaining one another with amorous tales and jokes during the plague, so after we polished off the delicacies and I was half tipsy on the good *calva,* I began to talk to her about Russian concentration camp literature—the work of Solzhenitsyn, Shalamov and others. I said that in the East, humankind underwent the ordeal of privation. Many of the higher human functions were eliminated. In the U.S.A. you had, instead, a population confined to the lowest of human interests—the emphasis in Russia being on the abolition of the higher, in America on indulgence of the lower. On a superficial view, that's how it may look. Educated opinion in the U.S.A. envies the East its opportunities for more cultivation and development because *there* they suffer more deeply. Here suffering is trivial. Nobody gets hacked to pieces for his ideas. This means you might as well be playing backgammon. Well, maybe so. But *Homo sovieticus* is a boring entity. Through no fault of his own, I grant you. It's mainly a question of how the human spirit was defeated by the so-called Revolution. However, there is a special Russian asset, which is the belief that Russia is the homeland of the deeper and sincerer emotions. Dostoyevsky among others promoted this reputation for unlimited passion. The West was nothing but a hospital for emotional-frostbite amputees and other cripples. Well, there *are* Russians who tell us we have been sold a bill of goods. Lev Navrozov, who is nobody's fool, says that for irrational and purely emotional behavior, America is in the twentieth century what Russia was in the nineteenth. There is far more display of feeling here than in the Soviet Union. It's not an altogether pleasant feeling, but there's plenty of it. He even accuses Dostoyevsky of being an ideologist who was personally a cold and calculating rationalist, ninety percent spleen. But we can skip that if you like, Mom.

She didn't agree with a word I was saying. She thought I was off the wall.

Therefore I gave it still another shot, instead of backing off. The East has the ordeal of privation, the West has the ordeal of desire.

This shocked her too. Probably thinking of Dad's amorous career, she said I was crazy. An ordeal, was it! It wasn't *his* ordeal, it was *hers*! For years she put up with his hanky-panky, and now I come and tell her that *he* was the sufferer. It was bad enough that I was born a bit deaf; I didn't have to be an idiot too. "You mean to compare London, Paris and New York with Magadan and Kolyma? Or this very camp we're sitting in? I shouldn't have eaten all that fancy stuff you brought." Suddenly Dad was paraded in front of us with all his chicks in various states of undress. *That* was an ordeal!

There are agonies and agonies. She hadn't read that D. H. Lawrence poem about the screaming turtle, "crucified into sex." Also, she hadn't read her Proust, though the shelves at home were filled with Proust. She thought, in surroundings like these, that I was heartless to weave theories and indulge myself in paradoxes.

I might have told her (in a spirit of gentle correction) that Russian suffering was, in a large historic view, suffering in its classic form, the suffering mankind has always known best in war, plague, famine and slavery. Those, the monumental and universally familiar forms of it, must certainly deepen the survivors humanly. My temptation was to try to make Mom understand that the sufferings of freedom also had to be considered. Otherwise we would be conceding a higher standard to totalitarianism, saying that only oppression could keep us honest. Free personalities getting no help from either deaf heaven or neutral earth were facing mortally dangerous choices which would determine the future of civilization. Here, as an aside, I mentioned Uncle's pain schedule.

Mother was studying me with real concern, as if I had lost my marbles. She wasn't as old as she looked. She put on agedness when she stopped trying to be a fashionable lady. What she wanted to talk about was the crowding of forty thousand refugees into a camp set up for two thousand; water being trucked in from thirty miles away; a shortage of tents; families trying to shelter under a roof of boughs; Ethiopian militia on the other side of the border snatching the children of the Oromos, raping the girls; the Somali officials trying to force refugees to return so that the Mengistu forces, organized for even greater atrocities, might finish the job. Instead, her only child had arrived to lecture her. In this regard he was like his pa, in whose list of pleasures lecturing came right after sex. Her visiting son was talking up a storm about 1905, the Russian fear of Mongolism in the late years of the old regime; about the medieval Russia that repulsed the Golden Horde of Asiatics in the Battle of Kulikovo. Blok had written a great poem on this. Bely was passionately absorbed with its prophetic meaning, the danger of sinking into primordial depths of chaos unless a spiritual sun shone, unless the Bronze Horseman had successfully leapt over history. The meaning of the Revolution was that Russia had attempted to isolate itself from the ordeal of modern consciousness. It was a sealing off. Inside the sealed country, Stalin poured on the *old* death. In the West, the ordeal is of a *new* death. There aren't any words for what happens to the soul in the free world. Never mind "rising entitlements," never mind the luxury "life-style." Our buried judgment knows better. All this is seen by remote centers of consciousness, which struggle against full wakefulness. Full wakefulness would make us face up to the *new* death, the peculiar ordeal of *our* side of the world. The opening of a true consciousness to what is *actually* occurring would be a purgatory.

"I should never have let you take Russian from that old man on the Rue du Dragon," said Mother. "He marked you for life."

I suppose I shouldn't have brought my preoccupations to this land of famine and genocide. Mother was scandalized by my theorizing. When I spoke she still heard the half-deaf kid. I could see it her way. She would by far have preferred me to say, as a sign that I had grown up at last, "I've got a scheme for pushing Flora Lewis off the op-ed page and taking her place." I was too feckless and foolish to do that. Maybe old Yermelov (and my uncle) had unfitted me for a productive life.

But I'm not going to linger in Somalia.

Uncle and I were in Kyoto (I am drawn from one part of the earth to another), and Uncle's host, Professor Komatsu, another botanical giant, came to the Tawaraya Inn to take us on a tour of the famous shrines and temple gardens.

A gentleman in his eighties, gaunt and brown, he wore a far from new kimono and sandals. Melanin spots covered his scalp. His wire spectacles were of an earlier age. He had studied at Oxford in 1925. The hired limousine he arrived in also belonged to that epoch. I think it was a Vauxhall, and except in silent movies I never had seen anything like it. Uncle Benn's mood had changed. He made lighthearted remarks and couldn't do enough to express his happiness. He seemed to want to help things along with his hands, never quite touching the objects that pleased him. It was spring here, wet but mild, nothing like the streaming rains of Seattle. An intermittent drizzle came down from a lighted sky, not a gloomy one. When you were under the trees you heard it dropping through the transparent new leaves. Professor Komatsu had brought a large maroon umbrella.

There were no wide horizons, only wooded hills, small fields. Industrial Japan was completely out of sight. It knew its own place, which of course was vast, but not a single factory window so much as glinted at us. The professor had prepared a special treat. He had translated some of his own poems, and when we were locked into the old Vauxhall he asked permission to read to us. His verses had a single theme: the old man's nurse—his nanny, whom seventy-five years ago he had deeply loved and who had passed away in 1912, when he was six or seven years old.

"The love of your life?" said Uncle.

Old Komatsu couldn't accept this Western formulation.

The chauffeur slowed down during the recitation. I moved over to the jump seat to get out of the way. Uncle's face was contorted with polite attention. Both of us watched the play of the old man's lower teeth, bits of teeth like pomegranate seeds when they dry out and go brown. When I was introduced to the professor, Uncle had assured me, in the lowered voice in which he made *genuine* statements, that Komatsu was a biophysicist who had given the world papers of real scientific power. That such a person should write lyrics devoted to a woman so long dead proved that love enjoyed a high rating with some scientists—people trained to read in Nature's book of infinite mystery. As God got a boost when Einstein mentioned him, so the credit rating of love, now at an all-time low, rose when the professor stood up for it.

The antique car built on perpendicular lines (long before airflow was a selling point) entered a hollow in the woods, where a band of women, all in dark brown, were doing manual labor. Those who are familiar with American assembly lines where people sometimes perform their tasks under a cover of marijuana smoke will get quite a different notion of work in Japan, where people throw themselves into it without seeming to reserve anything for themselves. These small ladies, bending over trestles on which tree trunks were laid, had stripped the bark and were scraping, washing, rubbing and polishing the wood. Old Komatsu explained: "These are houseposts, of special significance in the construction of traditional dwellings."

"Ah, yes. Specially cultivated, I suppose," said Uncle.

"And inspected, and seasoned. Then prepared by these women with the prescribed material, probably ground pumice and oils. All by hand. It amounts to a cult."

Uncle's comment was spontaneous. "Women who do this work might make wonderful wives."

You could observe the gradual change of Komatsu's countenance, as one by one large creases of appreciation entered it. He raised his face towards the roof of the limo and laughed. I thought he was about to pick up the speaking tube and translate the joke for the chauffeur. Instead, he crossed his arms (his lap was full of poems) and said, "This is one of the humorous remarks for which you are famous, Dr. Crader. To transfer this treatment from houseposts to husbands. If the husband should be willing to exchange places with a tree trunk."

"Oh, Professor, there are times when I would willingly do it. Today it would seem a paradise."

Things that Caroline would certainly not have done for him. Nor poor Della Bedell.

"Those ladies would have callused hands," said Komatsu. "Those would take time to become tender. I think you have come out with a fairy tale conception, as in *The Magic Flute*, where an ugly old creature is changed into a beautiful young wife."

"Still, planned, rational choices don't seem to work," Uncle said. I knew his moods well. *Uncle* speaking of rational choices? He was very high, he was enjoying himself.

Old Professor Komatsu became playful with him. The old man said, "Our feudalism is very seductive to you people, but Americans who shop for docile wives here often are disappointed. After a year or so in the U.S. the ladies are Americanized. Roles are reversed. In a short while, Professor Crader, *you* might become the attendant, rubbing a supine wife where she commanded you."

Yes—well, even that would have been better than what happened later to Benn. Suppose I had asked Komatsu to recommend a reliable Japanese matchmaker. Then there would have been no Matilda—no Layamon family.

A funny populace—ours, I mean, not the Japanese. Oh, theirs is funny enough. Tokyo and Osaka are *villes fourmillantes*, they swarm. Any door you pull releases hundreds of people. You can't open a closet without finding somebody sitting in it. Lift a manhole cover and they come streaming out. But we are funnier, in our country, looking to gratify so many desires, turned loose on the world to live it up. Or to obtain the money to live it up with. Or to prove that you can live it up on the money of others. To touch one of my own bruises, Treckie had said to me in Seattle, "I've gotten used to multiple choices." Meaning what?

She made me think of that friend of Stendhal's, mentioned in his memoirs, for whom the sex act was enjoyable only once with any woman. Twice, at most.

But we are in Kyoto, having a guided tour.

The limousine was parked below an ancient temple and we ascended to the gardens, often stopping for a rest. I was jet-lagged; Uncle, the more experienced globe-trotter, was feeling no strain.

Nothing afterwards in Japan was nearly so agreeable. My seniors, the two botanists, exchanged information about leaves and blossoms, while heavy drops fell from the trees on the professor's umbrella as fast as the Morse code. Presently the sun came out. When the clouds drew apart, there was a moment at which I was reminded of the way Treckie sometimes brushed her hair down one side, over her brow. When girl images come like that, you have a sign from the skies that you've been singled out for trouble. Or that you've singled yourself out, as though others weren't already giving you plenty of heat.

The old Japanese professor said to me while Benn was walking ahead that Uncle had a special gift of observation. It might not be "scientific" in the accepted meaning of the term. There was something *visionary* about the distinctness with which "plants came before him." You could have a thought that was ultraclear, but there was a further stage, in which it was not merely ultraclear but became visible, as if it were drawn or painted before your inner eye.

I wasn't sure that I could understand this. The professor wasn't entirely sure that he did, either. Could a thought also be an object? Well, Euclid made diagrams of thought. The French had flowers they called *pensées,* he said. That didn't count; it was a sentimental usage. The language of love in flowers? In Ophelia's mad scene it was touching, but apart from amorous heartbreak and filial grief, there was nothing in it but maidens' folklore. I was careful not to offend Komatsu, who might have used flower language in his poems. What I did get from the old man was confirmation of my hunch that Uncle didn't see as the rest of us saw things. No wonder he had often reported to me that from his perspective plants were queer beings, a branch of life for which you needed special, almost divinatory powers. Highly structured, they gave no signs of consciousness as we understood it. Atop a world of rock, they were succulent, they breathed, they reached outwards. By contrast, we were inwardly enfolded—think of the intestines or the enfolded brain.

Uncle was busy near this temple, and happy. I watched him

as he bent down to inspect leaves or blossoms. His Russian back more and more looked as though his jacket covered a wing case, and if he chose he might take off a few clothes and fly around the garden of this shrine. But it wouldn't do to leave his human friends behind. He was a very polite person.

Again the question came up: What if there should be similar powers of insight into human beings? What if he should have some himself? There may have been an influence, a green overlap, as it were, when human faces came into his field of vision. However, he couldn't make the psychic transfer to human relations. This quickly became apparent in his second marriage.

I'll be taking this up very soon—introducing Matilda Layamon.

First I must describe a very different sort of outing in Kyoto.

Some of the old professor's junior colleagues took us out for a night on the town. They said, laughingly, that they would make up to us for Komatsu's nanny poems, with which he pestered everybody, and they asked whether Dr. Crader would object to a girlie show. So picture this now: a seer in the vegetable kingdom invited to a strip-tease. "Real hot stuff," one of them said. Uncle commented, "I thought this was one of the holy cities of Asia." They seemed to think this was very funny. I could see that Uncle's reputation as a humorist may have been based on cross-cultural misunderstanding. The junior colleagues laughed a great deal, perhaps out of politeness. (Once again, politeness: Politeness gets funnier the more the rules of order disintegrate.)

Uncle's experience of lewd shows was very limited. Such performances were not his cup of tea. Actually these young scholars were putting him to the test. They wanted to see how the famous American botanist would react to the girls. I myself was curious about that. Even now I can't really say how sensual a person Uncle was, innately. I knew that women were on his mind but not what they were on his mind for. He didn't have my dad's interests, I could swear to that in front of a notary public. Did he have pagan tastes? Was he erotically motivated in the old Greek sense, was he a Dionysiac? Well, to begin with, he was Jewish, a Russian-looking Jew. I suppose there have been Jews like him forever. And like Dad. Like me too, skinny dark ones, keen to get to the bottom of things, mixing candor with slyness. But we've never had a historical moment quite like this one, sexually; different from Babylon or Rome, different from ancient India. This would be a really worthwhile research topic. So few people have the intelligence to find a real one.

The theater the junior colleagues took us to after dinner had no seats. Standing room only. There was a stage in the very center, and crowds of men surrounded it. The usual Japanese numerosity, crowd density. Most of the public were young executive types and dressed like their American counterparts, in business suits which the British used to call lounge suits, as if anybody was lounging at IBM, Mitsubishi or Sony. A multitude of what looked to be upper-income, well-dressed Japanese, black-haired, most intense but most restrained, were staring up at the stage. The performers were identified on placards as Miss Osaka, Miss Tokyo, Miss Nara, Miss Yokohama, Miss Nagasaki. They wore brocaded kimonos and ceremonial obis, they had on clogs and carried paper parasols, their hair stood high, their faces were chalked and painted. Each little maid from school sang in a sweet tremolo. After this preliminary put-on they got down to business, like strippers the world over. These were particularly pretty, dainty girls. Then two at a time, these young things entered a plexiglass cage. The cage was raised to the ceiling, where it was connected to a monorail. As it crisscrossed and circled the theater, spotlights followed the performers, who were romping, tussling, embracing, kissing, sticking out their tongues, dying in ecstasies. For them it was a romp. The men, so many barbered heads turned upwards, were the somber ones. It was heavy going down below, especially when the plexiglass love cell returned to the stage. Then each of the girls in turn stooped, opened her knees, and dilated herself with her fingers. Dead silence. A kind of static insanity descended on the house. You could have drawn the lines of force straight from the eyes of the men into the center of desire, the chaste treasure fully opened. Everybody had to see, to see, to see the thing of things, the small organ red as a satin pincushion. The men were packed together, too well disciplined to push. All these business and laboratory wizards rivaling the Germans, the British and the Americans, these high-tech and management types, not one of them drunk, not one opening his mouth, had come to see what these girls were displaying. Miss Osaka and Miss Nara put it in front of you, as literal as it was possible to be, and the more literal it was, the more mystery there seemed to be in it. The junior colleagues who had brought Uncle here to study his reactions weren't looking at him at all. All these botanists, engineers, inventors of miraculous visual instruments from electron microscopes to equipment that sent back pictures of the moons of Saturn, cared for nothing but these slow openings. They couldn't look enough. The girls felt the weight of the attention they were getting and seemed to know how much suffering they caused and how shaken their audience was. I was shook up too. There was no help for it. And Uncle standing bulky in his nice light gray suit—he was in a state.

It was more than he could take. He lost a lot of ground in Kyoto. He made no bones about it. In the morning he said he was ready to leave.

"You didn't sleep well?"

"I took a Dalmane capsule. I'm ready to go now. Look at us, having breakfast on the floor. A week of this is plenty for me."

"You've seen girlie shows before. A man over fifty, these aren't your first strippers."

"Of course not. But I don't like the way I felt yesterday."

"How many times have you gone around the world?"

"More than Jules Verne."

"How *did* you feel yesterday?"

"Turned on and off, then on again and off, to the point of disintegration."

"It's intricate, this Japanese outlook on sex. Their premises all are different."

"I'm sure that's true. It really isn't any of my business, though."

"Japanese businessmen arrange international sex tours for themselves. The wives stay at home, the husbands fly to Latin America for special entertainment."

"That would be very interesting to an anthropologist, but it isn't my specialty. Let them make what they like of it. For me it's too much of a strain."

"Our friends from last night want to take us to a club. There's a performer there who ties a knot in his cock."

"Well, I don't want to see him," said Uncle. "When people decide to put their ingenuity into any special field, they always go too far. It can become a kind of inferno."

He was badly rattled, or he wouldn't have expressed himself so strongly. I should have sensed that he was looking for protection. Perhaps he was recalling (as I myself was) those Japanese maidens whose pubic tufts grew straight forward, a rich silken black around the little satin crannies. Uncle had no ironic distance; he lacked worldly tempering. Everybody now gets the entire world set before him, for his judgment, with the implication, "Tough luck if you don't get this right." Well, then, it's universal tough luck, because nobody does get it right. As for sex, Uncle wasn't one of the truly qualified players. He'd never be a real contestant. It wasn't that he was so innocent. There is no such thing. Just think of all the day care tots who testify in courts against elderly matrons in sex-abuse cases, perhaps sending respectable persons to jail. What's the origin of these infant wiles? And the decadent practices of the Remy de Gourmonts, the "English" vices of the Swinburne set, the *Jardins des Supplices* of the last century. All that is as common and as cheerful as dry cereal at breakfast. As for "innocence," I don't give myself any of that stuff since learning what Ponomarenko, who was Stalin's deputy and boss for Byelorussia, had to say about preserving the innocence of the masses. "Purity" is the favorite camouflage of the deeper varieties of criminality. (And certain forms of insanity too.) So then, bringing it back to Uncle, he wasn't innocent. He was strangely finicky, fastidious to a degree, hard to interpret, eluding the categories available to me. Of course he had read classics like Forel and Havelock Ellis, Kinsey and the other sexual Ellis—Albert, the Thomas Paine of the sexual revolution—plus Masters and Johnson, and whatnot else. I'm sure I've mentioned the trouble he went to in keeping up with herpes, AIDS and other venereal infections. And can I pretend without faking that he had no taste for the Dellas, Carolines, et al.? He said once that in the sexual embrace

Caroline would cry out, "Oh, you're an angel! You angel, you!" Why would he have told me that unless his purpose was self-characterization? *She* was the weirdo. He was the scientist and child-man (the innocent, the angel) who lent himself to her needs. . . . I couldn't possibly go along with that.

He had been genuinely attached to Aunt Lena and he had been a faithful husband. But I allow myself to record one of his confidences here—there's no harm in it now. At one time, when he was in his thirties, he did make one small experiment, not with another woman but with a drug. One of his colleagues in the medical school had given him several shots of testosterone. Experimentally. No effects were noted for a time. But one day—Lena was out, marketing—he was attacked by raging sexual sensations. "I lay there not knowing what to do. All at once I was infantile. A pair of tiny fists, tiny infant feet, and all the rest of me was one single swelling, nothing but tumescence. Enough to turn you into a weeping babe—weeping because there was nothing you could do about it."

"What did you do?"

"I waited for it to pass. What else was there to do? I never took that stuff again."

In my opinion, he didn't need it. And now he was in his fifties, and still tormented, a full-scale example of the ordeal by desire. I had had it in mind while speaking to Mom. In late middle life people were still enchanted by the blazing sexual fireworks from which, in other civilizations, they turned away when the time came. They took life stage by stage, with dignity—so I am told—not sobbing with grief as some of our poets, even the greatest, do in this period of sexual anarchy. But then, every age has its gross hazards: The odds are heavy that when they pick up momentum you will be done in by them. Think of the Black Death or world wars or forced labor. When these get under way, few can hope to escape. It may seem odd to list *our* gross hazards, the erotic ones, for instance, with war or forced labor, but whatever it is that snatches souls away by the hundreds of millions has to be reckoned with. This needs to be stated at a time when "intelligent observers" are warning America that in order to cease being a superficial monster she must prepare for bad times.

America therefore requires an ordeal of major scope—an old-style ordeal. If M. Yermelov's angels coming to instill higher love into us, and finding us unprepared, inject it directly into the physical body so that we immediately fall into the most brilliant but terrible forms of corruption (which in our blindness we take for *pleasure*!), your only ground for refusing to consider it an ordeal is that you aren't *conscious* of it. From this you can see why I put so little trust in "intelligent observers," in intellectuals. A poor lot of people. Brainy but ignorant of the fundamentals.

But I'm not going to pursue this here. Here I state the simple fact that Uncle was profoundly upset by a succession of sexual miseries. There was no good reason why Miss Yokohama and Miss Nagasaki should have thrown him so badly, caused him such pain that he determined to settle his life once and for all. About this he didn't level with me. I suppose he didn't want to put himself into my hands. These are choices that a man has to make for himself. I can see that. I can see why it might drive him crazy to discuss matrimony with Kenneth Trachtenberg. What I can't see is why he should have picked a woman like Matilda Layamon, if what he wanted was *calme* or *ordre*, let alone *volupté*.

Anyway, at Christmas, while I was abroad, he married this lady in a private ceremony in the home of her parents, Dr. and Mrs. William Layamon.

I had gone to see my mother in East Africa and my father on the Rue Bonaparte. When I came home after the first of the year, I found the wedding announcement. It was marked "Do Not Forward." Now, announcements of this quality have to be ordered months in advance. You don't crank out such Tiffany-style engraved invitations. It was clear enough that they had been ordered long before I took off. When Uncle drove me to the airport, plans had already been made. Yet not a word was said about Matilda Layamon. I didn't even know he had been taking her out. And he had *met* the woman through me. I had been introduced to Matilda by my mother. Mother liked to advise American girls in Paris, and Matilda was one of Mother's protégées. Having lived so many decades in Europe, Mom was a valuable source of guidance and information—of useful connections as well. If you were good at getting around her, she'd introduce you to people, even give a little party for her favorites. By opening her doors to pretty women, Mother might also have been showing Dad how fearless she was. Who knows? I don't believe it was in her mind to be his accomplice. Certainly she was aware that she was married to a genius (an amorous genius, which he remains to this day). How many truly remarkable people does one meet in a lifetime? The case of Uncle Benn offers a parallel. He, too, was outstanding, although at this moment in my account of him I don't much feel like conceding it. Somewhere, I'm still sore because he cheated on me—broke the rules of our relationship.

Matilda, by the way, never became involved with Dad. She was on Mother's side, not that her support was solicited. Mother's relations with Dad came under the official secrets act. Matilda wrote to Mother in East Africa, but in none of her letters was Uncle Benn ever mentioned and Mother's invitation to the wedding didn't arrive until February, signifying that Matilda was making sure there would be no interference from that side. Mom had often made fun of Benn's troubles with women. As a Crader, she had inherited her share of the family wit, and she had said once, "In love, my brother is the kind of hemophiliac who would shave in the dark with a straight razor." When at last Matilda informed Mother that she and Benn had fallen in love and that the Christmas wedding had been beautiful, she also said that a special blessing was to have become the sister-in-law of so good a friend. Even Mother with her weakness for flattery felt this was overdone, and when she wrote to me about it disclaimed all responsibility, concluding, "It never entered my mind that a girl like Matilda would see marriage prospects in a fellow like Benn."

In a long postscript, Mother commented on this marriage, with animadversions on my relations to my uncle and my tendency to imitate the man. She believed that Uncle was dependent on me. "He has tied you up by the affections (and delusions) and prevented you from developing your ambitions. Now you won't be seeing so much of each other and you, too, will be tempted to marry. Treckie would *not* be a suitable wife. She belongs to the Ken Kesey acid culture and all that craziness which now is *passé* and doesn't yet realize it. It has created no *avant garde*, which would have been its only excuse. When you were here, you spoke of a young woman named Dita Schwartz. You probably are unaware how often you referred to her. Evidently she is glad to listen to you for the sake of her education. You had every cultural advantage in Paris, whereas she is merely an American girl, from the Middle West at that, so she has everything to gain. This may mean, as a corollary, that you have everything to lose. To tell your only child to be circumspect usually provokes more recklessness. But now your uncle will need you much less than formerly. . . ."

This last statement proved that she was in Somalia not only geographically but mentally as well. Uncle had never needed me so badly as now.

To go back very briefly, for purposes of placement: Matilda had come to Paris to collect information about cultural activities under the Nazi occupation. She was especially interested in the big figures, like Ernst Junger on the German side, and Céline on the French, together with Drieu La Rochelle, Brasillach and Ramon Fernandez (a pity that Fernandez, a gifted man, should have joined the literary fascists). Mother was able to introduce Matilda to Marguerite Duras (long before Duras became a celebrity), and Matilda spent weeks taking notes for a Ph.D. thesis. She spoke French unusually well for a graduate student, she had first-class references for an American, she was a beautiful woman and also one of those gripping listeners, just the type for a garrulous informant. As a collector of information she was tireless and, keyed up herself, she won the confidence of the hysterical persons she interviewed, crooks, most of them, whose strange idea was to reconcile the atrocities of the war period with the highest goals of France as a civilization. For instance, to get information for the Resistance you slept with a collaborator, or after a double-dealer was shot you might discover that you truly had loved him after all—that way you could have it all: pornography, heartfelt *douleur*, corrupt love, patriotism, and a fine literary style, so that the purity of French culture was preserved. Rotten through and through. No reasonable person would pursue such a subject.

When Matilda returned to the home base (her father was a medical big shot and very rich) she looked me up, and it was through me that Benn became acquainted with her. He and I took her to dinner together. He observed that she was handsome—an objective statement with no particular affect. He couldn't have meant to mislead me. At that time the thought of marriage hadn't yet entered his head. It was early summer then, and he was doing his Arctic lichens, relieved to get away from the harsh sexual experiences of the past year. Occasionally, avoiding technical complexities, he would tell me how lichens could take nutrition from the atmosphere as the air masses moved from zone to zone, carrying a mixture of nutrients and toxic substances. I was pleased to see him get back to work, suspecting nothing. He was okay in the green. There wasn't much that could hurt Benn the botanist. Matilda had told me at dinner, when we took her out, that she still corresponded with La Duras, without, however, pursuing her research. She had come to see that it was beyond her, unless she was prepared to submerge herself in the subject for five or six years. I gathered that she had given up a number of such projects in the past. My surmise was that she didn't need to see these enterprises through. Social exploration was her real purpose. She was now in her thirties, had never been married, was not too old to have children, and what she was looking for was a husband. It never entered my mind that Uncle Benn might be thought a candidate for matrimony by this glittering, nervous, Frenchy-Midwestern woman. I see now that his academic weight and scientific fame offered her a stable base of operations. She had been around a long time, too long to marry impulsively like a young woman in love. In any case, she had asked Uncle not to mention their courtship to me. Discussions between us would embarrass her. She hated to think that the man she loved was talking about her. I might be a dear person, and obviously Uncle doted on me, but nobody could deny that I was a bit on the weird side and notorious for the kinkiness of my theories. Even Mother had hinted (more than hinted) that I was somewhat unstable. "And in marriage a man ought to make his own uninfluenced choice," Matilda told Uncle, "and follow his deepest instincts."

"So you kept me in the dark," I said, as if admiring his ingenuity. I wasn't about to tell him that he had betrayed me, welshed on an agreement which was the very foundation of our relationship. That I was burned up.

Well, what's all this about a "relationship" and its foundation?

To tell it as I see it, and as briefly as possible, it's about the dreariness of what Swedenborg called "mere nature," the boredom of eternal enclosure in a fixed circle, whether cosmic or personal, which makes prisoners of us. A fixed world of matter and energy, don't you see. The Solomonic wisdom of "nothing new under the sun" or "eternal recurrence"—a closed circle, and a closed circle is a prison.

My parents (with filial respect) were closed circle types. Hence the attraction of my uncle. He apparently was not inside the usual circumference but made forays into the vegetable kingdom, and sometimes beyond. Well, we formed an understanding. On an elementary level, neither would let the other walk into a whirling propeller. And our habit, developed over some years, was to tell each other (with a liberating ease) what was going on at any level. To start with a basic example, Uncle would say, "I can't get rid of this *pruritis ani*." "Try sitz baths." Now, catch an Othello talking about his itches. But we're no longer at the glory stage of great wars. We start at the other end. Yet it's still the same human power of penetration, whether you start from the top or from the bottom. The intervention of an Iago will bring you down to the salty monkey level, you can depend on that. Anyway, Uncle and I were trying to cover the whole range of human concerns between us.

We human creatures should be at play before the Lord—the higher the play, the more pleasing to God. I doubt that it can interest Him much to watch the shits at their play. I don't refer now to the Iago type but to people of ordinary stunted imaginative powers. The work of psychology is to explain and excuse these shits, but the Divine Spirit knows that the principal conditions are epistemological and metaphysical, and have to do with the prison, the hell of the closed circle. "Before the earth was made," says the Book of Proverbs, I was with the Lord "forming all things, and was delighted every day, playing before Him at all times, playing with the world. And my delights were to be with the children of men."

"I had to cancel some office hours," said Uncle, resuming his well-rehearsed rationalizations. "I'd pick her up from her dancing class, or after her analysis, and then we'd spend an hour in the park conservatory, or in Frankenthaler's genetics lab."

"Places where you'd never run into me."

"Actually I wasn't thinking of that."

"Somebody was."

"You don't have to sound so betrayed, Kenneth. Or as if I were three years old and you caught me playing with matches."

Well taken, this. I changed my tone. I surprised myself by the irritation, vexation, the vulcanism of my reaction. I felt like a father who had released the hand of his child, and the kid immediately bolted into traffic and was hit by a truck. Grief, rage, out of proportion to the event, was no way to deal with Uncle. But when I came home the wedding announcement had thrown me badly. I had a "high-dignity" reaction from olden times. I *sent* for Benn. From his department secretary I found out his new number and left a haughty message on the answering machine. He was staying with his in-laws in their duplex penthouse, at the peak of a newly constructed building in what passes in this town for a "fine old neighborhood"—a cluster of residential condominiums, many of them tawny pink, so that in full frontal sunshine they made you think of the Sons of the Morning who shouted for joy (joy over all the dough they had piled up). On Dad's side I have other uncles who might have fitted in here. However, this particular uncle had no business in such a location. Very soon, he returned my call. Naturally he had given my reactions much thought; many sleepless hours were spent deciding how to square himself with me.

I wouldn't meet him in his old apartment (just under the rooms where Della Bedell had died). He came to my bare, devoid-of-comforts place in the dormitory. As I waited in my damaged recliner, I was not simply miffed but aggressive, preparing and editing accusations and backing Uncle into one guilty corner after another. What the hell did you think you were doing? You wouldn't have hidden it from me if you thought you actually knew what you were doing! . . . But all of a sudden I caught myself out, making the most of this opportunity to beat up on Uncle, who had troubles enough already.

Tired with travel just then, in a room without curtains or carpets, I was perhaps tempted by the Russian publications covering the floor into a Russian mood of live and let live. In the Soviet Union these would have been luxurious accommodations . . . the usual diversion with hardships, toying with them just because my spirits were low. The sense of myself was that of a figure in a sketch, somewhere between Cruikshank and Rembrandt—skinny, long-faced, sallow and greenish (reflections from a Dutch canal). Modern life, if you take it to heart, wears you out, and I was only translating inner poverty into outer because of certain expectations that had suffered a setback. If I had been a young woman, I would have had a refreshing cry over it. Furthermore, that morning nothing seemed to work. Even my hearing aid was off, and when I fiddled my finger under my long hair and tapped on it, something like a sonic boom went off in my skull. Then—I can't say why—an old joke about an Ed Sullivan show came to mind. It's probably nothing but folklore. This was the one about the poor spastic girl for whom Sullivan had raised funds from the bighearted American public to give her therapy. The girl was treated, and she was supposed to be shown in an improved state on TV. To prove how much progress she had made and how well she was coordinated, Sullivan handed her an ice cream cone. She said, "Thank you, Ed," and took the cone. But instead of bringing it to her mouth, she stuck it in her eye. A cruel bit of fun aimed not at pitiable spastics but at myself, my impaired hearing—a shaft of enraged wit.

Arriving, Uncle confirmed that I looked greenish with jet lag (maybe spleen). He would stay only a few minutes and let me catch up on my sleep. He stayed for quite a long time. "You weren't sick in Ethiopia, were you?"

"This refugee camp isn't in Ethiopia, it is in Somalia, at Tug Wajale. I see you didn't get my postcard."

"Oh, yes, I got it."

Uncle wasn't normally in touch with world politics and certainly didn't know what Mengistu was doing in Ethiopia. From the start Mengistu was a terrorist. He had the adolescent children of opponents murdered and left at their parents' doors. After this he raised other kinds of hell. Meanwhile, back in the Middle West, Benn Crader, Ph.D., became wedded to Miss Matilda Layamon, daughter of a prominent physician. (There are ordeals and ordeals.) Now, my aim is to be totally truthful about Uncle. I had often envied him his life in science. He was wrapped in nature. The whole vegetable kingdom was his garment—his robe, his coat—and that to me meant fundamental liberty from low-grade human meanness, it meant universality. Still, Uncle's garment was incomplete. It didn't quite button. In Paris, attending a concert of modern Russian music, I had heard a quartet by Shostakovitch, the fourteenth, which made me feel the incompleteness of the art garment. This incompleteness exposes one tragically. The human being now simply can't close his elected garment about himself. Obligations to one's fellows perhaps prevent full buttoning by artists. This is how I interpret the cries of the strings in the fourteenth, the broken passages, the impossibility of concluding, or closing. How many can go even so far in work, or in utterances?

To put aside more distant reflections: Today Uncle wasn't wrapped in nature, he was wearing a tailor-made suit—eight hundred bucks, minimum. And when he started to talk about Matilda he was not the fellow who could claim a decent place in the larger hierarchy for himself; he was simply a schnook. The daemon who had moved him to give the junkman his nickel and buy *Great Mother Forest* was on leave, or something. What Benn said about Matilda you could have read in the Ann Landers column. I saw how he was struggling, but in the first moments I felt pitiless.

"So you love this lady?"

"Oh, I really love Matilda. She's the greatest."

It's not that I'm cynical about love; just the reverse. I was checking into this thoroughly for the sake of love itself, to be sure his was an authentic instance. Here was a man all but engaged to a lady (Caroline) who would come to town with a bagful of X-rated videotapes, which he would watch passively, without comment. True, he knew enough to escape when she closed in on him, he wasn't so passive after all, but I would have had to be an idiot to buy what he said about Matilda. It wasn't that he was incapable of loving a woman or that he had been crippled by this selfish, low-down age; it was that he was so inexperienced. Those people, the Layamons, weren't exactly the cast of an old Bing Crosby movie—*The Bells of St. Mary's* or some such sentimental piece.

"All this while, you and I have had a project, Uncle."

"Have I ever forgotten that? It was a top consideration with me. But there are things you can't consult anybody about. Different imperatives—you can see that. What if I had let this opportunity slip through my fingers just because you were in Ethiopia?"

It was better for the moment to assume that he was on the level; otherwise I would have been forced to suspect that Matilda had supplied him with excuses. Either he was in real earnest, or he wanted with all his heart to believe what he was saying. This must be emphasized because Uncle had the deep-down gift of knowing exactly what he felt. Therefore, I mustn't drive him into unbearable hypocrisies.

"Well, if it was such an imperative—okay, an imperative is an imperative. Now tell me, have you given up your old apartment?"

"Not yet."

"So the Layamons' duplex penthouse is only a visit."

"Getting acquainted. Their only child, and all of that."

"They want to inspect you close up."

"To see what Matilda sees in me? Maybe. And I'm observing them too."

"You're supposed to be a genius morphologist, but that's with plants."

"I have some feeling for people too. You, for instance . . ."

You don't deny a claim like this; it's too unkind.

But if he had found happiness with Matilda and the Layamons, some outer signs were missing. The tailor-made suit didn't sit comfortably on him. He was pale, his cheeks were thickened by trouble and doubt. When examined, he fell back on clichés. And in a silent interval this was what I read in the light and shade of his face (roughly translated): You can't just sit still. Something has to be done. We have to die, some sooner than others, and as condemned men, it's only natural to try for peace—two human beings bound together in love and kindness, and so forth. He didn't like hearing me say that he had been a sex-abused man, a mere victim of so many Dellas and Carolines, not to mention the Rajashwaris and other ladies of the Third World. I would never have said that to him. Many causes had driven him to take sanctuary with a wife. As in a stifling sexual Sicilian summer you hurry into the cool church of marriage.

"And don't you think Matilda is a good match?" he asked.

"Me? I haven't said anything against her."

"You wouldn't deny that she's beautiful. . . . Slender women aren't your type. There's Treckie, of the opposite build. And your friend Dita Schwartz."

"Who said that life was a beauty contest?"

But I granted him that Matilda was a beautiful woman. It wasn't her beauty that I questioned, it was the Edgar Allan Poe stuff he was giving me about her—the Nicaean bark of yore in perfumed seas. Too much of the marble statue in the stained-glass niche. Once or twice I let him get away with it, and then I said, "It's counterproductive, Benn. Poe in prose was a maniac about women. Besides, that Clemm girl he married never even reached puberty. You're quoting me the wrong author."

"Whom would you recommend instead?"

"Oh, William Blake, for instance. 'Blight with plagues the marriage hearse.'"

"Do you call that more appropriate?"

"No. I take it back. *Je rétracte*. But you haven't said anything about life with the in-laws in that classy penthouse. How many servants have they got?"

"No more than your mother used to have in Paris."

"These ones cost a hell of a lot more than ours, you can bet."

"They have a cook and a maid of all work, one Polish, the other Mexican. Being waited on is very uncomfortable for me. However, we're leaving in a few weeks."

"Going where?"

"To Brazil, for a short term."

"On the run again? I thought marriage meant you were settling down. And you didn't like Brazil the first time."

"Not like a *whole country*? You'd have to be pretty spoiled to reject such a big piece of the continent. Anyway, my behavior there must have been good, because I have a standing invitation to come back."

"Matilda wants to go," I said.

"To escape the winter. To honeymoon in a warm climate."

"Also, to have you to herself for two or three months."

I didn't add: "To cut me out."

"And besides, the new flat has to be redone," he said, "and we'd be living in a mess."

"After twenty years you have to give up your old apartment?"

"The time has come."

"A change in your social position. Also, to get away from the ghosts of the ladies you used to entertain there."

Uncle said, "Those are things I never discussed with anybody but you."

"You don't have to worry; your confidences are respected here. Where are you moving?"

"That huge cooperative building, the Roanoke. Matilda's old aunt left it to her in her will."

"The Roanoke! Sixteen Venetian palaces piled on top of one another in a towering heap. That's pretty wild—stockbrokers' baroque circa 1910. Like bourgeois heaven. About twenty rooms apiece?"

"Haven't counted. I haven't even been there yet. Anyway, we're off to Brazil. You could stay in my apartment and get away from these bare dormitory walls for a while."

"I could water your plants."

"Not fair, Kenneth. My assistant does that."

"Of course he does. I've become adjusted to this bleakness. In spite of the rock music below, this pad is home."

"How nice it would be if you'd take my apartment over. Keep it in the family. You'll tell me you can't pay the rent. But I'll miss the old place."

I kept a narrow watch on Uncle Benn. I knew his face backwards and forwards. When he was well, it was like the moon before we landed on it; when he wasn't, his gaze was disturbed by a kind of squibbing or fizzing, and by the hyperactivity of his figure eight or diabolo eye frame, working and winking. This I reckoned as part of his attempt to present his delirium as stability. Here was the meaning of the answers he gave to my questions. What I had to determine was whether the delirium—or let's call it instead the fantastic reality—was pleasant, unpleasant, or a mixture as yet unassayed. For instance, he would have liked me to take over his apartment—as an escape hatch? "I can't move now," I said. "Especially not into your old surroundings."

"The history of all the mistakes I made there? But a happy marriage might be the result for you too."

"We aren't exactly alike. You had a way of giving equal time to all the ladies that applied for it. I don't do that."

After a thoughtful moment, he said, "They weren't *all* mistakes. Many were important human contacts. . . . I *did* like Caroline."

"A woman who would stuff herself with paper and then put on full makeup before getting into bed with you."

"That's an exaggeration."

"There isn't a single word of it that didn't come from you. Even more, during the act itself she would look and behave as if she was sitting in the Dress Circle at the opera and you were the starring tenor."

"What about the times she said, 'You angel'?" Uncle ventured to ask.

"You'll have to explain that yourself. There are plenty of men who don't care *how* the woman behaves—couldn't care less. But you're not one of them. Anyway, Caroline isn't a real option anymore. You're a married man now. Happily married; by some miracle, considering how finicky you are."

When I said "Happily married," he listened hard to ascertain to what degree I really meant it, whether I accepted his propaganda. Because I'm an erratic talker, I might talk myself, with a little steering from Uncle, into buying it. He tried to get my preoccupations to work in his favor.

I wasn't quite there yet, by any means. I said, "So now you're living in Parrish Place. That's a ritzy neighborhood. How do you feel about it?"

"Where does a world traveler feel most out of place?"

"In his own country?"

"In his hometown," said Uncle. "To kids from Jefferson Street, Parrish Place was out of bounds. We had to change three streetcars to get there, to see how the rich lived."

"This was before they built the high-rise residences with the tinted windows."

"The old buildings are still intact—marquees, doormen. They've added video security monitors. In the old days, when we hopped off the streetcars the cops would keep an eye on us to make sure we didn't vandalize property or commit a nuisance in the alley. I told Matilda the morning after the wedding, waking in her room, "This is an experience for somebody from the other side of the tracks."

"What did she say?"

"Well, she looked at me with her big eyes."

Matilda, whose face was slender, had huge eyes, as notable as Uncle's blue ones—monstrously large or, as they say, humongous eyes. Benn wasn't wrong about the classic face. You might or might not care for it, but you couldn't dispute the beauty.

"What color are those eyes?" I said. "That crazy Poe says 'hyacinth hair.' Hyacinth is a kind of amethyst or sapphire."

Uncle was pleased with this sign of interest, a preface to acceptance or friendliness, perhaps. "They're a lilac color."

"Frosted lilac. A pale lilac. She's a remarkable-looking lady," I said.

"About the tracks . . . I probably said that oftener than I should, and she doesn't like me to say strange things. That is, she doesn't like to hear that things strike me as strange."

"She doesn't care for your imaginative background music?"

"There's nothing so imaginative in the poor-kid slant. She reminded me, 'The tracks are gone; there *is* no more wrong side of the tracks.'"

"She doesn't care for that far-away-and-long-ago stuff."

"That's it," said Uncle.

The city is the expression of the human experience it embodies, and this includes all personal history. But Matilda didn't like Uncle to look back, cling to the past. It wouldn't do to call her a futurist (the machine-age, high-speed, early-Mussolini stuff), but she seemed to have a progressive orientation.

Uncle sat in my uncomfortable sling chair, his stout knees widely separated. "She said she knew this vanished streetcar rigmarole from her father. Doctor was raised near the old produce market. 'Believe me, pal,' she said, 'this isn't the town you grew up in.' Sure, the old urban Midwest is finished. I told her, 'The model city for these days is probably Beirut, if you're looking for what's authentically contemporary.'"

I took the trouble of recording Benn's conversations from his other life (the Layamon one) as he reported them to me, and I've kept the notes. At first he was reserved, intent on making an impression. With time, however, he began to go into greater detail, consistent with his habit of mind.

Matilda quickly began to set him straight. She said, "You like to picture yourself as an outsider, positively a greener. It's not that you came over as an immigrant; that was your parents. But you have this steerage mentality—you've got the whole Russian-Hebrew-Aramaic routine, and this includes Egypt and the Babylonian captivity. Let's try to be a little more real. Sure my folks have a luxurious setup here. They own this duplex outright and it's done over by a decorator every few years for big bucks. So what! When you were in Zurich lecturing at the *Hochschule* and we stayed at the Grand Hotel Dolder, I watched you. All those silk featherbeds and the plush and gilding and glitz? With a private funicular for the guests? It didn't impress you one single bit. You're as far from the slums as anybody I ever saw. You think you have to remind yourself that you're a poor kid still. . . ."

Matilda wasn't absolutely wrong. She refused to let him hold himself aloof or play the dumbsock. ("Gee whiz, I don't dig how these rich guys live.") She said, "Don't go on doing the same number, Benno." And it was perfectly true that Benn was not intimidated by the Layamons' penthouse. Wandering through endless fields of furniture, strange surroundings, yes, but he was not so impressed as Mrs. Layamon probably felt he should have been. It wasn't the difference in station that got him; not the class idea "They're bourgeois"; his mind didn't work that way. It wasn't the objects that bothered him but the persistent sense of being in a false position. This was what these articles of furniture symbolized. He took all this in with the motive of reporting to me; he put it down, but he *was* excited by the novelty of his surroundings. He confessed that he had to "live up to it" there—that is, he didn't come out of the bedroom in his dressing gown or unshaven. Today he was wearing one of the suits that Doctor's tailor had made for him, an Irish tweed—a rich gravy color with twists of seaweed green all over it. The cloth for once conformed to his shoulders so that his wing-case hump didn't stand out when the coat was buttoned. "The in-laws do have their magnifying glasses on me," he confessed.

I myself can't wear shaggy tweeds that irritate the skin. In overheated apartments, they can be hell.

"All I was trying to explain to Matilda was that as a kid I had been on the outside looking in. Suddenly I'm staring at the city from the summit, in Parrish Place, looking down from the fiftieth floor. And the city is better to look at than to be in. The streets everywhere smell so bad. The water is low in the sewers, that's what makes them fetid. I've given up trying to locate Jefferson Street. All I can see is that Ecliptic Circle Electronic Tower, dominating those miles of rubble. And everybody is so proud of it. . . ."

"Built on land we used to own. Out of which Vilitzer made a pot of money," I said.

"So the Layamons are always saying. It's a theme at the dinner table. I reminisced once about those premises, how we moved there from Jefferson Street, and what life was like when Dad died and Mother made the place into a home for old invalids. That helped put me through graduate school. And now this landmark skyscraper owned by the Japanese stands on that site. Those double television masts that relay programs over the whole region. Pillars of fire by night, as seen by the children of Israel . . ."

"That's not the kind of language the Layamons use at dinner," I said.

"No, but I can't sit there and suppress everything. Then I couldn't make conversation at all. I'd seem dull."

"How could you hope to interest them, Uncle, with their outlook on life?"

"Don't tell me there's *no* common ground. None at all? It can't be true."

"Common ground? You and Matilda married for love. That's for starters."

Uncle wouldn't take me up on this. He looked very edgy. He hadn't yet begun to understand that by marrying into the Layamon family he had carried me with him. Through my attachment to Benn I had hoped for an enlargement of personality. We were moving in the opposite direction instead. I wasn't ready to go into that aspect of things with him. I mustn't add to his difficulties: That was my policy in those first days, and even later.

He said, "Unless you pull the drapes, the Electronic Tower is staring down at you all during dinner. So it is a topic. I have my own connection with it. I tell them that I was my mother's handyman back in the fifties. In that comfortable dingy place, I tended the furnace. Sometimes I slept in the cellar."

"And now there's this mighty construction in that space, and you refer to the strangeness of human experience."

"Yes, that's what I said. I had plants in lots of those rooms. Some of our invalids hated the sight of them, others were glad to have a gloxinia or some potted lilies."

Uncle never would be as closely fitted by the Irish tweeds as he was by "the strangeness of life." Matilda objected, raising both hands and looking skywards. "Not again with the strangeness!" Those huge eyes of hers gave him a frequent thrill of precisely this, of "unknowable sources." And that frequent reaction was definitely connected with his botany. Of a plant that absorbed his attention, he would often say, "*There's* a curious existence for you. Try to think of it not as an evolutionary result but as somebody's invention. What sort of mind would have dreamed up *that*?"

When he described the wedding ceremony to me, he mentioned that it had been performed near the Layamons' Christmas tree. Although dusted with plastic snow, the tree itself was real. You couldn't fool Uncle about a tree. It was a balsam fir, and to this bristling little plant he connected himself somehow. It was like a sister to the bridegroom, the nearest thing to a relative standing up at his wedding. It was a significant transfer, come to think of it, the blood in his veins going out to the fluid in a conifer. If while he and Matilda were being united by the judge Benn closed his eyes and swayed slightly, it was because his imagination was enlarging in his head the heavily cutinized epidermis of the needle leaves—the stomata beneath the surface, the mesophyll, the trabecular projections, the resin canals, the procambium. If you didn't know him better, you might ask why a man with such extensive sympathies for a different kingdom of nature should offer himself in marriage, or should be a bridegroom at all. A fair question, and I have to answer it. Human attachments held a clear priority with him. A Christmas tree if you took it to bed wouldn't hug back when you hugged it. Never mind that relationships, otherwise known as human entanglements, would be moody, fickle, capricious, daemonic, scheming, heartless—all of that made passionless affinities (to plants) more appealing than they ought to be. Uncle was sure, he strongly believed, that nature had an *inside,* and a trumpet vine might have it as well as a dog. Think of the nausea music provoked in Darwin; or of Matthew Arnold three parts iced over; or of M. Yermelov insisting to me that in each of us there was a small glacier demanding that we thaw it. Carrying such a glacier in the bosom, one might be attracted to the saps of the flora. Uncle often said so. Sap is a temptation because sap is passionless. What demands can it make on you? Limited. Blood is charged with longing. The red blood is egotistical, with terrible powers, with desire and perverse impulses, and carrying strange wastes that demand purgation. Blood is that in which the Self lives. Keeping the various kingdoms in balance was a factor in Uncle's "strangeness." Assume that vital contents are pouring into the personality and have to be assimilated. There must be something inside to do the job. This was why Uncle laid a special emphasis on "strange." He presently stopped repeating it, when he saw how testy it made Matilda.

"So the little tree gave you the strength to go through with it."

"There was a mob at the reception—doctors, lawyers, brokers, builders, newspaper people, politicians."

"Did you invite Uncle Vilitzer?"

"Naturally he was on the guest list, and he was sort of the absent star. It was the wedding of Matilda L. to Boss Vilitzer's nephew, as far as the crowd was concerned. That goddam Electronic skyscraper, on the other side of the downtown district, edged up on us until it looked to be right across the street. After dark, when they light it up, it fetches loose and drifts towards Parrish Place."

"Matilda's dad, the physician, seems to be into politics too," I said.

"He's a powerful person." Uncle took a high view of his in-laws. He was impressed, excited. They were bringing him *out*, as if he were a debutante. Dr. Layamon belonged to the big city network. The power brokers were his acquaintances. Some of them were pals. "Doctor's connections are fantastic. Don't look skeptical, Kenneth."

"Who, me? I'm not a bit skeptical. I read the papers. I'm probably more with it than you are, Uncle. If I didn't follow Wall Street, sports, TV, Washington and the political scene right here, I wouldn't be able to understand my own subject." By this I meant the St. Petersburg of Blok and Bely in 1913—and their preoccupations: the satanic darkness, the abyss of the Antichrist, the horrible islands of gloom, granite and ice, the approaching Terrible Judgment, the crimes of Immanuel Kant against human consciousness, and all the rest of that. I have a big stake in keeping up with triumphant America. Doctor's intricate money-and-power didn't surprise me at all. "Okay, Uncle," I said. "You want me to get your new picture. I've got it. You've married a beautiful woman with rich, high-placed parents. They threw one hell of a reception for you. But you didn't exactly feel at home with their hoopla, so you were clinging to the Christmas tree."

"When I tell you something confessional it's understood that you don't turn it against me. As for the rich part of it, make no mistake, the Layamons aren't giving away any dough. They had the wedding budget figured down to the penny."

"All you have to do is live a while longer than the old folks. You're already wearing the best tweeds in town, and a real necktie, not one of those rags from the engine room."

There was a silent interval, both parties considering how to come to better terms. For a while our eyes were held by the display of falling snow put on by Winter—bit upon bit upon bit, white particles doing everything acrobatically possible, the bigger flakes suggesting the astral storming of one of Van Gogh's night skies.

"Did you really expect old Vilitzer to attend?"

"I thought I'd be doing him credit, for a change. Not that I missed him."

"He's written you off as a science ninny. Your biggest worry is what makes grass look green—I imagine that's how such a guy would dismiss you."

"I don't think he's written me off. He hasn't forgiven us for suing him. Now I have one fact more to tell you."

"Yes?"

"The judge who married us? Well, he was the judge in that case—the same judge!"

At this, my legs dropped off the recliner and I sat upright and turned my head to hear better. "That can't be right, Uncle Benn; you must have misunderstood what they told you."

"No. Take it from me. The same fellow. Judge Chetnik."

"You're sure, now? One of Vilitzer's stable of judges? You recognized him?"

"You forget, I was away in Assam and never attended the trial. But the name was Amador Chetnik. I wouldn't have forgotten that."

"Was it after or before he tied the knot that you found this out? Was he friendly?"

"Those people always are superfriendly, no matter what they've done or are about to do," said Benn. "He was pompous. A vulgar face, especially the nose, a disfigurement, but no matter how rugged they look, they've all got that smooth manner."

"Did your in-laws know about this?"

"Well, I'm not sure. All I can assume—being fair to all parties—is that they didn't make the connection. I wish I were in a position to make a valid guess."

"Well, if you're offering me one free guess, Uncle, I'd guess that your father-in-law, at least, knew."

"Is that a way to kick off an era of good feeling?"

"He may have intended it in your best interests—in a big perspective. We can't expect to figure the ins and outs. Still, I can't imagine how else to put the parts together. The man *did* rule against you, and you and Mother were done out of a lot of money. It *was* a fixed case. Mother has that on solid authority. The legal word for it is 'impropriety.' If that was what happened, how do you account for the fact that he was willing to perform the ceremony? No hard feelings? Nothing personal? Just the way things always have been done in this town?"

"I'm not exactly in a position to interpret. I realize that I'll have to take this up with Matilda by and by."

"If her father knew, wouldn't she have known also?"

While this was bound to be said and must have been expected, Uncle looked hectic, jerky; he pulled at the expanding strap of his wristwatch, then drew the sleeve down over it. Under his breath he said, "Bureaucratic." Checking the time was bureaucratic? But this was quintessential Uncle Benn, to stick himself sharply in a single word. What this showed was that under it all he was aware of the true facts. He said, "Before I can bring up unpleasant subjects, she and I need to have the pleasant side of the marriage in order. Goodwill has to be established first."

"I expect you'll know how to take care of yourself," I said, without believing it. "Well, let's hope this Chetnik wasn't Doctor's idea of a joke."

"Doctor *is* a sort of humorist. He isn't a smooth type at all. But it may have a tactical meaning we can't see yet. Fence mending of some kind."

"I hope it's not like the kind of fence Stravinsky's grandfather was climbing when he broke his neck."

Uncle wasn't altogether himself. He was under alien influences. The whites of his eyes had a medicated tinge. In becoming the husband of this classy, extraordinarily desirable woman (like a *Vogue* photograph), he was excited, he was challenged. He was ambitious, he asserted powers that had never been called upon before and he wanted me to understand that he was capable of holding his ground against those influences. I helped him out by asking him to describe the wedding reception.

"I suppose there were upwards of a hundred people. A first-class caterer laid out a beautiful spread. . . ."

"Quite a big attendance. It must have been a long-standing puzzle in town whom Matilda eventually would marry, and people came just to look the fellow over. Such a choosy doll . . ."

"With quite a lot of experience, you might as well add. A modern woman in her thirties, what would you expect?"

"Well, you beat out the whole field, so there must be something to you."

Uncle's face was lowered to conceal his smile (the shade of gloom in it). "Old boyfriends must have been at the party. I was aware of that."

"And the bride herself?"

"Wearing a long, gold-green thing, her face gold-white. She was at full voltage. Against . . ."

"Well, against what?"

"A background of second thoughts, probably. Which a woman might well have, in a case like mine."

"I don't see why. She's a clever lady. Clever ladies are all nerved up; that's common with quality women. They may tremble, but they're resolute. I suppose the parents are happy?"

Uncle said, "I don't believe they have anything much against me. Her dad does talk about matches that she might have made, and I can't kid myself that I was really the hoped-for husband."

"Come on, Uncle, you sound like Jane Austen, with your matches. You've dialed the wrong historical period. Why don't you hang up and try again?"

"It's the attitude of the parents. You asked me to describe it."

Well, the wedding was behind him now, but the magnificence went on, and there was Uncle in this fantasia of opulence, every morning wandering in the long rooms of Persian rugs and decorator drapes, lighted cabinets of Baccarat and Wedgwood, and schlock paintings from the eighteenth century of unidentified (and I'd say uncircumcised) personages from Austria or Italy. Were *they* ever out of place! And Uncle perhaps was even more of a misfit than the portrait subjects, acquired by purchase. By feeling anyway, to judge by his reports of the Layamon "life-style." "You wouldn't believe the thickness of the bath towels," he said, with an intensity suitable for a confidence. "Or the force in the faucets. All the toilet seats are upholstered—plastic seats with padding. The kitchen cabinets are cinnamon with a red trim, and there's a floodlight over the butcher block. . . ."

"The cook is Polish, you say?"

"Decent, down-to-earth person. Not much English. And the Mexican woman has a husband who tended bar at the reception."

Benn wasn't comfortable with servants. To sit idle, or even to read while they worked, was a burden to him. Any well-informed person will tell you, if you press him to define "bourgeois" and "postbourgeois," that "bourgeois" implies a servant class. But the Layamons didn't much care which they were. They had dough and they weren't going to stint, they were lavish—at least with Baccarat, with interior decoration. They absolutely *were* thinking about a match for their only child—never mind my crack about Jane Austen, or Uncle's remarks about people who were ignorant of Balzac and therefore didn't speak the same language as cultivated readers. Basically, he didn't even want what they wanted—the money. As many dollar bills as it would take to fill the Grand Canyon wouldn't have been enough for them. Plant morphology satisfied him. So how were they to understand one another? As I interpreted things, he was simply the latest problem their daughter had dragged home.

They would try to fit him into their lives, if only he would keep his mouth shut.

I said, "What's their behavior towards you?"

"Oh, definitely friendly. Mrs. Layamon is reserved, but she's correct. Well, she's considerate. But remember, she's only eight years my senior, about the same age as your mother. Instead of a son-in-law I might be her brother. I don't expect her to show affection until she's certain that it will work out."

"What about Dr. Layamon?"

"Doctor acts affectionate, but with him it's more like a style."

"They have to psych you out. That's natural. At the same time, anything but agreeable."

"I wouldn't say *dis*agreeable. Their conversation isn't quite what I'm used to. I have to prepare for it, and if I didn't bone up on the *Times* and the *Wall Street Journal* I'd just have to sit there and feed my face, nothing to say. Fortunately, I don't have to say much, because Doctor is such a great talker. He talks! Thank God he talks so much! About the private clinic where he's the senior partner, the hospital, those patients who are such big operators: developers, bankers, junk bond experts, 'greenmail' raiders—what are those, by the way? Matilda keeps an eye out and covers for me. She's got what you always call 'ironic distance' on her parents and she's teaching me how to be amused and not oppressed. But I'm getting an education. What a country this is! I should have known these things long ago."

"If I were you, Uncle, I'd try first of all to find out why that crooked judge was brought in to marry you. I'd like to talk to Fishl Vilitzer about that."

"I doubt that his father would tell *him* anything about judges. He won't even see him."

"But there's not much worth knowing about his old man that Fishl doesn't know. You didn't invite your cousin to the wedding, having asked Uncle Vilitzer? That figures."

Being educated in a new branch of knowledge was Uncle's all-purpose justification, and "education" could reconcile him to almost any sort of abuse. I believe that Dr. Layamon intuitively picked up on this, and immediately put on a special display of his proclivities and powers, in some degree mistaking Benn's polite, "learning-experience" attentiveness for inertia or submission. Layamon was in his own way a clever, aggressive man. He had a great deal to show for himself. Look at the picture: a twelve-room duplex penthouse; a winter residence in Palm Springs. Among Doctor's acquaintances and golf pals were Bob Hope and President Ford. Norman Lear had the Layamons to dinner. Matilda, slightly sardonic about this, said that Doctor had felt he had to kick in a contribution for the Civil Liberties Union: "As payola." Still, it was a class connection. Tilda thus might have chosen a husband from any of these spheres. According to Doctor, she passed up a national network anchorman, then a fellow who was now on the federal appeals bench, plus a tax genius consulted by Richard Nixon. The list was fairly long.

Mrs. Layamon, accepting Benn on approval, gave him every formal courtesy. Doctor was more forthcoming with his son-in-law, and I saw him as more of a problem. In his person, Doctor was lean, slender, more mechanical than organic in movement, flat in construction, almost two-dimensional, wide in the shoulders, a touch hectic in his color, almost hypertensive, mobile and urgently clever in facial expression, and with a tendency to bear down on you in conversation—almost as if he were putting you through a pretrial interrogation. He had a thin, gabby mouth, and when he wasn't speaking he sometimes wore a look of violent primness, like an actor in a Shaw play, forced briefly to listen to the other guy but thinking how he would rip into him in a minute. "His thing is to punch the fat out of you," said Benn. "He takes pride in being straight, even about his daughter. He says he wants to brief me. It's an ethical thing. His responsibility to his daughter is ending, mine is beginning, therefore it's only right that he should level with me. Matilda knows that he's doing it and she can tolerate it because she understands her dad's principles, his honor system. Everything up front. There shouldn't be unpleasant surprises later, or occasions for reproach."

That Benn should share this with me was perfectly right. Uncle said that he wouldn't even understand the phenomena (Doctor's logic and his sincerity) until he had described them. So this was why he submitted them to my judgment. Benn gave the impression that he was glad of his new family, proud of them. Such interesting and highly placed people took him seriously, welcomed him into their circle, invited him to participate in their fascinating lives.

He and Doctor had had several private conversations, man to man. There was, or had been, a Texas builder who flew up from Houston in his private jet just to take her to dinner. But what do you think! At that time she was mixed up with some Croatian prick who needed a green card, and she preferred this weirdo illegal immigrant. Go figure it out! He must have had something the guy in the ten-gallon hat couldn't match. But then Matilda just naturally drew men. Consider her assets—not just her figure but her taste in dress. Substitute Nature for Teller—you're holding an H-bomb of beauty invented by Nature, and you aren't a dumb superpower, either, you're a brilliant, independent woman. At first she didn't realize. She didn't have to futz around in Paris with all that postwar sleaze. This girl had brains enough to be chief executive officer of a blue-chip corporation. With her mentality you could manage NASA. When Mondale announced for the presidency she sent him a campaign blueprint, and if he had been smart enough to put her in charge he might be in the White House now. Her head is like a computer bank, and all she ever used it for was to contrive more personal trouble, a migraine for her parents, lasting more than three decades. On the chance that there would be less trouble to get into in higher education, they sent her to the best institutions. As a result she has more degrees than a thermometer—all useless, worth shit. Both Yale and Harvard admitted her to law school, but she preferred Croatian romances, speaking French top speed and writing at that book she never got finished—up all night beating on her tinny typewriter in the wee hours and saturating the curtains with tobacco and pot. And by the way, what did Benn's nephew Kenneth think of this French of hers?

Boastfulness was the frame for all this conversational freeform modeling. First Doctor bragged about himself, about his wealth, his connections, and then about his daughter. He poured it on. When the current became too strong, his control was temporarily taken from him. He turned on his daughter and began to bitch about her. From childhood—hell, from birth!—she was demanding, moody, contrary, tetchy, a complainer and a schemer. She was bad enough in high school, but when they sent her to Vassar she took up with town punks in Poughkeepsie and did everything you read about in the papers. (By "papers" he meant the *National Enquirer* and other checkout-counter publications.) "In Italy I swear she would have joined the Red Brigades. Normal people like you and me can't begin to picture what kind of sex activities they had. We never combined the sex with LSD. The youngsters' visions don't even start until they've been at it for two hours. That's the way the Manson killers practiced in the sack for those stabbings and human sacrifices. Governments also seem to be into this, and that's how come a Manson-type Turk shoots down the Pope. Well, to get back to Tilda, thank God this is behind her, finally. When I say 'behind' it's not a sexual joke. I'm just being frank. By choosing you she showed that she wanted to make her life stable at last. At last! So bless you both, and good luck!"

This was not the conversation here in the dorm that Benn and I should have been having on such an occasion. Doctor's talk, while it was "fun," was also insidious. It injected you with fears. Benn ought to have been describing his delight, shining with happiness—or if "happiness" is too romantic in these distressing times, at least glowing with mature satisfaction. Benn and I might have had a good laugh over his maneuvering his skeptical nephew out of the way, and then some drinks and congratulations. Only I'm good and tired of watching high-quality people fuck up in practical life, to the gratification of the vulgar. But no, the quality people are always knee-deep in the garbage of "personal life." What, Uncle too? But perhaps I was prematurely bitter, jumping to conclusions.

My private thoughts: Swedenborg severely separated Good and Evil, Heaven and Hell. William Blake's view was that Good and Evil were commingled. His radical statement on this is to be found in *The Marriage of Heaven and Hell*. A connubial sexual angelism is *not* what we creatures generally experience. In any case, I wasn't about to give up on Uncle on this early evidence. Nor was *he* giving up, by any means. After all, he did right to marry, to break away from the tyranny of sex abuse. It was too soon to judge Matilda (in spite of Doctor), and perhaps that time would never come. As some wise Roman said (Cato, maybe), "Only the husband, the man that wears the shoe, can tell you where it pinches."

Meantime, over a few sessions, Uncle gave a fuller account of Dr. Layamon's ambivalent judgment of his daughter. Layamon couldn't resist the dual temptation to boast about her and then to tear her down. He praised her mother, he praised himself, he had nice things to say about Benn. Then he got a little wild. His fluency was intoxicating, and he began to utter flatteries lacking in specific reference, like a virtuoso playing all possible variations, crossing his hands on the keyboard from an upside-down position, with his shoulders resting on the back of a chair, like Mozart drunk and entertaining the tarts with his tricks, in that moving picture. Brag, derogation, complaint, followed the inner movements of the Doctor's character and mode of thought, and presently you saw a reality (of a kind) rising before you. The way grains of sand follow the wind into undulations, and form dunes or rippled deserts. This very nicely dressed elderly party, the Doctor, before you knew it, before he himself was aware of it, was confiding, professing love and admiration, being superintimate, hooking Benn close to him as he talked. He was very physical with people. He dropped a hand on your knee, he caught you by the cheek, he worked your shoulder. He played every emotional instrument in the band. You couldn't, however, depend on the music. Suddenly a wild bray would break up the tune. He complimented Benn on his eminence in botany. Then he'd say, "Too bad those overlapping front teeth weren't corrected"; or else: "Either you're wearing a tight shirt or your *pectoralis major* is overdeveloped—big tits, in other words." At dinner, when Doctor passed behind Benn's chair, taking his time about it, Uncle couldn't doubt that his bald spot was being inspected. And when they were using old-fashioned urinals at the club, Doctor set his chin on the high partition and looked down through crooked goggles to see how Uncle was hung. His comment was: "Fire-fighting equipment seems adequate, anyway."

Benn was sufficiently rattled to speak of this to Matilda, who got a good laugh out of it. She said, "I noticed that he followed you pretty quick into the gents' room." A little more seriously, she added, "Genitals are a common fixation among doctors. So many are obsessed with men's tools, and also women's things."

Benn wondered, "Is that so?" This was one of the fascinations Matilda held for him: unexpected points of view, new horizons. Besides, it gave Matilda the satisfaction of making memorable remarks and cracks, such as a fine creature ought to make.

"How are botanists that way?" she said.

"It's true the reproductive organs of the plants have gynecological names, but some of us wonder whether this may be a misleading projection."

"Daddy is sexually curious about me. Has he asked you what kind of lay I am?"

"Not yet—not quite."

"I've always been the channel for his unclean fantasies."

It was her style to have swift intuitions. They came with an unexpected break. Her cleverness pleased Benn, and it was the sexual aspect of it that most intrigued him. He may have thought that he had married in order to rid himself of damaging distractions—health risks, abuses. I held a different view. Uncle had gotten into the "fresh mode of experience" movement mentioned earlier. There were carnal matters he was driven to explore. There was a special pathos in this, for he was a man who really did have something to do—other than trouble others, which seems to be what so many of us are here for exclusively. He was a noble person of passion and integrity. The question was whether he valued his own gifts and whether he would defend himself for *their* sake. Self-defense was not even the main consideration for such an individual. I consider Darwinian self-preservation to be a vulgar ideology. Its leading exponents are sadists who are always telling you that for the good of the species and in conformity with the law of Nature, they have to do in the gentle spirits they encounter on life's way.

Doctor's comment in the gents' room stung Benn, and Matilda, instead of theorizing about the hang-ups of physicians, ought to have spoken a word of solace and reassurance to him. Edgar Allan Poe's Helen standing in her niche had nothing to say. The representative of beauty was dumb, a terrific advantage for a sensitive devotee of classic figures. Especially if the devotee plans to run in the great contemporary sex marathon.

I turn to Uncle for masterly guidance, and what does he give me? He gives me vulnerability in a field in which my father had his greatest triumphs. All I can do now is treat the Layamon phenomenon as a lapse, predictable, venial and requiring patience. (And patience is not my strongest suit.) If it was erotic master classes I needed, I oughtn't to have come to the U.S.A. I could have had them from my dad. In this department an American finds his greatest advantages in Europe. Anyway, I didn't molest Benn with my opinions. In the end he would voluntarily tell me everything. Once begun, he couldn't bear to keep anything from me. I even foretold that he would phone me in the middle of the night to add some trifle to the record. So I couldn't have been more fully informed.

Benn insisted and repeated, "I am happy with this woman."

"Good. I'm delighted for you."

What I had told Benn about Treckie now applied to him—the power of a repeated declaration. You announce what you're going to do. Then you do it. Then you publicize what you did. At last it becomes a fact. In lawyers' language, it's *res judicata*.

Meanwhile Doctor hammered away at Uncle, and there was nobody to shield the poor guy. "You're a high-grade scientist, and I'm an experienced physician. We not only can speak freely to each other, but we must. The women never will. It's important that *we* do. You love Matilda. . . ."

"Oh, yes!"

"Of course. I figure you for a cocksman who had sense enough finally to stop the chasing. Maybe someday you'll tell me about some of the women you scored with."

The late Della Bedell, with her electric light bulb.

"My daughter will organize a life ideal for your final years. She can be a real bitch, but her bitchiness will be working *for* you. What more can you ask? Right now, it's honeymoon time. You should have a great holiday in Brazil. Let me ask you: Is there some particular reason why you didn't want to go back? Is there a woman in Rio who'll make a scandal?"

"No. There's nobody with my special interests in Brazil for me to talk to."

Doctor said, "It may do us some good to exchange views. You can speak your mind to me. We have interests in common. Pool our headaches, that's the smart thing to do."

"I appreciate that," Uncle answered, lamely. What Doctor had said about the "final years" distressed him. Just married, he was starting life anew, and Dr. Layamon already pictures his decline. Were there signs? Was he speaking generally or diagnostically? Did he mean a stroke? Alzheimer's disease? Failing potency?

"Matilda says that living in high style makes you talk about coming from the other side of the tracks. Which side do you think I'm from?"

The problem was not with opulence and luxury, the Jacuzzi bath, the Rosenthal china, the tortoiseshell toilet articles. The penthouse Matilda was very different from the lady he had courted. During the courtship, he had thought her, like himself, an early riser, but now in her own room she slept in. She was never out of bed before eleven o'clock. Waiting for her to get up, he killed time. He met the newsboy at the door and read the *Wall Street Journal* in the kitchen until the Polish cook arrived. Then he wandered out into the showroom of furniture and sat with his newspapers near the Christmas tree, while it lasted. Afterwards he sought out the cut flowers. Mrs. Layamon kept potted plants in her office. This little room was off limits to him. "I look in on her azalea now and then."

"What does she do in that office?"

"Writes notes, makes appointments, orders the food, and she tapes poetry for people in nursing homes."

"Could be useful," I said.

"Nice for them to put on a Walkman and listen to Robert Frost."

"Or William Blake."

I pictured the moribund as prisoners of the TV. Much better for them to hear the words of the Psalms. Recitations from the Book of Proverbs, Ecclesiastes, extracts from Shakespeare, *Songs of Experience*, while they were being woven into eternity. I asked, "What does she read them?"

"I'll find out from Matilda. Mrs. Layamon does have a gorgeous azalea in her sunny den. It does wonders for me. I mean, when the going is rough I stand in the doorway and stare at it. One of the funny rules of the house is that nobody goes into this sanctum of hers."

When he spoke of staring at the azalea, the twist of his gaze altered his entire face—again a physiognomic peculiarity of one of those passionate natures who long to find and to see what perhaps does not exist on earth. That's how the Russian poet Blok once put it in a similar case. He also observed that in such persons one eye (usually the left) is smaller than the other. (The loops of the figure eight are not identical in size.) Such a hunger to see lasts all through life, up to the grave, perhaps beyond the grave. By such signs I understood that the Citizen of Eternity is not cut off from his inner sources. I still didn't understand why he needed to be in this place, the Layamon penthouse, at all, any more than I understood the

Chinese mountains, Indian forests, Amazonian jungles, that used to take him away, when he was lost to me for months at a time.

Yet there he was. He waited for Matilda to rise and he read papers. Damn if I knew what he was making of these Qadaffis, Imeldas and Waldheims, or Washington's budgetary trillions. His one unchallengeable affinity there was with the azalea plant thirty yards away and around the corner. Another affinity, with Matilda, was (we hoped) still in the formative stages. Her need now was to sleep, and it was necessary to bear with her. He was careful not to disturb her, and he therefore hung his pants on the back of the bathroom door so that the jingle of keys and coins wouldn't reach her. All morning the cook cooked, the maid cleaned, Mrs. Layamon recorded Marianne Moore or Wallace Stevens on tape, and Matilda in her maiden bedroom was wrapped in her silk eiderdown. You saw only her profile as she slept, the child of wealth cleared at last for total rest. After much agitation, defiance, prodigal or neurotic wanderings, she was reconciled to her home. This was where Uncle Benn came in. Marriage to B. Crader restored her. She found rest. She resumed her earlier ways and privileges, as it were. She slept. She was an extravagant, luxuriant sleeper, fully abandoned to sleep. You could think of it as Psyche embracing Eros in a blind darkness. This was how Uncle put it, to my surprise. "Psyche" was also from that Poe poem, with which he was then obsessed, as he was to be later with the Charles Addams cartoon. At first, mistakenly, I thought, "Here comes more of that crazy Edgar Allan Poe with his marble Psyche. Only this poor nerd, who happens to be a nerd I love, could drive himself nuts over it. All this second-class imagery, so much self-indulgence. And so far, far from his botany, where the best of him should be invested."

I was dead wrong about this. *He* had a glimmer of the truth. If she was a Psyche, the Eros she embraced in sleep was not her husband. Indirectly, he was telling me this. He was the cause of her rest but the substance of that rest might be something else again. Another man? No, of course not. Something, not someone. There was no other man. Only that thing, her Eros, was not Benn Crader. Of course Poe's

Psyche was all marble, and represented Ideal Beauty. The Poe lady was there to be contemplated, not embraced—Beauty in contemplation. (What are Jews doing, getting into all this Greek stuff, anyway?)

"Well, let her catch up on her sleep. I see she needs it. I don't want to ask her 'Why do you sleep so much?'"

"It gives *you* a chance to catch up with the contemporary world," I said.

"Let her sleep herself out," he said. "Nobody, in the ultimate sense, short of death, really gets the rest he needs. So when she makes up for lost sleep I expect to get some of the benefit of it."

However (for the time being, maybe), her waking was not happy. When she drank her coffee, she was snappish, morose. Her big eyes were still back in the sleep world. Little was said. Before she spoke, and as her mouth was opening, Benn noticed how sharp her teeth were. But you can't fault people for their teeth. If the opening of a beautiful woman's mouth is a noteworthy occurrence, that in itself may testify against the observer rather than the woman. Still, I always took Uncle's powers of original observation to be one of his strengths. All such notations were pregnant with insight. Ever since I had asked him to lend a hand with my studies of the Russian symbolists he had been absorbed in authors with whom I had no great patience. I depended on him to abstract their arguments for me, and he became a great reader of Soloviev (on Plato), Fyodorov, Berdyaev, Vyacheslav Ivanov *(Dostoyevsky and the Tragic Life)*. Based on this reading, he would say things about forces from the interior of the earth acting magnetically on the spinal fluid. He referred to the earth as being charged (giving his Russian references) with Luciferic electricity. And his first wife proved to have influenced him with Swedenborgian notions, after all. The correspondence theory, for instance: A tree is not merely a natural object, it is a Sign. There are correspondences. Objects, beautiful or ugly, are communications. A human face gives information, as do colors, shapes, fragrances. So Matilda is opening her mouth, right? And Uncle Benn notes that a woman of great beauty may have four bulges in the gums, at the base of her canine teeth. This defect, if it was a defect and not rather an indication of perversity in the perceiver, an impulse to quarrel with perfection or a quirkiness that indicates resistance to the potency of beauty, may be a sign of weakness. High beauty may be a torment. It tears at our hearts (some of us), and then we frantically fight it. We superimpose a Medusa on the innocent face of a girl.

What's the use of talking!

A morning type by nature, Benn was liveliest when he woke up. Then he tried to help Matilda over the pains of her waking. He read the *Times* and the *Wall Street Journal*, picking out items for her, conversational themes for the breakfast table. "That terrorist whom Craxi set free, he went to Yugoslavia, and they put him on a plane for the Middle East." Or: "Reagan says it's okay for Star Wars researchers to profit privately from discoveries made while on federal subsidies. Of course, with his belief in free enterprise . . . And speaking of that, there's a funny piece about Milton Friedman. Somebody asks him, 'Are you sure that Economic Man *is* completely rational—can we depend on it? Many qualified thinkers have asserted that the behavior of *Homo sapiens* is distinctly paranoid and some even say that there is a widespread physiological condition described as *schizophysiology* and producing effects of *schizopsychology*. Koestler made such an argument. Now, how does this incontrovertible insanity square with your theory of Economic Man?' Friedman answers that no matter how crazy people are, they still remain sane about money. What do you think, is this fact or faith? Well, he doesn't speak of Good and Evil. He doesn't even discuss psychology, which is greatly to his credit. All he seems to say is that between humankind and full chaos there stands only the free market. Belief in the invisible is narrowed down by him to the Invisible Hand."

Here Friedman sounded to me like Caroline Bunge!

"Ho, ho," said Matilda, bitter. She didn't take Benn's views seriously. And it's true that he was trying to coax her into a better temper. He made these efforts in a spirit of pure appeasement. But she hated waking—*hated* it.

"Like a brilliant thundercloud, a charged cumulous rage-cloud comes over her," said Benn, rather admiring. A passionate woman—admirable!

The breakfast rolls were icy in the middle, and she burst out, "It's the goddam microwave. Why the hell doesn't Irina use the gas range!" Anger, beauty, blame. Benn caught it in the face, so to speak.

"I'll take the buns to the kitchen," he said.

"You will like hell! . . . Irina!" she called.

She didn't like Benn to be on good terms with the help. About servants he didn't know damn-all and had to be taught.

These breakfasts were more trying than they should have been. Was Matilda already dissatisfied with him? Was she reconsidering? In his place I wouldn't have put myself out for her. I'd have avoided breakfast altogether; gone to the lab; spent the morning in a conservatory. He shouldn't have been hanging around.

At about this time, Benn said to me (he had said it often), "I wonder what life would have been if I'd had the same gift for human beings as I had for plants." Take for instance the matter of Matilda's sleep, which reminded him in some respects of the plant world. Deep sleep is devoid of consciousness of any kind, and so is plant growth, evidently. In crystals and in the plants, intricacy of design occurs without any trace of conscious intelligence. Yet intricate metamorphoses suggest an intelligent intent. One may be tempted to suspend consciousness in a divinatory effort to get into those strange (silent? but they're incapable of sound) plant organisms. With Uncle I assumed that the penetration had preceded any tempting. Moreover, the power of Matilda's sleep may have drawn Uncle's imagination towards the plant analogy. For all I know, he viewed her as a sheaf of ferns bound up in the satin edging of the eiderdown, and expanding at the top, fronds of long hair coming down over shut eyes.

But then he hadn't married a plant. Matilda might remind you of a fern or a lily of the field, and maybe the plant element *was* strong in her—the trouble she had making the transition from sleep to waking suggested a struggle between two natures—but she did wake, however reluctantly, and came out at last in her gorgeous housecoat, a brocade of Far Eastern design. Sometimes she shut Benn up altogether. She said, "Oh, for Chrissakes, Benno, don't make heavy conversation before I'm awake. It gives me such a headache."

Well, he was sad already—out of his milieu, out of his depth, under orders not to speak. Sitting in the breakfast nook, all he could do was look out at the city, which fills so many miles. All those abandoned industries awaiting electronic resurrection, the colossal body of the Rustbelt, the stems of the tall chimneys nowadays bearing no blossoms of smoke. One of your privileges if you were very rich was to command a vast view of this devastation. From the top of the Electronic Tower you had an even more stunning view. Mrs. Layamon's opinion, given at dinner, was that the tower was an "important piece of modern beauty." Benn could see no beauty in it, but he wasn't about to disagree; he kept his mouth shut during such dinner discussions. Occasionally he repeated during the meal what they had paid no attention to the first time: "We used to live on that spot. We moved there from Jefferson Street when I was about twelve. The city took the building from the former owner in lieu of taxes and my dad bought it on Uncle Harold's advice. I think he paid seven hundred bucks. It came with a nice yard. There were two big mulberry trees and they attracted lots of grackles in June." Little notice was taken of this natural history. "Very fine trees, the kind with the white fruit. The purple mulberries have a better flavor." Expressive looks passed among the Layamons. Uncle was aware of these but interpreted them as signs of boredom. There he was definitely wrong, as we shall see.

From the breakfast nook, then, Benn had a privileged view of the city, its caved-in streets and ruined apartment blocks. At the center there were buildings under construction—renewal programs. "I wonder where my mother-in-law heard this, about the 'important piece of modern beauty.' Once or twice I was tempted to say, 'That's what your *daughter* is.' But I didn't want to get out of line, referring to her daughter as a 'piece.'"

Nor perhaps would he have been entirely sincere in saying it. And there was a carryover at dinner from the orders he was under to keep his mouth shut while Matilda drank her breakfast coffee—cup after cup of the strongest *caffè espresso*. Just then, he wouldn't have taken an esthetic view of her. He would have been wondering rather: Is it something I've done? Perhaps even: Is there something she wants done that I'm not doing?

"The first honeymoon was four days in Aruba," said Benn. "The hotel we stayed in belongs to a group. Doctor is in on it."

Doctor's patients and pals were big-time developers, and now and then one of these people with whom he played rummy or golf let him have a piece of the action—a new office building in Dallas, a shopping mall, a luxury condominium, time-sharing apartments in a Florida resort, an astrodome in Oklahoma, a city contract to tow away abandoned cars. A percentage point here, a percentage point there, said Matilda. Papa's fortune was made up of bits and pieces of such enterprises. Tilda had put together a comprehensive picture of his holdings, although Doctor refused to give her any information. Doctor told Benn, "She's a hell of a challenge that way. You can't keep anything from her. She'll go around and talk to people, have drinks with them, and before you realize it she's found out all about the deal. She's always watching from her satellite. She's never been too absorbed in the French junk to lose track of economics. Then again, it's something of a comfort. When Jo and I pass away, no officer of a trust department will be able to snow Matilda. I pity the guy who tries."

I said, "He wants you to know that Matilda is a rich heiress."

"It's all Matilda. I'm hardly ever in the picture. But I don't need to be."

Just then, before she left for Brazil, Matilda and her mother were busy every afternoon with bridal registry choices, deciding between Lalique and Baccarat and also linens and kitchenware. A more experienced housekeeper than either of them, Benn had ideas of his own about pots and pans and dishwashers. He held curiously strong views on many matters remote from science. "Nosy," he said about himself. However, he wasn't consulted, nor did he try to put in his two cents. "We're going to assume in this case that Matilda knows better," he said. "I don't expect her to be a homemaker. But she's buying as if she were preparing to open a small hotel."

Freshly shaven every evening, Benn turned up at dinner in the role of the botanical professorial bridegroom and son-in-law—Dr. Chlorophyll. I was there one night and watched. Old Layamon and Matilda did all the talking. Afterwards a gang movie was played on the VCR, *Godfather II*. And I was able to see for myself what Benn had been telling me about the Electronic Tower. It drew close in the night, a mass of lighted windows bigger than the *Titanic*, and the fiery masts like a sign to the Children of Israel. That evening, Matilda was very lively, not a trace of the enraged hard-to-wake beauty silently warring against bright day and full consciousness. I had to admit that she was (objectively speaking) attractive, witty, with a nipping high manner. The lesson she taught was that you don't often have beauty which doesn't carry some affliction for the beholder. The kind of woman I prefer—I've made no secret of it—is built closer to the ground. For my taste, Matilda had too much elevation. To hold nothing back, I kept wondering, How long do those legs go on and where and how do they attach to the trunk; what happens at the point of attachment? You've got no truth to life if you omit such masculine conjectures, and you will see that even Uncle, for all his vegetable reveries, had entertained similar pictures. Anyway, I wondered how Benn obtained his happiness from what I was imagining. But here, trying to guess, even the eagerest third party will only wear himself out. The only sign I ever had from Benn in those days was this, that he said to me, "It *ought* to be possible to gratify a woman's wishes. We'll do what *she* wants. I can find out only by going along with her will. Then I may be getting somewhere." He went shopping with her and kept his mouth shut when she bought a GE dishwasher. "For only a hundred bucks more, the Kitchenaid is a thousand times better," he told me. "I'm not going to say, 'I told you so.'"

Matilda needed measurements from the apartment at the Roanoke, the place she had inherited from her aunt, and brought Benn along to help with the tape. This was Uncle's first view of the place. He reported that my Venetian palace comparison was right on the money. You could imagine a building like the Roanoke—bourgeois baroque—also in Vienna or in Rio. Even the house key looked Venetian. The front door of the apartment was a foot thick, easily, and embossed with plumes and spears. The hinges were superheavy. "The air that flowed out smelled like sickrooms," he related. The old aunt had died more than a year ago, and the place had been locked up. Either Matilda didn't notice the staleness, or else the joy of ownership made a fragrance of it. She had worked on this legacy from the time her uncle died, a matter of fifteen years, beating out two other scheming nieces. So it was a substantial victory.

"Matilda gave me the conducted tour. 'This is where we'll live. What do you say to this layout?' I didn't want to ask, had the old lady been incontinent? Did she keep cats or dogs? All I could say was that it was pretty lavish."

"Trying to picture yourself here—such a long way from Jefferson Street?" said Matilda.

And she began to spell out the advantages of the Roanoke: walking distance from the university; Benn could have a lab right here, at home, if he chose—all the plumbing was in place. All they had to do was tear out some tacky old sinks. He told me that the space she offered him would have been ideal for a photographer's darkroom. He answered her that it was a great suggestion but that he was used to working away from home. Also, he needed that walk to campus as an aid to reflection.

She asked whether it hurt to give up his old apartment, "the scene of your first happy marriage."

A second happy marriage now had begun, he said with tact.

"Then giving up the place where you entertained so many pretty girls. Including me."

There was no reason to mention anyone like Della Bedell and how she had pounded on the door, shouting, "What am I supposed to do with my sexuality?" Neighbors might be thankful that *they* didn't have to answer. Poor thing. Now that she was dead it would be simple courtesy, charity, to forget how she had carried on.

Here we are, however, the living, inspecting our grand residential legacy. Benn sized up the scale of the rooms, the spread of the chandeliers. He took in the wallpapers and fabrics, some of them hanging in strips, the swelling fatty porcelain of the bathtubs, where silverfish flitted; the weighted drains plated in German silver—all first class once. It was different from the wealth that Scott Fitzgerald had admired—established country-house wealth, polo ponies in the stables, muscular fair-haired players, best schools, Lafayette Escadrille. No, the Roanoke was the indoor, closet-type wealth of

German Jews whom the Long Island rich would have called *Shonickers*. Uncle Benn didn't even begin to be in with either category of the rich. He ran out of comments as Matilda was showing him around. "This is the living room," she told him. And he said, "It's the size of a pasture. It's gorgeous. Is this carpet white, or oyster-shell colored? It's like fleece, only it's turning yellow."

She told him that cleaners would come and steam away the discoloration. She said, "This is a safe building, guards and doormen around the clock. The chairman of the Physics Department is overhead, and the woman whose father invented artificial sweeteners is underneath us. Now let me point out one feature you're sure to like. We're low enough here to get traffic noises from the boulevard, but also the windows look straight into the treetops."

Right she was. Benn inspected the sycamores along the side of the building. Here he'd have the leaves for company during half the year. Matilda, having fun with him, was, however, right on. The thick sycamores he gazed into were pale and brown. The root systems, like hairy mammoths, spread under pavements, around the sewer system and other installations, working underground and drawn towards the core of the earth. He spoke of this to me—his keenly listening, sharp-faced nephew, who was trying to dope him out. Occasionally he made avowals to me—almost confidences—about plants. A true plant man diffused his personal essence into leaves, internal tissues, and sent himself from the root-clutched soil to the highest extremities. As if talking to himself, he spoke of forces from the center of the planet, akin to grief, driving green impulses to the surface and into the sun, which act was applauded by the leaves. I'm not sure he actually knew what he was saying. He trusted me enough to ramble, to put unaccountable thoughts, inadmissible notions, into words. Familiar as he was with the anatomy of these organisms, he had a special conception of them. And I said before when I spoke about Matilda's long legs and their attachment to the trunk (at the husband point), I said that you got no truth to life if you brushed aside such conjectures. In this spirit, I can't omit the last remark Benn made about the sycamores. As he stared at them he thought he heard a moan coming from behind, from the pasture-sized room at his back. What would it be moaning about? (It was not a human sound.) The only responsible interpretation was that it was a projection, pure and simple, inspired by the bare sycamores. This throws doubt on "responsible interpretations" per se.

He himself would have made such a sound if he hadn't been on his best behavior. But on this visit to his future residence, he was being the ideal husband. This vast place put up in 1910 by dry-goods merchant princes—its rooms, he said, made him think of cisterns of self-love that had dried out, now that the original occupants had moved to the cemetery. But it was harmful to indulge such fantasies, so he began to examine the furniture—any number of sofas and other very large pieces. He said to Matilda, "The upholstery has had it. It's saturated with smells."

"I don't smell anything."

"Oh, definitely. Bad smells . . ."

"Aunt Ettie left a few fine pieces. But her will ordered that after the funeral her relatives and friends were to come straight back here, right away. There were tags on every object and the people who inherited were supposed to take their property then and there."

"Immediately?"

"You've got it. And some of my cousins got beautiful antiques."

Recalling this, he said, her "filaments still glowed" with outrage.

"Somebody outsmarted you."

"Ah. They got around the old girl."

"Were there any hassles?"

"No, not just after a burial, but there were plenty of sharp contacts as they carried away their loot. So what you're looking at is the unlabeled stuff, which all was mine. Lots of valuable pieces were lost. As far as the old girl was concerned, these sofas were built for the ages. Everything has to be replaced. The thrift shop of Daddy's hospital will come for these davenports and easy chairs."

"A hell of an expense, refurnishing," said Benn. "We could bring all the passable articles into the main rooms. Maybe have slipcovers made."

"No, dear. No," she said.

This "dear," the "dear" of contradiction, was laid down like a cement block, Benn reported. The blue-eyed portly man didn't appear sensitive, although he was a veritable apparatus of complex notation, equipped with innumerable fibrils.

"Where would you find proper furniture? Scandinavian design wouldn't look right here."

"Maybe in Rio. They must have marvelous stuff," she said.

"What about shipping costs? Five thousand sea miles or so?"

"Air freight might be cheaper. And there are always some deals that can be made. For instance, you lecture in public for the U.S. Information Agency. That way we'd see the country too."

"I see you've given this thought. How would we wangle a diplomatic passport?"

"You're being ironic with me. You are an international celebrity in the field—kind of a monument. A big shot. They'd do anything for you. You yourself don't really know. . . ."

It was gaunt winter that day, gray skies that made nature's bones stand out white. But the building had a fat form covering all bones in which you could ignore the outer environment. The radiators put out lots of heat, too much, in fact, and old-fashioned sounds and smells came with it, exhalations of the matter that composes our own mortality, and reminiscent of the intimate gases we all diffuse. The message of this place was: "Don't worry. You'll be taken care of here." But the Roanoke wasn't simply an apartment. You couldn't just live in it. If you tried, you'd decay. It really was, as I had said, a palazzo. You had to give parties here—dinners, private concerts—otherwise the surroundings would have a disembodying effect on you and pretty soon you'd be a spook, haunting the pantry. What Tilda was saying as she guided Benn through the bedrooms and servants' quarters made it pretty plain that they would be entertaining a great deal. Whom? Desirable connections in this town. (For what purpose? Benn didn't ask, but he thought it.) Visitors passing through, people like Dobrynin, Kissinger, Marilyn Horne, ballet dancers, Günter Grass—on the road, and no better place to kill an evening—would discover a civilized haven.

"Won't that be expensive?" asked Uncle, as if he didn't know. He was nothing but a professor on a salary of sixty thousand dollars or, as I said before, just about what it costs to keep two convicts down in Stateville. Out of this he had saved about ten grand per annum, so that he had assets of roundly two hundred thousand or so, plus his annuity, which he couldn't touch (luckily) until retirement, and Lena's insurance, which it wouldn't be right to squander on the Roanoke (entertaining Henry Kissinger or Pavarotti, her successor's pals). Matilda only smiled at his anxieties. Obviously she had a master plan.

With prompting from me, Benn reconstructed the conversation he had had with Matilda in those empty rooms.

"You need to approach this place with more imagination," she said. "It looks grandiose and schmutzig. But I have memories of its better days, and I'll tell you, if it was on Fifth Avenue it would be worth a few millions and you'd have to be a Lehmann or Warburg to afford it. It's probably the most gorgeous residential building between Pittsburgh and Denver. To say the least. Even here, it's a protected landmark, and can't be demolished. Maintenance is low, and the taxes are relatively trivial."

"I'm all for it, if you want it," said Benn. "Why not? Still, I need to know what we're getting into, darling. Where I live has never been so important to me." (Not entirely true; for thirty years or so he had been at home in his corny old flat.) "Can I swing it? That's the question. This fifteen-room leviathan will swallow my whole salary, and then some."

"Now just hold on, and don't get frightened," she said.

"Oh, I'm not in a tizzy over it, just asking."

"Naturally I've considered this from all sides," she said, smiling. "I thought it would appeal more to the Don Quixote in you."

Benn said, "Quixote was a bachelor."

"I meant that the irrationality of it might appeal to you."

"What we might do, at first, is fix up the front, the showy part, and you and I can live in the rear."

"Eating out of tin cans?" Her humor was on the sly side. "Or maybe going on food stamps?"

He said, "Suppose that you were to sell it—what kind of price would it fetch?"

"That's unrealistic too. Before putting it on the market you'd have to fix it up. In its present condition you wouldn't get near full value." She wasn't offended that he should ask; she gave him one of her down-under smiles while she lowered her face, easing the elastics of her underthings through the material of her dress. During a conversation, she would do this at the waist or behind her back. She humored him, that was soon obvious, and she had no intention of giving up this splendid place.

"No kidding," said Uncle to me. "The living room could be the hangar for two, three private planes. Her lifetime plan for married happiness included these—what looked to me like museum halls. It's a three-cornered match: Matilda, me and the Roanoke. I hadn't realized that. Well, how could anybody, beforehand? Still, remembering how Doctor praised her brains and said she could have made Mondale President, I started to inquire about available resources. Like: 'Do you expect your parents to kick in? Did your aunt Ettie leave money for this purpose?' But that got me nowhere. I couldn't believe that these sharp people from Parrish Place had made no calculations. But I couldn't get any direct replies from Matilda. Well, all I can do is set my own ceiling for expenditures. And I believe it's going to take a while to make out the whole design, the figure in the carpet."

"Sure they have calculations," I said. "That on your salary you should pay for such an establishment never could make sense, and those shrewdies know it. They can't expect you to kill yourself to please the woman you love. And as she certainly loves you, she doesn't want you to do yourself in. So I think the best attitude is to take this for now as a charming mystery. That's my advice."

"Well, yes. The conclusion of our financial discussion was that I was going to go into it all with Dr. Layamon. She's setting up a lunch downtown for us."

"To talk finances."

"I think that's it."

I didn't believe that Uncle would be representing his own interests very ably at lunch. Too bad he had become involved in such matters. Earlier I cited Churchill on the British Empire, that it had been acquired in a fit of absentmindedness, and I drew a parallel with Uncle Benn's marriage, but I don't take much stock in this absentmindedness theory. The secret motive of the absentminded is to be innocent while guilty. Absentmindedness is spurious innocence. In the case of a man like my uncle, whom nothing really escaped, it was not an acceptable rubric. As for the figure in the carpet, Uncle would never discern it as long as he himself lay on that carpet. As of this moment, in my admittedly tough judgment, he wasn't on his feet. I ran through the facts as I then knew them: A beautiful woman unites herself with a world-famous botanist. He may think it will serve *his* needs. No, all the while she has been thinking what she can do with *him*. And I fancy myself back on the Rue Bonaparte, working it all out with Kojève—just the two of us present. I choose him because he is a relentless, merciless reasoner. Benn was a botanist looking for a wife, and he found a wife who wanted just such a botanist to be a host to celebrities—the spouse who went with the house. His motive was longing. *Such* longing! You can't expect longing of such depth to have, or to find, definitive objectives. For her part, Matilda had quite clear objectives. She knew what she wanted and she got it. He didn't know what he wanted, and he was going to get it.

My work was cut out for me: I was to help my dear uncle to defend himself. I didn't suppose that the Layamons meant him great harm; only they weren't likely to respect his magics or to have the notion of preserving him for the sake of his gifts. There was quite a lot at stake here. I can't continually be spelling it out. As: the curse of human impoverishment as revealed to Admiral Byrd in Antarctica; the sleep of love in human beings as referred to by Larkin; the search for sexual enchantments as the universal nostrum; the making of one's soul as the only project genuinely worth undertaking; and my personal rejection of existentialism, which led me to emigrate and which makes me so severe in my analysis of motives. That has been indicated.

I said to Uncle, "As a favor to me—because I'm so curious—this time, ask Dr. Layamon about the judge who performed the ceremony. You said you were going to."

"So I did. And I'm making a note of it now." He took out his wallet, looking for a scrap of paper. Nothing was available except an American Express charge slip. He uncapped his pen and printed AMADOR C. across the back. His accountant would ask, next April, whether he had treated this party to dinner, and was it deductible. He tucked it in among other bits of paper with foxed corners, and I thought he'd never look at it again. I commented to myself skeptically (I was learning not to nag at him), "That's the end of that." But he did in fact remember to bring up the subject at lunch. I was pleased by this, a sign that he took seriously what I said to him, and also that he could assume the initiative.

Doctor took his son-in-law to the Avignon, which served *nouvelle cuisine*. One more skyscraper summit, Benn said. Apparently Layamon enjoyed being at the top. They came into the glass-enclosed dining room on the seventy-fifth story of one of the newest high-rises, the windows with a plum tint to cut the glare. Doctor, fresh from the barbershop, had his thinning hair washed and center-parted, his fingers just manicured. He walked in like the commander of an armored division, holding his shoulders stiffly—"Damn near two-dimensional, those shoulders," Benn said repeatedly. Such attributes were important to him. (Just as a tree was not a tree, merely, but a *sign* as well.) And he gave me a characteristically detailed description of the man. Doctor had a slender and mobile neck, which "urged" his face towards you whenever he wanted to drive home a point. He added, still on Layamon's face, that it was small relative to the length of his body, and in the middle of it there was something comparable to a reflecting watch crystal when it caught the sun, a flashing spot. But when you looked for the source of this, you couldn't find one.

Lunch didn't get off to a good start. Doctor wanted Benn to appreciate this three-star treat, and to respond properly. "*Nouvelle cuisine*," he said more than a few times (*nouvelle cuisine* is now on the way out!), and Benn couldn't get the note of TV brightness into his responses. On the contrary, he made a gaffe, or goof, immediately. When you entered you were shown the featured dishes of the day, each course arranged as it would be served—fish or chop, pureed carrot or squash—and the items named in French and translated into English. The display was covered by a glittering plastic material. "I believe it was Saran Wrap," said Benn. Doctor thought it was very smart, but Benn said it reminded him of what the bereaved are shown when they have to choose a coffin for a parent. Doctor was vexed by this. ("Turned as stiff as the rods they reinforce concrete with," said Benn.) If there was anything Doctor couldn't stand about his son-in-law, it was this associational anarchy. There was a paprika color under Doctor's eyes; he walked fast and Benn followed behind the maître d'. Uncle said he couldn't help himself. The veal and sole meunière laid out cold like that. But appointments had had to be canceled, and when you added up the office hours Doctor was sacrificing and the tab for this lunch, it came to a pretty good piece of change. Besides, as Matilda later commented, Doctor hated having death brought into the conversation, especially at mealtimes.

"For a minute, there," said Benn, "he could have murdered me, Kenneth. I saw it all come up on him at once. He was putting himself out for me, and it was no use, because I'm simply a natural fuck-up. But he recovered his control. Fatherhood won out. And also the forces of Positive Thinking."

"He believes in that?"

"He often says so."

They were installed in a booth upholstered in leather, like a Porsche or Lancia, and Doctor took up the wine list. "White or red—France or California? It's an occasion." A bottle of sparkling Vouvray was ordered, and Doctor's toast was: "Welcome to our family! Jo and I are proud of Matilda's choice! We believe you love the girl!"

Benn declared, "I *love* her."

"Of course you do. And intend to be straight with her."

"I was with my first wife."

"I know that. What you did *between* the first and the second is nobody's business."

After a glass of wine, Doctor became himself again; he got over his vexation about the coffin crack. He had a preference for physical closeness, and in the booth at the Avignon he was right on top of Benn. Not ordinary proximity; you couldn't tell whose breath was whose. "If I'd been a girl, he would have hooked me by the neckline and looked down the front of my dress," said Benn. Doctor's eyeglasses didn't sit level and his glances, too, were skewed. The two sides of his face, along a vertical axis, were not quite matched. His skin was arid, his mouth long and gabby, his eyes uncoordinated. At the hospital, his nickname was Motormouth. He held Benn in the crook of his arm like a hearty rancher, feeling and squeezing. "Maybe he was gathering medical information," said Benn. "He even fastened his fingers on my underthigh just above the knee. Where they put the hand in the Old Testament when they swore an oath." Physically Benn recognized that he was no match for Matilda. Uncle belonged to an earlier somatic type, that of immigrants and the first generation of their children. In a country which breeds and vitamizes (poultry and cattle), and dazzles the world with the teeth of its children, their healthy skins, their aerobically developed arms and legs, Benn with his domehead and the Russian curvature of the back was like an illustration from a book on the evolution of the human form—about three or four figures below the peak. Matilda *was* the peak, Doctor's golden child. (We shall see that Benn, in some hard-to-reach atrium of his labyrinthine mind, didn't really agree.) So why had Matilda picked this *zhlobb*! This was what Doctor longed to know. They finished their first glass and ordered lunch; the waiter poured more Vouvray and Doctor twittered like the bird house at the zoo, so many winged families represented, having nothing at all in common but the noises they made.

"To go back to our subject of the other day," said Doctor, who had never left it, "I've just about stopped trying to keep up with the sexual revolution."

"Then again, why should you keep up?" Uncle said.

"Put yourself in the position of a fundamentally old-fashioned dad with a daughter, and an only child at that. As a physician also, dealing with patients who bring up complicated syndromes. You're obliged to try to understand the context. How do you expect a doctor to react to the facts of life? In the office, then at home." I could picture Benn, very distant (not aloof), watching Doctor from afar, from an elevation. "Kids without parental supervision, watching lascivious TV," Doctor went on. "Or listening to porn rock music. 'On your knees! Gonna nail your ass to the floor!' Records that sell up in the millions, when they go gold. Figures in a class with the national budget. . . ."

"I hadn't really thought about it."

"You pure-science fellows, you don't have to."

Uncle said, "It's among the things private citizens can't do much about—the bomb, for instance. After the atomic one, the orgastic one was dropped on us."

Doctor was pumping and prodding him, as usual, trying to fish out information about his daughter—a complaint, a confession, a scandal.

"*You* didn't dive into a shelter," Doctor said. "You got your share of it." As he saw Benn preparing to protest, he hastened to say, "I'm not blaming you. It brought certain benefits, and there's no reason why you shouldn't have had your share of pleasures and kicks. I always advise patients never to quit, even those that are getting too old for it. You'd be surprised how many come to me to say they're not up to it anymore, and what do I think about hormone injections, so they can go on satisfying their wives. I tell them, 'Look, as long as you have a knee, an elbow, your nose, your big toe, given an affectionate wife, as long as you did your duty by her in the days when you could get it up, she will take whatever you've got now, and you don't owe her any more than that.' Of course these old fools are afraid some karate instructor will sweep their old biddy away, and they start asking about prostheses. Or maybe a little air bulb so you can inflate the member. Like a blood pressure cuff, you know."

Benn (we can be sure of this) had a look of thinking it over, but he couldn't really figure all this sex talk out. He suspected that Doctor was so heavily involved with his daughter that he couldn't let the sex alone. Benn himself was not in a position to state that he had had no trouble in that line. It would have been a protestation, a defense, not a value-neutral statement.

"Now listen, Dr. Layamon—"

"William."

"Okay, William, why are you telling *me* about hormones or inflating the genital? You think I'm going to make you some medical confession?"

Doctor reddened—not an ordinary red; he was orange red,

the color of one of those newts you see on country roads. "Why would I . . . ?"

"I don't know why you would, or if these hints are supposed to give me an opening. Or if Matilda has broached the subject with you."

"Nothing!" said Doctor. "You mustn't lose your cool."

"These days, women, you can be sure of it, don't marry without a trial period. Matilda joined me in Switzerland last summer for a month."

"It was no secret. She sent us pictures."

"Of what?"

"Postcards of Zurich and Geneva, saying she was very happy. You've got me all wrong, Benno. Jo and I have a pretty fair idea about you, that way. Don't be annoyed, but we ran a little check on you, purely private and absolutely discreet. You can't blame us. These are kinky times and Matilda is our only child, and will come into a pretty tidy inheritance. Matilda didn't like it and said it wasn't necessary, she had looked into your past herself, in her own way. She had a pretty fair idea about the ladies you were previously interested in."

"So you retained an investigator to find out whether there were any abandoned women or illegitimate children all over the place?"

"Hell, boy, you move around so much we would have needed the CIA or Interpol. If there was anything bad we wouldn't be sitting at the Avignon together. Also, if there was serious stuff in the fellow's report, he would have gone to you and tried to sell it to you first. That's the customary blackmail. One expects it. You retain an investigator and the sonofabitch gets the best price he can out of the fellow he's investigating."

"I hope he socked you with a big bill. Did Matilda read the report?"

"I wouldn't show it to her. Besides, she didn't want to see it. She said you two had a deal not to pry into the past."

"I guess the fellow just vacuumed up local gossip around the university."

Had the investigator gone to Caroline? Even now Uncle remained mysteriously attached to Caroline. She had certain feminine peculiarities that he valued—a kind of subcutaneous ripple of the lower throat and the breasts. He didn't miss Caroline; he now admitted that she was a nut case. But for that reason precisely she was easily upset. She may have been all twigged out, but he had embarrassed her and he felt for her, poor thing—his very words, as I find them in the notes I made after our conversations. He said that in our "mentalities, most of us, most of the people we meet, are mentally on skid row. One stumblebum after another." Take Dr. Layamon himself, that medical swell and hotshot: Much of the time he didn't control what he was saying. Out of every ten sentences he spoke, only three seemed to come from his conscious mind, and the rest were from some other source. "Like the second self that told you to give the junkman your nickel?" (I go by my notebook.) "Something like," said Uncle. "What you like to call a daemon. I looked this up in Plato, where it says that Eros was a broker spirit between the gods and human beings. But I don't see why we should drag poor Eros into this squalid stuff."

So Doctor wasn't responsible for what he was saying. He was a Charlie McCarthy, a dummy for subconscious forces. Except when he talked about money. This was proof for the Milton Friedman view that dollars and cents are what keep us rational. But then, think of the oceans of money spent for sexual purposes. Can the case be made that that *spending* is rational? As rational as *making* the stuff? Uncle was always trying to recall the name of one of my Russians, the one who said that sex might be a diabolical way to recover paradise, a "poisoned ersatz," a parody on the beautiful and the sublime, a false light shed for our destruction by the sexual Lucifer—if indeed great spirits like Eros or Lucifer are still bothering with us human nut cases.

What it comes down to is that men and women are determined to get out of one another (or tear out) what is simply not to be gotten by any means.

As for Caroline, Uncle needn't have felt so bad about her. Obviously, his escape on her wedding day was not among the most startling or picturesque events of her life.

"Now don't get sore, Benn," said Doctor. "People of means have to have special intelligence reports prepared for them. Hiring investigators is routine."

"Depends on what questions the fellow asked," said Benn, coldly.

"Do you think I'm such a jerk as to send a man to find out how a *woman* felt about you? I haven't practiced medicine forty years without discovering that women have different reactions altogether, way beyond the horizon of some shamus with an FBI background. I'm not a complete fool, only somewhat irregular in the way I talk."

"I don't like to be at the mercy of third parties," said Benn.

(Whatever could that mean? Only second parties had the right to cut him up?)

Doctor said, "Listen, son, you get more information—and it's straight—out of me than I paid that shamus for. I've told you myself what a bitch Matilda can be. Or was, until now. Marriage to the right man is going to change her—has changed her already. You're a special personality, and don't think I'm not aware of it. Those hairstyled anchormen who learned everything they know in a communications course—it's true they draw down staggering salaries, but I'd just as soon marry my daughter to a slice of quiche. In about a month she'd be throwing up at the sight of him. Different with a man like you. She'll always be able to look up to you, learn from you and be able to attract people to her home because of you."

"Why attract?"

"Because you know plants backwards and forwards. That's a big draw. . . . Finally! Here's our lunch. The way they fart around in these glitzy restaurants . . . I have the veal, and my guest has the sole. . . . I guarantee that your life will be enjoyable if you can learn to like company. You're kind of a solitary, but Tilda is very social. She's like her mother in that respect, and a wife, especially a physician's wife, can make or break a man. I don't care if you're a genius diagnostician; if your wife is one of those selfish neurotics that won't go out to people warmly and entertain, you'll never have a first-class practice. You'll end up taking blood pressures for an insurance company or massaging coal miners' prostates. A woman has to be able to bring together the right people and make conversation. If you haven't noticed it yet, you will when you set up house. Matilda is great with brilliant people and she can invite them because of you, a big name in your field. The first time they'll come because of you, and afterwards because of her. It's not that you're so asocial, but a man who likes people doesn't wind up in the Antarctic."

"That wasn't why I went. . . ."

Doctor, cutting up his *paillard de veau*, said, "What *were* you doing there, if it isn't classified information?"

"No. I had a special project with lichens. They draw nutrients from the atmosphere and I was working with meteorologists who were studying world air currents."

"You always speak differently when you speak of the Antarctic."

"Do I? I always had wanted to go there. The ends of the earth. Why . . . ?"

And Uncle, in silence, listed his reasons: Because it's a land of epic, explored by heroes like Shackleton, Scott and Amundsen. Because there men sacrificed their lives for one another. Because the South Pole gives a foretaste of eternity, when the soul will have to leave its warm body, and down there you can practice the indifference to temperature you will need when that moment comes. Uncle never would attempt to give such an answer. It couldn't, it wouldn't, register. Whatever you offered Doctor, he would throw it away impatiently if it didn't relieve what was eating him. Speak to him of the soul leaving the body and he'd stare at you as if you were bonkers. Don't speak of it, keep silent, and you seem antisocial.

Their lunch was half over. They ate. Their sky-top restaurant was in an unthinkable location—as high above the streets as steel beams could be assembled. Engineering made this "easy"; conversation, however, was difficult. Intransmissible notions, strange spontaneous expressions like "orgastic bomb," *nouvelle cuisine* dishes under Saran Wrap compared to a display of caskets, put Doctor off. His face was still contracted. But, fundamentally dissatisfied, he still talked.

Doctor was saying that there had been a cute item in the paper about a couple applying for permission to marry in the Antarctic so that the bride might have a totally white wedding. "What's the North Pole! Anybody can go to the North Pole. There are regular helicopter expeditions, and you can fly up for lunch and be back in civilization for cocktails; but the South Pole is a different proposition. It still has mystery and romance." And speaking of romance, it wasn't only wonderful that Benn and Matilda had fallen in love, it also was a providential moment. This was the time to marry. To stop chasing. Random sexual contacts now were more dangerous than ever, when medicine was stumped temporarily by viruses like AIDS (an epidemic in the making, a regular plague) and other, less publicized venereal infections. Monogamy was coming back. He hoped that Matilda was planning to become pregnant in Brazil. "Son, this will be your last opportunity to have a family. Even she's already old for a primipara. I've always been curious about Matilda's biology. In the delivery room, when she was born—and I remember this well—we physicians had to puzzle over the baby. Was it a boy or a girl?"

"You've got to be joking," said Benn.

"I'm only saying that at first nobody was exactly sure. Some kids are smooth and beautiful at birth, others look as if they were delivered by an avalanche."

Dressed in strange garments, lunching on strange heights, his normal appearance altered by the hairstylist Matilda had sent him to, Uncle wasn't sure of his bearings. Still, he had presence of mind enough to say, "Well, set your mind at ease, Doc, she's female through and through."

Here at the Avignon, the Electronic Tower was again very close, the next great structure rising above the rest, and after the Avignon had stopped, in the view from the penthouse, its companion or big sister still went on soaring. "There's your old home again," said Doctor, gesturing with his glass. "Never thought in the old days, when your mother ran that home for incurables, that one day it would become this gorgeous monument, didja?"

Benn was riled by this and said, "That's not a fair description. It was a family kind of place, and mostly the people were old friends from Jefferson Street."

"You don't have to tell me; I interned in that neighborhood. Those old-fashioned immigrant women would pull their skirts over their faces when they were examined so you couldn't see them blush. How different now, in the stirrups . . ."

But Uncle was not about to let Doctor run away with the conversation again. He recovered the initiative, and fastened his cobalt-blue gaze on his father-in-law, knife and fork in fists. "I want to know why you brought in that Chetnik man to perform the ceremony."

"Why, Chetnik is an old family friend; we went to the same high school. He clerked for Bonaccio, the mouthpiece for the syndicate in the great days of Prohibition."

"Never mind the history part of it. He was the judge in our case against Vilitzer."

"I am aware of that."

"Then the question is why you asked him to do it. A fix had been put in."

"You want to be careful. You could be in big trouble, making such statements."

"I'm making them to a member of the family, not in a press conference. I found out during the reception who he was."

"And you were shocked," said Doctor with an edge of satire.

"I was sore. *He* must have gotten a kick out of it. First he shafts me in the courtroom . . ."

"And what—he gets a second shot at you?"

"Do you realize how many years it took us to pay the legal bills in that matter?"

"Thank your sister for that, and the dummy lawyers she retained—what firm was it, by the way?"

"We're not discussing that."

"Well, the lawyer was a jerk, or he would have known better than to fight the Vilitzer case in Chetnik's courtroom. He should practice law in Tasmania; he doesn't belong here. But he was good at billing, hey? Well, that's why Moshe Dayan had lawyers in the first attacking wave, because when he yelled 'Charge!'—boy, nobody could beat those lawyers at charging."

Benn was not stopped by this poor joke, he told me.

Doctor then said to him, "I expected you to go after me on this, and I'm kind of pleased if you're interested in my reaction. Glad to see you stand up for yourself."

Down from sublime regions, where you had no access to him. Now, owing to self-interest, you could get a grip on Uncle. The Layamons had set themselves to bring Benn in, that is, to bring him back to the one great thing America has, which is the *American*. You can't have a son-in-law by your American hearth who has another habitat—extraterrestrial or some such goddam thing. What's more, Benn had *wanted* to come down, he had a special wish to enter into prevailing states of mind and even, perhaps, into the peculiar sexuality associated with such states.

"Did Matilda know that Amador Chetnik was *the* Chetnik?" Benn asked.

"She may have had some idea, although he's been a family friend for so long that to her it would be natural. . . ."

"William, don't give me that stuff."

"Well, yes. It took a little persuading, but when you put an advantageous proposition in front of that girl she can grasp it in a minute. There was absolutely no harm done. Bygones are bygones. Nobody was gloating over you. In the midst of romance nobody wanted you to bother your head with such things. Chetnik himself is in the middle of a switch, changing loyalties. He still insists, though, that your wild-ass uncle had a strong case."

"What, as executor of Mama's will, buying the property from us through a phony company which he himself owned?"

"I'm sorry a prominent scientist like you has to have such an undesirable family connection as Vilitzer. He was on the Zoning Commission and he did have advance information on the site," said Doctor. "It's true that your uncle made Amador a judge, and for years he could unmake him by taking him off the judicial ballot."

"I'm still waiting to hear what the advantage was of dragging him into the wedding," said Benn.

"Not letting up," said Doctor, quite satisfied. "Relentless. I like that. No wonder you didn't get along with Uncle Vilitzer; he's used to ass-kissers, and he always had plenty of them. Well, as you will have figured, with a brain like yours, the object is to recover money from Uncle Harold. That's the overall game plan."

"For the purpose of refitting the Roanoke palazzo?"

"Right! And *then* some. Ettie left a little money for maintenance and such. But her financial ideas go back to the days of old wealth, when prices were low and services cheap. The old lady could nickel-and-dime a person to death. Modernizing that place will cost a good three hundred grand. You couldn't expect Matilda to go to Brazil and leave this responsibility just hanging in the air. Got to have some resolution. That's her way. Do you realize what Harold got out of this multinational—mostly Japanese—conglomerate, Ecliptic Circle, that bought your land?"

"How would I realize any such thing! Maybe Chetnik realizes. He didn't do this *only* to stay on the ballot."

"You can't expect Amador to tell anybody what, if anything, he was paid for throwing the case. Nor can you expect him to turn to me on the fairway at the club and say, 'Harold Vilitzer owns me.'"

"Well, I have no experience with people in this kind of life, but now that I *have* to think about them, I discover that I do have some aptitude for it. So then, old hands in the community understand that Vilitzer owns Chetnik. Naturally Chetnik can't say it."

"Doesn't have to. Also, I'd put it in the past tense: Vilitzer *used* to own Chetnik. As far as your aptitude is concerned, you come by it naturally. It might even be a talent—hereditary. Now, I won't tell my sources, but the price paid for your parents' slummy old property was at least fifteen millions."

Benn brushed this away. The sum didn't matter; it was only one of those sums one is forever being quoted, like the number of cocaine addicts in the country, of the dead in the Great War, or a figure for the daily loss of brain cells.

Doctor said again, "Fifteen biggies—didn't you hear, son?" Comprehension was what he was after.

"I heard, all right. You said that Vilitzer *used* to own Chetnik. A thing of the past? When did he stop owning him?"

"When the U.S. attorney for this district took out after Chetnik in real earnest. Insiders could tell you that a federal indictment is only months away. Amador has his own ass to cover. The Justice Department . . . and it's the old story, a Republican administration out to nail the local Democrats. So for you to discuss this with your uncle would be advantageous now."

"No, no, I couldn't do that. He's over eighty years old."

Dr. Layamon, his wrinkles reset—a different configuration—seemed scarcely to have heard him. "When a smart prosecutor hits top form, he's running the grand jury *and* the press, he's timing his announcements, leaking to the TV guys. He's got a full nelson on the other guy and can break the poor fucker's neck. That way he goes to the statehouse, while the wrongdoer ends up in the slammer. So you send Vilitzer to jail, and you have a clear path to the U.S. Senate. Or you become governor and you're even mentioned for the presidency, maybe. That's how our present governor did it."

Doctor could have given a master class in significant staring. The veal and the Vouvray were pushed aside. He was looking to Benn for special commendation. Shows you where his real passions were. He never claimed so much for medical achievements as for political smarts.

"Now, just what am I supposed to discuss with my uncle?" said Benn.

"You'd point out that this would be a bad time for you to reopen your case against him."

"I see. And with Amador Chetnik, now going in reverse, coaching us on the legal side. Yes, I get it. And this was why you asked the judge to unite Matilda and me."

"Oh, very good, you catch on fast," said Doctor, tapping his hands twice in applause.

"But I don't want to harm Vilitzer—he's my uncle. Sure he's been rough. Still, he's my uncle—he's Mama's brother."

"A funny time for family feeling."

"You have family feeling for Matilda," said Uncle.

"My own child, that's different, and even then, if she were to put a bad move on me, as bad as Harold Vilitzer did to you, she'd have a fight on her hands, and she knows it. And she, believe me, is a toughie. Not towards you, naturally; love is the great exception. You're *her* big child. I mean to tell you, though, they could use a mind like hers at the War College. Then you wouldn't have fiascos like Grenada, with all the softies from the rival services colliding. She's a mastermind. What a girl you married, hey?"

"Is this her idea, about Vilitzer and Chetnik?"

"Of course not. What do you mean? The main consideration is justice. You were gypped out of millions. And it turns out that your new family is protecting your rights, and by rights you should be set up in a place like the Roanoke. You're entitled to live in style, a rich scientist and not just a research rat."

"And she wants me to twist Vilitzer's arm? I must discuss all this with her."

"Harold would be the first to understand your motives, a seasoned old angler like that."

"Dr. Layamon, it wouldn't feel right, threatening him. Especially since I don't quite see all the angles, the hidden ones. I need to think this over more."

"I'd start Vilitzer at five millions, ready to come down to three. I'd estimate his total net worth at a hundred million."

"That's no concern of mine," said Uncle. "What you want me to do amounts to a threat. I don't agree that it would be so damaging to him to reopen the case. It wouldn't do him much good, but why would it do him five million dollars' worth of harm? What if he were to laugh in my face? And do you think I could enjoy high living on extorted money?"

"What extorted! Put it that he swindled his sister's children. And the federal prosecution is ready to kick the shit out of him if certain parties give the word. Then again, what if *you* are subpoenaed to testify? Your sworn testimony would send him away, and you wouldn't get a penny out of it."

"I'd also have to say that Amador Chetnik committed an impropriety."

"Well, the main injury in that would be that Uncle Harold paid him off. And we're embroidering too much. You couldn't document this on the witness stand. Let's go back to fundamentals. Matilda wants a brilliant position for herself, no more than a woman like that is entitled to. You're earning what—sixty grand?"

"Quite adequate," said Benn.

"Why, that's nonsense. Why, just the other day Margaret Thatcher said that if the U.S. lowered its tax rate to twenty-seven percent while England was taxing the hell out of everybody, the creative scientists in Britain would run away to America. They'll leave their *country*. While you won't even pitch your uncle for what's yours by rights."

"In plant morphology, sixty grand is good pay. Now, I love

Matilda. I'd do anything within reason for her. But I don't want Uncle to die in jail while I live in that showplace Roanoke. I'm willing to approach Harold peacefully."

"Peaceful! You come with an olive branch and Vilitzer will snatch it from you and stick it up your ass," Doctor said. His face kinked up with laughter. It was more than ever baked from within by his hyperactive temper, or by the heat of connivance. Inside, he was superheated, needing a superconductor way below absolute zero. "No!" he said, becoming severe again. "You'll have to come to him with a strong argument if you want money, real money, big money. The olive branch will get you zilch. Maybe the person to send is a smart lawyer."

"No, thanks!" Benn was firm, he drew a definite line. "Whatever happens, I'll take charge myself. No third party; I'm not having any."

"Well, it's your uncle. I see you're in earnest. In that case you're going to need a lot of briefing."

No amount of briefing would help. Besides, there was nothing to stop Doctor from sending his own emissaries to Vilitzer. He had plenty of agents for the purpose, which was to hold Harold's feet to the fire. They could and would say they were doing this for Benn, with his consent.

Ever so briefly, I allow myself to put in my own two cents: Inasmuch as I became a participant in these events, meeting with Vilitzer's son Fishl, reporting back to Uncle, and so forth, I am not observing from a theoretical satellite. What needs to be said is that from the standpoint of a Dr. Layamon, Uncle was totally incompetent in negotiations of this type. You might as well give a Melanesian aborigine a new Yamaha motorcycle with an operator's manual and turn him loose on the expressway. He couldn't even start, much less stop. Thus Uncle was roughly equivalent in Doctor's view to the Russian masses as Ponomarenko, Stalin's boss for Byelorussia, had seen them—an innocent in whose interests historically unavoidable, indispensable crimes must be committed. Uncle was a wimp: I don't say Doctor thought it all out; I am thinking it for him. And it's obvious, Uncle was a professor, no different from other professors, therefore operating from a soft morality (herd morality, in Nietzschean terms, soft, squalid, foolish—not that Doctor would ever have gone on to speak of the degradation of man and the morality of timidity—I'm not going to be sidetracked into *that*, never fear). Doctor saw himself as somebody who was on top of things, nobody's fool. There was a sexual angle too, and I think that he even knew it. He veered between humor and rage when he dealt with the husband Matilda had chosen to lie on her body. Benn had applied for this outrageous privilege and Doctor was going to see to it that he paid the price. "If you're going to share the bed of this delicious girl of high breeding and wallow in it, you'll have to find the money it takes. And it so happens that the single most valuable piece of real estate in this town was your property until five years ago, when you were screwed out of it, chum. We think you can be made whole. So here goes."

The rest follows from this.

Here I could pay myself a compliment (as people are forever doing) and say that I didn't want to interfere in Uncle's affairs. But that's simply not true. The complications were forbidding, and I couldn't have been effective. Besides, he wouldn't have taken the right advice even if I had had it to give. So more for my own sake than his, I made a date with Vilitzer's son Fishl.

Fishl shared office space downtown with another erratic character, and was listed in the phone book as "Vilitzer Associates—Seed Money for Beginning Entrepreneurs." In Uncle Benn's opinion, which seemed right to me, Fishl would have done better to leave town after his father broke off relations with him. There was no access to old Vilitzer through his son; he wanted no part of him and made no bones about it. For fifteen years or so, Fishl had been entirely on his own and he had organized quite a few colorful failures for himself, some of them right on the edge of felony. Not very long ago he had conceived of a combined yoga-style and commercial venture. Describing himself as the local representative of a West Coast maharishi, he put out an investors' manual and mailed it to a substantial number of subscribers. The general idea was to play the market from a spiritual base. Meditation, by reducing the oscillations of consciousness, made you a more capable investor. Some success attended this, until the idea hit Fishl of telling his clients to get a large number of credit cards, say five hundred at a minimum. By borrowing a thousand dollars on each card (short-term), you obtained half a million dollars, paying little or no interest. With this capital you went into the options market, and with nervousness expelled by meditation, you could make quite a pile of money—at least a thousand per thousand invested. You traded on a daily basis, for safety, avoiding the risk of extended commitments, and within a month you had half a million dollars of your own. The banks affected by this took immediate action to block these cash raids and their lawyers came down hard on Fishl's counseling service, in a case widely reported in the press. Some government agency also got into the act—maybe the SEC—and before it was all over, old Vilitzer, with plenty of troubles of his own, had told the press, "He's no son of mine!" Demoralized for a time by this failure, Fishl next studied Chinese acupuncture, and presently set up a special practice as an acupuncture abortionist. Again he was sued, this time by a woman who had had a baby after receiving treatment. You can always count on litigation. A Philadelphia jury has just awarded big damages to a lady who was robbed of her psychic powers after undergoing a CAT scan. After long years as a medium, she was forced to close up shop. Say what you like about America, but few countries have welcomed originality more warmly, and never before has it been a mass phenomenon.

My specific purpose was to learn what I could about old Vilitzer's relationship with Amador Chetnik. I got Fishl on the telephone, and he said he'd be glad to see me.

My friend Dita Schwartz, who had a doctor's appointment, drove me downtown in her green Dodge van. She had taken Russian courses with me. Long an office worker, she was self-taught in Russian, and she had actually learned a great deal before coming to the university. Independent, complex, determined, imaginative people always give me the greatest pleasure. She soon took an M.A. in Slavic Studies. That brought her a job in the city branch of the state university.

With just an edge over me in calendar years, she makes a more youthful appearance—a mature-looking woman, pale-faced, black-eyed, she has hair that grows with Indian force. Both her parents were factory workers and she had a proletarian upbringing—another vanishing breed, the proletariat: bye-bye blue collars. Dita had an eye on me, that couldn't be denied for one moment, though there would have been some advantage in denying it since there was a degree of awkwardness in it for me. At the same time, I couldn't help welcoming it. For the sake of self-esteem. In that department, Treckie had done me some harm. But it's a tiresome preoccupation, self-esteem. Something has to be done to limit the number of people whose opinions can affect us. Unless they care for us, or have done us some good, or hold out some promise, why should their views matter?

I allowed myself a full hour with Fishl, assuming that he had the time to spare.

He had all the time in the world. The appearance of the lobby of the old building where he had his office told me that he was unlikely to be very busy. These premises went back to the beginning of the century. The elevator with its squiggle ornaments was slow, and I had lots of time for observation—on the first floor a taxidermist specializing in birds; on the second, a shirtmaker dating back to Edward VII, and a homeopathic pharmacist with flagons of pink and green fluid, and also jars stuffed with herbal remedies; next a sanatorium thrift shop with old waffle irons, electric percolators, cocktail shakers and antique golf clubs—mashies, niblicks and cleeks. Fishl's office shared a corner of the corridor with a men's lavatory.

Amid these old objects, Fishl himself was an up-to-date person. Plump and suave, he wore a three-piece suit and moccasin loafers. His head was the fair, fluffy-bald sort. His back hair was more abundant than it should have been, for my taste. He was fat in the face and had a double chin and also an imperial, somewhat Roman profile. He was a bit of a babyface, but his blue eyes, which reminded me of Benn's, notified you not to take too much for granted, nor to judge him by the surroundings. The eyes, to go with the double chin, were pouchy, but the look was keen. You were on warning not to presume too much. The man was no softie. He proved to be very smart.

While I looked him over, he (to use an expression of his own) was logging in the data about me. What he observed was: a member of the family; age thirty-five; education foreign; communication powers mediocre-to-low; hearing impaired; not stupid but hampered by singular preoccupations. Getting together pleased us both, on the whole. I didn't have the all-too-common tearing-at-the-gut feeling that I must escape as soon as possible from somebody. If he had really been the piercing executive type he wanted to be taken for, I would have been out of there in fifteen minutes, going down in the obsolete elevator.

He tried from the first to take control of our conversation by asking the questions. Good communicators understand how important this is, and Fishl, as I quickly perceived, was an advanced communicator. He was one of those people—an increasingly familiar type—who explain what they are doing as they are doing it, like Dale Carnegie or Norman Vincent Peale; part of their ideology is technique. To them the method is just as intoxicating as the message. I soon realized that he had me answering him, and I tried to capture the initiative and keep him at bay with questions of my own. How was the family? Great-aunt Vilitzer had passed away a few years ago, but Fishl was on fair terms with his brothers. They had profited by his quarrels with their dad, and did a big business with the city. They owned an insurance agency and wrote lots of municipal policies.

"None of them into politics?" I asked.

"No talent in that line. Not much future in it either, for whites. In twenty years, black politicians will be running everything, so no more sweet insurance deals from the city. Diversification is what this family needs. I try to tell them, invest in the suburbs, get rid of the real estate all over town."

Fishl's views were firmly held. No appeal was possible. I gathered, however, that his brothers weren't taking advice from him. The credit card scam, the yoga, the acupuncture, had reduced his credibility.

"How's my cousin Benn? Now that he's married, are you two still so close?"

"Too early to tell. Naturally, right now he's closest to his wife. And how is your dad?"

"As you must have heard, I don't get to see him as much as I would like. Too bad. His heart isn't strong, and he's taking a lot of heat politically. Now is when I could be useful to him. You follow the local scene?"

"Not as much as you. I couldn't."

"That's right—you came here to give Czarist Russia some serious thought. St. Petersburg, 1913. So you once told me. You might as well study that here as elsewhere."

Fishl smiled at me, and for the first time I noticed what a treasure he had in teeth—beautiful, the enamel in perfect condition, not a stain, not a twist, not a single filling.

"What heat is your father taking?"

"He has powerful enemies. One of them at least is a crusher."

"Where do you get all your information?" I said. "Or is it floating downtown, in the streets?"

"I get it from political pals of his who have known me from childhood. Some are interesting types. They always have inside dope. All of them are barbarians, naturally, but they're awfully shrewd too. Also, they have less and less to lose because they're on their way out. When you have a hostile administration in Washington, the Justice Department always investigates and prosecutes the locals. City Hall is full of soon-to-be-convicted felons. Everybody has been stealing for years. The grand juries can pick and choose their targets."

"I'm not changing the subject," I said, "but did you attend Benn's wedding?"

Fishl wouldn't have said that he hadn't been invited; it would have been a sign of social weakness. "Unfortunately I couldn't make it," was what he told me.

"I asked because I wondered whether you know the judge who married Matilda and Benn."

"A judge, was it?"

"Judge Amador Chetnik."

His double-chinned composure became so perfect, he was so silent, that I saw I had taken him by surprise.

I said, "No comment?"

"Strange choice for the Layamons to make," said Fishl. "Chetnik was the judge in Benn's case, wasn't he?"

"Yes. Ruled for your father, didn't he?"

"Was Benn aware?"

"He soon found out. What do you think of this?"

"I think it's a strange way to operate. Your only daughter's wedding . . ."

"The only child."

"They might have stopped scheming at least for fifteen minutes, those people. That old Layamon—I've heard about him. They say he's got more angles than the geometry book."

"I thought I should ask somebody more familiar with the way things are done locally," I said.

"Chetnik's secrets aren't exactly secret now. There are fifty people in town who could tell you how much trouble he's in. His indictment hasn't been announced yet by the U.S. attorney, but it soon will be and Chetnik will be in the judicial wing of the Sandstone penitentiary. Plenty of our judges in the federal prisons."

"Your father couldn't protect him?"

"He wouldn't even try. You see, it's Dad they're really after. He must have heard that the bride's parents asked Chetnik to unite his own nephew to this woman. Her father was using the judge to make a statement. So it's twice now that Chetnik has had your uncle Benn in his grip."

My information had had a powerful effect on Fishl and he had fewer disguises or prepared reactions than I would have guessed. Excite him, as I had just done, and you would have glimpses of a very different Fishl. "You ought to tell me more, Kenneth. This may be important," he said.

"There isn't much more that I *can* tell. And I don't think the judge has had Uncle Benn at his mercy. It's hard to imagine what form power over a man like Benn might take. He can be manipulated, yes. But can he be *had*? Had as those people understand it?"

Fishl evidently liked this elevation of the perspective and he took a different line with me, talking more naturally and warmly, so that I began to understand him better. At the moment he was in disgrace, renting space in this all but abandoned building—on the fourth floor, near the century-old lavatory. The owners of this valuable land probably were bargaining with developers. Fishl's position appeared weak. He looked like a funny fatty with a high entrepreneurial manner who *talked* about venture capital, seed money—he was doing just that now, as he described his activities. "What I'm into at this point in time . . ." From this description I realized that he admired and loved the entrepreneurial spirit, and was thinking continually of people who shunned a conventional career path—energetic, single-minded, imaginative, bold personalities who dared, who presumed, to take on the biomedical, aerospace or communications industries. I was fascinated by the entrepreneurial jargon he used. It was his jungle gym, his trampoline, his trapeze, his church. And he appeared weak only if you judged him by his business failures. These were accidental, transient. "I don't *recognize* failure," he told me. "High-energy types *never* do, they just don't care about it." He saw himself as a clever, resilient, solid and dedicated person bound to be a CEO—in the big time.

"But let's look at Chetnik for a moment," he said. "On a salary of seventy grand, how come he owns a four-bedroom condominium here, with a Mercedes for himself and a BMW for his wife? How does he also manage to buy a house in Florida? Who gives him free Hawaiian holidays, and other beautiful perks?"

"Not your father?"

"No. Dad bought Chetnik when Amador was a young lawyer ringing doorbells to get out the vote, before he was even a precinct captain. He bought him and put him on the bench. What you need to know in addition is that there are guys who come to the court building and then ride up and down in the elevators. These tempters know the county judges' schedules and wait for the opportunity to say a few words in private. Chambers can be bugged; that's why they pitch them in the elevators. Now, these guys carry special offers, like big interest-free loans that never have to be repaid. They have an exceptional nose for corruption potential."

"Are you speaking of petty-graft fixers?"

"Not at all. These are dependable, influential, solid parties. They're often the senior partners in big-name law firms. They plan to bring major cases before their favorite judges, that's all. A brief encounter one-on-one in the elevators, and the deal is cut."

"Is *that* how it works! Very obliging of you to share this information with me."

"All this I understood before the age of twelve," said Fishl. "Your mother should have consulted *me* before suing Dad over Electronic Tower. I was a mere undergraduate when some of this happened, but I could already have recommended a better lawyer. Above all, your lawyer is to blame. He was either a flake or else running up a big tab with no expectation of winning. I don't blame Benn for this. With his commitment to creative output, his sense of directedness, he couldn't possibly interpret a situation which leaves you confused even after a lifetime of exposure. Benn's capabilities seem to keep on unfolding. I'm very fond of my cousin Benn. I used to be even fonder. My dad was suspicious of him, and some of that suspicion rubbed off on me. Benn and I were too much alike to suit him. And there *was* a similarity. We faced the same question, Benn and me: 'What will I do with my creativity?' Did he ever tell you that in college he and I tried to patent an invention?"

"Never knew it."

"Yes. It was a bamboo bicycle frame, very light and also collapsible. You folded it and it fitted into your car trunk. Damn ingenious. We didn't have the savvy to get a patent. Of course, that was just a momentary challenge. Botany was his fate. He was too inner-directed to be a true contemporary type. Inventing a bamboo bike was merely his entertainment. Making a killing was *my* motive. Not that I was one hundred percent outer-directed. I was inner-directed also—in secret. That's the heart of my problem. I felt that Benn was better than me."

I said, "How do you account for that?"

"He didn't invest his whole life in a struggle with his parents. I meet people of eighty who still are furious over their toilet training, or because their dad wouldn't take them to the ball game. Imagine such an infantile life! Such bondage to papa and mama. A whole life of caca-pipi! No self-respecting person would submit. Part peacefully from your parents if you can, and if you can't, tell them to fuck off. You have to go your own way at twenty, at least. I'm typical, still pursuing my father at the age of fifty, hating and loving and begging him to let the prodigal come back. By now I've tried a dozen prodigal careers, each more sensational than the last. Benn had it better. Without thinking twice he stepped out at a higher level. He's a natural contemplative."

"You see that!"

"Why, sure, I always did. He may have loved his parents, but it never even crossed his mind to make his whole life an acceptable offering to pa and ma. While at the same time cursing them, as millions of Americans do. They'll even do this for vicious dogs—an unhappy puppyhood. No, Benn stepped out at a higher level without looking right or left, as if walking out of a fiftieth-story window, and he never got hurt. Talking about the esthetics of botany saved him—the beauties of plant life."

"He still does it. He plans to write on that subject."

"When he married Matilda Layamon, he followed those esthetics onto the human plane," said this amazing Fishl. "She's a beautiful woman. I used to see her now and then. I never dated her, I wasn't good enough. Just an agreeable acquaintance."

I said, "It's true he's fastidious about women. He got mixed up with all kinds, and couldn't marry any of them because they didn't meet a standard."

"Based on what?"

"That I can't say, Fishl. Can't be a botanical standard, because there are plenty of ugly plants. Some are gruesome. And there's no agreement even among birds and insects, for instance—hummingbirds seem to love red flowers, so do butterflies. Wasps are supposed to favor dark brown, while flies prefer flesh colors or yellowish browns. So each species has its own idea of the beautiful or the disgusting. I'm leaving out the fragrance preferences."

"Well, take this specially developed high type of complex man and have him united in marriage by a judge who once did him out of millions of dollars. It's the stuff of drama. You came to me because you're concerned about him. And I'm concerned too, about my dad."

"You'll have to tell me why you're worrying."

"Sure. You'll understand in a minute. Have you heard of immunity offers? I see you haven't. Well, when a prosecutor is out to get somebody, he can offer the privilege of immunity to key witnesses. The law says that a witness who refuses to testify may be held in contempt and sent to jail. This was intended to be the government's answer to Cosa Nostra, but the practice has become much, much wider. Now, here's this fellow Amador Chetnik—the U.S. attorney isn't really interested in Chetnik. He's after bigger game."

"Like Harold Vilitzer."

"You've got it. Chetnik testifies against Dad and he gets a reduced sentence. Now, suppose that Chetnik tells the truth about the Electronic Tower case . . . You can finish the sentence for me."

"Old Layamon can reopen it, and recover millions for Uncle Benn."

"We're a brainy family. This is alien subject matter, but when it's laid out for you you see the heart of it quickly."

"Millions for Benn means millions for Matilda. That's why Chetnik was invited to tie the knot."

"Look, chum. I'm the unhappy Edgar, cursed by old Gloucester, his father. That's why I'm in this shit-house office while my brothers are up in pig heaven. Bind fast his corky arms! Put out his eyes and spurn them with your foot! My dad has never been exactly a good guy, but I'm his son and long to save him. Be reconciled. Behind it all is Donovan Stewart."

"Which Stewart is that?"

"Goddam academics, they never know shit about what goes on locally. Governor Stewart, of our own state. In his time he was the U.S. attorney here, and every single successor has been one of the young guys from his original team. Guess for yourself whether or not Stewart has influence on the present incumbent."

"Fishl, what has Stewart got against Uncle Harold that he'd send him to jail at age eighty?"

"Oh, it's nothing personal that he wants to do him in for. It's just an opportunity to extend his control. You come in as the reformer-conqueror, drive the corrupt politicians from their stronghold, and then you take away billions in revenues—a couple of hundred franchises out at the airport, for instance—capture millions of voters . . . you build a regular empire. My father and his guys are in retreat, their clout is lost, no chance now to hold the city, so they've been stripping it, but good."

"To get back to Chetnik, what's in it for him?" I said.

"A reduced sentence, plus he gets to keep his boodle, and maybe a fast parole deal. Maybe also a cut of what Benn can recover from Dad."

"And you believe that Layamon and Chetnik already have schemed it out?"

"I haven't got second sight, Ken; all I've got is savvy. Plus, I want to do what can humanly be done for that poor fool, my aged dad. I want to prove that there's only me, the rejected son, defending that rugged ogre, that I'm the devoted one, not my coddled wimp brothers."

"And I'm devoted to my uncle Benn. What I don't see is why your dad had to treat Mother and Benn as he did."

"I agree. But once a man has scrapped the old ethos, he has to kick and stomp it and try to finish it off once and for all. Harold Vilitzer is a crook. Don't expect the man of sin to have boy scout lapses for his relatives. The rule is 'Don't spare anybody.' Now, then, does Benn want my father to give him millions of dollars?"

"That's not Uncle Benn. It wouldn't be characteristic."

"He could become uncharacteristic for the sake of his wife."

"No, he didn't marry for wealth, just for beauty."

Fishl now was no longer the entrepreneur and seed-money man with me. He was changed altogether by the information I had brought him. He didn't even look like the double-chinned suave man who had received me in this naphthalene-smelling office. The eyes, the nose, not a single particular of his appearance remained the same. I thought, You don't even begin to know a person until you've seen the features transformed in an overflow of feeling. A totally different Fishl came before me as soon as he saw that he might be in a position to defend his father, save him from his enemies. And as I registered this change, I couldn't help thinking that the heightening of my own powers of receptivity was due to Uncle's influence. Uncle had said, "a second person inside me . . .

told me to give the junkman my nickel." Perhaps there was such a second person also in Fishl. There was no more talk of "logging in the data" or any of the high-tech business jargon. He now was straight—very curious for a man who had elaborated so many fancy tricks. He said, "I have to think what to do. I would suppose that Layamon wants Benn to go to my father."

"Or get somebody else to do it, saying that Benn was willing to reopen the case. It's your dad's own rule not to spare anybody. Suppose that Benn were to go on the same standard!"

"Benn shouldn't lend himself to that, shouldn't agree to adopt totally new motives at his stage of life."

"Consider his position," I said.

"I would, if you'd tell me more about it."

"I'm acting on my own," I informed Fishl. "What he tells me, he tells in confidence. I can't say more than I've already said."

"What we have to find out is what Chetnik is being offered by Dr. Layamon. Chetnik is bound for prison. He can get a reduced sentence by finking on Dad. Or he can keep his mouth shut and settle for a chunk of money. He'll need it when he gets out of jail. So the price of keeping Dad out of it might be so much for Amador and so much for Benn. Two, three, four millions. Matilda could buy a seat on the stock exchange."

"The exchange? Why would she want that?"

"It wasn't a week ago that I heard talk of her going into a brokerage house. Fingal Brothers and Hockney."

"Going into?"

"Negotiating, probably. It's a mutual fund. She'd need some training. There's a mad search for gifted women. These companies aren't directly subject to affirmative action pressure, but it does them credit to have a lady wizard in an executive spot. . . . Is this the first you hear of it? Hasn't Benn said anything?"

"No, nothing. A lot of what I get from you is much like the pictures you see when you run a fever. A heat-oppressed fancy . . . Why would Matilda need so much money for a brokerage apprenticeship?"

"Buy a million dollars' worth of their shares. Then they'd have to advance her quickly. You must be thinking how this will affect Benn."

"Well, his basic rapport is with the plants, as you know. No reason why our world should affect him too much. Naturally this isn't what Benn married for."

"Sounds as though the lady acquired *him*," said Fishl.

"Conscious intentions always predominate," I said. "And who was he *not* to be acquired? That's another sphere of speculation. Still, there's no telling what goes on between two people. They may have found more in each other than any outsider ever could see. Have you been married?"

"Oh, quite a few times," said Fishl. "But I wouldn't care to go into it at this point in time. Would you put it past Dr. Layamon to have had this in mind from way back? After all, Electronic Tower is big stuff. Worth having a shot at that kind of money."

"Wait a minute, Fishl," I said. "Matilda is very desirable, could have easily married rich. . . ."

"Yes, sure, but she wouldn't have had the same control. I won't argue it, Kenneth. But a famous professor is always a good catch for a woman who doesn't like vulgar society. The best husband for most women is a composite. Try this sometimes in a conversation. I've done it, and the results are damn curious. Candid women will tell you, I'd like some of this and some of that—a little Muhammad Ali for straight sex, some of Kissinger for savvy, Cary Grant for looks, Jack Nicholson for entertainment, plus André Malraux or some Jew for brains. Commonest fantasy there is. Unfortunately you have to limit your catch to one, and an absentminded professor isn't so bad, if he has the prestige and isn't too absentminded, so you don't actually have to check his fly in the morning before letting him out of the house. Now she's Mrs. Benno Crader, and she can draw interesting people to her set. There's probably more than one hostess in this town who snubbed her when she was single, and she'd love to give them the business. But what kind of salary does Benn earn, and what latitude is it going to give his wife? Her father isn't giving away a thing, that's his reputation, and think how thrilling it would be to turn the son-in-law into a millionaire, which he might have done himself if he hadn't been such a creepo. Any normal individual will protect his interests—what's so distinguished about letting people screw you?"

I really liked what Fishl had said about the composite dream husband, each man a dish on a table of delights, a smorgasbord. Fishl's ideas or insights were much better than his chosen style of conduct. They made his conversation curiously enjoyable. But when he suggested that he take charge of things, I became more reserved. He said, "Why don't you leave all this in my hands. Give me a week or two to check out how my father feels."

"Why ask me?" I said. "I'm on the outside."

"You could put it to your uncle Benn. Say to him, 'Don't do anything on your own. Fishl has offered to investigate.' Or: 'Fishl is on your side. He knows his way around with these types. Let him map out a campaign that will respect your unusual needs.'"

"Seems to me that Uncle is tired of everyone telling him that he's incompetent, that he's positively fated, programmed by fate, to go off course. That's why getting married was his own decision. Nobody was consulted."

"Okay. But he's not the only party affected," said Cousin Fishl. "There's my father too. I grant you that Dad was stingy with the Craders. He should have given them half a million apiece. Throwing them contemptuous scraps was very bad. Your mother felt insulted."

"Just a few hundred thousand bucks, it came to, and most of that went for legal fees."

Fishl said, "Point out to Benn how useful I'd be to him. Otherwise he's completely in his father-in-law's hands."

"And Matilda's hands. Only I can't say that to him."

"You must have considerable influence."

"I can *put* it to him. I agree he needs smart guidance. But if he thought you were orchestrating something elaborate, he'd run like hell."

"What is this 'elaborate'?"

"I figure that to be your inclination."

"If you refer to my business schemes, I have to say that you've heard nothing but louse-ups, ignorant gossip and standard misinterpretation. That's the worst of journalism. It isn't the gossip that offends you, it's the stupid mismanagement of the facts. Right now what worries me is my father. The bad guys are after him. And you don't want the Layamons to take custody of your uncle totally."

"Teach him a lesson," I said. "Let him find out what he got himself into when he rushed into marriage without talking it over with me."

"Angry words," said Fishl, very sensible. "You don't mean that. That's not the real Kenneth speaking." Coming from him, with his pale fat imperial face, this made a curious impression. The real Kenneth? Was there a real Fishl? As I watched closely, the singularity of this seemingly comical fatty seemed to detach itself from him and, with a tremor, move away. I give my impression of this just as it came to me. Another Fishl was sitting there in the fully buttoned vest, his feet in the moccasin-seam loafers meekly crossed. Intimations, maybe, of a second Fishl.

"I guess I brought you an opportunity today," I said. "You may see a way now to get together with your old man and prove to him how smart you can be about the rock-bottom essentials. No fool. And concerned about him. And also that you love him as nobody else does."

"Well, don't stop there. Finish what you started to say."

"Okay, I will. You must figure that he's in decline, the wild bull he used to be is old, so he's ready to open his heart to sentiment. But you yourself said before that his motto was 'Don't spare anybody.' Which I translate as 'He's of a modern type of mind.' More modern, maybe, than his eldest son. Conciliation and united hearts may not be uppermost with him."

"When I approach—if I can manage to—he may tell me to fuck off. Still, whether he wants it or not, my impulse is to approach."

"Good luck on that," I said, and got up. "My ride is waiting. I'll be in touch."

"Above all, tell your uncle not to go to my dad on his own. Warn him against it."

As I was going down in the huge, slow elevator, past the taxidermist with his display of owls and bobcats, past the herbalist with his jars, I was unusually fertile in notions. This strange Fishl in the seed-money business had planted a variety of suggestions in my head. Although he teased me about moving to the Middle West in order to study Czarist Russia in its final phase, damn if he wasn't himself, in his cockamamy office, similar to a Russian of that epoch. In his emotional development, at least, he was flavored with essences belonging to that period of Rozanov, Meyerhold, the late Chekhov, Mandelstam and Bely. Moreover, this American metropolis on the prairies was rich in resemblances to St. Petersburg, 1913. Here, too, there was a mixture of barbarism and worn-out humanist culture (granting that the latter had never had much of a chance to flower in these parts). There was even a population of peasant immigrants from Eastern Europe whose development was arrested at the 1913 stage, who spoke dialects of Polish or Ukrainian no longer spoken in the Old Country, even though they drove Japanese Hondas and wore J. C. Penney underpants. These were exhilarating reflections. Sexually, too, there were parallels. For instance, a cerebral animalism or primitivism; crazy drug cultists pursuing visionary ecstasies once experienced only by mystics; sadomasochism (raging abuse inflicted or endured, and identified with love or pleasure). A further similarity was the proliferation of a multitude of false worlds to whose rules people were earnestly committed. They could draw you along because they seemed to know what they were doing. All the while they were in a deep trance but still spoke authoritatively for the "real." A man like Bely's Ableukov, for instance, under the influence of a group of conspirators, agreed to plant a time bomb in his father's bedroom. He didn't really want to be a parricide. An apparent ethical logic drew him on. But by and by it became evident that the metaphysics that had long supported the ethical order had crumbled away. To me this similarity with St. Petersburg was a stimulus. There were intoxicating analogies. Oedipal ones, especially.

I stood waiting in the street for Dita to pull up in her green Dodge van—a handsome, well-made woman operating a trucklike machine. She was generously built, slightly ashamed of such abundance and trying to tone it down by acting dainty. On our rendezvous corner, there was a caramel-corn shop, and a warm, sticky fragrance came from the copper cauldrons.

They were as big as kettledrums and gave an agreeable warmth and a copper shine to the street. To be in a crowded place was agreeable also. Inner communion with the great human reality was my true occupation, after all. It was a field without much competition, so few took it up. I did it out of a conviction that it was the only worthwhile enterprise around. As earlier stated, unless you made your life a turning point, there was no reason for existing. Only you didn't *make*, you *found* the turning point that was the crying need (unconscious, of course, as the most crying needs are) of humankind. I was just beginning to admit that I myself had meant to do (or try to do) for human subjects what Uncle Benn did for the algal phycobionts of the lichens. My meeting with Fishl Vilitzer had brought this home to me at the moment when I saw (or thought I saw) the "officially presented" Fishl detach itself with a tremor of the face, and move away, leaving behind a different individual altogether, another creature than Fishl the kookified promoter of strange deals. I have to admit that it gave me great pleasure to experience such a thing (or, to defer to the principle of objectivity, to imagine that I experienced it).

Speaking more immediately (in my own person, quickly recognizable as a lean, long-haired, slightly saturnine but in reality naively motivated man in his mid thirties), I was looking out for my uncle's interests just as Fishl—to borrow words from the Canadian anthem—"stood on guard" for his father. Fishl was setting himself to engage and outmaneuver Dr. Layamon, Judge Amador Chetnik, and even—in a remoter perspective—Governor Stewart, who allegedly managed all the grand juries in this federal district. Fishl had the nerve to consider himself a match for these stars, this killers' row. As Uncle's self-appointed guardian spirit, I, too, had to try to interpret their motives and anticipate their plans. I'd have to take counsel with Fishl, of course. I couldn't try to cope alone with these hard, savvy, politically wily personalities or hope to outwit such intricate wits. It was vanity to think of attempting it. What was I up to? How could I win? What would be won? Yet through one's own pettiness one might enter—and not superficially—into the petty aims of others. I envisioned such aims (no longer altogether petty when they were so profuse and engaged so much ingenious energy) being towed along like tiny crabs enmeshed in seaweed. Everybody—but everybody!—had quantities of such weed in tow.

Well, now Dita Schwartz in the right lane was edging up in her Dodge van. The traffic was very heavy and she was making finger signals to me through the windshield. Instead of thinking obscurely, I'd have done better to buy her a bag of caramel corn. She always spoke fondly of Cracker Jacks. She was, however, like so many self-conscious types, a weight watcher, and anyway the opportunity had passed. There she was, a full feminine presence. Getting into the Dodge, you felt the warmth of her bust before you felt the heater.

"Hi, my dear," she said. "You had a cold wait. Should have come to the parking lot, or even the doctor's anteroom."

She could say "Hi" in a friendly male manner, but her breath had a feminine flavor and the look of her dark eyes was a woman's look entirely. You noted this because her skin was not distinctively feminine. It was not a good skin, it was like a mixed weave, a layer of scar tissue from some fiery adolescent disorder. Even in the frost, she had a white face. She preferred to seem indifferent to it. But sometimes she was sullen or indignant about her complexion—a defect; she had a sore heart about it. Still, it wasn't altogether bad to have your worst feature up front, not hidden, so that you had to tough it out. It's the hidden defects that make the worst trouble for you. (What I have in mind is my own sexual inferiority to my father, the phallic cross I've had to carry.) Dita was pale because her skin was too dense to show color. She had once asked to see photographs of Treckie. The only one I had was one of those Instamatics, in which Treckie, with bare shoulders, was laughing—glossy teeth, blue eyes, a pink face. The pink face was what Dita concentrated on. She only said, "What kind of a name is Treckie?" I asked about her own name: No, it wasn't short for Perdita, nor even Edita; simply Dita—from a true-love story her working-class mother happened to be reading in the maternity ward. Dita and I were, at the time of this conversation, teacher and pupil, on friendly terms. She was willing to listen to my troubles, and to put up with my divagations and aberrations, my absurdities, which in fact pleased her. To persons of a normal outlook I would have sounded off the wall, but Dita and I had read so much Gogol, together with Dostoyevsky fantasies, Sologub and Andrei Bely, that tall conceits and screwball ideas didn't faze her. She was used to my way of trying things out. As E. M. Forster once said, "How do I know what I think till I see what I say?" This is true, as far as it goes. Englishmen, however, are so often pleased with a striking beginning that they stop right there. The next requirement is to carry your thought forward, to take it out of the category of bright sayings. Dita often saw well in advance what I was getting at and met me more than halfway. She asked me how I had done with Fishl. While I hadn't taken her into my confidence, I had been all atremble during the trip downtown. "How was it with your cousin Vilitzer?" she said.

"The way it is with all of us barbarians and hybrids," I said.

It was unnecessary to spell this out. She knew my opinion—namely, that in general this was a century of hybrids, and that if you weren't one, if you asserted that you lived by a classical, traditional standard, as some people took credit for doing, you were out of it. (I see I am nevertheless spelling it all out.) You might be an estimable person, but you were living "elsewhere"—pre-1914, even pre–eighteenth century. That might feel nice, certainly, but it meant that you had excused yourself from the present age, you had opted out. (This may seem more divagation, but wait a minute.) The Jews, insofar as they had lived in isolation within their ancient code, had done that for millennia, back into the fossil ages. But then they began to come voluntarily into the present epoch, and later they were forcibly dragged into modern history, riding into it by the millions in cattle cars, thus becoming aware (those who had the time to be aware) that for them there was no genteel option to declare that they stood clear of contemporary civilization. I can't press on with this now, I have other urgent priorities. But it is legitimate as background, explanatory of my description of the conversation with Fishl Vilitzer. He and I were barbarians or hybrids of a peculiarly American type. If you venture to think in America, you also feel an obligation to provide a historical sketch to go with it, to authenticate or legitimize your thoughts. So it's one moment of flashing insight and then a quarter of an hour of pedantry and tiresome elaboration—academic gabble. Locke to Freud with stops at local stations like Bentham and Kierkegaard. One has to feel sorry for people in such an explanatory bind. Or else (a better alternative) one can develop an eye for the comical side of this.

I wouldn't discuss Uncle Benn's troubles with Dita. We were friends, there were no love complications, so we could safely talk about all kinds of things. Still, Uncle's marriage difficulties and sexual torments were confidential matters. I wanted like anything to discuss them with somebody, and Dita would have been ideal for the purpose; she had an excellent head. But I couldn't even talk around the subject, since she would very quickly get the drift.

I asked, "What kind of doctor were you seeing?"

"A dermatologist," she told me. She said this lightly, so I didn't guess that she had anything serious in mind (for instance, an attempt to change her looks so that she could rival Treckie). I was so much involved with Uncle Benn, the riddle of the Roanoke, the grand juries, and the rest of it, that I was slow to understand the signals Dita was giving. When she mentioned a dermatologist, my sole reflection was: "She can't be thinking of a face-lift, she's much too young. Must be a rash in some unmentionable place." I let it go at that.

When I got to my small Slavic Studies office, I found a message under the door from my uncle. "At home, this P.M." I didn't even take off my coat. I knew what "home" meant and I went directly to his apartment near campus. These days, he was not often there, having committed himself to Parrish Place for the idealistic purpose of establishing a relationship with Matilda's family. Dr. Layamon seldom went straight home after office hours. He played cards at his club for fair-sized stakes. Matilda especially wanted Benn to cultivate her mother, to form a personal connection with her. This was not so simple as you might suppose, since Jo Layamon often sat in the off-limits office, and when Benn showed himself in the field of furniture beyond, she didn't acknowledge his presence. As for knocking at her Dutch door, he was too shy for that. If he glanced in occasionally, it was more to see the red azalea in the far corner than his mother-in-law at her desk.

At any rate, I found him in his own smaller and much

darker rooms, surrounded by his botany books and framed prints of plants with Latin names, or of morphological cross-sections that didn't look like much of anything to me. Uncle himself wasn't in great shape. He wasn't thriving, that was obvious, didn't look well. He poured me a drink of Wild Turkey. He wasn't keeping house now, so the glass was foggy. A year ago he would have set it in the sink to soak in Calgon, and reached for a clean one. The cardiologist had put him back on Quinaglute for his arrhythmia, he said. His breathing was somewhat melancholy too, and as an outstanding "noticer" (there is such a type), he was definitely aware of it, because he presently said, "The respiration is a little cramped today."

"Not unhappy, are you, Uncle?"

"No. Not really."

"Post-honeymoon adjustments?"

"Don't hint around with me," said Uncle. "Am I sorry about marrying? The answer is a clear no. I did an excellent thing."

"I didn't say it wasn't. I haven't been married myself, ever, but I'm told that in the early period, when people still are feeling their way, changes are noticed. I don't want you to think I'm teasing or putting you on, Uncle. Just normal concern."

"That's all right, Kenneth. Your views on love are pretty familiar to me—that everybody is on a separate system."

"The *petit système à part*?"

"And in every breast there's a glacier that has to be melted, otherwise love can't circulate."

"I don't deny that we've discussed this in these terms. Which are dark terms, no question about that. I didn't mean to depress you, Uncle Benn."

"I didn't think you did."

"And when I asked about post-honeymoon adjustments I was only remembering what Benjamin Franklin once said. His advice was, before marriage keep your eyes wide open, after marriage keep 'em half closed."

"Are you saying that having them wide open afterwards is a bad mistake?"

"Franklin is famous for this sensible, humdrum, middle-of-the-road formula for a contented life. Why do you think he got his picture on the hundred-dollar bill? I only meant, Uncle, that you seem a little down."

"A few nights of broken sleep, that's all."

"New anxieties? Seeing yourself filling up all that empty space at the Roanoke? Or is it the Uncle Vilitzer business that worries you?"

In putting so many questions to Uncle, I recognized a carry-over from my earlier conversation with Fishl Vilitzer, the entrepreneurial tactic of keeping the upper hand. It wasn't really fair to practice this on my uncle. I dropped it *toute de suite*. Uncle, not being too truthful, said that he wasn't terribly worried about Vilitzer. Nevertheless he was keen to hear about my interview with Fishl. "You didn't give him any information about me, I hope?"

"Not beyond mentioning that Amador Chetnik had performed the ceremony. That got him talking about Chetnik. Chetnik is under investigation, because he's too rich for a judge."

"We knew about the investigation," said Uncle, impatient.

"To lighten his sentence, since he's bound for jail, he might be willing to tell the authorities what he knows about Uncle Harold. Harold is the one they're out to get."

"Yes, but he's survived so far. As my father-in-law says, knowing how to steal is the difference between the men and the boys in politics."

"As long as their machine was intact, the Vilitzers could get away with anything. But it's badly damaged. The only safe base for a Democrat now is in the House of Representatives, which is still Democratic. And even there, the glory days are over except for chairmen of the big committees, the guys with the clout, the strongmen whom not even the Ethics Committee can touch. So I've been told by people who ought to know. Here, locally, Uncle Harold has been gerrymandered out of power and that's why he no longer can protect himself. He's one of those old guys that were in control since the days of FDR, and now they can't even hang on to the money they stole."

"This sounds more like Fishl than yourself, if you'll forgive me saying it. What's your impression—isn't Fishl a freak?"

"Not more than most of us. The main point is that he's determined to protect his father."

"For you that would be the most important fact. That's what wins your heart. I was hoping to get a better understanding of it all. I'm ashamed to say that I don't even know what gerrymander means. Up against these people and these sums of money, I feel weak and ridiculous."

How well I understood what he was talking about! People like ourselves weren't part of the main enterprise. The main enterprise was America itself, and the increase of its powers. Submission to those powers made something of you. Even opposition to them counted (if you were a cocaine user, for instance, you absented yourself from the work force but you came nevertheless to the market for dope, so that your resistance to society was bought and paid for, somehow). But where did Uncle, with his Russian stoop, his large head, his infinity-symbol eye frame (the blue lemniscate gaze), fit into the picture? Did he understand what Paul Volcker was saying about interest rates? Or anything to do with jet propulsion? Or electrical engineering? Why, the very spies that sold technical secrets to the Russians were ahead of Uncle, because they could read blueprints. If Uncle had done something or other in television, in mutual funds, in advertising, in commercial music, in hydraulics, in protein chemistry, how different the attitude of the Layamons would have been! But he was nowhere with a blueprint, with a balance sheet, so what were they to make of him? He came haunting around the edges of the Layamon world, drawn by his longings. These longings can be further broken down, as admiration of beauty; desire to be bound to a woman in love and kindness; and finally, sexual needs, which, let us speak frankly, are seldom if ever free from crotchets, if not downright perversities.

I suggested to Uncle, "Why not say no? No to everything. Why don't you say that you don't want to move into the Roanoke? And you don't want to do a number on Uncle Harold. Just refuse."

"How can I? I have a certain obligation to Matilda. She's so beautiful, so spirited, and so on. I can't tell her that she has to lead the dull life of a professor's wife. It would do me harm too, in the end."

I couldn't reason severely with him or take a hard position, because I was compromised by my own attachment to Treckie, and open to counterattack.

"What does Matilda want you to do about Vilitzer?"

"She doesn't expect me to negotiate with him. Somebody else will have to do that."

"You're only supposed to say that this somebody else is representing you?"

"Well, Kenneth, the old man wasn't fair to Hilda and me."

"*You* couldn't have gotten fifteen million bucks for that property."

"He treated me with contempt," said Uncle.

"What of it? What's contempt? He's an old party now. You really don't want to threaten him . . . ?"

"Matilda says he won't come to any harm. She wouldn't allow that."

"Uncle—Fishl would like you to let him handle his dad."

"No, no, Kenneth. I prefer to do it myself, if it has to be done at all."

"Fishl, I gather, is worried about his father's health."

"Maybe so. Then also he wants to appear to his dad like a savior. And I can't think of a single thing that Fishl ever succeeded in. Matilda says he was in a terrible mess over something she called livestock futures. He bought on margin, whatever that is, and there was a blizzard and hay couldn't be brought to the animals. They died. So Vilitzer had to come up with half a million dollars to keep Fishl out of jail. That was *it*, as far as Harold was concerned."

"Why did Amador Chetnik marry you—does Matilda talk about that?"

"Nothing to it at all. A friend of the family. He's gross, he has a gross nose, but he's no different from a dozen others. Anyway, a wedding is something you go through for the sake of the parents."

"She didn't realize that Chetnik was the judge who found against you?"

"A new bride, Kenneth. Less than a month, and bluffing already? I have to take her word."

I was about to say that in some cases the bluffing never stops, and if a wedding is a convention, so are words like "true" and "false," but this was no time for bandying sophistries with my uncle. He was not himself, he was carrying unfamiliar and heavy burdens. The inward labor I observed in him was a great worry to me.

Uncle said, "Matilda and Doctor feel that I should be made whole. I never heard that expression before—downtown language, I guess. Everything looks different from Parrish Place. I've never lived so close to the center of things. And every time I come near a window, I see that goddam skyscraper. My old life is lying under it—my mother's kitchen, my father's bookshelves, the mulberry trees. It's like one of those drowned villages in the TVA valley, where you'd have to be a scuba diver to revisit your childhood."

"I've never been inside the Electronic Tower. Maybe we should go and look around, just to demystify the place. I think that on the next sunny day we should ride up to the observatory."

"You'd better tell Fishl that he's not acting for me. He's just an aging hippie, still trying to break into the business world. He should have accomplished that twenty years ago."

I said, "That's not the main part of Fishl. It's only a subcontinent, so to speak. In the basics, Fishl is sound."

To this I appended a few private reflections:

The first was that Benn and I had nobody *but* Fishl to turn to. He had a pair of keen eyes, but their setting (fat face, imperial double chin, fuzzy baldness) was *not* a hundred percent reassuring. I grant you that right off, or as they sometimes say in my native land, *tout de go*. However, you couldn't judge by the particulars. Those particulars flowed from a single source. If you couldn't find the source, you had nothing but assorted lips, noses, ears, hairlines, skulls, et cetera—*disjecta membra*. Well, I thought I had a grasp of the source, in Fishl's case, and he was fundamentally predictable and trustworthy. Far more trustworthy than the Layamons. I conjectured that just as soon as Doctor had learned of the Vilitzer connection he fell into a state of conspiratorial inspiration. He could make Matilda rich without it costing him a penny, and this dodo botanist Crader, instead of a mismatch, would be the *grand prix* husband the Layamons had virtually stopped hoping for. The biggest matrimonial computer in the world couldn't have found such an ideal man. He had incalculable advantages, one of which was that he had no dollar smarts. Besides, he would be indebted for his millions to the finagling in-laws. And you could leave the rest to Matilda. She would work out the possibilities, and tie up all the loose ends.

This was very likely how the Layamons viewed Benn, who was, to me, a man in a million, a genuinely special case. They didn't appear to know exactly who he *was*. Did he himself know? He did in part. And I didn't like to think that such a person, having magics or mantic gifts, had to consent to be preposterous in real life. This fitted too neatly into the postulates of "pragmatists," those insolent types who see themselves as the only true interpreters of reality and who are allowed to get away with murder by the inattentive "special cases." Now, those special cases have no business to be so inattentive. If you ask me, they are perverse themselves, too submissive under degradation. In this connection I often recall a side remark of W. H. Auden: "Trouble is attractive when one is not tied." What did he mean by "not tied"? Not engaged by real necessities? Lapsing from one's vocation? Submitting to trash because there is so much of it in the foreground? Oh, so much human thread being wound on the most trivial spools. If you drive off the distractions long enough to think about it, you begin to have sensations of profound distress, and it's just as Uncle said to the newsman who interviewed him on the dangers of radioactivity from Three Mile Island and Chernobyl—something like: "Sorrow at heart killeth full many a man." And it's a safe guess that there *are* more deaths from heartbreak than from atomic radiation. Yet there are no mass movements against heartbreak, and no demonstrations against it in the streets.

Above all, however, I hated for Uncle to let himself be used against Harold Vilitzer. Vilitzer beyond a doubt was a powerful operator. His main objective was to pile up a huge personal fortune, and the hell with everything else. Personally I had nothing against him, but if the logic of acquisition dictated that he should be brought down too, then let it happen. It makes perfectly good sense that those who take the sword should perish by it. Ditto, those who take the penis or whatever else. Where you have drawn the line you must prepare to go down, by a law all reasonable persons recognize as irrefragable and just. This law ought to apply to Vilitzer, why shouldn't it? What I really disliked was that Uncle should be made the agent of it. I could see that as one of the consequences of his position, the complications love and marriage had gotten him into—or, if you prefer, sensuality, carnality, the karma of eroticism. I never was completely certain that Uncle was impelled by an overpowering sex drive, or whether he was claiming his dues or paying his dues. Poor old Della Bedell had been a claimant ("What am I supposed to do with my sexuality?"). Uncle, on the other hand, may have been submitting to exactions ("You've got to come across as all other men do"). And I never shall be fully certain, although Uncle did eventually tell me what his relations with Matilda really were like. As I said earlier, the old boy told me everything he could think of telling.

I thought it was corrupt of Uncle to agree to put pressure on Vilitzer. In the original lawsuit he had only nominally been a plaintiff. For professional reasons he was away in Assam, and he hadn't much cared how the case came out. It was the Layamons who were telling him that it was shameful to let yourself be swindled. "Can't let this man make a *putz* of you, even if he is a blood relative," said Doctor.

Still, under it all, I couldn't help feeling that I had done right in immigrating to America. What I had told my parents, "The action is *over there*," turned out to be true. I couldn't say that I wasn't getting my money's worth. Even at a time like this, with Uncle in a rapidly developing crisis, placed in a false situation, sitting before me in one of those new suits they had ordered for him, confined by *their* will, by the will of the Layamons, so to put it, in his clothing, he was still a person of unusual resonance, he was still a major figure, possibly one of those Citizens of Eternity, a mysterious being—a mystery he perhaps projected upon the plants. Yes, botany. Botany was the big thing. Yet it had a rival, which was female sexuality. He couldn't leave the women alone. When he traveled around the world, his professional cover was roots, leaves, stems and flowers, but actually there was a rival force of great strength. Part of his Eros had been detached from plants and switched to girls. And what girls! A phoenix who runs after arsonists! was my spontaneous and startling thought. Burnt to the ground, reincarnated from the ashes. And after all, every return of desire is a form of reincarnation. For after desire departs, no man can be certain that it will *ever* return. It's like the Yeats poem: "Many times I died,/Many times I rose again."

Choosing a bright day, I took Uncle downtown and by a series of elevators we went to the hundred-and-second-story observatory at the top of the Electronic Tower, once the site of the Crader Home for Invalids. On the ground floor was the Burke and Hare National Bank, with its multilayered steel vaults. This institution, Benn—these days such a close reader of the *Wall Street Journal*—was able to tell me, had been bailed out by the federal government. Too many bad loans to Third World countries ruled by what that same paper called kleptocrats—i.e., military or bureaucratic officials who transferred these borrowed billions to private accounts in Switzerland. Anyway, here was the great and clean monument, anchored God knows how many hundreds of feet in Permian or Triassic strata. Certainly an impressive metamorphosis of anybody's old homestead. Admission was a dollar fifty, one of the least expensive tourist attractions in town. To me the visit was genuinely diverting. Any number of disorders can temporarily be forgotten at such a height—a crime you committed long ago, a fatal error of judgment. Even the secret birth of cancer cells occurring in you when you are rapt from yourself by such a view from the hundred and second floor . . . Any amount of human queerness, I mean to say, may be checked for a moment as you face an Egyptian pyramid, or a Sistine ceiling. I silently followed Uncle as he inspected his native city with that cobalt gaze of his—empty factories, stilled freight yards, upended streets, stretches of river where the water was as still as a fish tank; and then the countryside, prairies liberated from the darkness of the city, farmlands under white icing, and skies suggesting freedom and eliciting ideas of flight or escape. I wonder whether Uncle wasn't thinking something like that: what a perfect day to flee, as he used to do; but now no flight; and a wife is not a valise. No hints were given. Scientific thoughts perhaps came and went, or sentimental ones. Maybe he remembered the book by Haym Vital on the Tree of Life, which was lost when the old house was wrecked. Buried here, perhaps. The single remark Benn did pass was about his father's death, somewhere under us, twenty years ago.

In the lobby before we left the building, we glanced at the directory: insurance companies, engineering and accounting firms, foreign consulates, national merchandising chains; no pharaohs entombed here. Uncle wanted to give me lunch at a landmark restaurant—Skelly's, near the produce market—but there was no sign of any market now, nor was any Skelly listed in the yellow pages. Skelly had gone to his reward—at rest in a Catholic cemetery—so we parted without lunch, silently, each with private preoccupations, and didn't meet again for several days.

I myself was unexpectedly and not always pleasantly busy. Uncle and I had only perfunctory telephone conversations. Just now he had enough troubles of his own and I didn't want to bug him with mine. A Mrs. Tanya Sterling had been in touch with me. She was Treckie's mother. A few days earlier I had received a note from her. She was coming to town for the housewares show at the Convention Center, and would be staying at the Marriott. Could we get together? Naturally enough I had to consult Treckie about this, and I had no number for her at the VA Hospital where she worked. Because Seattle was two hours behind, dinnertime calls were inconvenient since I was seeing a lot of Dita Schwartz, who was not well just then, and needed help from me. The one favorable circumstance in that troubled week was the excellent winter weather. I am very weather dependent and have hang-ups about the climate, seasonal moods, happy or downcast. But now we had a series of favorable days, keen and sunny January afternoons that gave me a musical ringing in the head. These were particularly suitable for contemplation. Unfortunately, I was too busy to contemplate and the opportunity was spoiled by worries. When I did finally get an answer in Seattle, there was a man on the line asking who I was and what I wanted. With interpretive skills sharpened by suspicion and jealousy, I judged that the fellow was in the middle of his supper, and Treckie was called away from the gas range: "Treck? Some guy wants to talk to you." This was no evening visitor; the man was well established there. The baby in the high chair may have been taking him for a daddy. She was working over the stove for his dinner. The stained-glass fixture—yuppie Tiffany—would be making the table center glow. I could picture that. *I* never had been invited to a meal by Treckie in Seattle. There was nothing in what she generally served that I regretted missing; frozen gourmet dishes from the microwave would be on the menu—either those, or fried beef patties with frozen Green Giant peas. If she was cooking, the room would be filled with smoke, and her tough friend I pictured in his undershirt, like Kowalski in *A Streetcar Named Desire*. To this squalor I had contributed a baby girl. Served me right, and would teach me not to come on with so much "dignity," be so polite and high on principle, with parties on whom it wasn't going to register. I could by rights have spoken boldly to Treckie. "Who is that man!" and so forth. But it was just me versus contemporary circumstances, and against those I never had a chance. So the position I adopted was, in legal language, *nolo contendere*. Which I translate freely as "hoping for a light sentence."

"You're having dinner," I said to Treckie. "Sorry to bother you. I have a date of my own in half an hour, and so I'll make it short."

"That's all right, Ken. What's on your mind?"

"It's your mother. She's coming to town and has asked to have a drink with me."

"Oh, has she. . . ."

"So I had to ask, how much does she know?"

"Oh, she's been here already and seen Nancy. After five years in Costa Rica, she got a spurt of interest in her daughter again. Nothing now to keep secret, if there ever was."

"Oh, Costa Rica? You did mention that to me some time back."

"She was playing out a romance with some Robert Vesco type the government hasn't been able to extradite. I guess he finally succeeded in spinning her off, so now he's free from the IRS and Mother too. Ken, what else can I tell you?"

"Baby all right?"

"Doing just fine at the child care center."

The skinny, diffident biological father out in the Middle West, not having prepared a conversation, couldn't think how to keep her on the line any longer. Himself a mysterious creature (no exception, either; most of humankind are far outside the shallow systems of psychology), he was eluded by the even more unfathomable mother of his child. "Do you object to me meeting with Tanya? What do you suppose she wants to talk to me about?"

From the tone of her voice, I knew exactly what Treckie was doing with her shoulders. As on the occasion of our first embrace, when they were bare, and she shrugged, challenging me to inquire about her bruised legs, I would have wagered that the shoulders were rising now. I can be very acute about telephone tones, in spite of my hearing defect. I can tell what people are doing two thousand miles away. She said, "Tanya came here to pick a fight with me. That's always her main motive for visiting. I couldn't care less what you say to her."

"Was she pleased with the kid?"

"Women like that always make a grab for the grandchild. The statement is: 'My granddaughter will be everything my own child should have been and damn well is not.'"

To me Treckie was neither friendly nor unfriendly. Our intimacy had slipped ten or twenty notches, now that she had a heavy boarder in the house. Her way was to be embarrassed by nothing which under the rules of olden times would have been embarrassing. For what I felt she took no responsibility. Contractions of the heart were my own lookout. If they bothered me to that extent, I could go to a doctor and ask him to prescribe pills. If I felt she was getting away with too much, it was up to me to design an appropriate response. I even thought (what a thought to have at such a time!) that somebody should do a study of meekness, one of the least successful of all religious policies. If I thought my behavior was commendably decent, who was going to do the commending? What I really wanted was to catch the next flight to Seattle and kick some sense into Treckie. Throw out the man who was shacked up with her, beat him up, concuss his head with a hammer and fling him down the stairs. Some of these violent fantasies, I now realize, arose from my indignation over Uncle's accepting abuses as routinely as a conductor collecting transfers. But there's no having *any* relations with people; none at all, if you won't accept abuse.

Treckie said, "I'm holding the receiver between my shoulder and my ear. These burgers will burn if I don't use both hands. So call me later, if you like."

I couldn't tell which of us hung up first. I believe she beat me to it, perhaps sensing that my politeness was drying out and that I had strong words to say, like: "Who's the rude bum that answered?"

Well, I wanted to see her mother. If she was at war with Tanya, I could get information from the old girl over cocktails, learn things which until now I had refused to admit into evidence. So I phoned the Marriott and left, or tried to leave, a message. You can reach places all over the earth by touching twelve or fifteen numbers, but it's no simple matter to leave word. Some months ago, for instance, the chairman of the County Board was approached at a fund-raiser by a frantic woman who feared for her life. Well, instead of listening to her then and there, he said, "Call my office." Probably she did call. The odds are that the message didn't get through. She should have said, on the spot, "A thousand-dollar contribution for your campaign if you'll give me ten minutes right now." But she didn't understand politics, and lost her life. Four months later, she was found murdered, sitting at the wheel of her car under fourteen feet of water in a county-maintained canal. (It was among twenty-seven automobiles sunk by their owners, who then filed theft claims with their insurance companies.)

Next day Tanya Sterling returned my call, but I was busy just then with Dita Schwartz.

From a conviction that she had to compete with Treckie's smooth face, Dita had gone to a downtown dermatologist and he said that he could help her. Owing to an adolescent case of acne, her face was uneven with scar tissue and deeply white. Hair and eyes were just as dramatically black. I realize now that I had aggravated her lifelong dissatisfaction with these blemishes by telling her with thrilling minuteness what I felt for Treckie. Well, Dita had now decided to make her move. It was her skin, she was convinced, that put me off. I was high-strung and fastidious, subject to a complex flow of attractions and repulsions. She wasn't so much offended as rueful with me that she should be entered in a beauty contest (I, who had told Uncle Benn life is no beauty contest!) with a girl like Treckie, whom she considered to be a dimwit, utterly without class. Class, in more senses than one, was an issue here. I think I said earlier that Dita was the daughter of a Jewish foundry worker. She was in fact a superior woman, and on the basis of cleverness, dignity, feminine warmth, daintiness, princess-style behavior, capacity for attachment, I would disinterestedly have voted for Dita. Only disinterestedness has nothing to do with this. If her bad skin was a deterrent (I once said this to Uncle when we were lightly discussing women), you could do as schoolboys used to say, cover her face with the flag and bang her for your country's sake—I doubt that Dita, with her mixed patrician-proletarian manner, would have been offended by such a joke (if the joke hadn't been on her). She herself used street language as easily as Presidents do in the Oval Office, and she looked up once from turning the pages of a fashion magazine to say, "I don't understand this rage for titless broads." On the other side of her nature, however, was a taste for poetry and the language of philosophy, and she was a woman of serious interests. I myself had trained her in Russian literature, and she was writing a dissertation on Scriabin, Kandinsky and other art mystics. She met all the higher criteria.

Last autumn, she and I, together, had watched a television program about a Swiss clinic specializing in dermatology. Rich women came there to have old skin layers surgically removed from their faces, and lay in their beautiful beds for as long as it took to grow new tissues. The process was long, painful and expensive. It was, for Dita anyway, a gripping movie, done in tinted art film, the colors delicate as in *Death in Venice* (a cheap piece of pseudo Platonism). The ladies were shown in their opulent sanatorium rooms. They looked out on mountain peaks and Alpine clouds, those who weren't too hugely bandaged to see out. In the early stage after surgery, they resembled wasps' nests. Later they still were veiled, like lady passengers in the first automobiles ("touring cars"), protected in their delicacy from the dust of the road.

This movie got to Dita, by which I mean that it reached one of her deeper fatal places, and she returned to it as often as Uncle Benn later was to come back to the Charles Addams cartoon. "You aren't thinking of this for yourself?" I said.

"On my salary? Teaching elementary Russian at the junior college level? I couldn't pay even the air fare to Zurich," she said.

Right she was. It would have to be the wife of some Third World kleptocrat struggling to recover her lost youth. Those rooms with gladiolas in Chinese vases and people sipping tea from Wedgwood wild-strawberry cups. With a new skin, the now glowing lady would go home (where people were dying of dysentery), perhaps to find herself replaced, if she hadn't, to begin with, gone into the treatment to beat out her rivals. (One must keep all such combinations in mind, or else the tragic career of mankind will have nobody to observe it.)

Here in the Middle West, Dita shopped around for a bargain, and like the working girl she was, found a downtown fellow who made her a price to remove the top layers of dead skin right in his office, under a local anesthetic. He scrubbed her cheeks, her nose and her chin with a sander, a revolving disk. As her eyes had been covered, she couldn't tell me whether the gadget resembled an electric drill (my natural question). It made a hiss like sandblasting, she said. She knew it would hurt when the novocaine wore off, but the removal of the bad skin was a liberation, purifying, and you had to pay the price (a very small instance of the ordeals of the West, which I tried to discuss with Mother in Somalia). When I saw my friend and pupil with the offputting rind removed, like a kiwi, alligator pear or Ugli fruit, I might fall in love with the angelic face of the real Dita.

I had taken her downtown that morning, without really understanding what was going on, and I waited outside in the Dodge van, a light but dull green ten-year-old model with the body pretty badly banged up and the odometer stuck at 120,000 miles and fixed like the evil eye. I couldn't park while waiting. The traffic cop made me circle, because near medical buildings there's always a crowded hack stand, and in our town, the drivers now are from the developing countries and gotten up like Jihad terrorists, acting that way too, hollering and spoiling for fights. I could understand why Dita wouldn't want to go home in a cab. Then, after an eternity of steering around (I'm not a gifted driver), I came by and recognized her by the winter coat. I had no idea that she would appear in the downtown crowd wearing such a hive of bandages, standing taller because of it. There were peep holes, and an opening for the mouth, but the entire unit had slipped, and the anesthetic was now wearing off. By the time I helped her into the van she was fainting with the pain. As I was clipping her seat belt, the hustling cabbies behind us had a fit, beating their horns with their fists. I didn't give a damn about them now, since Dita's bandages were already soaking with blood serum and I was afraid that the gauze would stick to her face and began to think of taking her directly to the nearest hospital. The doctor had given her sample packets of pain pills. His nurse had guided her down to the lobby and through the revolving doors. I was going to stop at a drugstore for more dressings, but she managed to tell me that she had stocked up on them beforehand, and please to go straight home. Her building had an underground garage and the car jockeys who used to proposition her (half joking) kept off today. Seeing her in this white cone, and a high-shouldered skinny with long hair stalking beside her, they made no passes, for once. I got her upstairs, dug the keys out of her purse, assisted her to the sofa bed, removed the coat, took off her shoes. She seemed for a moment to pass out—hard to be certain of a faint when you can't see the face. I was about to dial for an ambulance, already asking the operator for the emergency number, when

Dita said, "Don't do that. Just sit with me." So I spent the rest of the day there. I wasn't much of a nurse, I need hardly say, but even if the success of the treatment was in doubt, you didn't remove the coat and shoes, you didn't open the hand the sufferer reaches for, without touching a new level of familiarity, with warm attachment flowing in very quickly. You immediately see "teacher and pupil" for the thin stuff that it is when the "man and woman" forces present themselves. Somewhere on my psychic premises there was grief for Treckie still. I can't deny it. But I had to take care of Dita. She became my charge.

Over her protests, I removed the swathings when they were soaked. Hard to understand how the fellow could bring himself to brutalize her face with those high-speed disks. He was probably, I thought, one of those old-time clap doctors or mastoid specialists put out of business by antibiotics, and setting up for a dermatologist. When I took off the surgical yashmak he had wound her in, she looked as if she had been dragged over the highway on her face. Those ladies in Switzerland never could have been like this. Cheap is cheap, as the old lower-class wisdom has it. Just her proletarian luck. I felt this all the more sharply, as I rewound her in fresh gauze, because I was the cause of it myself. She wanted to be in a class with Treckie. Or Matilda. She knew Matilda too. She used to call her "that recliner empress." Still, these were ladies lucky in their exquisite faces, and for whom Uncle and I were ready to make sacrifices. So Dita came forward with a sacrifice of her own. These torments and martyrdoms to which women submit their bodies, the violent attacks they make on their own long-hated faults or imagined deformities! Gladly assaulting themselves. The desperate remedy. The poor grinding their own faces.

However you describe it, I wasn't worth this suffering. Treckie wasn't worth it either, as a rival. In most respects, Dita was effortlessly superior to us both. She had ten times more heart in her, and this produced a kind of beauty we were unfamiliar with. I thought I would have it out with Uncle Benn on the whole subject of beauty. Something was wrong here, off the wall with the classic face, the grandeur of Rome, the glory of Greece. Poe, this poor genius nitwit married to a moronic and forever prenubile girl . . . here was a poet who had run straight into a world rolled flat as a pizza by the rational intellect (and at a primal, crude stage of capitalist development—let's not leave out capitalism), and he fought back with whiskey and poetry, dreams, puzzles, perversions. Then also Baudelaire, Poe's successor, with his vicious madonnas, taking the field—sickness and sensibility against mechanization and vulgarity. As you see, the usual thought suspects were rounded up.

Still, for several weeks I had something worth doing. I went to the supermarket. I rather enjoyed this domestic stuff, and taking care of a patient. Keeping house for Dita wasn't a demanding job. Housekeeping obviously wasn't one of her stronger interests. The back of the bathroom door was hung with unwashed personal things. I fussed in the kitchen, brewing coffee or boiling packets of Knorr's dehydrated soup. I bought a bottle of Wild Turkey, which was the sufferer's basic remedy till the worst of the pain was over. For several days I fed her broth through the bandages, using straws, and when she was well enough to go out she was still too unsightly to be seen. Strips of drying skin hung from her face. One of them was the size of a roof shingle, and she was splotched with bruises, scratches, scabs. Touching was absolutely forbidden; you must wait for the happy morning when you found the scab in your bedsheets. Little kids know what a thrill that is. In any case, I continued to shop for her and to straighten up the kitchen and the bathroom, in the course of which I learned how little Dita minded a ring in the tub, or mustiness, or streaky windows and spotty mirrors, or cared how many tin cans for bacon fat she had back of the gas range. More to keep busy than because I was myself so strong on neatness, I borrowed Uncle's Dustbuster from his apartment, and also his Windex and 409. Presently I switched from Knorr's soup to pizzas, which I could order by phone, or Chinese food, from time to time cooking an omelet. Unlike Uncle, I wasn't much good in the kitchen—more like an unhandy alchemist, pouring from the measuring cup. As an undergraduate, Uncle had been short-order cook in a Greek one-arm joint. If the Layamons had let him make griddle cakes, he would have been more cheerful in the penthouse.

Their Polish cook was a gloomy personality. Her employers, who were afraid of her, treated her like Rostropovich, a great performing artist—extradeferential.

In the end, Dita didn't have a new face. The extreme pallor went away; the coarse weave, however, remained. It mattered less now, for if the experiment didn't succeed, there was a broader relationship between us, we were on a more intimate footing. If she didn't cure herself, she cured me anyway. As a patient, Dita didn't wear much clothing. She didn't show herself off deliberately, no flaunting. Still, her bathrobe fell open while I was holding the soup bowl. A woman whose head was wrapped in gauze couldn't be expected to keep herself pinned up to the neck. Making herself known to me bodily seemed to give her satisfaction of a deeper sort—I could see her as she was beyond the face, and after all, there's more to a woman than her face. At her bedside, then, I ate warmed-over egg foo young and drank Wild Turkey with tap water while we discussed Scriabin and Madame Blavatsky. Here was a woman who for my sake had submitted her face to a brutal sanding, and while I was pining after Treckie, Dita had made me a love offering of her own, so I wasn't absolutely on the street.

Pondering it again, I began to consider that a man might either give women and love what time he had to spare from his major undertakings (for instance, the struggle for existence, or the demands of his profession; also vainglory, fanaticism, power—each person would have a list of his own) or else, released from work, enter a feminine sphere with its peculiar priorities and directed towards very different purposes. Here is an example everybody will understand: If you weren't at war like Marc Antony, you were in love like Marc Antony; in which case you left the battle and ran after Cleopatra when her galley fled at Actium. I don't actually in my heart of hearts care much for this Roman stuff—i.e., Roman law, Roman political organization, Roman citizenship. Remember that from obstinate motives of their own, the Jews alone in the ancient world rejected the imperial offer of citizenship. . . . And I will remember that I am here not to lecture on history but to relate the strange turns in the life of my uncle Benn.

Anyway, the time had come for my drink with Tanya Sterling. I expected that Treckie's mother would have much to tell me about her daughter, about my successor and about the outlook for my little Nancy, amongst those changes that Treckie saw fit to make.

I hunted up my credit cards in the sock drawer and rode the bus downtown—late afternoon, a big winter glow in the west, banks of snow in the streets and many forms of radiant ice along the way. The bar of the Marriott, where I found Treckie's mother, was a different scene altogether—an indoors hanging garden with fountains, ferns, mosses, gardenias, all flattering to the executive class (in softer moments when it wants splash and fragrances). Mrs. Sterling was a youthful woman, relatively. She immediately said, "I was a child bride," a statement in which there was an implied carryover. She was still a sexual woman. She wasn't asking, like poor Della Bedell (since Della had a chip on her shoulder), What shall I do with it? There are very few people willing to declare themselves out of the running. Stop running, and you join the census of the dead. Hence the sexual craziness in the moves and motives of men and women. If they don't have specific sexual intentions in any given case, then they are rehearsing, continually trying something on, preparing, practicing their grips: just like cats when they wrestle with each other in fun.

There were a few sensational facts about Tanya Sterling. The most prominent was the makeup that she wore—a violet-bluish raccoonlike mask, wide blue circles about the eyes, which were gray and somewhat bloodshot. She seemed to have no eyebrows of her own but two bars made with a Magic Marker. Yet she was a pretty woman, downright attractive, with genuine personal emanations. I don't speak now of the heavy perfume she used—Arabian musk, patchouli or what have you (I am not trustworthy here, can't speak *en connaissance de cause,* as my dad could easily do). I speak of rays, waves, frequencies of emission, the irrational female music, twanged, breathed or bowed. Although Tanya was not a tall woman, she was wide in her person, handsomely dressed, with fine hands; not so small as Treckie—she had never had that intoxicating full, small body, I decided. Cordially smiling, informal, confiding in manner, *sans façons*. When retirement rules had been stricter, she would have been overage for the charm signals she still made. But it's only in museums that you can see the widow's cap. Octogenarians with osteoporosis still call themselves "the girls." But here I am pushing Tanya too far. She must have been in her late fifties, no more. To hold myself to a more conservative account, she was gracious in her behavior. As she said, there was a bond between us. I was the father of her one and only grandchild. "Until a few months ago I didn't know I had one," she said. "Five years in Costa Rica, and somehow I lost touch. Even in New York I would have been out of touch. Those young hip types speak such a gibberish and there are no dictionaries for parents. We can't make sense of them and *they* can't make sense of themselves." Tanya went on in this style, saying how adorable Nancy was and how much she resembled me. She didn't mind saying that I myself was no disappointment to her in appearance or manner. Especially my cheekbones and the odd setting of my eyes appealed to her. She wouldn't have advised a man in his middle thirties to wear his hair so long, but then it took an unusual turn over the temples, and the combination of olive and ruddy color was unusual, the commoner color being olive-sallow. To this I had nothing to say. No comment was expected.

Then she, too, stopped for a while, richly humming, not to be musical but because the generator was still running. All that was in her throat. She turned the daiquiri glass by the stem.

Like General Patton, I couldn't help thinking, she was deciding what side to hit you from next.

By and by she said, "When did you last speak with Treckie?"

"Last week," I said. "She told me about your visit."

"Was that all?"

I realized then that Tanya intended to speak of my successor. Well, why not.

"I told her we were going to meet."

"No mention of Ronald? She might as well have, since he moved in with her."

I said, "There was no need. He answered the phone."

"You must be upset," said Treckie's mother.

I answered her that I naturally was. But I'd rather not talk about my feelings, I told her.

"Of course, since you don't know me at all. Still, you'd have to be."

"I don't like to build a general conversation around private emotions."

"That tells me you were in love with her. Can't be a pleasant thing, with a person like my poor child. For her, an exclusive relationship is too confining."

"Who is this Ronald?"

"Oh, kind of a bruiser type. I thought he was disagreeable. He used to be a slalom champion and then a ski instructor. Being on the slopes does something to women, I think, and the instructors have all the sack traffic they can handle. Well, this winter-sports idol now works in snowmobiles. He says it's a new growth industry. I said that at fifty miles an hour, if you weren't sober, you could be decapitated by a wire fence. The fellow just laughed."

"Then he's a rough man," was my comment.

"You would have been too gentle for her taste."

Maybe I'd have won Treckie by kicking her in the shins. I didn't have the heart for it. I didn't think I was all that humane. Perhaps it wasn't my type of cruelty. Yet I suffered through the next moments.

I don't know how warmly sympathetic she *really* was, but Tanya sent me a message of womanly compassion. With her winsome teeth, which gave an effect of sympathetic adolescence to her grin, you almost forgot the width of her face and the breadth of her figure, and I really didn't mind her wrinkles since, although she had covered them with raccoon circles, she wasn't trying to put herself over as a young person. She had a sort of FDR cigarette-holder informality with the swizzle stick that dated her. If she had been a child bride, she must have become one during the New Deal.

"Meeting you in person, Kenneth, I see that my daughter has no plan for happiness. She's a fool. However, I would guess you have too much self-respect to eat yourself up with grief. You may look mild, but you're a fighter. Not much of a drinker, nursing your sherry. You're more my kind—special, not showy."

"Thanks," I said. "Good for the self-image to have your qualities noticed."

"Treckie actually was a sweet child, until she started her development, and then, *Bam! Bam!* Tiny as she was, she was looking for action. You never can tell which of the elements is going to dominate in the mature woman." Tanya now opened her big purse, which had been resting between her feet. She lifted it to the table with a habitual movement of her full figure, more like a quake than a practical action, as if she were drawing a bucket from a sensual well. Probably I was reading too much into this. When she opened and examined the purse she was disappointed. She said, "I brought family pictures to show you, especially Treckie as a small girl. I must have left them in the room. Let me bring them down."

"Don't trouble yourself."

"No trouble at all. I know you'll want to see how pretty she was, a lot like our little Nancy. The shape of the head is all you, but around the eyes she's just like her mother."

"I'm sure there'll be another occasion."

"Treckie said you were brought up in Paris. I might have guessed. There's a manner that tells. There's breeding. The present guy is a boor. Girls who are turned on by rough treatment are a puzzle to me. When I try to imagine what they get out of it, I draw a blank. They are a throwback to peasant life."

She definitely was referring to her daughter's bruised legs.

She went on: "A girl I knew at school has had her arm broken twice by the fellow she lives with. Two ambulance trips to Bellevue, and she goes back for more. Yet people tell you there's been no great change, and it's always been like that."

"Your view is that sexually these are exceptional times?"

"You'd better believe it."

I took her opinion seriously. She spoke with authority. She reminded me somewhat of Caroline Bunge, Uncle's friend. If Caroline had had all her marbles, the resemblance would have been closer. Where Caroline was absentminded, Tanya enjoyed full consciousness. Both had had a considerable experience of men. Together they had probably seen more nude males than the U.S. surgeon general. I do not mean to be pejorative, only to come to clarity on a most significant problem which cries out for answers. Old M. Yermelov on the Rue du Dragon had tried to get me reflecting on it when I was a kid at the Lycée Henri IV. I might have learned something from Gide, Proust and others whom as a Parisian adolescent I had read as a matter of course. But not even Proust had covered the ground as the ground now was: The sexual tastes of the aristocracy, the misbehavior and hanky-panky of the *haute bourgeosie*, the animal embraces of the proletarians and the peasantry (see Zola's *Germinal*, and so forth), were not in the same class with the contemporary democratized-plus-Third-World erotic mixture. Millions of persons had been freed from labor, routine, vows, incest prohibitions, and the rest of that to invent freely, and all the ingenuity of mankind, or as M. Yermelov used to say, intellect without soul, was turned loose—the will of the insane to suffer pouring into erotic channels. You could well believe that a divine master plan for the evolution of love had miscarried, that the angels in their innocence had got the signals mixed up and inculcated all the wrong impulses into mankind. "Eruptive forces from subsensory nature," as old Yermelov would say. Standing on volcanic terrain in Italy, if you set fire to a piece of paper you would draw smoke out of the soil immediately, he told me. I have never seen a volcano.

Uncle Benn and I had our work cut out for us, let me tell you. Could it be that a special class of women had selected us for special attention?

For now Treckie's mother took an utterly unforeseeable line with me. "There's no reason why that girl should do exactly what she likes and get away with it."

"Brought to justice?" I said. "Well, it would be nice to see an example of justice finally, in a case like this. Or in *any* case. Although not many might recognize it for what it is."

"You'd have to take a strong line," said Tanya.

"Like what?"

"We could turn the tables on that girl. Nancy is your kid too, and Treckie really isn't fit to be trusted with motherhood. You should bring a suit for custody."

"I'm in no position to do that, Mrs. Sterling."

"Tanya . . . Together, we might be in a position if—for the purpose, and only for the purpose—we were married. I see this startles you."

"You're right."

"It would be a formality, just as W. H. Auden married Erika Mann to save her from the Nazis."

"Not the same at all," I said. "Courts are nutty too. You should hear my cousin Fishl—not a first cousin but a family connection—on judges. I wouldn't depend on the effect of reason in a courtroom. There are forces around us which nullify reason. It doesn't seem to have the social base it used to have. Also, Tanya, I think you might appreciate what Fishl told me not long ago about women putting together an ideal man for themselves, part of this, part of that—a Sugar Ray physique, Mastroianni charm, romantic courage like Malraux, scientific wizardry like Crick and Watson with the double helix, millions like Paul Getty, plus a Spinoza brain. You ask why this is relevant? Well, I had part of what Treckie wanted in her composite, but she needed more."

"Kenneth, you're evading me. I don't understand why I think so, but if you saw those photos you might want to make a move to obtain custody of our Nancy. I can't forgive myself for leaving them in my room. Would it be too much bother to come up with me?"

I took hold of my watch to study the time.

"You're about to say you have a date."

"Taking care of a friend who isn't well enough to feed herself."

"You could do it and come back by cab."

"Or else see the pictures another time."

"You think they're a pretext to get you upstairs. That would be too crude. Both parties have some delicacy. It's time now for civilized candor. You would have been my son-in-law if my daughter hadn't been a little tramp and idiot and not able to spot a man who has a valuable ability: being nice to a woman. Only a person who's seen life can say how rare that is. At least twenty percent of the women you meet, if they sense this, would be glad to have you for their husband. But then there's the perverse element that would despise you and abuse you precisely because of the quality you have. You'd never be able to please *them*. Take a girl like Treckie. You have to do her will. She doesn't want you to please her. Even if you spent your whole life trying to be agreeable, if you invested fifty years in the effort, she'd still have no use for you. For a different type of lady, it would be bliss if you didn't do more than hold her hand. Marriage on the terms I have in mind would be a protection to you. Yes, I am your senior by ten years or so. But that's why we could have a relaxed relationship. So that if an aggressive woman put her moves on you, you could say, 'I already am married.'"

"And what would you expect of me?"

"Only what you were willing to do. If you held me in your arms in bed, I'd be happy."

Ten years my senior? The real figure would be more like twenty plus.

"Think of Nancy too. Well, I shouldn't advise you to think. If I may say so, you're the type of person who thinks things over until they disappear entirely. Let's go back to you and me. The pleasant nights we'd spend together would give us strength for anything. Would you like to try one to see what it might be like?"

I said I was certain it would be a wonderful experiment, but I wasn't prepared to make it just yet.

"Only to lie in bed. Talk or not, as you please."

She smiled at me with her peculiarly winsome teeth. She actually was an attractive woman, never mind her paint job of raccoon or badger markings. Also, it would be against my rule of truthfulness to conceal the fact that I am fond of preposterous people.

And what stunning offers you can get from the insane! That's what went through my head as I raised my long arm to the next cab in the queue under the warm rods of the Marriott marquee. A long way west, above the frosty fog of the straight street, there was a winter-blue crystal setting for the declining sun, with a red nucleus inside it.

Walking me through the lobby, still saying erratic things, Tanya Sterling had among other statements told me, "One look at this Ronald and I could see how much he'd been around. If you've had three hundred women, what's the difference between two hundred and ninety-nine and three hundred and one?"

At that hour the express bus no longer ran, and I spent twelve bucks in cab fare to avoid the local, which made thirty stops, its rear fumes giving me a diesel headache.

In his old apartment next afternoon, Uncle and I exchanged accounts of our experiences on the previous day. It turned out that he also had seen a thing or two. I said to him, "Well, it's too bad all this love stuff has been debunked, disowned and discredited. For a long time the world made love promises to young women, like 'All will yet be well.' It was a con—a betrayal! And now, naturally, women are angry and have turned against it. As for serious men, they have to ask themselves too, 'What the hell are *we* doing here?' I can understand entering the love world—understand, I mean, that for hard-minded people the justification is merchandising: shoes, dresses, purses, jewels, furs, styles, cosmetics. Also, there's psychiatry; there's so much money in that. Anything except love itself, for the natures that could love have become too unstable to do it. People with 'role models' or 'self-images' aren't up to it because they're fabricated, or constituted."

"Yes, yes, yes, yes," said Uncle, mainly to shut me up. "Now let me tell you about yesterday."

I had been thinking aloud in the usual way, and until he interrupted I hadn't altogether realized how upset he was.

The very ends of his hair showed it as well as the blue gaze of his disturbed eyes, very much dilated in their figure eight frame. The tilt of his upper body when he said, "Let me tell you about yesterday," made me say to myself, "Oh-oh!" And the roundness of his head took on a different aspect. It had never occurred to me before, but a head as round as that was born to roll.

This was the onset of his crisis.

He began by telling me that he had had a date with Doctor. The place was the hospital where old Layamon was on the staff. The purpose was to hold a strategy session. They were to have a sandwich together and afterwards drive back to Parrish Place in Doctor's Bentley.

"What hospital is that?"

"The old Moses Maimonides. When I was a kid that was a *schrecklich* name. Both parents had their surgery semifinals there, so there are as many bad associations as your heart desires. Since then they've put up lots of new buildings. There used to be a nice old garden, but they needed the land for a clinic for dope addicts. Instead of decent old tailors and storekeepers, needle-trade workers, you now see zombie types, prepared to do anything that might occur to them. Why not?"

"Bad scene, eh?"

"One of those places where it all bubbles out. The modern additions make you feel, 'Don't worry, modern medicine is in charge. All will be well.' So I pray, I hope and trust they're right. In the middle of it is the original Maimonides building, pretty well decayed. I was supposed to proceed to the Message Center. More than half the doors were locked for security, and there were so many detours underground that I was tired out when I got there. I had Doctor paged, as instructed, and sat down with a magazine. Finally he marched in. You know the way he sways."

This was accurately observed. Doctor oddly worked his shoulders, in rhythm with his stride and his head stiffly held back. He had served in the Pacific and there he may have picked up a few Douglas MacArthur traits; on Guadalcanal he had been Major Layamon. So he swayed in, wearing his white coat. He said to Benn that he hadn't quite finished his rounds, he was behind schedule.

"He apologized," said Benn. "I told him, 'That's okay, I can wait. I'd be glad to. Plenty of old magazines here.' 'No, no,' he said. 'I'd like your company. This will interest you.' I was supposed to put on a white coat and pretend to be a doctor."

"Which you didn't refuse?"

"I didn't see how I could. I was being treated like an insider, which was a sort of honor. I was reluctant, sure, but he laughed me out of it. He had done this before and people got a kick out of it, mostly, masquerading as doctors. Roughhouse medical student type of humor was how I saw it, going back about forty years."

"Well, now and then a little malice is good for the soul."

"Don't start theorizing on me, for God's sake!" Uncle said with a rare tone of sharpness. "He helped me into the white coat and put a stethoscope into my pocket, and he said, 'You *are* a plant doctor.' I could just see myself trying to find the heartbeat of a tree." Uncle didn't laugh at his own joke; his stare was too wide for that. "Damn awkward," he said. "Pose as a doctor? He was dragging me through it out of mischief, and his rounds were in the oldest part of the original Maimonides, full of horrible associations and especially awful memories of your grandmother, because all the patients yesterday were old women."

"Women only?"

"Nothing but old ladies. He had saved them up for me. They were all hip cases, pinned hips, and they didn't need more than a glance, so it was all very quick, double time, in and out of the room, just long enough to pull off the sheet and have a look. Funnily enough, the ladies didn't mind how they were treated. Being exposed didn't faze a single old person. Not a face changed its expression. Doctors can do as they please. Once in a while Layamon would say, 'This is Dr. Crader, my associate'; nobody cared about it. Out in the corridor he was as gabby as ever—Motormouth Layamon—and I guess he has normal eyesight but the eyes don't seem coordinated. He was barging in and out of the rooms, pushing away the door and everything else, yanking off the covers. The ladies' hair was dyed and set, they had on lipstick, other makeup, they wore lacy bed jackets, and then there were the stitched scars, and short thighs, and warm, shiny shins, the mound of Venus and the scanty hair—all those bald mounds. But the old people might have been knitting or sewing buttons, they looked so complacent. So what had all the shouting been about, and all the men who loved them, dying to get them, crazy with jealousy, desire stuck in their hearts like cloves, and pleading and weeping, and the women also in an agony to decide which man was the right man? After I had stared at six or seven of them I began to have a dizzy sensation."

"Like what?"

"Like what! I might have been flying over the Badlands in a helicopter. I began to have arrhythmia, my heart was misfiring, which I interpreted as engine trouble, and the copter was about to crash. Maybe it's time for me to have a pacemaker put in."

"What are you talking about? You just married a young woman—you don't need any pacemaker. You simply aren't tough enough to face what the doctor faces routinely year in, year out, and that's probably what he wanted to impress on you—how he pays for the luxuries and services the womenfolk take for granted. It's still a hell of a thing to do to a bridegroom."

"Maybe he doesn't think I'm a bona fide bridegroom, and I'm closer in age to those fading things with broken hips than to my bride. He kept shooting me looks across the bed. . . ."

"Those unbalanced eyes of his."

"Out in the corridor, I thought he was talking wildly."

"What was he saying?"

"He said, 'I get a pretty girl once in a while. As a patient, don't misunderstand. It's not always old snatch.'"

"It gives disciplined people relief to act bonkers sometimes. With you he allows himself to give in to the impulse."

"I felt very bad about the old ladies, and how awful they'd have felt if they had known I was there just for laughs, as Doctor intended by this prank."

"They'd never give you a thought. I think they have a kind of understanding with doctors—something parasexual. As for him, I don't believe he knows what he's up to, what's eating him, some kind of erotomania. You should tell him to consult a psychiatrist."

"Not me!"

"You're too respectful, Uncle. You shouldn't be so diffident. I mean that. You won't admit that you're *sui generis*, a man in millions, and you have a duty to your exceptional status to reject what the Layamons are forcing on you."

"No, because then I'd have to think as they do, and I won't touch their premises."

"Because you took a beautiful daughter from them?"

Uncle was deeply uneasy.

I said, "You don't have to get into battles with them, only protect your special gifts. They don't understand—aren't conscious of them."

"There's nothing they can do to *those*. I don't like people who make a temperamental fuss over themselves."

"All right, Uncle. Let's pass on this one for the time being. So you followed him on his rounds."

"Followed is right. He led the way, and I was keeping up. I never before realized how wide his shoulders are. From the shoulders alone you could identify him as Matilda's dad. Not thick, kind of two-dimensional, and very elevated. Did you ever, as a kid, try to see over a fence that was a few inches too high for you?"

I couldn't reply to this. He was in such a state then, so singular, that no reply was called for.

"Now, it's off the wall, as you sometimes say, to attach such importance to backs and shoulders. That's *sui generis* too, and it's not a very high-class genus."

He was right, there. At the time I didn't know how right he was, or what "right" might signify. That I was to discover a little later. Standing on tiptoes, wanting to look over a fence, but what was there to see—a baseball diamond, a gravel quarry, a Steinberg landscape, a rare collection of Arctic lichens?

"Yes, seen from behind, they're alike in build." Hiking up his coat sleeves and moving the band of his watch on the inner side of his wrist, Uncle applied his fingertips to his pulse. Still the arrhythmia? Every third beat was delayed, and he would have to go again to Dr. Geltman for an EKG. Being unwell made him impatient, and he never took cover behind a cloud of illnesses. Medicines—tranquilizers, beta-blockers—interfered with his scientific work. He had no patience with hypochondria. He hated hearing people speak of psychoneuroses.

"Still," he said. "It hit me very hard to see that similarity in father and daughter—Matilda so beautiful and Doctor just the opposite. A person with such shoulders is one of a type."

"What do you mean?"

"I can't say what I mean. A type. I seem to mean something eternal."

"Is it like somatology?"

He said sharply, "No. It's not. Let's not be so learned. I'm not talking anatomy and character."

I tried to fathom what he might mean by "something eternal," and I could see how painful it would be to a man of science to be subject to such intimations or magical suggestions. He was unable to beat them back or expel them from his mind.

"Okay, Uncle, now the rounds are over and you have a sandwich together. He talks to you about the Vilitzer business."

"He thinks I should confront Uncle Harold."

"First he shakes you up by exposing those poor old ladies . . ."

"I still am shook up."

"I see that. But I doubt that it was deliberate. He's not that consciously diabolical. He's a hard-driving, basically crude man. He senses your weaknesses, he doesn't psych you out. Now, how are you supposed to take on Vilitzer? What are you supposed to say?"

"I'm supposed to say that my father-in-law believes I was short-changed and that I feel the question should be reopened." Then Benn veered away from the subject briefly, saying, "Physically Doctor is an odd person. The parts don't match. Maybe that's why his manner is so intimate—the way he takes over and feels and examines and squeezes when you're lunching with him in a booth. He wants to know why you're put together differently. And don't you find his color strange? Sometimes he's that funny shade of orange that you see in little newts—family Salamandridae. Or do I find fault with him and hit back because he criticized my overlapping teeth?"

"He doesn't think for one minute that you can stand up to Vilitzer."

"He tried to brief me about politics in this town. The main part of what he said was a regular megillah."

"And he lost you."

"In two minutes," said Uncle. "What he wants is that I should personally tell Uncle Harold that the way the property was sold is unacceptable to me."

"And that you think you should be made whole."

"That's it exactly. Goddamn these bastards, will they never stop fighting about money! All I wanted was to settle down with an affectionate wife, in a civilized style. Do my work, possess Matilda . . ."

"Whom you love."

"Respect *and* love. Through love you penetrate to the essence of a being," said Uncle. I was used to his irrelevant way of darting out, but the leap he took in this last statement was a considerable surprise to me. He seemed to be talking through his hat. He certainly was not himself, and he made me feel that he was like the Pick-Up-Stix game, where a sheaf of skinny spindles drops in all directions helter-skelter to start the play. This, I thought, was about to happen.

"Can you reconstruct the conversation with Doctor?"

"You must think you're talking to a nitwit, Kenneth. It went like this: I said, 'Maybe I should write Uncle Harold a letter.' Doctor said it wasn't done that way. Never put anything in writing; around here they didn't do business that way. Then I said, 'But he'd never agree to see me.' 'Oh, we'll find a way.' 'I'd like to wait until his son Fishl can sound him out.' 'That's not such a hot suggestion, son. You're leaving for Brazil in less than a week, and besides, Fishl is a wimp and disowned by his old man. Like in disgrace.' 'I'm trying to think how you can disgrace a family like the Vilitzers, famous for dirty dealing.' 'Even for those types, you'd be surprised, there's a code. I grant you it's hard to have a bad reputation in this town—take our sheriff, who has kept proven hit men and other kinds of killers on the payroll; he's running for reelection and still he stands high in the polls—but acupuncture abortion just lacks class. Old Vilitzer has a lot of pride.' I said, 'I'll take your word for such things, Doctor. You understand them, I don't. Still, I'd be more willing to play my part if I grasped the master plan. Couldn't you give a fuller outline so I'd know what I was involved in?' 'Well, the essentials must be clear to you—that your mother left you real estate worth real money and all Vilitzer gave you was peanuts.' 'What kind of pressure do you plan to put on him?' 'The kind he'll have to pay attention to. His political gang ran this city for fifty years. Now they're on the way out. Over eighty, why does he need the hundred million or so he stashed away?' I said to that, '*I* don't need it, either. I can't even grasp what there is to do with such amounts of money. I already have everything I need. I look at the magazines that come to the house'—Jo subscribes—'and I just can't understand all the spending. Like: "You only live once, live it in Revillon natural Russian sable." Or Waterford hand-cut crystal and sterling silver for your dressing table as well as your dinner table. This never has been among my personal life objectives.' Doctor told me, 'Listen, son, women have to have suitable activities. If they aren't *engagées* (there's a word my daughter used until I picked it up myself), they can get into bad, and I mean really very bad, scheming and double-dealing their menfolk. It's better to let them have these ego satisfactions.' I said, 'Yes, especially if they were brought up that way.' 'Matilda wasn't brought up, she *got* up on her own. If the woman he loves has special needs, a fellow meets them, if he knows what's good for him. That's just elementary. Besides, give her the start that she requires and she'll do the rest herself—make you happier than you ever dreamed of being. You'll be left totally free to work, fool with your lichens as much as you want. She'll be in the financial district all day. She comes home—beauty and love enter the house. What the fuck else could you ask for? She'll take off the business wardrobe and put on the dine-at-home *schmatte*, perfume herself.' Now, Kenneth, when he came to this part, the dream life, he gave upside-down knuckle knocks on the table. He would have given anything to be the husband of such a wife, and he became so rash in his looks, laying it on the line, that he seemed what you sometimes call demonic. Action! That's what the demonic part of it is. Get off your ass! Take hold, get a grip on things."

"Well, what kind of grip are you planning to take, Uncle?"

"Within reason, I have to go along, seeing that it's a new marriage and the first thing necessary is to accommodate the bride's wishes."

"Up to what point?"

"You can see for yourself that I don't have a big range of choices, Kenneth. Above all, I have to show goodwill."

"What I can't see is the goodwill the Layamons are showing. So what's Doctor's plan?"

"Vilitzer won't see me. But there's a public hearing coming up before the state parole board, and Uncle Harold is a member, so he'll probably attend. I asked Doctor, 'Why would Vilitzer be on a parole board? I'd expect them all to be old wardens, criminologists, retired cops or sheriffs, social workers and such.' It seems that Vilitzer asked for the job years ago to help political buddies get an early release, and sometimes there were big operators in prison, as in the racing scandal some time back, or in the construction business, so the parole board connection was important and even lucrative. . . . What would *I* know about this kind of shuffle? The growth rate of Arctic lichens, an hour or two of daily sun for centuries, more than twenty years to expand to an inch of diameter—so fifty years of finagling, for Vilitzer, while the organisms I study may have a lifetime of five thousand years. Anyway, the governor has let Vilitzer keep his place on the board, the open hearing is next Friday at the County Building, and I'd like you to come with me."

"You'd like *me*?"

"What's the surprise? Your mother would want you to, and she's part of this."

"You're crazy-scared to face up to him alone. Why should it take two of us?"

"Put it any way you like. It's true I'm not myself, completely."

"You should bring Matilda along. Since she's put you up to this, it's only fair that she should face some of the heat herself."

"I don't want her to take over. She'd get into an argument with Harold."

"Make threats. Probably so," I said. "I'll come, then. Promise me not to get into family sentiment with him. Play down the blood emotions."

"First of all, I intend to be all business, and secondly, I'll ask for *his* viewpoint."

"Fishl thinks it's a mistake altogether for you to approach him. He's terribly worried. The old man has dangerous cardiac complications."

"Kenneth, you and I hurting Uncle Vilitzer? A couple of chipmunks could as easily damage a hardened missile site."

"We'd just be the advance men, Uncle. Fishl feels this is serious. I suppose he wants Vilitzer to last long enough to change his will—changes in the will might be an alternative. But I see that you're bound to try to corner him at the hearing, and I won't let you go alone." I felt competitive. I was as concerned for Benn as Fishl was for his father. And Uncle couldn't resist the pressure exerted by the Layamons. His vitality seemed depleted and I worried lest he fall apart. There were threatening signs. For instance, he thanked me elaborately for promising to attend the hearing, nodding with a kind of china-doll formality. (Unnatural!)

"Without you it wouldn't be easy."

"Just out of curiosity, Uncle, to give me a fuller picture of what goes on, tell me what the rest of yesterday was like. You had a snack at the hospital cafeteria. . . ."

"Doctor seldom goes straight home from Maimonides. Usually he gambles at his club."

"Even he doesn't like that beautiful household too much—maybe. Gets out before dawn for surgery and doesn't show again till dinnertime. Where did he take you?"

"There's an estate jewelry outfit downtown. They had bought stuff from the nizam of Hyderabad or the akhoond of Swat. Doctor needed a birthday necklace for Jo. We went straight to the inner sanctum of Klipstein, one of his rowdy oldtime pals from the army. A real heavy-security place, with TV monitors, mirrors and push buttons, God alone knows how many alarm systems for the rubies, diamonds and artworks. Maybe twenty Buddhas in a row and crowds of painted elephants and other exotic toys. Doctor spent better than two hours joking, rapping, sparring and bargaining, and then he bought five thousand dollars' worth of opal earrings with an option to return. On the way home, Doc said that Jo would get a separate appraisal tomorrow from Cartier; Klipstein expected that. Traffic was so thick that it took another hour to get to Parrish Place. Then we appeared minutes before dinner, when the ladies were all dressed up, but Doctor was ordered by Jo to change his shirt before she would even look at his present. Finally, the four of us in the deep upholstery of barrel-backed swivel chairs sipping gin and tonic, sherry, a Bloody Mary." (Happy Hour for the Layamons, but not necessarily for Uncle.)

"Did Mrs. Layamon react to the opal earrings?"

"Moderate reaction. She's a cool type."

"Then dinner?"

"Palm-heart salad, which is Doctor's favorite, with pimentos. Lemon veal; wine, Sauvignon sec; dessert, Polish claffouti with quince filling. Conversation, dominated by Doctor—how the Congress appropriates billions and has also grabbed the power to force the President to spend them. Every year they have this Pike's Peak of tax dollars to spend, and they pass the money around to their favorite industries in return for campaign funds. Every second year it costs double to run for your seat in the House. Jo Layamon eats, drinks and talks in a refined style. Matilda winks at me to keep up my spirits."

"Why, does she know you're heavyhearted?"

"It's never been discussed."

"And then?"

"Then we have television or videotapes. Last night we first had Dr. Teller and Dr. Bethe on opposite sides of Star Wars, having it out like wicked wizards, two ancient faces disputing the ultimate question of human survival and the fate of the earth, with heavy discussion of laser particle rays or X-rays produced by atomic explosions. Then we looked at *La Cage aux Folles*—homosexual camp and screaming transvestites. I kept seeing Bethe's mask face, like human features painted on the sole of somebody's foot, and Teller like the atomic Moses coming down from Sinai with the Commandments on hydrogen tablets. Then Matilda, trying to please me, switched to

Clint Eastwood and some perverted killer swapping the heads of the women he murdered. I slipped away to the bathroom, and afterwards wandered around, made a tour of the lighted crystal cabinets and all the Wedgwood, Quimper, glass art from Sweden. I had a look at the red azalea in Jo's office. I don't go in, you understand."

"Funny rule, that little room being sacred to her."

"Still, it's a beautiful plant and does me good. The original word means 'dry,' maybe because the shrub is brittle or perhaps does best in a dry soil."

"And you commune with it while . . . A hell of a thing to be mooning over azalea blossoms when you have a gorgeous and brand-new wife."

The eyes, and he responded only with them, were filled—overfilled—with silent comment. In the arts of concealment he had never gone beyond the elementary stage, and in talking to me he wasn't going to assume skills he didn't have. And then, as might have been expected, given our attachment, our habit of openness (not to mention the close watch I kept, and the silent encouragement I gave him), he began at last to open up. There was such a glitter of trouble about him. Even the symptoms of his tension were brilliant. "I suppose I'll have to talk to you about this thing. I was hoping to manage by myself."

"Why would you have to?"

"Because people do; they must. Also it's disgraceful, that's why, humiliating to talk about. On the other hand, I don't want to carry it all the way to Rio. Alone there, it would be very bad. Too much for me."

"Alone?" I said.

He raised his voice. "Don't put me on about Matilda. This is no time to score points because I didn't notify you about the marriage."

"It wasn't meant as a dig, Uncle. What is it you can't manage? We've had hundreds of conversations right on this spot, and neither of us ever broke confidence." I referred to the sober books, the drape-darkened light and the leather chairs that dated back to Aunt Lena's time—Uncle's true habitat, the one I had chosen over any number of more attractive settings in Paris because I anticipated that here human life was making essential advances. Here I could expect real clarity.

Benn began by telling me that he was convinced that Matilda was just the woman for him. He spoke slowly at the start, feeling his way as if his job were to explain constitutional checks and balances to an acquaintance from Prague. By October, when I had already taken off for Paris and East Africa to see my parents, he and Matilda had decided that they would be married during Christmas week. To give himself more latitude, Benn had arranged an easy teaching load. He was giving a single course in morphology. His assistant could fill in for him whenever he had to get away. Matilda, who said she loved the country, proposed that they spend a week in the Berkshires, enjoying the autumn colors. She had friends somewhere between Barrington and Canaan who were in Hawaii and said they'd be very happy to lend their summer house "for a pre-honeymoon holiday." Lots of delightful villages in that moneyed corner of Massachusetts. Benn of course knew leaves backwards and forwards. So the couple walked the back roads. Splendid, cool, bright, bracing, blue, wood-smoke-smelling mornings; pancake-and-maple-syrup breakfasts; plenty of ripe, chill apples on abandoned trees. Some late flowers which Benn capably identified, careful not to be pedantic—this was their first opportunity to be alone. A certain amount of shooting in the distance by deer hunters. To be on the safe side, they wore red caps. No trouble on that score. The dirt roads were hard and dry. "That classic profile under the visor of a baseball cap." But after a few days with the maples and birches, "listening to me drone over them," other entertainment became necessary. There was an old car on the place for shopping and local excursions. No television, not much action after dinner, and Matilda wasn't used to going to bed at nine. The local paper stuffed into the RFD box listed the movies in town. A golden oldies series caught Matilda's fancy. "Why don't we drive in to see *Psycho*?" she said. "The original Hitchcock one. I've seen only those sequels."

"I saw it back in the sixties," said Benn. "It made a negative impression. I understand it's become a big thing—a cult. It doesn't take much to do that."

Matilda's cajoling answer was: "Sitting next to me, you may think better of it than you did some twenty years back."

So they drove in for the six o'clock showing. It was already dark, said Benn. Each day like an art exhibit of fields, fences, roads, woods, but closing earlier and earlier. Listening to Uncle, I must have been at my Frenchiest—long-faced, fitting in verses from the *lycée: "Nous marchions comme des fiancés. . . . La lune amicale aux insensés."* At least one of the fiancés was tetched, it's dead certain; I'm getting to that. And no, Benn didn't think better of *Psycho*. The second viewing was much worse than the first. "It was a phony. I hated it. I hate all that excitement without a focus. Nothing but conditioned reflexes they've trained you into. That's what stands out in the video films I've been watching at the Layamons'. Logical connections are lacking and the gaps are filled with noises—sound effects. You have to give up on coherence. They keep you uneasy and give you one murder after another. You presently stop asking, Why are they killing this guy?"

His memory of the picture was accurate nonetheless. He remembered the old tourist home resembling a funeral parlor, the tacky antiques, the terrible grounds. "All the bad ideas we have, the crippled thoughts we all think, producing a vegetation which is spiderlike. Coming up through the soil, part plant, part arachnid. That's what was covering the ground in that nasty sunshine around that nasty house."

Then came that pretty girl, the image of a sweet junior miss but a criminal herself, and on the lam. She rents a room, where she undresses and steps into the shower. There she's knifed through the shower curtain—stabbed, stabbed, stabbed, and the camera is fixed on the lifeblood going down the drain. Feeling chilled (what need was there for summer air-conditioning well along in autumn?), he put his hands under his thighs for warmth. Matilda offered him the popcorn box. No, thanks, he didn't like the stuff, it got between his teeth. He said that if he had been more alert he would have taken note of a vaporous haze of trouble forming inside his head and been forewarned. But you never know enough about yourself. He loathed the film; Matilda was enchanted. There was just enough light in the theater to show her elegant profile. Without having to look, she took the handkerchief from his breast pocket and wiped the salt and butter from her fingers.

The death of the pretty girl was followed by the murder of the detective who was trailing her. As the doomed man climbed the stairs, the camera concentrated on the back of a static figure that waited on the landing. This person, as improbable as the house itself, wore a long Victorian skirt, and a shirtwaist of dark calico was stretched over her shoulders. Those shoulders were stiff and high, unnaturally wide for a woman.

"Matilda!" Identification was instantaneous. That person seen from the rear was Matilda. This was as conclusive as it was quick. For Benn it would always be what it was at first sight.

Shocked at himself, rigid at the atrocity committed by his mind (perhaps by the "second person" inside him), he watched what he already knew was coming. In a moment the killer would go into action with a jump. Then you would see the barbarous face of a man, false hair piled on the head, a maniac. Murdered, dead before there was time for astonishment, the cop would fall backwards. Anticipating this, Benn said, he had already tried to take some evasive action, not so much against the "crime" (which after all was rigged) as from the association with Matilda. That was low! to see her in this transvestite. What was he trying to pull off here! Which of all the parties was the craziest? Benn said that if this had been one of the usual thought murders that go flashing through us—well, a thing like that can be set off by the sight of a kitchen knife on the sink. Just as great heights suggest suicide. We can deal easily with these flare-ups. No harm meant, not *really*. But merging Matilda with Tony Perkins playing a psychopath—that was a deadly move. It came from a greater depth and seemed to paralyze Benn. "I couldn't distance myself from it," he said. This wasn't one of your fleeting mental squibs, or flirting, playing with horror; it was serious. The woman was his fiancée. The wedding was planned, invitations were being engraved. And this vision in the movie house told him not to marry her.

What was worst about it was that the association was fixed upon him, too actual to be cast off. "The way I felt?" he said.

"In addition to being sick at heart? I remembered a demonstration in the zoology lab long, long ago. It was done with the hydra, just the simple freshwater polyp. You'd soak a dot of paper in a weak acid solution and put it on the creature. Then the tentacles near the mouth did everything possible to get rid of the irritant. Showed you the nervous system at the elementary level."

Part of what got him was that a bad movie should set him off like this—cynical Hitchcock camp laced with sexual inversion—that the message from his heart should be released by this box-office crap. What did this tell a fellow about his heart—that it was activated by trash? Sometimes he'd feel angry in the morning over the stupid dreams he had dreamt. Those showed you up, when they were especially moronic. However, dreaming was involuntary, whereas what had just happened, happened in full consciousness, in a movie house not far from Tanglewood, where music lovers came all the way from Boston and New York to attend beautiful concerts, and he had got himself poisoned by this Hollywood ptomaine. Maybe he shouldn't blame the movie for dragging him down; he may have dragged himself down. He couldn't escape the sense that he had committed a crime.

"I *have* to tell you this, finally," he said.

"I can see why."

I had now and then indulged myself in imagining that his eyes, so remarkable in shape and color, were prototypes of the original faculty of vision, of the power of seeing itself, created by the light itself, as if it demanded that creatures should see light. Right now his eyes were too dark to be classed as blue, and coming from them was sorrow. Certainly it was sorrow, and he didn't try to make it the most creditable kind. He hadn't meant to do Matilda such an injury. You can't narrow down what a man's eyes tell you. Not too closely. Benn was convinced that he was guilty of a crime, and somewhat like Ajax after he came to himself and realized that he had been out of his mind and cut down so many sheep. Posthypnotic recognitions and torments! When a plant clairvoyant, which I had always taken Uncle to be, turns his attention to human beings . . . well, what is there to say? Some while back, I was hard on Feuerbach's vulgar maxim "You are what you eat," and suggested instead that Blake was truer with "As a man sees, so he is." The world as it appears to you classifies your mind. Assuming that imagination has an independent plastic power, nearly godlike in extent. But here is a case of what occurs when a world is imposed on you by a corrupted vision. And whether Benn could shield himself by pointing to *Hitchcock's* corrupted vision was the question. But he didn't try to do that. Hitchcock was not responsible for Matilda's shoulders, and Benn said, "It was the shoulders especially. Those shoulders were what did it."

The rest of the movie didn't matter, except that it took its time about ending. The intolerable thing *was* that it took its time, and you had to wait out all the tricks and the paces that artful Hitchcock put you through, "the boomboom part," as Benn said. Finally you saw the mad killer's mother in a rocker, like the famous Mrs. Whistler, except that she was mummified, with empty eye sockets and her skull covered in coconut-fiber hair. In this form, death couldn't affect you much. Death was not dead, as John Donne had said it would be. It couldn't die, since it wasn't even real. So then the lights went on.

As Uncle Benn helped Tilda with her coat, he faced her shoulders again—innocent in themselves. (Or *were* they!) She bowed a little as he did it, and she didn't slip her arms into the sleeves, she wore the coat draped and gathered the collar under her chin, unaware of the evil that had been laid on her. When he told me all this, he added that he had avoided looking at her great-eyed, low-browed, musing, beautiful face. She was concentrating on the movie, or more probably on the best way to open a discussion of it. Never in the world could she guess how depressed he was. (One of those mercies which permit the flow of life to continue. If it were ever to stall, where would we be?)

"Wasn't the flick better than you remembered?" she said.

"No, it wasn't."

He fell behind briefly. The crowd in the aisle was his excuse. "I was too lame to move my legs. They seemed to have gone to sleep in the seat. They were lame, paralyzed. I pinched them and used my feet to kick the life back into the calves."

On the street, he admitted to Matilda, "That Hitchcock for some reason depresses the hell out of me."

One of those bluish, slaty New England fall evenings, and a Sunday at that. Sundays always were hard to handle. He started up the car and drove down Main Street, which was brightly lighted. It was only when he turned the corner that they discovered their headlights weren't working.

He said, "No lights. We'd better go back."

"Why do that? There's no garage open now. Look, you can use the emergency flashers. Once we get to the dirt road it's only half a mile."

He was too downcast to argue this, so they proceeded by flasher at fifteen miles an hour. But before they could reach the turnoff, a big, powerful sedan rushed from behind and cut them off. They were forced to the side of the road. A civilian, not a trooper, came out cursing. "You shit-ass! You prick! You queer!"

"And who the hell are you?" said Benn.

"I'm making a citizen's arrest to keep you from killing somebody."

"This guy is drunk," said Matilda. She leaned across to the window and said, "You're a hazard yourself, full of whiskey and couldn't pass a breath test."

"Shut that broad up," the man told Benn. "Give you a choice. Follow me back or I'll shoot your tires out."

Matilda challenged him again. "Where's your gun?"

"You better hope you don't get to see it."

As they were driving back to Main Street, Tilda's high voice was shaky with anger and she said, "You shouldn't let a bastard like that talk that way."

"Nothing I could do."

"You don't have to take such stuff from anybody."

"He's packing a gun."

"You should have got out and kicked him right in the knackers."

"Matilda, you're under the Hitchcock influence. You said yourself that he's drunk, and he looks like a Vietnam veteran. Besides, we *are* a hazard on the road, in this old heap."

"Backing down under threats is a Holocaust mentality."

"I'm not going to fight this football player. I'd resist if he tried to do you harm. On unfamiliar roads without lights, we might go into a ditch. He has a deputy's star on the radiator."

"Deputies are known hit men, where we come from."

The town cops let Benn use his Triple A card to post a bond, and a hearing before the justice of the peace was set for next morning. Matilda tried to get a cab back to the house. Finding anybody to come on a Sunday was out of the question. Benn said it would be more convenient to stay at the inn, especially if the dining room was still open. Avoid a round trip in a taxi and also the inconvenience of cooking. Although she was displeased with him, Matilda let him have his way. (She disliked cooking, I should note here.) So they were accommodated at the inn, which was a pleasant one. There was a wood fire in the dining room. "The meal was fair," said Benn, "but they had hot Indian pudding served with ice cream—that cornmeal, molasses and spice mixture I'm so fond of. I remembered the Indian pudding at the Durgin-Park fish and steak house in Boston. I kept talking Indian pudding. I clung to the Indian pudding. And gradually Matilda forgave me for being cowardly with the drunk that arrested us. All I can tell you is that I thanked God we weren't going back to the deep woods that night."

"What was wrong with the deep woods?"

"I was all shook up, Kenneth. I was scared, to tell the truth."

"Of what? I thought you liked woods."

"I couldn't bear to think what might happen in the night. Sometimes people are violent in their sleep and do horrible things. What if I were to do something terrible while unconscious?"

"To her!"

"Don't force me to spell it out."

"For instance—what Duncan's grooms were accused of doing to the king in *Macbeth*?"

"They were drunk. All I can tell you is that I was frightened."

"You didn't think you'd strangle her . . . because of those shoulders!"

"I decided that if we had to go back to that gloomy house, I'd take a double dose of chloral hydrate. I always carry some for bad nights. I wanted to be sure I'd pass out. Once these suggestions take hold of you, you play *their* game. You get kicked around like a soccer ball."

"Nothing but nerves," I said.

"Maybe. That's why the inn was pleasing. There was a normal kind of cheer about it. I knew it was probably no thicker than the old-fashioned wallpaper, but it protected me. There was a polished double sleigh bed. Antique. Walnut. Then I looked at the patchwork quilt and thought, Patchwork! This is no setting for a crime."

"You could have beat it. The escaping bridegroom is the answer farce gives to this kind of thing. I've told you about the goofy fellow in Gogol who climbs out of the window just before the wedding. And Dad likes to tell the one about a postexpressionist painter and some charming girl who lived with him. One day she said, 'It's time to discuss this relationship seriously.' He said, 'Sure, but I have to go to the john first.' Then he crawled through the bathroom window and ran all the way to the L.I. station. Then there's Molière's George Dandin, who *should* have run away."

Uncle Benn had been married not quite two months when we had this conversation.

I said, "If it was no setting for a crime, *who* was going to commit one? Are you sure it would have been you? She might be inspired to murder *you*."

"Do me a favor, Kenneth, and don't be so effing rational with me. There's nothing more aggravating than misplaced rationality. This was an upheaval. I'm talking affective phenomena, and you're talking good sense. Worse than useless."

He had it wrong, I thought. But he was too agitated to be differed with. I was only saying that it wasn't clear who was threatening whom, which of the two was the more hostile.

A pair of psychopaths under one quilt.

Anyway, the sleigh bed and the country wallpaper, and the old gas fixture converted to electricity, the flowered pitcher and washbasin, released him from fear. No chloral hydrate was necessary. Any harm done to Matilda would have cost him his own life, and he was opposed on principle to suicide. All he had to do was avoid her shoulders, so he lay on his left side all night and slept soundly. In the morning—how nice!—

the sun shone and Benn and Matilda were on excellent terms. She had no toothbrush, he had no razor; the coffee was first-rate, though.

At half past nine they appeared before the justice of the peace, who was the complete New Englander—blue-eyed, dry; cheekbones chipped out of red brick; thin, comb-marked hair. He ran the hardware store and the hearing was held in his small office. He accepted Benn's explanation about the lights. Decent with out-of-staters.

"Better have those lights taken care of."

"Immediately, we will."

"The man who arrested us was very threatening," said Matilda. "He said he had a gun."

The JP said that Mr. Darns was a selectman and also a deputy sheriff. "Case dismissed. No fine. Fix lights."

"That man was drunk," said Matilda.

Benn said thank you to the JP. "He asked what was my trade? I said I was a professor of botany. He gave back my license."

Matilda said, "Obscene and abusive. Was he licensed to carry a gun? Isn't there a stiff gun law in this state?"

"I wondered if it wouldn't be better for him to lock me up," Benn told me. "He didn't answer Matilda, hardly gave her a glance. If he detained me, I wouldn't mind too much. Maybe he'd prevent a crime. Also, I envied the man and wished myself in his shoes. What a nice office! Wood walls with sunlight. White church steeple. Maples in color. Of course I understood: no Jewish JP in this old Berkshire village. Just as I couldn't be an Irish tinker or a Hungarian Gypsy. Easier to be a Jewish cardinal in Paris."

"What in hell was Matilda doing, Uncle?"

"Can't say. The grotesquerie might have done it. A high-flying pair like this, grateful to a yokel hardware merchant for letting them off! Better to pay a fine in disdainful silence. Or maybe she was being virile for me, since I was too schmucky to do battle for myself." Then he added a few words about her appearance—extra-large lilac eyes, the power of the hair growing dense from the low forehead, the forehead narrower than ever, and darkened and sharply lined. I asked myself why the physical characteristics should be so important, and came up with the answer that physical beauty was the foundation that supported it all. Before the JP she came on like a fury. I didn't ask whether her teeth looked sharp; he had already told me about the teeth. I asked nothing, since Uncle's spirits were more scattered than ever. Confession gave no relief. It brought the enormity into clearer focus and I felt great pity for him. Another and a harder man might have laughed this off. Uncle, after letting me into his secret, only felt worse. Maybe it's better to be an out-and-out nut case than to have a partial understanding.

I can understand why Uncle went through with the marriage. He couldn't surrender to a brain fit. He had a structure to maintain, a vested interest in stability. Absurdity had to be defied. Besides, his runaway thoughts had wronged the woman, and he was sensitive that way. Masquerading as a doctor among the lady patients when Matilda's father pulled their sheets off had made him feel bad. It was unethical to stare at their poor bald privates. Once you get into the erotic life, modern style, you are accelerated till your minutest particles fly apart.

What was clear to me was that his telling me nonstop, "She's a beauty. The classic face. A real beauty," until it came out of my eyes (the way they say it in France—*ça commence à me sortir par les yeux*—is more expressive than "coming out of my ears"), was a justification for this marriage, looking more and more like an immolation presided over by Father Layamon and Judge Amador Chetnik. Because, you see, he had been warned. Practically from on high (though Alfred Hitchcock and Tony Perkins were the effective agents), he had been told, "Don't marry her. She's not the woman of your heart." Now those big eyes of his, dedicated to science, so to speak, were crazed (just a bit) by sin and punishment. I realized that I must do nothing at all to irritate him. My theorizing was an irritant, so I had better not theorize at him. Theorizing was tantamount to "I told you so," "you were asking for it." (In the harshest form, Hamlet telling Horatio why he didn't care about Rosencrantz and Guildenstern having their heads chopped off: "Why, man, they did make love to this employment.") No, I couldn't do that to poor Benn. Anyway, you could depend on him to take full charge of his own tormenting.

"Do you think that Matilda has the slightest idea . . . ?"

"Is she aware of the resemblance to her father? She sounded exactly like him when she said I should have kicked that drunk in the knackers."

"No, no. It's the rear view of the shoulders that I'm talking about."

Uncle said, "I always assumed that women assessed themselves to a painful degree. The good points give them satisfaction and the bad ones agony, generally greater than the satisfaction by a huge factor. So she must be aware. You can trust a woman to know her measurements."

"Men also know their measurements."

"Partly true," he said. "Sixteen and a half, with a thirty-five sleeve."

That wasn't exactly what I had in mind, but I kept my mouth shut.

And what if she wasn't the woman of his heart? He probably wasn't the man of *her* heart, either. There are people who advise you to leave the heart out of it altogether. It shouldn't figure, it's untrustworthy. In some cases the heart takes early retirement. A philosopher over at the university surprised me once by saying, "Your heart also can be a sophist." That one puzzled me for some time, but I think now that I perfectly grasp his idea. It's not a dependable criterion. Everybody pays the heart lip service, of course, but everybody is more familiar with the absence of love than with its presence and gets so used to the feeling of emptiness that it becomes "normal." You don't miss the foundation of feeling until you begin to look for your self and can't find a support in the affects for a self.

"It'll work out, Uncle," I said. "A man like you can't be expected to cover all the bases. Botany absorbed you. Then you had terrifying attacks from the sexual side of things—longed for a woman's love but didn't have the preparation you needed. Nobody is educated for it. You were right on the nail when you told that interviewer that bad as radiation is, more people die of heartbreak, yet nobody organizes against it. And you can't send for the Roto-Rooter man. Well, call me any time of the day or night. I can't figure how to help you, but I'm always available."

"Well, thank God for that."

"You were brave to tell me what's going on. Couldn't have been easy."

By the time I got back to my dormitory quarters I was in a mood which refused to be identified: mystified by Uncle, sad for him, but also—and this was odd—in high spirits, *angry* high spirits, assailing everybody, including myself. First of all, coming into my comfortless sanctuary, I wanted to throw out all the books and papers—the same books on which I depended for clarification, for keeping up with the twentieth century. After so much mental fussing, nothing was clear anyway. I had counted on Uncle Benn to set me straight on certain essentials, instead of which he needed help from me. He was burdened, bowed to the ground by the weight of Matilda Layamon's shoulders, which were heavier than solid bronze.

Well, here were my two rooms, the imitation-Gothic windows with a bleak north light, the gray plastic squares of the floor crying out for a carpet, with vermicular swarms of ingrained dirt. I had given up on creature comforts, without great gains from the sacrifice. I had a kitchenette and a tiny toilet (WC), and shared a shower with undergraduates. The college believed that it was good for the kids to associate with their learned elders; just as I had expected to benefit by associating with Uncle, a man of quality from whom there was so much to learn.

I used the bathroom and then, for quick energy, I ate a slab of Hershey's chocolate before sitting down to record my conversation with Uncle. Instead of throwing papers out, I added more papers.

In black and white, the facts looked terrible. Nobody bothered about Uncle as long as he was a harmless morphology freak, no more challenging than a collector of bird calls, but when he made a bid to enter society at a more significant level, he engaged the interest of people whose attention it was better to avoid. Could he plead unworldliness? No, because he perfectly understood anything he would set himself to understand. He simply preferred not to get into worldliness. He chose instead to be the harmless, innocent botanist who had married a high-stepping beauty, refusing to identify Matilda as the fatal emblem of something until his imagination took things subversively into its own hands. I don't understand why these quality minds have to justify the contempt in which they are held by the general public. Why was it necessary for the Father of Cybernetics to have his zipper checked by his wife before he left the house? And why doesn't the quality compel the respect of the bums who surround it?

At this moment, night having come down on Parrish Place, Uncle would be letting himself into the Layamons' apartment, go looking for his new wife and find her dressing for dinner. She might or might not say, "Hallo, there"; sometimes she was preoccupied with her fingernails, or shaving her legs, doing her hyacinth hair under the glow of golden boudoir light bulbs. Even when she was tending herself she was slightly fretful. What did she *really* think of her husband? Did he meet her expectations? Uncle never could be certain how he was doing. Matilda evidently thought it best to keep him guessing, and maybe it was this ambiguity that set loose those dark, unconscious forces, fusing her with Tony Perkins. Dressing, Matilda moved from mirror to mirror, chatting about arrangements still to be made for his lecture tour of the interior of Brazil. She would be (he was himself the first to say it) more beautiful than ever. Her low forehead—not unintelligent; many thought lines cross it—is intoxicating. But he is standing behind her and there again are the shoulders, still wide, still high, a curse and a doom. Can I get over this? he asks himself. He tests himself inwardly against this barrier, checks out his powers inwardly; the place at which he checks is becoming sore. He locates this at his diaphragm, since he is uncannily acute in self-observation. The muscle between the two rib arches now is painful to the touch. Surrounded by mirrors, he doesn't raise his eyes to look at himself, afraid to see his gloomy mad face. "Absolutely bonkers!" as he will later tell me, taking it all on himself. He goes out to the bar, which like her dressing room is illuminated glass, and pours a tumbler of gin to get him through dinner. Then at dinner he feels, he says, like the Sunday-supplement kids' puzzle—what is it that doesn't belong in this picture?

Out comes the palm-heart salad again, Doctor's favorite. That he should get what he wants is only fair, considering how hard he works. Matilda and her mother tell how the Bridal Bureau screwed up on the dessert dishes. The crates will be delivered to the Roanoke and stored in the pantry, where Jo will inspect them for breakage. Between courses, Benn dandles his head on his hand. Since he's seldom asked for his opinion (the oddity of his answers makes Matilda's parents fall silent; they don't know where the devil *he's* coming from), Uncle is free to brood. You can leave the talking to Doctor, who can be funny when he goes after those *yutzes* in City Hall, gets those salamandrine streaks on his face and lifts his brows like a Shavian wit. As usual, the Electronic Tower floats closer till it's right on top of them, bigger than ten *Titanic*s lashed together, every single window lighted and on a dead course for the penthouse. Sick with repulsive gratitude to the Layamons for letting him be one of them, choking on lies, accusing himself before God, crying out, "What have I done! Why am I here!" Benn works himself over. Most of his anger is directed at himself ("intrapunitive" is the clinical term for this) and he stares at his own evil, but since he always seems to be staring because of the anatomical idiomorphy of the eyes, nobody takes notice. Uncle wouldn't have been sorry to be rammed by the Electronic Tower right here at the dinner table. Let it happen! In this fancied Cecil B. De Mille collision, no harm would have come to Matilda. Only he himself would be deservedly punished.

I was going out to dinner myself. There was nothing to eat in this cold dormitory except the chocolate stashed away with my shirts. Dita had asked me over. She wasn't yet well enough to be seen in a restaurant, and on these winter evenings I was her only company. Next Monday her sick leave ended and she was going back to work. My dad had given me a bottle of Gevrey-Chambertin from his cellar. When I was a kid, a wine salesman used to come to the Rue Bonaparte to take Dad's order. I don't suppose there are any of those left even in Paris—such *bien élevé*, deferential civil people, in natty topcoats and polished shoes, wearing a homburg and holding kid gloves in one hand, and pretending that my father was superknowledgeable in wines. The smell that rose from the fellow's head when he removed his hat was so agreeable!

Dad handed me the wonderful bottle (Côte D'Or, Domaine Roy), saying, "This is good old stuff for a special occasion. Take it back to that damned city with you. It's good for cuts and bruises too, but you should use it internally." When I moved to the Midwest, my father took a subscription to the hometown paper and was better informed than I was myself. He occasionally referred in his letters to people stabbed in the streets, beaten to death in their beds by invaders, shot in city buses. He was worried for me although I lived in a protected enclave on which the university spent three million dollars a year for supplementary policing. I joked about it. "At least it's not Saigon or Beirut," I said. "Lots of people still live here in great comfort." I suppose I was referring to the Layamon category. Residential buildings like theirs, or the Roanoke, were under heavy security. Thanks to my studies, I spent more mental time in Petersburg, 1913, than in this Rustbelt metropolis. Men of my type do tend to fall back on books and theories. If you're an astrophysicist, it will never even enter your mind to spend a morning at the Violence Court. If you're an economist, you depend on market forces to predominate over local disorders. Disorder will disappear when the money supply is sensibly controlled. As for types like my own, obscurely motivated by the conviction that our existence was worthless if we didn't make a turning point of it, we were assigned to the humanities, to poetry, philosophy, painting—the nursery games of humankind, which had to be left behind when the age of science began. The humanities would be called upon to choose a wallpaper for the crypt, as the end drew near. And if there is no turning point, it will soon be time for the "esthetic" call. Thoughts like these are nearly as undermining as the problems they address.

> The tom-toms beating inside our heads, driving us crazy, are the Great Ideas!

I was preparing dinner conversation for Dita. She enjoyed this kind of thing and counted on me to provide it. I myself had a great weakness for table talk. Understanding amounts to nothing if you have nobody to communicate it to, and since there was no talking to Uncle now about such matters, Dita's value for my mental life (my secret life, if you prefer) rose considerably.

I put the bottle in a brown paper bag, hoping I wouldn't have to bring it down on the head of a mugger. One never knows in these streets, and I had one vacant lot to cross. I opened the door to the stone dormitory staircase, which smelled like the Middle Ages, and then remembered that I hadn't heard the telephone messages recorded on my machine.

The first message was from Fishl, my kinsman, who sounded hyper. I could tell from his voice alone that he was unshaven. He was wildly distracted. His dry, rapid lips told me, "My dad is coming up from Miami for some kind of business. He shouldn't take this trip in winter. Bad for his heart." Business? Fishl didn't know that his father would be attending the parole board hearing next day. "Does Benn know about his flying up? If so, be sure that he doesn't talk to Dad until I've worked out the right approach." Too late for that now. Dr. Layamon had given Benn press passes for the hearing. I was going to meet him downtown.

The second recorded message was from Tanya Sterling: "Housewares show is closing and as of this time I have not received the courteous reply I expected, I made you a bona fide proposition. Have retained private investigator in Seattle. Please communicate with me."

As to the bona fide proposition, she was not kidding. She was making a bid to take me over, just as Matilda had taken over Uncle. The very thing that Caroline Bunge had attempted. No way—no takeover. Not for me, thank you, ma'am. I clasped the bottle under my topcoat, actually looking forward to Dita's dinner. My room was so crummy, I might as well have been in solitary. I ran across the vacant-lot shortcut. In spite of the snow, some autumn burrs stuck to me. My tactic was to protect the Gevrey-Chambertin in case of a fall on the ice. My father wouldn't have approved of my sprinting—it shook up the sediment—but I was glad to get to Dita's door safely. Chambertin had been the celebrated Kojève's favorite wine. Father had always served it when he came to dinner.

Dita's apartment was very different from the Rue Bonaparte, but I was grateful for the warmth and color, the cooking odors. I wasn't always so big on domestic comforts, but tonight the weather was fierce, February sweeping over us with burning blasts from Montana. Her place was not up to Uncle's standard for cleanliness. Well, now he was in a penthouse with two servants. I didn't mind the hanging personal articles on the back of the bathroom door when I washed my hands and combed my hair at the basin. I came out and opened the wine to let it breathe, happy to be there. The cork was old but came out in one piece, and the wine was as good as my father had said it would be. "What's all the fuss in Europe about corks?" Dita asked. "I don't really know. Just a ritual," I said.

Dita did not set more store by cooking than by housekeeping. She was an intellectual woman, the kind that seldom eats well. Women who live alone lose all feeling for the kitchen. But the pilaf was tasty. "You're late," she said. "I took the pilaf out of the oven because it was starting to scorch. I tried for lamb, but all they had was mutton. Taste it and tell me what it needs."

It needed nothing. This dish was just as I like it, an accidental success, nearly burnt and therefore crusty.

"And this Chambertin is a present from my dad. It was a favorite with the great Kojève."

Dita was very pleased. "How nice to have you to myself these evenings."

Through me in this impressive but barbarous metropolis she enjoyed a connection with Europe, with Parisians and with Russian civilization. She looked attractive tonight, wearing a turban. (I suspect that she didn't like washing her hair. She used convalescence as an excuse. The shampoo stung her still sensitive face.) A woman with a well-developed figure, she had lips of the Moorish type, a nose perhaps fuller than my own criterion for noses could come to terms with and a solid face with nothing masculine in its solidity. Excepting some negligible defects, she was terribly handsome. Her skin was almost healed—an ice rink scarred by skate blades, was my figure for it. The scars would presently go away. When she had served the food and seated herself, she looked across the table with a woman's eye radiance directly informing me how much satisfaction she took in entertaining her teacher.

Teacher's thought was that his uncle was crying out to the Electronic Tower to ram the penthouse and put an end to his life.

Dita was saying, "This beautiful wine is wasted on me. In my family we drank boilermakers—whiskey with beer chasers. I'll stick with the Wild Turkey. You're the one with the palate, you drink the wine." I didn't argue with this; instead I reflected that drinking this Kojève wine, I might fall into the temptation of talking like Kojève and natter away about posthistorical man.

"Tell me," said Dita, "how's your uncle doing? He's a lucky man, to my mind. No, not because he became the husband of that recliner empress but because you love him. You came all the way from Europe to live near him."

"He was worth it. I still believe I did the right thing."

"You didn't follow that girl, Treckie, to Seattle. You didn't plead with her not to move. You stayed with your uncle."

"You think pleading would have made a difference? I stormed, I begged. I would have thrown myself in front of the airport bus, but in language she's an Esalen type, and in that jargon there aren't any words for certain things."

"I just can't see you throwing yourself in front of a bus. You might be able to think yourself under the wheels; that's as far as it would go. No matter how you tried, you couldn't do enough to suit her. She needs clutching, grabbing and rudeness. She'll never understand the motives of a person like you, nor put out the effort."

It was a melancholy subject, but it didn't make me feel bad altogether. I chased down the last grains of rice with my fork. Two thirds of the sensational wine had already been drunk. I didn't need to be told, I knew what Treckie was like, and although Dita was an interested party her opinion was not unfair, not unwanted. Treckie, that pale girl-aborigine, was a primitivist, she needed primitive sexual encounters. In a decade or two her tastes might change. I might, if I liked, hang around twenty or thirty years and wait for this reform.

Dita was wearing a cocoa-brown velveteen costume buttoned to the throat, the sleeves puffed at the wrists, not exactly suited to the kitchen. Her manners with the flatware were ladylike, she handled the fork with working-class delicacy, yet she opened her mouth wide for the food. She was a fine, strong, handsome woman who was afraid she didn't have enough breeding or elevation. You could hear this concern also in the downgliding of her phrases, and the made-up Anglo-Irish rise at the end. All that was forgotten when she laughed. When she laughed you saw her tongue and the fillings of her back teeth. Her color wasn't at all bad, that much the sadic dermatologist had done for her. Her black hair, all but the front covered by the turban, had a rising tendency, like quills. Still, she gave out womanly assurances of warmth—I mean intelligent, considerate warmth, sympathy with a man and true tact in dealing with him. This was what I call *basic,* the bottom line.

"Now, your uncle and his bride are going to Brazil?"

"In a couple of days, yes. He'll be back in May or June. Another long absence. After marriage he wouldn't travel so much, I hoped."

"Are you seeing much of him before he leaves?"

"As much as possible. Tomorrow morning we have to meet downtown. I have a great-uncle in politics—"

"Vilitzer. As if I didn't know."

"Uncle Benn needs to talk to him before leaving. Vilitzer is on the parole board and the board is sitting."

"Oh, that would be the Cusper case. Don't tell me," said Dita. "Being shut in, I read every scrap of print. It's been on television too. Is that where you're going?"

"They've given us press passes."

"Good grief, they're at a premium. It's the biggest show in town. The governor himself is running it."

"Matilda's father has lots of clout. He arranged the passes."

"I can't think of two less likely people for such an event. This is not your uncle's line of country."

"Nor mine?"

"Well, you aren't a hockey or football fan and don't follow the Indianapolis races or Dr. What's-her-name's sex-advice program on TV. She tells women with love problems to go to the grocery and buy a nice firm cucumber. You don't even watch Johnny Carson to find out what your fellowman is up to."

"I don't think I'm quite so out of it as Uncle."

"You don't belong to the full community. You and your uncle have been absorbed in each other. When I'm into research on Scriabin and Kandinsky, this kind of thing passes me by too. Do you know what the Cusper case is about? Of course you don't. I'll brief you. There's a young man named Sickle serving a sentence for rape in the state penitentiary. The victim's name is Danae Cusper. Her testimony put him behind bars. But she's been born again and she's had a religious change of heart. Now she says he didn't rape her at all, she made it up. Her spiritual counselor tells her she must speak the truth. This is what her conscience demands."

"How long has he been in jail?"

"Six or seven years. Such a noise has been made about the innocent young man that they've let him out on bond. Governor Stewart has taken personal charge of the deliberations of the parole board. The Sickle boy's rap sheet has been published. The paper must have paid somebody in the Police Department a pretty penny for it, and it's quite a document. Items like 'Criminal trespassing to vehicle.' 'Retail theft.' 'Nol-pros but with fine.' Then the big case, 'Aggravated kidnapping and rape. Victim forcibly abducted by three male persons and raped in the back seat.'" Dita had picked up the paper from the floor and was reading it to me. "'Suspect's underpants confiscated and examined for loose pubic hairs. Loose hairs combed from victim's genital area for comparative analysis by forensic experts.'"

"It's some sex show, then," I said.

"Why do you think it's such a big hit on TV? At the original trial, Danae Cusper gave convincing testimony. She now says she lied because she had been having sexual relations with another fellow, thought she was pregnant and was terrified of her strict parents. Now she can't rest easy until she has atoned before God. She asks the poor victim's forgiveness. They meet in front of the cameras and shake hands. She's a different person altogether, married to a fellow named Bold, a matron and the mother of children. Her heartfelt prayers for justice have moved many viewers. She makes a clean-living impression. Her true story has been sold to the movies by her lawyer for an undisclosed figure."

"So that's where we're going."

"Yes. And I wonder what your uncle will make of it."

"Him? He's seen some pretty raunchy shows in his time. Getting away from all this upsetting disturbed sexuality was what he intended."

"That's why he married Miss Layamon. She's a friend of Marguerite Duras, I hear."

"My mother introduced them."

"I read that woman's novel about the French girl-child in Saigon who did all that prurient sex with a Chinaman. Didn't she also do Hiroshima with sex? And the French Resistance with sex? At one time there's an affair with a French collaborator. It was more or less a patriotic duty. Wasn't that nice! I wonder what made your uncle think he was coming into a safe harbor with the American pal of this lady."

"I think she's through with that existential-political literary lechery," I said.

"When the newlyweds come back from Brazil they'll move into the Roanoke. I've been in that building. Also, I took the tour to Franz Josef's royal residence when I was in Vienna, and I suppose the Kremlin is similar."

"Oh, the Kremlin! After that Fanny woman shot him, Lenin was crying for death because he couldn't control his sphincters and was humiliated."

Dita made a graceful openmouthed pause before she asked, "What's the connection?"

Variously stimulated by the Gevrey-Chambertin, the comfort of dinner, by the warmth and color in the room, I was unusually—that is, emotionally—open to associations. It was esthetically intoxicating to entertain them all. Furthermore, it was characteristic—it was me: me as it excited me to be, fully experiencing the fantastic, the bizarre facts of contemporary reality, making no particular effort to impose my cognitions on them. I didn't especially wish to make sense; I wanted only to follow the intoxicating flow of those facts.

"Well, how will your uncle like it at the Roanoke?" she said.

"About as well as an egg likes cold storage. It'll keep but never taste good."

"And what is he up to professionally?"

"Morphological something of Arctic lichens. I never studied botany. All I can say is that lichens are both algae and fungi. At fifty below zero they freeze. As soon as the sun shines they perk up, millennium after millennium. It makes me think of the little glaciers in civilized breasts. Yermelov, my first Russian teacher and also my guru, may have been a poor old crank. He deposited this image of ice with me. Lots of Russian exiles lost their marbles in the West. There were shops in Saint-Germain-des-Pres doing a big business in Madame Blavatsky, Ouspensky, Hermes Trismegistus and the Cabala. Russians are very big on that. My grandfather Crader also talked about Jewish mysticism—the Tree of Knowledge and the Tree of Life. (That Tree of Life is buried a thousand feet below the Electronic Tower.) Uncle denies the influence of the Tree, but he may well have been influenced. I think he works like a contemplative, concentrating without effort, as naturally as he breathes, no oscillations of desire or memory: like calm waters, Yermelov would say, and deep—they are so deep. That's how he is with plants. But you have to reckon with the rest of life, and you'd better reckon shrewdly or you'll be sorry."

"Able to meet the requirements of science but not of women?" asked Dita.

"That's not a fair way to put it. They're drawn to him too. He carries a charge, and they sense it. I understand, by the way, that lichens can get nutrients from the air when they have to—like the mythical air-eating creatures. Jews are tempted to think of themselves in that way sometimes—accepting assignments of such difficulty. In the Old Country they didn't actually make it. I see where there are only seventy or eighty Jews left in Venice, and almost none in Saloniki and other Greek communities where mystical studies were pursued under the Ottomans. All that is gone."

"Sounds to me as if you believed your uncle would have been better off with the erotic part left out."

"I hope that by and by he'll tell me what that's been about. A funny thing about him is that he *can* tell you what's going on, once he decides to take the trouble. It's all there, in his head. I can't do that."

"You're trying to tell me what his attraction is."

"I can manage that, all right. Uncle is a true person. Never deviates from his original, given nature. He may try to get away, he'll dodge for a while, but in the end he'll come clean. He stands before the bench and tells all. I admire that. Also, I'm shocked by it, and sometimes it seems downright dumb. If you're all of a piece, and if they should find you an obstacle, they'll just cut you down."

"You don't like that beautiful Matilda, do you?"

"Why shouldn't a man want a beautiful wife? If he's going to renounce all others, he might as well get a beauty. Only the present happens to be an all-time world climax, a peak of genius for external perfection and high finish. Look at Delicious apples from the state of Washington created by pomologists, or a Bugatti sports car by Italian engineers. Heartless beauty has never been so wonderful. But with men and women, human warmth is poured into the invention. When there's light and heat in the eyes and cheeks of a woman, you can't positively tell if it's genuine. Does your beauty yearn for love, for a husband, or is she after a front man, a suitable cover for her beauty operations?"

"You don't really believe it's nothing but a trap."

"Of course I don't, but there are too many human variables to keep track of. For instance, Uncle may have known very well that he was going to be deceived, and he wills the deception as much as she does, because it excites him. Or else he will spoil beauty by exaggerating trifling defects. A crazy fastidiousness comes over him and he picks on the beloved. He fixes on her knuckles or the shape of her ears. Or else she's got a tiny birthmark, like the otherwise faultless beauty in the Hawthorne story. Aylmer, the crazy scientist, kills her when he removes the mark. Well, you know what the old books say—Dionysus and Hades are one and the same, the god of life and the god of death are one and the same god, meaning that life for the species demands the death of the individual."

"Oh, sure, all that was in the Soloviev course I took from you."

Not only was I her teacher, but she had taken my Russian Seminar 451 on The Meaning of Love. No wonder she had submitted her face to be punished by that devil dermatologist and his high-speed sandpaper disks. Never the same after my seminar. Another shadow on my conscience.

"Dita, I can't tell you how much this Layamon business has taught me. For instance, Dr. Layamon, talking to Uncle about impotency (and why did he do that!), said that a man didn't have to worry about gratifying a woman as long as he had a big toe, a thumb, a knee, the stump of an arm, a nose. Ladies are very accepting nowadays, they've learned it's the spirit that counts, and if they care for you it doesn't matter all that much to them. On the other hand, Vilitzer's son Fishl told me that it was a common feminine fantasy to put together an ideal man. No real person has everything they dream of, so they assemble parts and elements from here and there—a large cock, a sparkling personality, millions of dollars, a bold brilliant spirit like Malraux, the masculine attraction of Clark Gable in *Gone With the Wind,* the manners of a French aristocrat, the brain of a superman in physics."

Dita laughed wildly, and then said, "Don't do that to me. My face is still too sore for me to open my mouth so wide."

"Make your own synthetic person."

"Different from the true person you said your uncle was."

"Most are fabricated, usually by themselves."

"So you assemble according to your taste."

"You can also dismantle, dismember, as fetishists do. They don't want a full order of person, only a lock of hair, or a woman's shoe or her apron. The rest they don't need. Take it back to the kitchen."

"Now, who is going through that?" said Dita. "What makes you bring it up?"

I gave her a long, silent look—I wasn't going to betray Uncle's secret (those shoulders!) simply to satisfy her curiosity or to make myself interesting at his expense. She looked just as steadily at me and said, finally, "I think your eyes are placed higher and wider in the head than most people would consider normal."

"To go back to what I was saying, there's always some dislocation in the relations between men and women, some transfiguring intoxication, as M. Kojève would say—*enivrement*. The mirrors of Circe, their glittering magic. It's goodbye to reality when love sets in. Kojève would say such things when he was getting near the bottom of the bottle. . . . I wouldn't like him to hear me reporting him; I'm not a philosopher myself and I'm not sure I'm getting him right. I still trace my weakness for the big overview back to him."

"Right on," Dita encouraged me.

"On my way to the Rue du Dragon and my Russian-conversation lesson, a mere kid, I felt like a cosmic crumb floating in the streets of what used to be the capital of the world. The Germans were driven out before I was born. From the fighting in the streets, some buildings to this day are pockmarked by people who hadn't known much about aiming a gun. In the fifties there was still a kind of Chinese disorder about Paris, but we were comfortable on the Rue Bonaparte and Mother set a good table. I was allowed to sit in for dessert and listen to Kojève talk about the end of history and how Man was released now to be *happy*—maybe. He could play around, if he liked, with Art and Love. He didn't have to negate the Given anymore. He was freed from historical struggle to be the most privileged of animals. Kojève talked about abundance and security in the posthistorical epoch and he said that the modern project—enlightenment, science, democracy—had found its main expression and success in the U.S.A. America had done it all without a proletarian dictatorship. China and Russia were just retarded cases. You couldn't expect a mere boy to understand all this, but I was struck with it, and it was absolutely clear that I'd have to go to the U.S.A., where the action was. Russia was an underdeveloped U.S.A., it was the country mouse of materialism. The Americans are members of a virtually classless society, appropriating whatever attracts them without overworking themselves. Money, goods, sports, toys and sexual candy are the forms of the payoff."

"Back to sex again," said Dita.

"Not quite," I said. It was the ordeal of desire as I had attempted, without mentioning Kojève, to describe it to my mother. Only Kojève would have seen it not as our ordeal but as decadence.

At this moment I felt it necessary to get up from the table and reach for my topcoat. I had a big day tomorrow, and an early date with Uncle for breakfast, I explained, and I had had a lot to drink. Dita didn't try to wheedle me into staying; she was too fond of me to make difficulties. Only one remark she allowed herself, and this was: "You'd be wasting your time with a woman who didn't enjoy hearing you talk—a woman who had no clue as to what you were saying, or what you're all about. I see I'm going to have to rethink my view of your attachment to your uncle. I had it wrong."

"Take care," I said.

In the night there came an extraordinary phone call from Uncle Benn. The illuminated clock dial stood at two-ten.

"What's wrong, for God's sake?"

He hadn't committed a crime, had he? My first thought.

"I had to talk to you, Kenneth, to help me get a grip on myself."

"Are you in the penthouse?"

"I dressed and went down to the laundry room. It's a coin telephone."

"Let's have the number and I'll call back, otherwise we'll be cut off."

"Nine six two eight four oh five."

When we were reconnected, he said he had switched off the lights in the laundry room so as not to be seen by the night watchman.

"You couldn't call from the apartment?"

"I wouldn't take a chance on being heard."

"What are you in the middle of?"

"We had a conference last night about Vilitzer. I can't begin to tell you—"

"What matters is what Matilda is saying."

"She says Vilitzer *must* pay up. We aren't depriving *him* of anything, he won't live long enough to spend much of those corrupt millions, so it's just the estate—my cousins. *I* can't understand anyway what there is to spend the money on—what is there so great to *buy*? When I sleep in a hotel I wonder who did what in those sheets and nasty blankets. There's always a blanket odor. I can understand why Madame Chiang, Evita Perón or Imelda Marcos had to have their own bedding—silk sheets. But does that justify a dictatorship?"

"Your wife shouldn't be putting heat on you. Vilitzer did screw you, but the money he surrenders—if he surrenders at all—won't be under *your* control."

"I can tell Doctor has already made his arrangements with that ox-face Amador Chetnik. The judge is bound for prison and he's dying for a deal to shorten his sentence and give him some cash for a new start in life when he gets out."

"Yes, I understood that before. No use repeating. Did you argue with them?"

"I don't want Harold to come to harm through *me*."

"That's what Fishl said. The state of Uncle Harold's health. His heart condition is bad."

"Harold showed me disrespect in the Electronic Tower deal."

"That doesn't mean that you have to give him a coronary. In one of our talks, Uncle, one of us said that this big money gives you the maximum opportunity to abuse yourself. Yet somehow I feel that you want the money. *You,* for some reason, would like to have it!"

He cried, "That's just not true."

"Maybe not for the money's sake alone. I don't know. Schopenhauer said that money was abstract happiness. *Maybe* it was Hegel."

"For the love of God, Kenneth. Not *now*. I've always been satisfied with my salary. I never touched a penny of Lena's insurance. Some of it was in Homestake Mining, the only stock I own. Her personal savings account is still in the bank."

"Now, suppose you *had* money. The Layamons would tighten their grip on you. It would give Matilda more power. You can't hold much over a man who hasn't got anything. If there's nothing you can take away from him, what's there to threaten him with? I figure, Uncle, that if you do want money, it's mostly because you're looking for independent strength. But that's not the kind of strength necessary to cope with those Layamons. So you're better off without."

"I couldn't sleep. I'm too agitated tonight. I got out of bed. . . ."

"Does it upset you sometimes to be lying next to her?"

"I may as well admit . . . Those rooms are overheated too, and I sweat under the eiderdown. Do women need more covers at night than men? I had trouble breathing."

"In the Berkshires, you were afraid to go back to the woods with her after seeing that film. That's the upset I refer to."

"*That!* That comes and goes. I'm learning to handle it. I'm sure I'll be able to. I can live down those fantasy impulses. I'm not going to be controlled by anything so stupid."

"Then you're having an anxious crisis about confronting Uncle Harold."

"Believe me, I'm not afraid of Uncle Vilitzer. And I intend to put it to him nicely."

"That you're going to sue him? That Amador Chetnik will admit the case was fixed? *Nice* blackmail?"

"I don't intend to let it get out of control. Kenneth, listen, there was a movie tonight that upset me before bedtime. I have to tell *you* about it. These films are phony, but my heart beats faster nevertheless. This was a German thriller. The hero was a fat decent German with a thick mustache. He's taking lab tests because a fatal disease is suspected. The man doesn't have the disease. However, a French hoodlum comes to him with falsified data from the clinic and says, 'You're dying anyway and you have nothing to leave your wife and little boy. I want you to kill a man for me. There's big dough in it for you. I'll provide transportation, hotel, the gun and the plan. All you have to do is waylay him in the metro.' So the nice German goes and murders a stranger in Paris. Then he's sent to kill someone else on the Munich express. This I didn't follow at all. He's supposed to strangle his victim in the toilet, throttle him with a rope. An American buddy turns up to help. No rhyme or reason. Who is this American? A big moment comes when the nice German is trapped in the toilet with the corpse by the conductor knocking for a ticket. The German can't find his ticket. The corpse has one, though, so he slips it under the door. There isn't a single motive for any of this, not even the dream type. Nothing makes sense, except your heart racing, and you get a kind of prickly heat under the arms and even between your toes. What's that for? It ain't catharsis, that's for sure. It's just an inside adrenaline bath. If the characters tried to explain, you couldn't hear their explanations because of the sound effects—train engines, autobahn noises, jet planes, heavy breathing, sirens and guns, and even the little boy has toys that crackle while the grownups are scheming. Logic is removed from all behavior, no coherence. The people who are wasted, blown away, seem to deserve to die. They belong to the underworld, so who cares. Some guy wrapped in bandages like Claude Rains in the picture *The Invisible Man* is killed in a booby-trapped ambulance. There's an explosion and a fire. He must have been wicked too, so why take it to heart?"

"Did you watch until the very end?"

"Yes, and the nice German turned out to have that fatal disease after all. The viewer is affected physiologically, he pumps more adrenaline, but nothing more than physiology is affected. There's no judgment—only respiration, heart rate, blood pressure; prickly heat if you're more sensitive. And that's it."

"It shook you up."

"Well, I don't want to have to tell you. . . ."

"You went to look at your azalea in Jo Layamon's office."

"Of course, I touched base. It was the same with the balsam fir when we were married."

"Maybe the intoxication with Matilda's beauty was already wearing off by your wedding day. If you needed additional support from the plant world . . . In the Berkshires, you already were beginning to suspect that her beauty was a delusion. Your judgment was that she was a marvelous girl, but your instinct intervened and told you not to do it. Don't get into it! You were warned. So now you're all shook up by a mere movie—it's one lousy movie after another. Naturally you're aware that bad art can finally cripple a man."

"Just a minute, Kenneth—the watchman is shining his light

into this place. . . . Okay, he's gone, I'm in the dark again. The bulb in the booth goes on when you pull the folding door shut. It's true I was shaken when I got into bed. Undressing, Matilda talked about Vilitzer, while I was realizing that the luxury of the sleeping arrangements were alien to my style of life. I was scared to feel my pulse."

"What was she saying about Vilitzer, then?" I asked.

"Not to worry about him because this was the way he had always lived. He wasn't called the Big Heat for nothing. He had put the heat on lots of people. He squeezed one fellow's head in a vise. He's got to expect to perish by the sword since he took up the sword. He's a realist and I shouldn't apply my standards to people who piled up millions, because all along the line standards like mine gave them the openings they needed. Politics are special that way. He's been in politics for fifty years and I should leave it to politicians to deal with him. I should also consider that I have a family by marriage that at last will protect my interests."

I said, "I can't do much to help unless you level with me, Uncle. When you get into bed, or when you watch her getting ready for bed, do you still notice the shoulders? I mean, do they loom large?"

"Not always. I'm learning to live with them. I sometimes do have bad reactions."

"That woman's build is not quite right. Now that you've called attention to it, I can't shake off your vision of it."

"Oh, Kenneth, if only she resembled her mother in that respect, not Doctor."

"Uncle, in a way you're an artist and artists see nothing as it is, they aren't made that way. The way you see things brings out the independent powers of the phenomena. You can't be expected to control that, or discriminate sensibly. The higher the range of vision, the more your control is weakened. The way you saw Caroline, for instance, made it impossible for you to defend yourself against her."

Uncle cried, "Why are Matilda's breasts so far apart!"

"Are they so far apart?" He took me aback with this.

"She isn't wide only across the shoulders but also in front. There's a lot of space between the two of them."

"What difference should space make, Uncle? For some men more space might be the ideal. Don't you think?"

"Should make has nothing to do with it. It *does* make a difference. I'm not asking for a sensible interpretation, I'm telling you how it *is*. The distance between them has an effect on me."

"So you need them closer together. Excuse me, Uncle, but you knew this early on. If your heart went behind a cloud when you became aware of it, you still were single. If it was unesthetic, if it was repugnant—well, repugnant is a powerful judgment."

"Okay, but also she was very beautiful."

"A mistake has been made. You might have waited awhile. Were you in a hurry to ruin yourself, or what?"

"Ruin? What do you mean? I married a beautiful woman. Highly educated, lots of culture, all kinds of charm, wonderful company, a wife who'll be a credit to me. It's possible still to work out all these irrational reactions. I'm not going to surrender to them. Listen to me, Kenneth. I'm not completely naive. In college I read all those clinical sex books—Havelock Ellis, Freud, Krafft-Ebing. It's no news to me that men who marry beautiful women often are suspected of homosexuality. They count on such women to attract admiring men. But I don't like seeing Dr. Layamon's shoulders on her. I don't want to draw the attention of men. It was revolting to identify her with Tony Perkins. I *hated* that! Of course it was my mind, my own mind, that did it. It's one of those unaccountable desire-repulsion intrusions. Okay, beauty! What was it that arose before me that I'm calling 'beauty'? I was drawn to have sex with *perfection*. There was nothing homoerotic about it."

"You were going to do something sublime with her. Well, there's another side to it: What thing was she going to do with you?"

"I wasn't up to this *perfection*. Sexually, I didn't seem equal to it."

"Maybe she was for admiration, not for mating. But now you're pulling her apart, distorting her. I had dinner with Dita Schwartz tonight and we were talking about fetishism. Those unhappy sex cripples can fall in love with a woman's foot. You're a negative fetishist and fall *out* of love with Matilda's shoulders. But it's still fragmentation or disintegration."

"You're making more sense to me than usual now. I need ideas from you, Kenneth. Tell me more. I always had the power to fall in love. I knew it was in me."

"You loved Matilda?"

"I'll tell you, she had the makings of a beloved."

"Are you trying to tell me after all this that you truly loved her?"

"Not in every aspect, no. But in a way, yes. Hit me on the head with a hammer and I see ten Matildas. One of those I love passionately."

I actually removed the phone from me and wondered how such a thing could come out of the earpiece. I said, "This is one of the damnedest conversations I ever had."

"Is that so different from the way you love Treckie? Do you love the Treckie who shacks up with bruisers, one after another?"

The heart went out of me and I didn't want to continue. I wasn't *married* to Treckie. More to the point, she wasn't married to me, perhaps because she had made observations of me comparable to the ones Benn had made of Matilda. Some radical obstructions or unknowable impediments can turn us off.

When you're awakened in the middle of the night, your lower ego lords it over you. Your better self is slow to come back. Or maybe it's just vanity—your sleep has been disturbed and you'll look terrible tomorrow, rings under your eyes, a wrinkled face, a dull gaze. The lower ego is wildly narcissistic. If you're going to say mean things, you'll say them in these circumstances. In the present instance I spoke them in a soliloquy, reminding myself that after all I held Benn dear, he was in a crisis and it would be unforgivable to ride him. If there were harsh comments, I'd keep them in the vault. Thinking of Benn at the Roanoke as an egg in cold storage, I told him mentally that he could anticipate a zero life with Matilda. What had he to expect? Ten years in storage. And why should anybody impose a cold-storage sentence on himself and give away a whole decade of his life? In Russia the government will send you to Siberia. Here you do it to yourself. Now, there's a real *acte gratuit*. Benn was miles ahead of André Gide. Pushing a stranger off the express train is nothing compared to this. So what do big-shot Russian exiles mean when they say *their* country is on the rack? What's going on, a superpower rivalry over suffering? Or maybe it's we, on this side, who claim everything, the highest standard of living, and of suffering too. Certain Russians declare: "We on the rack, *we* have culture. You, nerveless flabby spoiled decadents, are out of it." This is what I was telling Mother (a haunting failure!) in Somalia, the peculiar ordeals on *this* side. It's true we don't make a good showing, the best we can do is a pain schedule, but that's because we don't face up to our unique ordeal. Anyway, this was the last thing that Uncle needed to hear from me.

He said again, from the dark laundry room, "I'm asking for your ideas, Kenneth. Scientists are so weak in the humanities. Lena got me to read a few books but she didn't have your chance at a complete education. Give me a psychological assist. Recommend something."

"I wouldn't advise you to get into psychology, Uncle. You don't need that. It's love that makes the difference, Uncle. These defects jump out at you because love punishes you for drafting it against its will; it's one of those powers of the soul that won't be conscripted. It makes beauty, it makes strength; sometimes for special purposes, when really inspired, it even produces new organs. Without it, critical consciousness simply reduces all comers to their separate parts, it disintegrates them. Many another man if he wasn't happy in his wife's bed, if her breasts or shoulders pained him, would brazen it out, he'd fake it, he'd make hypocritical adjustments."

"I don't know, Kenneth," said Uncle, very discouraged. "Why should I fight Uncle to obtain millions for a woman whose breasts are so far apart? It's getting beyond me. Maybe I can get the name of a good psychoanalyst in Rio."

"A Portuguese analysis on top of all this! Don't do it, Benn, stay away from treatment. Freud taught that love was *overvaluation*. That is, if you saw the love object as it really was, you *couldn't* love it. That's the clinical view of things, straight from gynecological wards. This was what Dr. Layamon was illustrating when he showed you all those bald old privates. At home, because he has a pretty daughter, he talks up love, but where he practices his profession and makes his money, at the hospital, where the real action is, he gives you an exhibit of the truth. Now, maybe a man does lie to himself when he's in love, but as Kojève sometimes would say—I think he got this from Nietzsche—in love he lies well and it transfigures him, it makes him rich, more powerful, fuller, it makes him an artist. Without it, only a fraction of him is alive and that fraction isn't enough to sustain a real life—that's why *teams* have become so necessary."

"*Not* to get help in Rio? I suppose I can wait till we get back."

"Uncle, listen. I'm going to tell you things I mainly keep to myself. You're an imaginative man, that's your strength. Don't go into reverse now. Most people start at the other end, by trying to cure their weaknesses of character and especially their sexual failings. They go back to birth traumas and sphincter control. Everybody is born weak and sick and oppressed by Oedipal forces, but they believe if they apply themselves to the experiences of infancy and focus strongly on their diapers and the crucifixion of helpless littleness, they'll become giants of insight, the great-souled men Aristotle talked about. Now, Uncle, why should you play this game nobody has ever won? You're already far ahead of it."

"I've got a light in the booth now and I've been taking notes on this envelope from the gas company."

"Don't spend your whole life exploring your weaknesses."

"You've been telling me for years that democrats take a low view of themselves, and are brought up to believe they're insignificant. But turn *that* around and you come out with megalomania, and we've seen plenty of examples of that too. One thing you and Matilda may have in common is that you both see politics at the bottom of everything. Well, the watchman is coming into the laundry room."

"Well, what about it? You live in the building, don't you, you're from the penthouse. Tell him you're having a conference with your stockbroker in California."

"Thanks, Kenneth, for listening to me."

"Go and get some rest. We're meeting at half past eight."

I turned off the bed lamp, thinking, Now we've got a front problem as well as a back problem. I felt low on Uncle's account, and a little on my own too. He was a naturally temperate and reasonable fellow, and the more he drove himself into ways he believed to be sensible, the more screwy he seemed to become. And look at me: He calls me to say he's drowning in troubles and I lecture him—my way of being helpful. I've got all this elaborate string on my fingers and I'm playing cat's cradle with him. "Here, you take this over, and then I'll take it from you and God only knows how complicated we can make it and how far we can go." As long as we're talking about democratic peoples, we may as well add that they're pedantic and sententious too. Ten minutes of action and the rest of the hour is a seminar. No, these cognitive efforts will never get us anywhere. What I had wanted to say to Uncle was that he should be more like—well, more like William Blake, whose life was governed by metaphysical and esthetic concerns. Put your strengths first and let the weaknesses catch up as they may. Blake was just the man for Uncle. He might begin with the poem called "The Crystal Cabinet":

> The Maiden caught me in the Wild,
> Where I was dancing merrily;
> She put me into her Cabinet
> And Lock'd me up with a golden Key.
>
> This Cabinet is form'd of Gold
> And Pearl Crystal shining bright . . .

But the next morning, instead of William Blake we got Charles Addams. Benn had torn the page out of Jo Layamon's *Monster Rally* and handed it to me, smiling—or the nearest thing to a smile that had crossed his face in days.

"What do you think of this?"

It was the cartoon graveyard with its stones and yews, the quirky figures on the bench holding hands:

> "Are you unhappy, darling?"
> "Oh yes, *yes*! Completely."

"Make me a statement on this," Uncle challenged.

"It speaks for itself," I said.

"Far beyond Alfred Hitchcock. Really contemporary."

"I hope you didn't show it to Matilda. I don't think it's so contemporary. You can find it in Shakespeare. Hamlet tells Ophelia to marry a fool, if she must marry, 'for wise men know well enough what monsters you make of them.'"

"Of course I didn't show it to her."

"Does she understand how hard you try to please her—how you knock yourself out, even sacrificing your science? And all you ask is some return of feeling?"

"It's true. I do long for the feeling. But she always seems to be departing. I come in, she goes out. The pursuit never seems to end. What did Hamlet mean by 'monster'?"

"I think he meant a cuckold—the horned monster."

"I don't think that would apply."

"You're the monster that deforms her in your mind—that's how you see it."

We were having one of our typical conversations, at a typical restaurant table with inferior coffee and not quite enough space for four elbows, not to mention two cups, an ashtray, a ketchup bottle, a plastic container of sugar packets and pink nonfattening sweeteners.

"Without you, Kenneth, I might not be able to face Uncle Harold. At the last minute, Matilda offered to come with me. She said, 'If you'll tell your nephew to stay home, I'll go downtown with you.' I told her no."

He wanted me to see how resolute he had been with her. All I could see was how shook up he was. The direct reference to Matilda's sexual habits had no parallel. Then, too, the resemblance to Sviatoslav Richter was stronger than ever, but it was a Richter who had been sick to his stomach in the night and was green and pale. Behind his powerful eyes the switch appeared to be disengaged, as if he were on the watch for something really worth looking at. A heavyset man silently transmitting anxiety, mortification. He drywashed his face with all ten fingertips and pressed the hinges of his jaw to relieve the tension. I knew him so well that I could interpret the least of his gestures. He was for taking a firm grip on life. It was a brief, blind thing and he thought it should be handled with spirit. He judged people by what they did with it. Present circumstances, however, couldn't have been less propitious, farther from the high level of his philosophy: We were about to join the parole board, which would hear testimony on a rape, and then he would have to corner Uncle Vilitzer long enough to state his demands. Hinted threats, not my uncle's cup of tea. Also, he risked betraying mismanagement of his sexual life. The tacit disclosure of damaging facts was a possibility hovering near. If he faltered or stammered, shrewd old Vilitzer would conclude that he was a sexually failed husband with a wife who had the whip hand, sending him on errands. With sex troubles, men *always* faulted the husband.

All that was implicit.

And then there was the building where the hearing was held, a new structure like a gargantuan glass pregnancy, expanded over more than a city block, the work of a provocative, controversial architect trying to outdo the excesses of a similar building in Chicago: "Making his statement," as Caroline Bunge enjoyed saying. You believed in eternity when you saw a skyscraper like this, if only for what comfort there might be in the thought that such a structure couldn't last forever. It *had* to come down at last. But all this curvilinear, bulging glitter was set in Japanese steel, so it was good for half a century at least, unless enraged mobs tore it down or the transpolar flight of a Russian missile (fifteen minutes from launch to target) disintegrated it. The interior made an even deeper impression. You could see why there had been a scandalous cost overrun. Some of the wild genes of the younger Brueghel or Hieronymus Bosch must have flared up in the architect. I did my utmost to grasp his conception. Billions of brain-born wasps working in the blue glass had made this mammoth round structure; it was designed in dazzling elliptic curves modeled on the celestial sphere and it showed what bold fantasy could realize, relying on the skills of engineers, on miraculous technology. *"Humongous!"* said Uncle Benn.

It didn't threaten Heaven, like the Tower of Babel, but subsided from the heights and melted downwards. A computerized bureaucracy no longer needed straight corridors. Bizarre surroundings didn't lessen its efficiency or its power to intimidate. We followed the signs to the great hall where the hearing was under way. The TV cameras were already in place and turning, the lights were beating down on the stage. Our press passes entitled us to front seats, but Uncle preferred to place himself to Uncle Vilitzer's rear. Vilitzer sat at the long table with the rest of the board, headed by the governor, who took charge (without precedent) of the inquiry. Witnesses came as summoned to a smaller table opposite the long one. Members of the board seldom if ever were asked to speak.

"There he is," said Benn, indicating Vilitzer with his chin. "Quite changed. The big ravages come between sixty and eighty, and he's past eighty now."

Vilitzer was smaller in stature than he had been five years earlier, but he still had the imperial bearing of big-heat politicians from these parts. He combed his hair forward too, in the manner of the television version of *I, Claudius*. (Excuse me for mentioning this, but the following is a matter of possible interest: Julia, the daughter of Augustus, represented in the film as profligate, recklessly licentious, seems in her orgies to have had a political intent, since she and her partners did the acts of darkness under a statue of Marsyas the satyr, and Marsyas stood for republicanism. Why a half-bestial sex demon should be a guardian of Roman freedom I haven't the slightest idea; all I can say is that Julia's debauchery was a political challenge to her father, the founder of the empire.) Anyway, Uncle Vilitzer had adopted the hairstyle of the BBC actor who played Claudius. It seems popular with the senior Mafiosi, whom you often see with a small, slightly curled fringe. Otherwise they have rugged faces, deeply tanned, as a rule. And that was Uncle Vilitzer for you too. He chewed cigars, he didn't smoke them. He mashed up some twenty a day.

In such a crowd, Vilitzer was not likely to spot Uncle and me. It had to be a big event, for it had brought out Governor Stewart himself. Governors can no longer afford to be so remote. In the old days, said Benn, you seldom saw them. Television had forced them out of their mansions. These highly publicized hearings were being viewed by millions this morning. Because he was away on a holiday during the big salmonella scare of recent weeks, the governor had been widely criticized, and this parole board hearing at which he was conspicuously doing public business was made to order for him.

(Raising his job-approval ratings.) I had never seen him in person. He was a loosely massive man. In his slackness there were highly organized tensions, and I would have said that he was a dangerous person, a mean fighter. His face was very large, with so many tucks and folds under his chin that if he had been a violinist, I thought, it would have been hard for him to decide where to put the fiddle.

We sat just behind the principal witnesses, and I recognized most of them from the newspapers Dita had shown me. Danae Cusper was a handsome, solid, fair-haired lady, mother of three children. Sickle, the alleged rapist, was not far away, with his lawyer. Years in prison had not given him the looks of a threatening criminal. The prisons no longer produce desperadoes or *louche* types with Bill Sykes faces. In public a young man like Sickle manages somehow to resemble his own mother's ideal picture of a fundamentally decent son. In the foreground were the crews of the major networks. On this morning the kiddies' cartoon shows had been bumped. For millions of children it was the parole board hearing or nothing. And maybe the kids would weather this better than Uncle would. Nor was it to his credit to be an innocent at his time of life. He had no claim to immunity. Remember, however, that when the Crystal Cabinet finally burst, the young man who had been locked in it became "A weeping Babe upon the Wild."

But never mind these abstruse considerations.

Vilitzer did not turn his head to observe his enemy the governor. He looked straight ahead. As for the governor, he ran the interrogations with relish and exhibited his finest skills, perfected in the courtroom. Before grand juries he must have been a formidable examiner—he was so big, sleek, thick in the throat, so smoothly groomed, fine as silk before the cameras but rough as hell in the interior.

His first witness was a young serviceman, formerly one of Danae's boyfriends. She had testified yesterday that she was afraid he had made her pregnant, and that the rape charge was directly due to her love affair with him. The governor asked, had he had sexual connections with Danae, the present Mrs. Bold, then Miss Cusper? Yes. Under what circumstances? When her parents were sleeping, she would let him into the house. How had she been dressed? In a nightgown. And the sex act? From 2 A.M. until daybreak. With ejaculation? the governor asked. No. She had insisted on withdrawal.

Uncle whispered, "Why is he going into all this?"

"Must be legally necessary."

I didn't believe my own answer.

"So," said the governor. "Your evidence is that you had frequent intercourse with Miss Cusper, but it was interrupted before the climax?"

"Yes, sir."

Miss Cusper (now Mrs. Frank Bold, her husband beside her) listened with the composure of a religious person. She was beyond all carnality now.

"Then you never ejaculated within her vagina?" said the governor.

"To the best of my recollection, no, sir."

The next witness was a medical expert. Through him the governor tried to establish how long spermatozoa would remain alive in the vagina. Three forensic experts followed with testimony on the girl's underpants, the ones she had worn on the night of the assault. The governor concentrated on them, returned to them insistently.

"Don't you think this is strange behavior?" Uncle said to me. "Harping on those pants?" He was upset. I, for some reason, was not. The thing was like a play or moving picture, except that the evidence had to be developed technically, and that took time and slowed down the action. Each of the experts had gone over Danae's underthings independently, examining blood and serum samples. One of them said that after six years it was still possible to find spermatozoa. The police had kept these articles of clothing under lock and key. (I pictured a warehouse with a hundred thousand storage bins.) The tails of the sperm had disintegrated, but the heads were identifiable microscopically. "The seminal material could have come from any donor of the Gm grouping," the technical witness said.

"And which is the prisoner's group?"

"Gm, sir."

"Do we have to go step by step through all this?" said Uncle, a little distracted. He made me feel like a Mephistopheles who had forced him out of his study and made him face life. That wasn't me, I thought. Mephistopheles never had such aches and pains. I was here for Uncle's sake. Uncle had come to go to the mat with Harold Vilitzer, who sat on the platform chewing his Cuban cigars—supplied maybe by one of his Las Vegas connections.

"This forensic stuff is science," I said.

"*Applied* science," Uncle corrected me. He guarded the purity of theoretical inquiry.

These were, however, distant colleagues of Uncle Benn's. Of course, the experts were putting on a show, that was what the TV crews were here for, but the suggestive undercurrents of their testimony carried the kinds of spoiled matter Uncle's system was least able to tolerate. I thought, You don't have to draw him pictures. He sees it for what it is. He's not all that innocent. Then I thought, Your absentminded man of genius is a copout. He knows exactly what everybody knows. He doesn't want any static from carnal nature interfering with his science.

This was partly an unfriendly reflection. I think I looked unfriendly too—dark, thin-faced, long-haired, my handsome father's features gone wrong in me. In the language of my native city, I may have appeared *sourcilleux*, slightly haughty or impatient. I had to harden myself for Uncle's sake, however. I prided myself on strong dependability. It was my responsibility to see Benn through this crisis in his life.

We had another witness now, from a different part of the country. Much care was taken to guarantee the impartiality of the testimony given. Being sworn, the stumpy expert, wearing a three-piece suit, looked like any lower-echelon guy in a giant insurance company. Sitting down and setting his elbows on the table so that his shirt cuffs showed, he read his prepared statement—technical stuff. Imagine such a life of lab analysis—skin, saliva, spattered brains, postmortem stomach contents. I said to Uncle, "I prefer your type of anatomy," but Uncle wasn't listening. His face seemed to have swelled, and it had a kind of histaminic flush, as if a flying bug from the tropics to which he was always escaping in his incessant flights had given him an allergic sting.

When the witness had read his introduction, the lights

were dimmed and the photograph of an object many times enlarged appeared on a screen behind him. It was a dark, brown something with maroon-colored stains and spots like moth-wing rouge. What was it? It looked like the Shroud of Turin to me. Just the opposite. A different article altogether. It was a picture of the undergarment the young woman was wearing on the night she was attacked. Posted beside it, holding a ten-foot pointer, the forensic expert identified it and then stood waiting to answer the questions of the board. However, nobody spoke except the governor. It was his show entirely. Watching him at work, you saw why he had been so formidable at getting out the indictments that had sent so many prominent politicians to jail. He made use of his size—a big man, his face corpulent, he bore down hard on the evidence, his questions were exact. In the examination you were aware of his boundless omniscient comprehension of crime and criminals. And yet he was soft in the face, too, and there was something paradoxical in it, a hint that perhaps the corruption was not all on the side of the defendants. And you couldn't be watched by millions, as he was being watched, without there being an element of showmanship in the event.

An article of intimate wear—kindly tell us what it is.

These were panties, sir, taken from the alleged rape victim.

She wore them on that night?

She wore them.

And now the scientific findings. Please identify the stains.

Uncle put on his glasses. What good would they do? They were for reading only. He must have wanted every possible aid to stare at that gloomy enlargement so they were worse than nothing. All those spatter marks, and ragged circles like spacecraft photographs of the moons of Uranus.

The pointer went from bloodstains to seminal discharges. The governor's questions were endless. Whose blood? Whose semen? More than one type of semen? Remember there were three men in the car.

I said, "The governor is really turned on by this."

"It's got to be distressing for the girl," Uncle said.

"We have to assume she knew what she was getting into when she reopened the case."

"The exhibits really arouse him," said Benn. "And after all, he's governor of a major state."

Lewd communications with the public, was my thought.

"Hard to fathom in the circumstances how Mr. Sickle would have been the *only* alleged rapist. There were two other young men," said the governor.

Danae Cusper Bold looked unperturbed. She belonged now to a religious community. She was sure of forgiveness, there was nothing to worry about. These crimes and sufferings belonged to the past. She was a full-bosomed matron. Uncle would never have had grounds to complain that her breasts were too far apart. You saw very plainly that they were close together.

My poor crazy uncle. This hearing at such a time of crisis was hell on him. He couldn't approach Uncle Vilitzer without first passing through these sexual agonies.

"Somebody should get Stewart away from those panties or he'll spend an hour on them."

I made a typical quite useless reply. "There's been such a shift in the sexual mores. Everybody is off on a Roman holiday."

Uncle muttered, "I hadn't realized it was going to be so ferocious, all this obscenity."

"Well, it's all those high-placed persons, the guys on the top of the ladder putting in for their share of the erotic recreations of the country."

"I can understand some of that," said Uncle. "But this is so raw."

Another slide came on the screen. This time it was Danae Cusper's belly, the girl's naked middle with crude letters on it, LOV, like graffiti on a viaduct, only these were made with broken glass. A policewoman had snapped the picture at the hospital. In her recantation Danae had testified that she had done this herself with a broken beer bottle, and Governor Stewart said with orotund scoffery that it would take fortitude, force and cool foresight in a young person, a teenage girl standing before a full-length mirror scratching false evidence on her own skin with a Budweiser bottle, then going to the hospital to accuse a man of a rape. Could she have made those letters upside down? Two of the experts thought it was feasible. Those were easy letters to do. This was bandied back and forth while the red scratches where the belly widened across the hips tilted like a Valentine's Day card made in a class for brain-damaged kids. This was of a piece with the *schizo-psychology* which, according to respected modern thinkers, had taken hold of us all.

"The governor is taking all the play away from these young people."

"And everyone else," I said.

On either side of him, members of the board, so many silent seated presences, had had all the initiative vacuumed out of them. He alone enjoyed full powers. The big man was toying with these juvenile offenders—juveniles no longer, but even now, a woman and a man looking like kids. Especially Danae, even though she was dressed and made up in the style of a respectable matron. Vilitzer, no dummy even in these circumstances, turned away from the governor's official (histrionic) display. The big unlighted cigar he chewed distorted the side muscles of his mouth. I kept an eye on him. I wanted to be sure that Vilitzer didn't slip away—disappear on us.

Governor Stewart must have asked for the stained-nylon slide again, for the scrawled belly moved out. The other forensic experts probably had to confirm the first guy's evidence. I think the belly with its LOV was the one that impressed Uncle more than the stained relic of the rape. He said, "If the kid did that to her afterwards with broken glass, his pals had to hold her down. They probably gagged her."

"I guess they would."

Uncle's eyes were inflamed. If you come downtown on a cold day when traffic is heavy and the auto exhaust is dense (it dissipates more quickly in summer), it burns your eyes; but of course I thought Uncle's were red from other causes. A man who filled out his clothes, he was wearing his tailor-made Layamon tweeds. Since he hadn't gained weight, there had to be other explanations for the bulging thighs and the expansion of his back under the jacket. What I affectionately called the insect wing case now was more like a wild boar's hump. The histaminic swelling of his face was part of the same distorting phenomenon. It not only disfigured his cheeks but got into his eyes. Knowing him, I would have sworn that he was inwardly finding himself guilty of the deepest viciousness. And this LOV scrawl was the cynicism that had the worst effect on him. I really believe that I could make out his feeling, and roughly put, it went like this: that Crime, Punishment, Justice, Authority, were satirized in this hearing. Plus Penitence. Plus Truth. If Danae hadn't lied at the trial she was lying in the retraction. So one way or another, Truth was taking a beating. Of course, that happens every day and you've got to be a botanical clairvoyant to have to wait till mid-life to find it out. But there was also the religious side of it—like: "Though your sins be as scarlet, they shall be as white as snow." This was very hard for a man like Uncle to take. The young woman was rebuilding her Christian chastity and publicly reconstituting her virginity. And what was devouring him now was his own complicity. He was involved in all this by the sensations he had had while watching *Psycho,* by the outrages his mind had committed, the discovery that he was probably not the husband of Matilda's heart, nor she the wife of his heart. Eternity itself had warned him, using Alfred Hitchcock as its medium, *not* to marry this woman. What wouldn't go down at this moment, I concluded, was that Danae had probably been choking on her own panty hose when the grotesque word LOV was scratched into her belly by those teenage maniacs. So there was *schizopsychology* for you—it seemed to be the only kind observable—and Uncle Benn, hitherto eligible to be described as a dear man, even a good man, assisting at the degradation of Love. Love, the very essence of the Divine Spirit and the source for humankind of the warmth of Heaven.

I knew how his mind worked, and even the vocabulary he had learned from Lena, his late wife. Although she was a student of Balzac, she was in her deeper interests as far from the contemporary world as her husband. When you come down into contemporary life, you can really get it in the neck. If on the other hand you decline to come down into it, you'll never understand a *thing*. I don't say that Uncle had made deliberate efforts to be above and beyond it. No, he had entered the present crisis under his own power, kept his decision to marry a secret from me, opting for the Layamons' penthouse, for the silks and satins, the eiderdown duvet of Matilda's bed, the carpets deeper than forest moss, the tremendous force of the taps in the bathroom, the whirlpool tub, the great view of the slums (like Sodom and Gomorrah the day after). Uncle had made love to his employment. Nevertheless I didn't want to see his head on the headsman's block.

That was a damn instructive hearing!

"Did you vote in the last election?" I said to Benn.

"I'm afraid I did."

"Well, why shouldn't a botanist also do his citizen's duty?"

"And I'm anticipating the follow-up question. Yes is the answer. I voted for the governor."

Sure, you face the machine in the voting booth and you don't realize what a phantasmagoria you're putting into place as (equating mechanism with order) you pull the lever.

But this was no time for theory—discussion: one of my deepest weaknesses, more harrowing to me than you might think (a haunting, perhaps destructive, habit). I had to remind myself forcibly *why* I had left Paris to live in the U.S.A. The action was here, and my uncle was the man from whom I had come to learn what it might be possible to do in this posthistorical world. And this role model was now in despair, that was why the reminding had to be forcible. But still he had those distinctive powers of *seeing*. Those he hadn't yet lost. He was a genuinely superior individual, susceptible of course to human weakness and unable to manage his sexual needs, or to be more accurate, his *love* longings, but I could retrieve even now from my personal memory bank those wonderful hours when, under his influence, not only my lungs were breathing but my mind breathed too. Some of his powers of seeing *had* been transmitted to me. So I saw. And a good many of my uncle's motives were visible to me. He had read Admiral Byrd's book and decided that he could not accept the explorer's account of the gloomy Antarctic X-rays of the human condition, the skeleton of the human soul. It would be a disgrace to make no effort to melt out the bosom ice, simply surrendering the heart to those zero conditions manifestly prevailing. (I remind you again of the Matthew Arnold statement that he was three parts iced over.) Well, not to stretch the matter out too much, Uncle had been fighting the humiliation of *not* being in love. Here was a man who *hoped*—hoped, for example, to marry the woman of his heart. Better to thaw *two* hearts while you were at it. What good was *one* thawed heart?

Clearly, meantime, the governor scorned the allegations of the twice-born young matron. She'd have to be born five times more to outwit these technicians, the forensic characters who had made a century of scientific progress since the days of Sherlock Holmes and his elementary deductions. The governor had to reckon carefully with the religious sentiments of the public, taking into account that her penitence at bearing false witness could not be dismissed. The public liked penitence. You couldn't easily eliminate it. And if young Sickle was indeed a rapist, he must have been gloating over this turnabout—being set free and a bonus of secret entertainment thrown in. What a big-time operator this little lady had become. And the governor wasn't going to send Sickle back to prison. Not now.

Sickle would be free. Enjoy the freedom of the city, like anybody else—you, me. Like Uncle, for that matter, when Uncle turned his attention to it. He seldom found the time for it.

Uncle while still young had found his answer to urban America, a neat way to step aside from the heavy burdens of social development imposed on the soul, there on Jefferson Street. He had moved the deeper interests of his life into the interior of plants. In the dullest weeds the powerful secrets of air, soil, light and propagation were hidden. So he took a transfer from curbstones to crabgrass and mulberry trees, the burdocks growing in vacant lots and freight yards. Then, after some years, he tried to move back again from roots, stems, leaves to human affections. He was not simpleminded. Nor was he an escapist. Suppose we grant the truth of Dostoyevsky's statement that nothing is more fantastic than reality itself. It follows that Uncle stood up pretty honorably to the tests of reality-fantasy.

The governor now got to his feet to announce before the TV cameras that the board would withdraw to begin its deliberations, so I handed Uncle his overcoat and said, "Let's get going before Vilitzer slips away."

Slipping away was not at all what Vilitzer had in mind. He

seemed to be expecting us. He stood behind the table, resting his weight on his knuckles and savaging his cold cigar. He scowled as we came forward. As Matilda had told Benn—he had said this to me at breakfast—*he* was the one who had been wronged, not to forget it and abandon the initiative to Harold. I had expected that Benn would attempt to strengthen himself by assuming the attitude she recommended. He didn't exactly do that. I suppose he was not feeling aggressive. He had no wish to fight. Surprisingly, his face wore a mild look—not especially conciliatory but mildly firm, as if he had chosen a course of moral suasion. Actually, I had expected him to be timid.

"You guys came to talk to me, hey?" Vilitzer pulled at his onion-shaped wristwatch, one of those monstrous Las Vegas gold articles with a band of flexible links. "I can give you fifteen minutes. That's all it'll take me to tell you off."

He led the way to an elevator, with no further explanation. You know how smooth and instantaneous these new installations are. You can't feel the speed of them. "Did Fishl get in touch with you?" I said as we were rising.

"I got the full message." Vilitzer, answering, stared straight before him. I wasn't even going to have the courtesy of a personal glance. I think I was more discombobulated than Uncle Benn, by far. On about the fiftieth floor, we stopped with an electronic *ping* and found ourselves in an environment of transparencies. Half the ceiling of the small conference room he had brought us to was blue-tempered glass resembling not so much a hothouse as a human forehead. Straight ahead of us stood the Electronic Tower, with its twin masts like the horns of a Viking helmet—it was very nearly as tall as the Sears building in Chicago.

"How is your health?" Uncle asked Vilitzer. "You had open-heart surgery, I understand."

"I'm strong enough," said Uncle Harold.

That I could believe. Rage is strengthening, if it's unmixed—devoid, I mean, of those flapping anxieties usually incorporated in the anger of weaker natures.

Harold said, "A nice visit from my nephew and Hilda's son—that's who you are, ain't it?"

"I'm Kenneth Trachtenberg."

"Oh, sure," he said, "the son of the great ladies' man. He's a big handsome fellow. You could hire out for a pallbearer, from the look of you."

I didn't take offense. To concede my father's superiority in his special field had been bred into me. Besides, I was intrigued with Uncle Vilitzer. I figured old age to have reduced his size by about a third. Still, he was fighting to hold his status as the Big Heat. He certainly was a fighter. He even had the face of a onetime boxer, with flattened cheeks, a nose with nothing left in it to be broken, and recessed eyes. Here, too, he stood at the table and was braced on his knuckles, bartender style. He wasn't going to sit. Not only was his white *I, Claudius* fringe curled under but his upper lip was similarly furled, you never saw it otherwise, and he showed his teeth even when he talked. His golden Florida color was misleading, because he was not in good health, actually.

"So they sent you to put the arm on me," said Vilitzer.

"They?"

"Your new father-in-law and Judge Chetnik, his buddy."

"The judge is your buddy too," said Uncle.

I gave my uncle great credit for behaving so reasonably. I wouldn't have been able to do it.

"Amador is a nothing."

"I understand. You made a judge of him, though, Uncle. And he ruled for you from the bench."

"He'd better have. And you and your sister had no business to sue me. You know what kind of profit you guys turned on that deal? Your parents bought the property for three hundred bucks cash. This was a deal that *I* touted them onto through the tax assessor. How would your father have heard of it? He had his nose in a book. I got you off Jefferson Street, where you were being surrounded by *schvartsers*. In the end you and your sister realized three hundred thousand dollars out of it. You bought a Depression bargain, which I tipped you off to. Well, they say no good deed goes unpunished."

"I wouldn't put it quite like that," said Benn. "First of all, my father said he paid seven hundred. Also, it might be more correct to say that from the first you had plans for that corner. Your position in charge of planning and zoning gave you the advantage of the larger picture, and you were able to decide on which side the downtown district would expand. You just allowed the Craders to hold the land for you. Which was nice too. I don't deny you were kind."

I'm sure that Uncle had assured Matilda and her father that he would hold his ground with Vilitzer, meaning, I now saw, that he would do it in his own way. Frankly, he surprised me. Considering what a state Benn was in, what with the somatic peculiarities of the Layamon build, the triple resemblance of Matilda, Dr. Layamon and Tony Perkins as the killer granny, plus the new complaint that his bride's breasts were so widely separated, with God knows what further forms of nuttiness marking time in his head, I wouldn't have predicted such quiet stability in the face of Vilitzer's rage. He expressed no hostility towards his uncle. And I want to note also, before it escapes me, that Uncle's strangely shaped and strangely colored eyes had grown as large as an aviator's goggles from the open-cockpit days, mirroring boundless daylight.

Vilitzer was saying, "You're too good to hustle. You let goofy relatives do the dirty work, and then you come around and ask for *yours*. If you were so interested in millions, you should have gone out for them on your own."

"You might have done better by your own sister's children," said Uncle.

"You see!" said Vilitzer, speaking to me. "He doesn't understand even the first basic principle. Where money is concerned, the operational word is *merciless*. I ask you," Vilitzer went on, still addressing me, "what's my goddam sister got to do with it?"

I have to say that it gave me a certain satisfaction to understand I was fit to hear such a message: Death is merciless, and therefore the ground rules of conduct have to include an equal and opposite hardness. From this it follows that kinship is bullshit. You can see how this would reflect on my attachment to Uncle, on Uncle's attachment to me. Against us there stood Vilitzer's exclusion of his son Fishl when Fishl's Chinese acupuncture abortions and his mental fire storms in cattle futures and in options trading made the application of the stern rule necessary. Fishl's emotions towards his father were further evidence of his unfitness, his ignorance of the conditions of existence.

"So they sent you to threaten me," said Uncle Harold. "It's not what *you're* going to do that's important, on account of you wouldn't know the moves to make. It's what the Layamon family will do, using you as their front."

The scattering light of the morning spectrum all over the glassy conference room surrounded this conversation with a contemporary equivalent of church illumination. The sun itself, without the usual obstruction of nature prevailing at ground level, transmitted directly a message about our human origins. Signals from our earth's star circled us in radiant threads. It was our option to take note of them or not. Nobody is forced to, of course.

Pointing over his own head at the Electronic Tower, Harold Vilitzer said, "I did a big thing, bringing that skyscraper to this town. I accomplished something for America. That is one of the biggest skyscrapers ever built. Without it this city would go on falling apart like the rest of the Rustbelt. Look at the thousands of jobs I created. Plus, I sold that multinational corporation on the stability of this town. By rights I should get a medal for this. Well, shit on the medals. I'd be glad if I was left alone. But the governor isn't about to do that."

"Why the governor?" I said.

"Because he made governor by the grand jury route, sending us politicians to the slammer. His personal team, now partners in the fattest law firms here, one after another have been the U.S. attorneys in this district. You'll never know from how many sides the sons of bitches are creeping up on me."

"That's what Fishl told me," I said.

"For once that little cocksucker is right on the money," cried his dad. "Okay, Benno, how much do you want? . . . I already know it's seven figures. You want me to make a millionaire out of you."

"*I* never said *that*."

"I been approached," said Uncle Harold. "As if it hasn't been hard enough on an old guy, with all the grand juries, they want to get me into a federal court with Amador Chetnik. Those guys will tear me like a herring."

Well, I could see it all. The new crooks were coming in, the old crooks in retreat. In four decades Vilitzer had stashed away millions. He did well out of the decline of the city, he swindled it to its knees. He had prepared for old age. Bay Harbor Island was to have been his Capri (I switch now from Claudius to Tiberius). But now shades of the prison house were surrounding the octogenarian. And whom should he see in the ranks of the enemy but his own nephew Benno—the blockhead botanist.

"What do you need two million dollars for?" asked Vilitzer.

I answered this in my own way, speaking to myself with that perfect clarity that sometimes *does* make me proud of myself: Benn needs it to pay for the mistake he made in connecting up with the Layamons. What the Roanoke required was an eminent scientist to answer the door, a prodigy to wash the dishes. Should there be a child to this union, an authority in plant morphology would be changing the diapers. Uncle was vigorous enough to have kids. Absentminded as Caroline Bunge had been, she was not so far out of it as to make plans for marriage with a dud. Even though she had passed him without recognition in the airport when he arrived, all heart, to meet her, still she had cried out, "You angel, you!" when they were making love. The sexual act probably was her last point of contact with reality. That lost, she would be finished.

"You won't answer this, Uncle Harold," said Benn, "but what did you make on the sale of that property?"

"You think I'm going to go into that with a man like *you*?" Vilitzer said.

"Why not with me?"

"Because you don't *know* anything!" Enraged as he was, he spoke also as a man proud of having dedicated himself to the high service of money, so that to discuss property and intricate calculations with Benn was demeaning. Could Benn read a balance sheet? Did he understand what it would take to piece off the other members of the zoning board? You should bear in mind that Uncle Harold had enlisted during World War II from love of country. Yes, and that he had made a killing through his PX connections and army surplus dealings was no contradiction, since Economy and America were just about identical. Uncle's question was worse than silly, it was virtually weak-minded. As if Vilitzer would ever name a figure! And even if he did, it would be off by as much as ten million dollars. Such ineptitude in Benn, considered in isolation from other facts, would seem like the last degree of alienation from your fellowman. And the other facts, the facts of Benn's strength in the realm of nature, could not be seen by a man like Vilitzer. As for myself, I couldn't have understood all this so quickly, so naturally, if I hadn't had a gift for business myself. This was a thrilling experience, this speed of comprehension. Yet from another side it was also disconcerting. It was a kind of treason to the higher life that it should come so easily to me. But then, there was no way to comprehend America without such gifts—and why horse around with America-comprehension if the aptitude was lacking? And I have this strong thing about being contemporary. Otherwise I might as well have been brooding about the Great Wall of China.

"Anyway, I'm not dealing," said Vilitzer. "Not with you—sure not—and not with Dr. Layamon, who's so busy finagling I can't see how he finds the time to treat patients."

"I thought we might settle it all between us quietly, without melodrama," said Uncle Benn.

"I wouldn't negotiate *anything* with you," said Vilitzer. "It wouldn't be final. You're not the boss over yourself. They're using you to beat up on me. As far as I'm concerned there's nothing *to* settle."

"Well, if you'd give Hilda and me the fair price of that land . . ."

Now we were just going round and round, I thought. The old man would die sooner than give up a single buck of the eighty million he had put away. Instead of an ethical structure he had a few ideas of honor, partly originating in the Machine—the politics of local government—partly in the Mafia, partly in cowboys and Indians. "I can still put up a pretty good fight," he said. "Bigger men than Layamon and Chetnik have been after me. If I scared easy I'd have been dead years ago. The other guys—and you know who I mean, all right, I mean the governor himself and his boys, all the way to the top of the Justice Department—have had my premises bugged from way back. It's been one investigation after another, and studying my tax returns from the year one. It's all new kinds of threats, new kinds of arm twisting, even new kinds of diseases. It's all kidnapping, hostages, ransom and terror. You don't have to look in Beirut; you can find it right here, where smart-ass organizers do it to corporations and television networks by organizing boycotts and all kinds of shit, and it goes all the way up to the White House, dealing with those Arabs that are snatching American citizens left and right. I mean to tell you, Benno, that's what you're into now: blackmail."

I was impressed by the old guy. This wasn't just raging, it was analysis and interpretation.

"Now I'm going to tell you—" Vilitzer cried out at us. "I've many a time been backed up to the cross, and my ass is full of splinters, but they haven't nailed me yet."

He now tried to hit Uncle Benn. He took a sock at him. I came between them and restrained the old man. When I held him he felt as light as an empty plastic egg carton. Not an egg left in him. He couldn't have had much expectancy, although his postoperative heart was banging away. There was a pacemaker fitted on his breast. This was registered by my arms as I held him, which I did only for a brief moment but long enough to be seen by Fishl when he came through the door. It was a moment made for Fishl. But before he could say, "What's this?" Vilitzer shouted at him, "Who the hell sent for you!"

"Why, Dad, I came to offer—"

"Stick it!" said his father. "I got a meeting with the governor to attend." Then he swept—tottered—out and we stood silent. Uncle was too stricken to say anything; he was immobilized in the upper body as if he were holding his breath. Fishl was silent because his emotional hopes had been pulled from under him. He had rushed in to save his old man and be reunited with him. And since I wasn't one of the principals, speaking would have been out of order for me. I don't know which of old Vilitzer's shots had struck and hurt Uncle most. Maybe "What do you need two million dollars for?" That must have been the most piercing. You come down on the aging brother of your late mother with a demand for two million bucks. What for? And it isn't even your own demand. You're stating it for somebody else. As an exact clairvoyant of plants, do you need that kind of dough? And especially if you study organisms as humble as the lichens, which get a livelihood out of bare rocks, currents of air, intervals of sun. And this was just the beginning of the emotional rendering—the *rendu émotif*—of the ordeal of desire, the peculiar trial of destiny prepared for us all.

Fishl, still in the grip of the entrepreneurial ideal, had to recover his entrepreneurial self-control and worked harder on mastering his feelings than Uncle. He reorganized himself rapidly and began to be himself again. I think I've said that he had a soft, calm look. The preferred image, the one he habitually projected, was one of untroubled composure. He had a smooth brow. When he wrinkled it he did so not because *he* was puzzled but because *you* were. When Herbert Spencer was asked how it was that after so many years of thought his forehead was unwrinkled, he answered that he had never been long perplexed by any problem. Fishl was the same sort of Answer Man. "Will you tell me," he said to me, "why you were grappling with my old dad?"

"I wasn't grappling, only restraining." And then I added, having learned that in entrepreneurial one-upmanship you took charge by putting the questions, "Why would I grapple with him? An octogenarian who's had open-heart surgery? I had to stop him from punching Benn."

"You mean to say that he tried to hit Benn?"

"He wanted to punch him."

"Didn't I warn you guys not to do this—give me time to prepare him?"

"The thing couldn't wait."

"You would have been better advised, just the same," said Fishl, in a tone of parliamentary debate. "Going by the results. Or maybe you figured that association with me would hurt your cause? I asked you not to fool with him. A poor codger on his last legs."

"Yes, of course he is," I said, "but still he can't bear to be crossed, and he was sore from the start."

"Because you're tied in with his worst enemies."

"Anyway, he hauled off at Uncle Benn."

My arms still retained a sensory memory of Vilitzer's lightness. He was scarcely even a tenement of clay; he was wickerwork, porous plastic. Only the pacemaker unit under his shirt had any weight. Still, he'd no more part with a buck than Michelangelo, sick and faint, would come down from his Sistine scaffold.

"All right, I'll go and wait by the office while the governor tells the parole board what it's going to do—there's a guy who knows exactly how to operate. Now lay off my father, will you? I blame you guys for putting him in this state. It's dangerous. And so many people are dumping on him. . . . And I'll tell you, Cousin Benno, I'd think better of you if you had gone after him on your own initiative, not on instructions from outside parties."

Benn took this in silence. Matilda, the spectacular beauty of Parrish Place, was not an outside party, and if you didn't do everything possible to please a woman in the first weeks of marriage, you might as well have remained a bachelor.

"If your old man weren't still wheeling and dealing," I said, "you'd have more justification. But he's still scheming and dealing at top speed, and what Benn did, trying to talk to him, was reasonable."

"If you can satisfy your conscience I congratulate you."

We had spoiled Fishl's big opportunity and he was bitter and heavyhearted. He couldn't bear that the old guy should die before they were reconciled. There I sympathized with him, this was a filial fantasy I could fully share, and I hoped it would happen.

"It's only me, the fucking prodigal son, that understands that old bastard."

Fishl said no more. He had to go. The governor wouldn't waste much time on the board. How was Fishl going to proceed with his father?

When he was gone, Uncle closed his eyes and let out an extended sigh. I said, "Anyhow, you gave it your best try."

"I wonder whether there *was* anything right to be done."

"No possible way to win, you mean?"

"One doesn't like to be in the position of a chump."

"What line do you think you'll take in Parrish Place?"

He shrugged. "I don't want to take any line. I wouldn't like to see Harold indicted. Would you?"

"It doesn't have much to do with us—they'll indict him anyway."

"I should have said, would you like to be a party to it? So what will I do in Parrish Place, you ask? There won't be any more discussions with Doctor. Matilda and I will settle it between ourselves. Just husband and wife."

"Would you care to predict what she'll say?"

No, he wouldn't care to do that. His look was uncharacteristically neutral. "We have to leave for Brazil day after tomorrow."

Did he think going away would resolve his problems? What would Dr. Layamon do, in his name, when he was gone? What would Judge Amador Chetnik decide? By implicating Vilitzer, Chetnik might shorten his sentence by as much as ten years.

"Do you think Matilda will be able to accept an alternative—give up her plans for the Roanoke?"

"You seem to have decided in advance that Matilda is an unyielding person," said Uncle.

The queer fact is that he didn't blame Matilda. His own faultfinding, notwithstanding the secrets he had confessed—first her shoulders, then the breasts (next it might be the inner curve of her thighs or, more embarrassingly, a directly sexual objection)—was not translated into faults of character. She was still his *beauty*. There he never wavered. Nor did he criticize her conduct. He didn't say, "She shouldn't have set me on Uncle Harold." So I figured that the enormity of his fantasies (afraid of getting into bed with her on that night in the Berkshires because he might strangle her in his sleep) forced him into compliance. He was blind to the offenses of others, couldn't enter into their wrongs against him, the reason for this being that he was engrossed in examining, policing, grilling, booking and fingerprinting himself. He never had an unkind word for the Della Bedells, the Rajashwaris of India, the Caroline Bunges. *He* was the one with the criminal motives. So he was paying Matilda because he had wronged her mentally. Let her have the Roanoke with its twenty huge rooms. He probably needed additional space for his bad conscience. If the thought of murdering her or any other mad fancy came over him, he'd be able to walk it off without leaving the house. "Put me away. I'm unfit to be at large. Not meant to be free."

I now think I was too hard on him. But I'm telling it as it happened.

On the way home in the hothouse of the city bus, I pictured the two separate endeavors—Fishl with his father and Benn with Matilda. There was not much chance that Fishl could make up with Vilitzer, and I never did find out whether Harold gave his son a chance to deliver his emotional statement. What I do know is that Harold flew back to Bay Harbor Island (Miami Beach) as soon as the governor had done with the board and that Fishl followed him. I'm better informed about the conversation Benn had with Matilda. He telephoned later in the day and told me about it. Luckily Doctor had gone to his club. When the weather was too cold for golf, he played rummy Saturday afternoons. He needed masculine companionship, gambled for high stakes and picked up essential political information in the gloomy cardroom.

"She and I had lunch alone," said Benn. "Jo had business to take care of in her office—that azalea room. So we had our sandwich in the breakfast nook."

Uncle was not a great luncher, and today his stomach was edgy. The downtown hearing was like the strip show in Kyoto in its effect. Hard-edged sex, one might call it, abstract excitement, maddening literalness when the girls invited the public to stare at their inmost secrets. Then Uncle turned to monogamy and domesticity for protection. So now his wife served him a breast of turkey sandwich on white toast. The Russian dressing he asked for didn't make the meat less dry. Sometimes he was affected by a retrograde esophagus—globus hystericus, difficulty in swallowing. What, in such a fine kitchen, with copper pots glowing on their hooks, the counter scrubbed, fit to pass an Annapolis inspection? Well, there was also the Electronic Tower coming up through a winter, sunpervaded haze, and its huge masts like a tuning fork. Uncle could always see the place where some of the best years of his life were spent, where he began to mature as a botanist, passed through lovesickness for the tailor's daughter—he didn't make too much of those times, sentimentally. I think

I'm doing that for him, prompted by the dry throat he told me about and his difficulty in eating and swallowing. No such demands were made on him in the days when grackles flocked to eat the white mulberries in the muddy backyard. Then he was a student, without possessions. Now he "had" something, and there were expectations, requirements. He had a wife. His wife had a family. They were going to "take care" of him. Matilda, to be perfectly fair about it, had to act for him where he wasn't capable of acting for himself. As she perhaps saw it, he needed things done and she was doing them. He had married an elegant woman and couldn't expect her to accept a drab life. He had never stated that he *didn't* want Vilitzer to give him two or three million dollars and make him "whole," as they say downtown. I believe she assumed that she and Benn had an affectionate partnership, and that he had married her not only for her beauty but also for her talents, one of which was a talent for management. She did what she was supposed to do, her duty as she saw it. She later told me that she perfectly understood how much it upset him to face Vilitzer downtown. She welcomed him home in a red dress he particularly liked, a very neat number with a Russian-type collar. Not red exactly but a ripe persimmon color, reddish orange, with slant pockets and a matching coral bracelet and carved earrings. She asked her mother to be busy and decline lunch. "I also put up my hair the way he liked it. He thought a woman should show her neck and didn't care for the hair to be down, schoolgirl fashion, what he called the Alice in Wonderland effect. Your uncle could make very special demands. Everything had to be 'just so.' In sexual relations also."

"Could you give an example?"

"I shouldn't. One thing—he didn't like a cigarette or whiskey breath."

"He was fastidious . . . ?"

"You can't have any idea how many conditions had to be met. In case you should have any doubts, I was good-humored about it."

"People do talk freely about things today. Thank God, the old reserve is gone. Think of your friend Marguerite Duras. For that matter, the Marquis de Sade," I said.

"Oh, nothing outlandish. Not your uncle. Don't get me

wrong. Nothing perverse. Only a kind of fussiness. He was fond of frilly blouses."

What I longed to find out was how seriously she took Uncle. How much weight he had for her, how much she believed in him. This she declined to reveal. I was allowed to infer that she was urged to put on a frilled blouse when they made love. Also that he had a decided preference for the foot of the bed and for one corner of the mattress. I took very little interest in details of this kind. As is evident by now, I have a weakness for the big issues. The meaning of human love. The sacrifice of egoism for the sake of the salvation of individuality. Like Soloviev and my other dear Russians. The egoist valuing himself so highly and crediting himself with absolute significance is in a sense correct because every human being as a center of living powers and as a possibility of infinite perfection is *capable* of possessing absolute significance and worth and one *can't* value oneself too highly. *But* it is unjust and evil to refuse this significance to others. So what does it matter to me that Uncle dragged the lady to the foot of the bed in order to enjoy her, since sexual relations represent love *par excellence* when they are *authentically* founded. But never mind that.

At this time, much later than the events I have described, Matilda was trying to get information out of me and spoke with some frankness in order to induce me to level with her. An aficionada of refined, advanced French literature, she had book knowledge, at least, of fancy fucking. It goes without saying that I had never seen my uncle at large in a bedroom (*that* would have been something to see!), but it would be a safe guess that foreign sexual practices would have confused him. Nor do I think that Matilda expected such behavior in married life, although Doctor had said provocative things to Benn about the erotic inventions of the younger generation, citing the Manson cult—drugs, copulation and murder, a father's nightmare, and a husband's too. Doctor was working Benn over when he said that a father would climb the walls, picturing what his gently bred daughter had been up to. But this was mere middle-class diabolism and, on the emotional side, it was a form of social climbing, since Layamon was no Augustus Caesar, his daughter no Julia, there was no empire to be seen, only a portfolio of investments, and for Matilda, a life at the Roanoke with Benn was no banishment. Anyway, the old guy's psychological sorcery had no effect on Benn. It simply didn't take. Benn thought of himself as the weary, wayworn wanderer in the Poe poem. That was his hang-up. Matilda wanted to be a tough broad in the brokerage world but also comfortably married to a respected professor, living in style at the Roanoke, where (a lady with fluent, current French) she could have something approaching a salon even in a vulgar town like this. Lastly, she had made a cult of deep sleep, and for that the Roanoke was the perfect setting.

That will set the orbit, define our limits again. I'm always worried lest they slip away. Benn called me several times to talk about their conversation in the breakfast nook and the turkey sandwich. No matter how much beer he drank, he said, his mouth remained dry. On the phone, he sounded very confused—wild talk, whirling words, inconsequent mention of Charles Addams. He dialed again after each call because something had been left out. Also on this weekend—such are the breaks—my own troubles with Treckie surfaced. Mrs. Sterling's private investigator in Seattle had given her new, highly distressing information. Treckie *was* marrying the snowmobile salesman. And that wasn't all. Since snowmobiles were a seasonal item, she and her husband-to-be were planning to go into the flea market business. They would operate from a base on Puget Sound and make the flea market circuit in a van or trailer or camper. Little Nancy would travel with them, naturally, although I was to be offered an option of taking her to live with me summers, when Treckie would be busiest. Mrs. Sterling, calling from the airport, took a biting tone. "You wanted to tergiversate!" There was a word from an offended woman! "This is a time when you could use help." A woman's help, she meant. Sure, but at what cost? Whichever way you turn there are costs, costs and more costs. By now the recording angels themselves will have to be cost accountants to understand what they're recording. Marry your little daughter's grandmother and your troubles will end. "What are you going to do about this—if anything?" said Tanya Sterling with a certain satirical weight.

Do? I'd have to fly to Seattle. Flight, five thousand miles of air travel, itself was doing something, and flying perhaps was the main part of the effort. How effective I would be on the ground was anybody's guess. However, I could catch an early plane and be back by midnight. Uncle and Matilda would be packing for Brazil. Before a long absence, Uncle always went to check out his will, with his lawyer. There were invariably last-minute codicils. Benn was sure to be busy. Besides, I mustn't assume that Tanya Sterling's urgency was realistic. Imperious people often hand you a timetable, and the nuttier they are, the more peremptory their orders. Well, this was not the best of days to leave town. I was badly needed here too. It even occurred to me that terrible things might happen in Brazil. A persistent and sharpening crisis, and nobody for Benn to talk to—how would he manage without me? I asked Tanya Sterling to give me the name of her private detective in Seattle. She went reluctant on me. He would think it unethical, she said. "It's not unethical if I pay him. Direct contact would be better. I'm getting my information at second hand," I explained. She said this was disagreeable to her, but in the end she gave me the man's number. Then I'd see for myself how straight she had been with me. She said she had taken me for a more trusting person.

I apologize for these asides. I have to tell the story as it happened. After all, I participated in it. Maybe I am distracted, because I have to make a real effort to get back to Matilda and Benn in the breakfast nook. So there they are, with the Electronic Tower in view. You mustn't think it was always an oppressive object. Skyscrapers, as we all recognize, also express an aspiration towards freedom, a rising above. They may be filled with abominable enterprises, but they do transmit an idea of transcendence. Perhaps they mislead us or betray our hopes by an unsound analogy.

However, the couple are talking, discussing Uncle Vilitzer. Matilda is trying to be decent as Uncle, shaken by Uncle Vilitzer's aging (and by the disintegration of human functions illustrated by the Cusper case hearing), tries to tell her how it has affected him. Well, Matilda had to be patient. It's hard to care about such things, and perhaps even harder to be called upon for the effort to care about them. We hear that hundreds have died, and then that thousands are dead. Now, what is the gauge of one's reaction to such increases? How much harder do we take the larger numbers? Is a thousand ten times worse than a hundred or do we, after people have fallen into the abyss, retract our feelings altogether? Nothing can be done about those—gone is gone. We must concentrate wholly on the living. Not that we do so well with those. So hearing about poor Vilitzer, Matilda brought out the tokens of sympathy and held them up to Benn at the proper moment. Get those over with.

"Baby, it *is* awful, isn't it, but what are you supposed to do?"

"Do we have to get that money out of him?"

"*Have* to? But your property was worth fifteen millions, and he gave you a few hundred thousands. It was unfair. It's damn unjust."

"Yes, but he lived a money life. He gave himself to it. I didn't."

"Those that take the sword, as you yourself say," Matilda reminded him.

"But why should I perish by *his* sword? Couldn't we live perfectly well without this dough?"

"It may be a theoretical possibility," Matilda said, *seeming* thoughtful.

"It doesn't have to be the Roanoke. It's a gracious place, yes. But it's worth half a million dollars, maybe seven hundred thousand. On such money, we could live elsewhere in style."

"Coming from the side of science, you don't see the thing as somebody like me would see it. *I'm* the one that will be judged by our address, the taste of decoration and style of entertainment. You'll be much happier if I feel my standards are being met."

"We could take a loan from Doctor, with the Roanoke as security."

"That's another front I wouldn't want to lose on. I need to be independent of Dad and Mother."

She spoke affectionately to Benn, sitting up straight, her bearing very fine, smoking her cigarettes but considerate enough to keep the ashtray on the lee side, seemingly aware that the odor had a slightly depressing effect on him.

"Something about these money discussions," said Benn. "It

wakes people up to make money; they're never more wide awake. Then, when they have it, the spending is dreamlike."

"Ha!" said Matilda. "If you applied that to the national budget, when *those* billions are being spent the mental light has got to be switched off. There *is* a fantasia aspect to it, isn't there?" She looked at the ceiling, taking pleasure in this, and blew smoke upwards.

"What else is there for me to do about Uncle Vilitzer?"

"You've done everything I hoped you'd do. I didn't expect him to surrender."

"And while we're away in Brazil?"

"The Department of Justice will go on with the case, regardless. That never was up to you and me. Vilitzer might have made his position stronger by keeping Amador Chetnik out of it. He shouldn't have hassled with him; he ought to have bought him off."

"I can't understand why that ox-faced clumsy bastard had to perform the ceremony."

"Oh, that was Dad's arrangement. He wanted the judge for class."

"Things going on behind my back," said Benn. "I get a creepy feeling. . . . Also, I've never been away so long from my work."

"In Brazil you can get back to your profession."

"What, traveling all over the country giving lectures? And when we return, there'll be the Roanoke to decorate. Settling in . . ."

"Well," said Matilda, cool, "you could do with more immediacy in your life. That's how everybody mostly lives, in the here and now, daily events. I don't say that you should fall in step. Part of your charm is that you don't. But the woman you married has a taste for the throwaway existence, and if you want to understand her . . . And if you love her you'll want to understand her. . . ."

Sure! thought Uncle (he remembered to tell me). If you have to marry a beauty you've got to expect difficulty. Only the brave deserve the fair. Call the difficulty understanding, or call it doing what she expects of you. Now make a brief rundown or summary. You have longings, the male Eros does that to you; you take the sexual path and it leads you into lewdness, lewdness opens up into insanity, a world of madness rushes at you full face. A vile movie brings you into this intimately, and the next disclosure is that you're as grotesque as the other crazies. Suddenly her shoulders loom over you like the Andes, you can't take both her breasts in one hand because they're too separate. Whether she has analogous dissatisfactions with you, you'll never know. Whether your genitals please her, or she decides to settle prudently and overlook such minor items for the sake of her marriage. And finally you're harrying your sick octogenarian uncle.

Uncle said to me, "These projections of a life plan, when your wife makes them in cold blood, kick the shit out of a man. You know?"

"Sure I know. Did you tell her you wouldn't push on against Vilitzer?"

"I sure did. But she said, 'The reason I wanted you to go to him was that Kolisko—that's the federal prosecutor—has just about got his indictment ready anyhow.'"

"Then maybe Amador Chetnik has already testified before the grand jury. Suppose that Uncle Vilitzer was aware that he had done that?"

"Bless you, Kenneth. That never would have occurred to me."

Why he had to bless me for an ordinary reflection, I couldn't see. What it meant perhaps was that I was standing by him, and he was pressing my hand over the phone. That was how I read him.

I got several more nervous follow-up calls that day. I also heard from cousin Fishl Vilitzer, who intended to follow his dad to Miami Beach. "The old man is sick," he told me.

"Have you seen him?"

"They won't let me talk to him, but something is cooking over there. What kind of a number did you two do on him?"

"Now, Fishl, don't treat us like the bad guys. How sick is he?"

"Plenty sick. I can't bear the thought of his death! It crushes me."

The nicest thing about Fishl was after all filial piety. His misconduct itself was caused by his wish to distinguish himself from his brothers with their frozen Birds Eye hearts; it was an attempted carry-forward of his father's career, a sincere offering. But his father hadn't wanted a successor, didn't care for attempts or offerings. He must have preferred respectability in his children. His crooked money was to be made straight by them.

Fishl said he would keep me posted from Miami, only I would have to accept a collect call—he was that low in funds. I said, "Yes. Keep me posted." It occurred to me that Fishl had nobody in the world to turn to. In emotional matters I was his last contact.

That night I slept badly. At three o'clock in the morning I surrendered to insomnia and got out of bed. The combined troubles were more than I could lay aside. I was heating a rum-flavored milk toddy on the electric coil when the phone rang.

"I woke you?" said Uncle.

"I wasn't sleeping. What's up?"

"Disturbance out of hand."

"Where are you now?"

"Down in the laundry room again. Around midnight, Fishl rang me to say he didn't know how long Uncle Harold would last. He's on standby out at the airport—can't afford full fare to Florida. Frantic! As if it were all my fault."

"His saying so is distressing," I observed. "It doesn't have to be true to be wounding."

"It's disorientation all around," said Uncle. There was more emotion in his tone than I could attribute to the news from Fishl. "I moved over into a kind of life I haven't been able to manage. I felt it was wrong even to think that. I should be able to stay afloat in any kind of water. You told me I ruined myself by this marriage and I was indignant. I said, What do you mean! She's a beauty. She's so gifted."

"Then you modified it. You said that if somebody hit you on the head with a hammer you saw ten Matildas, and *one* of those you loved. The natural question was: '*Which* one?'"

"That was just a metaphor," said Uncle. He was right to tell me that you shouldn't be held accountable for a figure of speech. "I was warned at the picture show not to marry. It was a sin to disobey the warning. But a man like me, trained in science, can't go by revelation. You can't be rational and also hold with sin."

"Oh, Uncle, that was the bunk. You didn't have the courage to run away. You're not a rational type at all."

"Yes, you often say that. Well, it's the dead of night, and there's nobody in on this but you and me. So tell me . . ."

"There's nothing rational about the way you see things. Others don't see what you see. You didn't have to defend yourself against what you saw in plants."

"A kind of childishness," said Benn. "When you're a kid you have an inner world of satin. . . ."

"I suppose advancing maturity was a threat. Your satin becomes threadbare. It gets soiled."

"Having to be false to get along. Question of survival," said Uncle. More questioning than saying. "You do have a gift for telling me what I most need to hear, Kenneth."

I couldn't quite picture what he was up to in the laundry room going on three o'clock in the morning, an hour often connected with the dark night of the soul. He was, by the sound of him, somewhere beyond the agitation I was familiar with. He was bringing himself to tell me something of unusual importance. He wanted me to remind him that he was a plant visionary, subject to plant-inspired trances. And sometimes he had asked, somewhat mysteriously, what if he should have this gift for people too? He may have had it but made a secret decision to cut it off, for you can't control what you see, when you see not only the phenomenon but the power behind it. You don't have to defend yourself from lichens, after all.

"So tell me, Uncle Benn, what's going on?"

"I will tell you. That's the purpose of the call. I'm in shock. I wouldn't wake you otherwise. Talking to Fishl shook me up. I was glad he didn't wake the family, but I couldn't go back to bed, and I wandered around the duplex. When it's as bad as that, I've often gotten reinforced by that azalea in Jo Layamon's office."

"Which is out of bounds."

"I went to the Dutch door and reached inside for the light switch. This time I really had to have plant contact. I'm not going to talk about the nature of the desire. It has something to do with my aliveness. Let that go. This time I slipped the bottom bolt, and I went in to get closer to the shrub. A few times in the past it drifted through my mind that you never saw it drop any blossoms. I put it down to my mother-in-law's neatness, because she's the faultless housekeeper. And then it hit me. That azalea is a phony."

"Hold it, now. An artificial plant?"

"Made of silk. Probably in Taiwan or Hong Kong. Damn near perfect imitation. False, though. A stooge azalea—a stand-in, a ringer, an impostor, a dummy, a shill! I was drawing support for weeks and weeks from this manufactured product. Every time I needed a fix, a contact, a flow, I turned to it. Me, Kenneth! After all these years of unbroken rapport, to be taken in." He cried this out—I could see it—among all those washers and dryers. "The one thing I could always count on. My occupation, my instinct, my connection . . . broken off."

"Not a good sign," I said. What else could I say?

"A sign? You don't grasp the meaning of a thing like this. I've lost it. Week after week of imaginary contact!"

The peculiar treasure lost! It wasn't that I didn't grasp what he was telling me. I grasped it only too well.

"I've been punished, Kenneth. For all the false things I did, a false object punished me."

"Easy, Uncle."

"Lost my bearings."

"You've still got the inside satin. I'm dead certain of it, Benn."

"I went for a different satin."

This may have referred to the show we had seen in Kyoto and had discussed in exactly such terms.

"Not at all. You were in love."

"Love shouldn't have led to this," was what he answered me.

"No use going round and round," I said. "You can't sit in the laundry room all night."

"I'd sooner be here than upstairs. There's a curse on that goddam penthouse."

"Take a chloral hydrate and pass out," I advised him.

"And be in a daze all day tomorrow? I'm not about to do that. I have to be clear in the head from here on in. Whatever else . . . Time I took hold."

When I lay down again and covered myself in my celibate

bed, I couldn't imagine what he might do to take hold. Before we hung up I had tried to console him, and I said, as usual, "Call me any time of the day or night." However, I couldn't think how to help. What had happened to him affected me as well. I could feel the perturbation widening and widening as I lay there and became aware that I had come to depend on his spirit. Without its support, the buoyancy went out of me, the city itself became a drag. The U.S.A., too, that terrific posthistorical enterprise carrying our destinies, lost momentum, sagged, softened. There threaded itself through me the dreadful suspicion that the costs of its dynamism were bigger than I had reckoned. I was warned to keep away. My parents both told me I was making a mistake. My father especially said I was too ambitious and wanted to put my ill-hidden hubris to the ultimate test by taking on America itself. I could, and did, fill in the details for myself. Your soul had its work cut out for it in this extraordinary country. You got spiritual headaches. You took sexual Tylenol for them. It wasn't an across-the-counter transaction. The price was infinitely greater than the easy suppositions of the open society led you to expect. Benn was a plant artist who was not qualified to be a love artist. Eros vetoed Matilda for him. He ignored the veto and married her. There seems to be a huge force that advances, propels, and this propellant increases its power by drawing value away from personal life and fitting us for its colossal purpose. It demands the abolition of such things as love and art . . . of gifts like Uncle's, which it can tolerate intermittently if they don't get in its way.

Of course, we all have these thoughts today instead of prayers. And we think these thoughts are serious and we take pride in our ability to think, to elaborate ideas, so we go round and round in consciousness like this. However, they don't get us anywhere; our speculations are like a stationary bicycle. And this, too, was dawning on me. These proliferating thoughts have more affinity to insomnia than to mental progress. Oscillations of the mental substance is what they are, ever-increasing jitters.

I wondered what Uncle might have meant by saying, "Time I took hold." When you've fallen from grace, what do you take hold of? I troubled my mind with that one until daybreak, when I got another call from Benn. He said, "I've decided to fly down to Florida."

"What about Brazil? Aren't you and Matilda taking off for Rio day after tomorrow?"

And what did *I* mean by tomorrow and the day after? I hadn't slept all night and was crossed up about the calendar altogether.

"We're flying via Miami, and I can meet Matilda at the Miami airport, right on schedule. Harold is in bad shape."

"How do you know that?"

"I called to check Fishl's story and talked to his brother Dennis in Miami Beach. Dennis said that Uncle Harold has collapsed."

"Does it sound really serious?"

"You bet. This may be it. I think that I should go there."

I was unable to understand what he expected to achieve in Miami. But it would have been a bad idea to question his initiatives. More than ever, he should be encouraged to act independently. To recover his equilibrium in his own way.

So I said, "How does Matilda feel about that?"

"She thinks it's perfectly okay. I should talk again to Uncle Harold."

Get him to sign a codicil or amendment with his dying hand? Deathbed reconciliation? Who could guess what she might have in mind.

"So it's goodbye for us?" I said.

"Maybe you could take a cab down here."

"And go to the airport with you?"

"That's the idea. Shouldn't be much traffic on the expressway. The commuters are coming in, and we'll be going out."

I told him it was a deal, to give me half an hour. Then on impulse I put a toothbrush and razor, a clean shirt, into my briefcase, and stuck the credit cards in my wallet. He was waiting in front of Parrish Place. The doorman had helped him with his luggage—the light clothing he'd need in Brazil, I assumed. "I had to pack in a hell of a hurry," he said.

"Matilda isn't seeing you off?"

"What for? I woke her in the night to talk it over with her. She's got a hard day before her. Anyway, we're meeting at the Miami airport tomorrow."

So she was asleep, rolled in sheaths of down and silk and in all the splendor of perfect beauty: the blue lids, the long eyelashes, the exquisite nose—the classic face breathing in profile on her pillow. There must be a separate metabolism, a metabolism of designs, schemes, secret intentions, which is parallel to the other physiological process, only science doesn't yet know how to analyze the by-products of this out of the breath of the sleeper. We haven't seen a thing yet!

Uncle and I got into the cab, the doors were slammed and we turned towards the expressway. I looked him over. You couldn't expect a man in his situation to look well. He had *lost* something. Of course, it must have been missing for some time. And why hadn't *I* observed the difference, if I cared so much about him?

"Is Vilitzer conscious?" I said.

"I hope so. The family may not be leveling with us. Obviously there's an advantage in looking as bad as possible. You often see big-time defendants wheeled into the courtroom with an attending physician by their side."

"And will they let you see him?"

"I am his one and only nephew. They may not. We'll find out."

"And what do you want to tell him?"

"Would I pitch a dying man for money? Stick my head inside his oxygen tent to argue with him?"

"It's been known to happen. For less than a millionth of the value of the Electronic Tower."

"No, no, that would be grotesque. He should see me—see family. I just want to show myself to him."

"Do you believe there's a change of heart on the deathbed? I always thought that was Christian mythology—never too late to mend. Of course, if the dying are surrounded by tender love they may open their hearts. Harold is just as likely to tell you to fuck yourself."

"Could be," said Uncle. "But there *was* a time of affection between us, when we went into the backyard and he showed me that mulberries were edible. And when there was still a vaudeville circuit, and we saw Jimmy Savo together."

"You'd have to get an archaeologist into his head to dig up a memory like that."

"I suppose so. But I'd feel better if I could tell him that I hold no grudges. Questions of property dwindle away. I doted on Harold when I was young."

"That was just the way *you* saw things, Uncle. That was part of your inside satin. Or the susceptibility of a mind subject to trances. The objects you looked at had more colors and dimensions than the others were ever aware of."

In this aspect, Uncle's feelings made sense. That inner world of satin was in those early times intact. He was only beginning to learn that a human being (thrillingly!) had in himself a mirror in which nature could see itself, something like a theater for the external world. But eventually he became involved with the Vilitzers on the Vilitzer types' own turf. Finally he got stuck there—bogged down in alien considerations.

"Several things I wanted to talk to you about," said Uncle.

"That azalea was shattering, I know," I said.

"Never mind the azalea, it's not for discussion right now. I was going to ask you to take over my old apartment. The bank has standing instructions to pay the rent. I kept Lena's account in her own name. The utilities also will be paid. It won't cost you, and it's important to me."

"I never did understand why that place mattered so much to you."

"Well, I don't understand why you hand over your salary to Treckie. She has no business to take it, and you're forever broke. But I'm not asking you to understand, only to oblige me."

"Well, if it's a request . . . If you put it that way."

"The leather furniture has to be treated with Propert's Saddle Soap."

"Lena used it?"

"Twice a year."

"You won't be gone that long."

"Leaving you instructions makes me feel less chaotic."

"And the plants?"

"Oh, yes . . . those," he said. "Ask the assistant, over in the botany building."

"Not to worry. I'll have them looked after."

We had a short interval of silence. He was compacting his

troubles, perhaps, making a space for such measures as he had decided to take. Reflecting, he was like an elementary reader who has to move his lips when he pores over a page. The truth is that he didn't look absolutely bad. There was one thing that was worrisome: the figure eight form of the eyes, so impressive hitherto, now seemed to me the mark of a displaced person. I hoped this would be temporary. Otherwise his carefully shaven face was as firm as a well-grown apple—one of those *pommes Canada* featured on Parisian dessert menus by the best restaurants. The only outright sign of distress was the inflammation of his eyes—literally desperate streaks of red. He had the composure of a man for whom the worst case had come to pass and who had no choice except to harden himself.

In this connection, I couldn't help thinking of Aunt Lena, since her bank account and saddle soap had been mentioned. It was Lena who had introduced me to the valuable idea that modes of seeing were matters of destiny, that what is sent forth by the seer affects what is seen. She liked to give the example of Whistler the painter when he was taken to task by a woman who said, "I never see trees like that." He told her, "No, ma'am, but don't you wish you could?" This could be a variation on "Ye have eyes and see not," an aesthete's version of it. One has no way to check this out, but it isn't too far-fetched to assume (the human crowd now covering such a vast span of possibilities) that people of a coarse constitution see only vile blobs when they inspect their surroundings and that they also project their inner deformities upon nature, whereas a heart like Uncle's made him a plant clairvoyant. He'd never dare to mention such a talent to colleagues, it would have blown their minds, they wouldn't stand for it. But I have heard that Werner Vishniak the naturalist would withdraw in summer to his own island in the Danube and that he'd been seen there nude, plastered with mud, wild birds sitting on his head and shoulders, so scientists are known to go personally beyond orthodoxy. I believe Uncle's intuition to have been that plants functioned as sense organs, collecting cosmic data for the earth itself. This would make him a communicant in a green universal church. To pursue this I would need more specific information than he ever gave me.

But then he had taken Mrs. Layamon's azalea for the real thing!

About this, in the interim, it has occurred to me that he came up against a different kind of genius, which is the Oriental genius for imitations. In the Far East, furthermore, plagiarism evidently is no offense. So some little woman in Formosa with her silk and scissors had taken Uncle in. This couldn't have happened if he hadn't been so shook up.

To get back now to our airport cab ride. During Uncle's silent interval I had time to consider poor Aunt Lena's principle, adapted Swedenborg or Blake. Suppose that what he saw was the measure of a man. Then what was Uncle now? A person like Benn can't be compartmentalized: a visionary with plants, a dub with the women. If you have peculiar talents you must be prepared to defend them. How many people in this (humanly underdeveloped) world have such distinguished abilities (a credit to *Homo sapiens*)? But this is what befalls talent when one tenth of the person makes galactic calculations, while his human remainder is still counting on its fingers.

After his many failures in the field of sex, Benn concluded that what he needed was a settled life with a beautiful woman. Well, okay. Nothing wrong with beauty. Not only is it estimable in itself, but he could harmonize it with the botany. And can you blame a man for preferring it—a joy forever, as Keats said? A man can romance mentally about his beautiful wife, in her absence or when she disappoints him. Should she give him the business, he can always wonder how the beautiful has become disconnected from the good. If nothing else, it keeps his misery at a high level. What was unforeseen in Uncle's case was that he would attack her mentally with intent to distort her beauty. By so doing, he startled himself. But whether in self-defense or in reprisal, he'd see Matilda, from behind, sometimes as Dr. Layamon, sometimes as a Hitchcock murderer—a very strange twist, a sophomoric impulse like that of schoolboys who disfigure madonnas in their textbooks with beards or penises. This is not the finest choice talent can make when it is called upon to defend itself. I'm not telling you anything you couldn't tell yourselves.

Now here was the airport coming up. Glass is a wonderful

building material. It makes you believe you can see everything. Plus, it's strong enough to withstand any wind force, or the severest jet blasts.

Uncle had begun to speak about his apartment—those heavily furnished, close-curtained, book-jumbled rooms with ultraviolet tubing for his flowering pets. "I never thought you liked my place."

"Maybe so, but I'm beginning to look at it from another slant," I said. And this was strangely true. It wasn't my idea of home. Of course, it was part of his defense system—what he had shored up against pavements, railyards, eateries, gas stations, hospitals, churches, paddy wagons, helicopters, and also the invisible human meanings quaking in the urban air-ocean, which we have to breathe, like it or not. But not all the leather chairs, books, copper pots, alarm systems, in the world could protect him from the Della Bedells who came to storm his doors. I wondered, natch, why his living arrangements should be so much on his mind today. With hindsight it's clear enough, but at the time I was heavyhearted for his sake and preoccupied also on my own account. At Delta Airlines I got out with him. A great deal of heat radiated from his open coat and even from his face. He was from a thermal standpoint very unusual, preferring light clothing because he threw off so much heat. The looks he gave me were oddly divided. He was both self-possessed and self-appalled. The figure eight form of his eyes, so impressive when he had his full powers, gave him the look of disorientation I had already noticed. I would have put my arms around him, if I had thought that he would stand for it.

"Where can I reach you tonight?"

"You want to call me?" He gave me the name of a spa in Miami Beach. "Right on the ocean," he said. "Doctor has an interest in it. His usual one percent of a big deal."

I told him, "We absolutely must stay in touch. You'll be away for months. There are lots of questions to set straight."

I saw him through the hidden-weapons checkpoint. Looking more Russian than ever on the far side, he pulled the strap of his blue garment bag across his shoulder. It went over the bulge of his back (more than ever resembling a wing case) and then he turned and saluted as if he were bound for Siberia. He was loaded down with luggage. An experienced traveler never checked his stuff, he took it all aboard. He went away looking from behind like a creature determined to walk although capable of flight. He had his long-armed Sviatoslav Richter look and wore an Irish crush hat, the last thing you would want in Miami or Rio. With some pain I watched him going off, wasting his strength, which was still considerable—but how long would it last?

When he was out of sight, I headed for Northwest Airlines and bought a round-trip ticket to Seattle. As it was a Sunday morning, we were two thirds empty. A Florida-bound plane would be crowded at this season. I gave one more thought to Uncle, at 35,000 feet: a man capable of living fully in isolation from the life of his time. Wasn't that a wonderful advantage? But he lost it in running after his contemporaries, not satisfied until he had gotten into the labyrinth of prevailing interests. Not so much the public or material interests as the sexual ones—acquiescing in the preeminence of sex, putting it at the heart of existence, bowing to the consensus. And this without having a gift for it. And I, too, lacked that gift. Otherwise would I be bound for Seattle? But there we were, seven miles above the earth's surface, on our diametrical course through this permeable alloy of pure colors. For our sins, both of us.

Sunday was the best day for my purpose. Treckie would be at home with Nancy, and probably the boyfriend would be lounging around. He, this Ronald of hers, was, I projected, a burly type, as ski instructors usually are, attractive to lady pupils. But somehow, in this setting, right in the middle of the azure world and five times as high as the mountains, I felt fierce enough to take him on. It wouldn't matter what he did to me; he'd have to kill me, not just beat me. As soon as he opened the door, I'd throw myself on him and mash his face against the wall, grab his hair and bang him until he was blinded. When he fell down, I'd jump on his arm to disable him, and then kick him in the head. . . . I think that planes contribute something to emotional rushes of this sort. The jets seem static, your whiskey glass doesn't even shake, but you're aware that you're making a ground speed of 650 mph. Although I was so intent, dead set on attacking him, I don't believe that my pulse was any faster than usual. The heartbeat seemed perfectly normal.

The weather in Seattle was ideal for my high-energy impulse to fight, to trample that man, as perfect a cold day, on the ground, as it had been in the Midwest. Owing to the time-zone difference, it was only eleven o'clock in Seattle—a sunny, freezing, clear morning. Long-haired, narrow and with a tall man's stoop, I got out of the cab, counting out the fare with penny pedantry, French style, making gestures which originated with my father (although my dad would never in the world set off on a flight like this, nor feel violent as I did about a rival, or a woman who didn't want him).

I rang the bell. Through the intercom, Treckie asked, "Who is this?"

"Federal Express," I said.

I was buzzed in, and then I heard her saying on the landing, "But there is no Sunday delivery."

I stepped past her, looking for the man I had come to fight. I saw only my small daughter, Nancy, at the kitchen table, holding a piece of bacon. She certainly didn't place me as her father. For my part, I identified her as my own—the long head and the Jesusy expression of face. That at the age of three she didn't identify me made me madder than ever.

"This is a hell of a thing, Kenneth, invading us like this."

I quickly opened several doors off the kitchen, hoping to catch this Ronald sleeping. I entered the bedroom, but there was nobody in the bed.

Treckie was pale, but she held her little body straight and said with a kind of smiling triumph, "He's gone to Mass. Well, suppose he *was* here—you want to fight him? Is that what you flew in for?"

I seized the bedding and ripped it away, grabbed up the sheets and pillows and threw them into a corner. Then I found my way into the bathroom and began to wreck it, knocking things from the shelves. Treckie was a great buyer of natural health stuff, shampoos, skin lotions, bottles of herbal medicines. She used to come to bed smelling of valerian drops. I emptied bottles of pills down the toilet bowl and flushed them away. I yanked at the shower curtain and brought the rod down. I squeezed her Weleda foot lotion on the mirror, wiped my hands on the bath mat, tumbled things out of the medicine chest, found the valerian bottle and broke it in the tub.

"And what next?" said Treckie from the doorway.

I answered nothing.

"Are you planning to tear up the whole place?"

Was I? I was not, but I felt unusually well. What went through my head was that Uncle might have benefited by doing in Parrish Place what I had just done in this small Seattle toilet.

"This ought to take off your edge."

"Never you mind my edge," I said.

I glowered dangerously still, but more than ever, the pale girl-aborigine Treckie really did have all kinds of natural attractions for me. Even now they worked on me. Somehow they got under my anger. With her there were always hints of Amerindian, indigenous, pre-Columbian origins. In spite of myself, I felt these influences. Hers was like a face (it struck me now) from a colonial family gallery—full brown eyes, puckers at either side of the soft mouth; she was perfect at the game of innocence and might have been painted wearing frilled pantalets, like a little nineteenth-century virgin who had been playing jacks or skipping rope.

But she was a sturdily self-possessed person. It took more than a wrecked bathroom to put her in a flap. In fact, the first thing she said—it took the form of an announcement—was: "I'm just not going to have ugly feelings. I refuse to. I've conditioned myself against them."

For me, the pleasure of being angry—intoxication, I might call it—was beginning to subside, and then I became aware of the lack of ventilation in the can. There was no window, only a small grille in the wall. The air was bad in here. It was worse than bad. The odors of a settled intimacy between man and woman (with a child thrown in) rose from the floor, came at me from the towels, the pipes, the base of the bowl, smells of human ammonia, sulfides, organic acids. If you didn't inhale this mixture of secretions, you didn't breathe at all. I still had on my hat and coat and sat on the edge of the tub with smashed bottles in it, considering what was what. These stinks, I thought, choking an intruder (me!), were more binding than a marriage license.

Treckie said, with no sign of ill will, "I guess you've made your statement."

Again, I said nothing.

"Anything else you want to demolish?"

I stood up and followed her back to the kitchen, where the little girl was still eating her bacon. I could feel my very eyeballs pulsating, a beating in the cornea, as I lifted the kid's chin and gave her a kiss. Her poor biological father would have to do what he could for her within the limits set by the human situation—or whatever you wanted to call it.

The primary aim never had been to become a father. It was to enjoy the girl who became the mama, to be turned on by a lady or child-woman with whom, owing to our respective heights, lovemaking in a standing position had been intriguingly difficult. It involved bending the knees, and why this exercise had been so exciting, why such a supermature kiddie type had so turned me on, made curious case-history material. I didn't think I'd ever figure it out—the charm of childhood sweethearts, the attraction of a half-sized woman. After all, Treckie herself had played it this way, piling telephone directories on her chair at dinnertime and also now and again referring to herself as a dwarf. I had had no business to knock Edgar Allan Poe for having similar tastes. I had done it to tease my uncle and bring him to his senses when he quoted me "Helen, thy beauty is to me." I suppose Poe had hoped to graduate from that poor Clemm girl to classic goddesses. But then what good is it to analyze such kinks? You mustn't allow things of this sort to become a "subject." And it's especially out of place to do that at a hippie-style breakfast table with its jars of fiber from the health food shop; dried yarrow blossoms, carob powder, herbal teas and whatnot else.

Treckie had gone to change out of her dressing gown and put on a skirt and blouse.

I suppose my overall purpose had been to bring her around gradually. Since she had had a child by me, I apparently assumed that the next step was to make a normal person of her. The premise must have been that she'd become normal by learning to appreciate my qualities and taking pleasure in my intimacy. But (and this was downright shocking!) she didn't want any part of me. I failed to turn *her* on.

Here are items that deserve to be listed on the pain schedule.

Or, if you prefer, the accomplished person (French educated, fully Americanized and an advanced student of Russian history and culture) was himself found to be knee-deep in the garbage of a personal life. The ordeal of the West!—which I went to such (useless) trouble to spell out for my mother in Somalia.

But now the little woman, mother of my child, was back. She was as respectable in appearance as a woman can be who doesn't bother with underthings.

"Feeling more like your usual self?" she said. "What a temper you turn out to have!"

"Yes, I do get angry."

"And wanted to fight Ronald?"

I admitted it. I'd have fought him now if he'd come through the door. But I said, "I came to check on the kid and find out what your intentions are."

"Ronald doesn't come back from Mass. Nancy and I meet him for brunch on Sundays."

"I'm due home myself. Classes tomorrow. You and I should agree about the kid."

"Oh, Tanya gave you reports. She hired that private eye."

"Is it your idea that I'm just an accidental father? Any other man might have been the one?"

"You'd be better off if you didn't take so much on yourself. Don't you like belonging to this species? You think you're about to die if you have no duty. That's why your mind is overloaded with generalizations. Much benefit you get from them."

I was not in good shape, my head ached, and I made no comment.

Treckie said, "Let me set Nancy up in front of the TV with the bacon and her security blanket. Cartoons keep her quiet."

So I waited—loose coat, straight face. In these surroundings, it was acceptable to keep your hat on. Under the coat I was still sweating, feeling the drops on my ribs, mortified now at the scene of rage I had made in the toilet. (In common use by the entire species.) Not exactly the place to be stung to the quick with high wrongs. I felt the heat of anger coming upward and the heat of shame descending from the head. But a change occurred when the two met. An interval of lucidity set in—anger-nourished, high-energy, impatient clear judgment. As tiny Treckie put the kettle on for herbal tea, I observed that she stood only bust-high to the peak of the percolator beside it. She had beauty plus handicaps, and you couldn't blame her for interpreting life accordingly. The childish inutility of her hands I still found touching in combination with her mature fullness. The funny part was how rich she was in physical blessings. They counted for more than the disharmony of sexuality and stature. A bug from Mecca might have made a pilgrimage and crossed all of Asia and the whole Pacific just to take a bite of her. I still was deeply affected by her figure. Schoolboys, being tough, might have called her "shortass," but I couldn't get it out of my head that her backswell revealed the nearness of a gravitational field. There was no reason why the planet itself shouldn't manifest its magnetism in relationships with persons who appealed to it. (There were traces of Uncle's influence in such perceptions or associations.) In this way I understood more clearly the attraction of Treckie. I had been intimate with her on a visiting basis. I wasn't what she was looking for, I only wanted to convince her that I was—bring her around by powers, persuasion and such personal charms as I had. None of these had worked. Was she married to Ronald? The formality was unimportant. The message of the bathroom pipes, the organ vapors (I mustn't allow those smells of intimacy to become a fixation), amounted to an announcement of wedlock. I had made my protest (I think it pleased her) and she believed that now we could be sociable and calm together. It's very elementary. I'm giving it to you in a condensed form.

What came to mind were the small fenced parks in European cities that you had to enter with a private key. Only subscribers had keys, and my subscription had run out.

As I dunked my herbal tea bag, Treckie answered a telephone call. I went to the parlor and gave my little girl a kiss on the head—hair fragrance mixed with bacon. As we watched together, a steamroller flattened an English bulldog.

He resumed his shape in a moment and ran after his cartoon-giant master. Nobody really was hurt. I pushed the remote control button and got a football game back East. Treckie, entering the room, switched back to the cartoon. She and I had unfinished business and we returned to the kitchen—the negotiating table. She had put on lipstick and pinned up her hair.

"So dear Mother kept you posted," she said. "I decided to be frank with the investigator she hired. What's to hide? We have a nice relationship. Lots of these fellows were in military intelligence, or say they were. Anyway, he's a pretty nice guy—our kind of people."

Treckie confirmed what Tanya had told me. She was leaving the VA job. She and Ronald were going to double in snowmobiles and flea markets, from a base on Puget Sound. The snowmobile territory was inland. Not much doing on the Pacific slope with its low snowfall.

And they'd be living like Gypsies, tinkers, hoboes, on the trailer-camp circuit. In flea markets, people bought one another's junk. Not much money in that, but then she didn't need much, she got so many dividend checks in the mail. "You don't care for this California-type stuff, I know that," she said. "You look down on things like applied Zen or group psychotherapy, Scientology. You've opted for a more serious life-style. You go by your uncle's preferences. He's your special thing, isn't he? I liked him, but I wasn't into him at all. How is he making out in his marriage, by the way?"

"I wish I could say how."

"What did he want to marry for? You take such a special tone when you speak of him," said Treckie. "It's always a matter of how this wonderful man is going to get the wonderful wife he needs."

"Do I sound like that? I suppose I do assume that he's special. Very hard for a man like Uncle to find a suitable life companion. And he has attracted lots of women, but there haven't been so many kinds of them."

"How do you see the relationships he gets into?"

"The relationship of rails to locomotives."

Smiling, almost pitying me for my quirky way of talking, as enigmatic to her as her way of looking was to me—I refer to the mingled warmth and directionlessness of her eyes, the strength of her hair wisps, the combination of ingenuity and unfathomable objectives—she said, "He's a famous man in his field, but he does make an awfully flaky impression when he sounds off. He was quoted in the paper on the Chernobyl disaster. He was one of the scientists interviewed about the radioactive threat."

"Yes, I've read that. He said increased radioactivity was very bad."

"But he dismissed it."

"He didn't dismiss it, Treckie. His comment was that more people died of heartbreak than of radiation poisoning."

"And isn't that a crazy remark?"

"Maybe not. If people were clear about it, more aware of their feelings, then you'd see a real march on Washington. The capital could never hold all that sorrow."

She laughed at me. "Are you talking about a demonstration? Actually, like Nuclear Freeze, or Greenpeace? That's just like you both, the two of you. You put your heads together, and what do you come up with?"

"I guess politics isn't really Uncle's bag."

Not mine, either, was my thought just then. I was referring to my Project Turning Point—that, really, conscious existence might be justified only if it was devoted to the quest for a revelation, a massive reversal, an inspired universal change, a new direction, a desperately needed human turning point.

"If he's so great in botany, then he should stick to what he knows."

"In botany, he seems to be what people used to call an adept."

"Something about religion?"

"I sometimes think so when I see him absorbed in plants. I can't tell you what the stems or veins of leaves mean to him."

"Wasn't he researching Arctic lichens?"

"He still is. I'm not able to tell you much about that, except there's an important, a basic life question at the bottom of his research. Those Arctic lichens are frozen through and through. Ninety-five percent of their existence is solid ice. But at the slightest warming they revive and even grow a bit. This can go on for thousands of years."

"You've told me that before. You said that we hadn't even begun to imagine how much there is to learn from the lower forms of life. You made me uneasy. I never was sure that to you I wasn't one of those lower forms."

"I can't see any grounds for that. It isn't as if we didn't produce a child together, or as if I didn't propose marriage dozens of times."

"To make an honest woman of me, even if I did have bad habits, or unacceptable personal needs, which you looked down your nose at. Still, they turned you on. No use denying, my sexual conduct excited you plenty. Other people's brutality. You better believe it."

"Your opinion surprises me," I said. "I promise to think about it. But right now I wonder if we can discuss a few more immediate things." I inclined my head towards the parlor and the cartoon sound effects—the bangs, whistles, buzzings, blams and tooting.

"You can see as much of the kid as you like, on my terms."

"I figured you to state it that way."

"The life-style around here doesn't meet with your approval. But the more facets to a kid's upbringing the better. We're a pluralistic society, after all. Multiple acculturation is what it's all about. At her developmental stage, you can't expect equal time, as they say. But you should have some input. I agree to that."

"How would you describe this input of mine?"

"You've got a certain amount of style. Even the way you use your arms and hands."

My God, I thought, that's not me gesturing, it's Dad—like a Stokowski conducting an orchestra of a hundred women.

"You're a gentle kind of person, on the whole—good intentions, but strictly inward. Sweet but guarded—uptight. I think your aura would be light blue. That's far from my personal needs. I have a character that calls for a partner with orange, red and purple, more of an extrovert and needing more action. Still, I was curious about you. I always was told that Jewish men were extraconsiderate with girls."

"I wouldn't be too sure of that. It sounds to me as if no one man could meet all the qualifications."

"No . . . not unless he was a case of multiple personality," said Treckie.

"That's because erotic practices have become diversified. Sex used to be like single-crop farming, like cotton or wheat; now people raise all kinds of things. As to Jews, for centuries they combined antiquity with modernity. You could almost see the archaic man in a contemporary Jew. But America has broken all that down."

"You've just given a perfect demonstration of what makes you hard to be with—drop you a hint and you carry it all over the place. It makes a woman feel she's slow-witted."

Yes. Nodding agreement. Nobody values another fellow's thoughts. He's apt to set great store by them. He ought, however, to acknowledge that really nobody wants to hear them. The oscillations of consciousness aren't thinking anyway, but mostly personal nervousness. It was different with Uncle. He had a subject. He really *knew* the vegetable kingdom. He practiced the scrutiny of secret things—total absorption in their hidden design. No doubt there were women who might have loved him for this alone. But where were they? I made no brief for myself. I think I deserve what I got. But Benn had merit. He should never have been somebody else's ticket to a desirable existence.

"Now, in your new life, how is Nancy going to fit into that?" I said.

"Kids like movement, and there's a lot to learn around flea markets. They attract scads of characters. Haggling is good training. Besides, so much stolen goods turns up that you have to be extra alert. One thing about you—you never had to apply your high intelligence to the lowdown specifics. If Nancy inherited some of your brain power, she may put it to better use."

"You wouldn't be receiving stolen goods, would you?"

"The FBI isn't out for waders, snowshoes, braces, bits, steak knives or old Latin dictionaries, to name a few of the objects that turn up."

"What does concern me more," I said, "is that she'd be living half the time in a camper with you and her stepfather. If we assume that your husband has a heavy purple aura, it mightn't be so wholesome for her. I could take the kid for part of every year."

"To live in a dormitory with you and listen to weirdo conversations?"

"I'm leaving the dormitory," I said. "There's an apartment available."

"Is that so? That *would* be a switch."

"My financial contribution would have to come down steeply."

Treckie was giving this serious consideration. She perfectly understood that scenes of intimacy in a camper, with Nancy watching from an upper bunk, posed certain problems. Tactfully, I made no reference to marijuana or the harder drugs.

"If you had her, you'd need some help from a woman," said Treckie.

"Naturally I would. I have somebody in mind. And one advantage for you, in this arrangement, is that you'd have a chance to explore your new relationship more freely."

And this was how Treckie and I concluded the matter. She said, "There'll be a closing on the Puget Sound house in about two weeks. We'll fix the place up—that'll take about a month. Then you could have Nancy on a trial basis."

"I'm glad you see it that way."

"You've got lots of warmth which seems to go begging in the wrong places. You could do worse than to put it on your own daughter. No reason why she should be emotionally handicapped."

"No disagreement there."

"I'm sorry you won't be meeting Ronald just yet."

I felt the battle that hadn't happened in the parts of my face that would have been punched—a kind of stinging. It seems that I had wanted to have a fight with him, and almost wished that I had found him at home. The one time when I was without a trace of fear.

"You did total the bathroom," said Treckie. "That's all right. As I figure, you had one tantrum coming to you."

There were highlights on her cheeks. She lifted her face as she spoke. An allowance of justice was made.

"You don't hold it against me?"

"A minor inconvenience," she said.

It might have been worse. It was to be the mutual quitclaim. What Uncle would sometimes call a Mexican standoff.

This was because she didn't really care a damn about me. For her, I didn't even exist.

That was nothing to get excited about, as it was one of the commoner human experiences—neither to give a damn nor be given a damn about. In practice it was accepted as a matter of course, though at heart nobody quite came to terms with it. There was a remote emotional holdover, in our case founded on the fact that we were the parents of a child. The meaning of the child lay somewhere between zoology, biochemistry and the Eternal Great Humanity Divine. But at the moment these were only notions which glanced off; I made no attempt to follow them up. I stopped in the parlor and kissed Nancy a third time. Under my chin she kept looking at the cartoon, taking no notice of me. Poor little kid, what was there for her to grow into? Maybe Dita would do something for her. Dita had enough of the romantic womanly about her to develop some kindness even towards Treckie's daughter.

After I had helped to zip the kid into her snowsuit, I set out for the Meany Hotel, where I had stayed overnight on my return flight from Japan.

Neither fists nor kisses for me.

I had tracked Uncle to the spa in Miami Beach and left several messages for him. At about 9 P.M. Pacific time, the telephone rang. Uncle's first words were faltering, so I knew at once that he had bad news. Well, one of us, then, had to be hard—firm, anyway. At a time like this, we couldn't have such faltering at both ends of the line. I was the more recently toughened through having perceived, that morning, that for Treckie I didn't even exist. So I said, "Well, Uncle, let's have it."

"It's the worst," he said, his voice rising, lamentable.

"The old man died?"

"Yes," he said. He wept for a while and I waited. There was nothing else to be done.

"Poor old guy," I said. Which old guy I had in mind was not exactly clear, even to me. "Okay, Benn. This is a difficult emotional moment. But he didn't really care for you, and I don't see why you're broken up over that old crook."

He raised his voice, probably to make himself heard over his own tears. "The last time we saw him he was in a bad way, but he was still a man, a person. Now he's just a packet of ashes, inside a black box."

"When did he die?"

"Twenty-four hours before I got here. It was the aorta that went. Fishl told me that."

"Fishl was already there?" I said. "He must have got lucky as a standby at the airport. The man was determined to make up with his father. Wishing the impossible as so many of us do. And the other Vilitzer sons?"

"They've all been sullen. When I got out of the cab, I didn't have any intimations. I wonder if the plant ambience here had anything to do with it." He now spoke more steadily. "That sometimes happens when you come from a winter climate to the lush subtropics. I never saw Harold's house before. It's a big, elaborate Spanish-style white building on an inlet, a cabin cruiser right in front. Palms, orange trees. There's a handsome fine *Quercus virginiana*—one of the finest live oaks ever. The Vilitzers' door was open, as it usually is in a house of mourning, I suppose, and people were going in. Was he giving a party? Condolence calls didn't cross my mind just yet. But it was too early in the day for a party. I still had no idea. Anyway, I went in too. Some of the people had a familiar look. They were retired officials from back home—like judges, City Hall types. I'd seen them in the papers, one time or another; either they were running for office or being indicted. Nobody I actually knew, only thought I knew, as you know the President though you never really laid eyes on him. Most of these fellows and their wives were elderly. They made me think of birds getting ready for a migration, when they gather late in summer. You've probably seen them flocking."

"But these, if I follow you, are tired old birds, and they're ready to migrate from their bodies."

"You've got it," said Uncle. "The empty skies over the water are waiting. But your eyes would never see it happening."

"Waftage," I said to myself.

"I went to the back and entered by the kitchen, where there were bottles, ice and glasses. I wasn't about to drink anything strong at that time of day, but I did need water to take my pills, and there was a black woman there who looked like Uncle's housekeeper—fat woman in a white outfit, keeping her opinions to herself. The pills for tachycardia—quinidine gluconate—if I don't break them in four, they stick in my throat, and these days I have a swallowing problem. The reflexes just aren't what they should be. . . . I'm getting on with it; I always have to say how things happened, Kenneth. I already suspected that Uncle Harold was dead. I asked the housekeeper about it and told her I was the only nephew, the one from up North."

All Benn got from the black lady was a silent inspection. Not everybody felt about relationships as Uncle did. People didn't care to hear about *his* relationships. Her reaction was not so favorable. When it came to family claims, she wasn't very different from Vilitzer himself. She was not about to take Benn in her arms and hold him to her bosom. When at last Uncle got her to open her closed mouth, she told him that Vilitzer had died within minutes of getting back. "Just made it up the porch steps and into the kitchen."

So Uncle was standing in the room where Vilitzer had died, and perhaps on the very spot. And where was Uncle Harold now? Had they taken him to the funeral parlor? Yes, there and back. He was in the living room. So it was a home funeral? She answered him that at two o'clock there would be a service. She gave him no directions to the living room, and the house was so large that you needed them. She turned away and went about her business. The less she had to do with outside people the better.

This waterside house was handsome and expensively furnished, obviously the home of a multimillionaire. Uncle (grieving Uncle, talking a blue streak, apparently relieving the soreness of his heart) gave me to understand that in this climate the sumptuous carpets and European antiques would have rotted without the dehumidifier—you could hear the machinery in operation, distantly. There were objects here which Matilda would have given her eyeteeth to have had in the Roanoke (it was Benn who said "eyeteeth," and I take leave to remind you that his feelings about her teeth did not leave him even now). These handsome breakfronts and fine chairs would have done credit to her Venetian-palace apartment. She would have said—so Benn observed—that *we* had paid for these objects with Electronic Tower dollars. A top decorator must have been brought in, maybe from Palm Beach. But where was Uncle Harold laid out? Benn (with his mourning heart) had worked his way through all of the ground floor and seen no coffin. So in the front hall, where there was a gorgeous skylight with colors of the spectrum similar to those in the glass of the state office building where we had had our meeting, he asked a drink server in a white coat (he and the woman in the kitchen were the live-in couple) where Mr. Vilitzer was laid out. The man said, "Right here, in this room." Benn had been looking for a casket on trestles, and for that the man gave him a high queer stare, as if he were dealing with a poorly functioning intelligence, and silently indicated where Benn should have been looking. Just inside the wide plantation-style door, there was a beautiful old umbrella-stand hatrack. It must have been Austrian, a bronze-antlered object. Hats and umbrellas had been removed from it, and on a red marble or porphyry shelf there was a box.

"A black box, Kenneth, no bigger than my binocular case."

"The ashes?"

"In there, he was," Uncle said. "I had been preparing to have my last look at him on this earth."

This surprise came up from the ground, as it were, and caught Uncle Benn around the knees, so that he had to sit down. The legs went out on him. The black man brought him a chair and offered him a shot of whiskey when he learned that Benn was the scientist nephew—close kin. Those were tough-minded people in this household. Sizing up Harold daily, gauging his life chances. Probably his death had long been expected.

Speaking to Benn of his reaction, I said, "You *can* love a man without loving what he did to you."

Uncle thanked me for the interpretation. But this was no time to indulge my commenting habit.

"What was the hurry to cremate him?" I said.

"Harold arranged all that himself. His order was immediate cremation, Fishl told me. The minute the death certificate was signed. Before sundown it was done, and he was brought back and set on the shelf. It turns out that he couldn't bear the very idea of a burial. Couldn't stand to be underground. He was revolted by it."

"There are some who can't wait to get rid of themselves. Whereas others can't bear to let anybody go."

"There you've put your finger on it," said Uncle. "It's true I couldn't bear to surrender Uncle Harold. It's also the way with my memory. Once my memory has fastened on to some phenomenon it grips it tight. There's a kind of obstinacy in it, which is an advantage in morphology but raises hell with your affections. It's especially resistant in a case of death. Well, I was sitting in this oval-backed chair in front of the black container when Fishl found me. Fishl and I were the only emotional mourners. You can't imagine how red he was in the eyes. He stared at me, and behaved as if I had shortened his father's life. I begin to think Fishl never was a stable person in any respect. It wasn't only his schemes. Sure, marginal business enterprises sometimes border on psychopathology. You can't help but wonder whether the real purpose of some enterprises is not to make money but to borrow plausibility from money as a cover for your crazy thoughts."

"Never mind that, Uncle Benn. What was he saying?"

"Well, first of all, we shouldn't have had it out with Harold. *He*, Fishl himself, understood him best and we ought to have given him time. It might have taken a little longer, but it would have spared Harold to us a while yet. What was the damned hurry? *I* let myself be pushed by the Layamons. Fishl, by the way, went into a long rant against Doctor. He thinks there's a special diabolical side to doctors and hospitals, and that there's nothing dirtier and more cynical than a big-city hospital or the operators like Doctor who take root there. He made a surprising statement which stayed with me, upset as I was. He said that places where human feelings come out, through suffering, attract a nihilistic personnel who see an opportunity there to give play to their nihilistic motives. He said he wouldn't be surprised if patients whose cases were botched were 'allowed' to die in order to avoid malpractice suits."

"How does that strike you?" I said.

"I'm not in a state to discuss subjects like these. Fishl called me a sex maniac."

"He didn't."

"Yes. Where does he get off, talking like that? I wonder what hang-ups *he* has about sex. Still, I was shocked by the amount of information he had about women in my life. When you get an outside view of your behavior, it looks horrible. Is it you that's horrible, or the viewers? Your torment is left out. In front of his father's mortal remains, he let me have it, that I was too old to be cunt-struck and had to try twice as hard as a man half my age. That an experienced beauty like Matilda had all my readings, down to a micromillimeter. He said I might be a leader in my science, but in the sack I was a dirty old man. And what was *she* putting down that enchanted me? His guess was that she was a con artist, ninety-nine percent gestures and come-on. But I was the weaker party, and I had robbed Uncle Harold of two or three golden years. And besides, I had actually lifted a hand against the old man."

"Why, the fellow is seriously disturbed. This is clinical. Off the wall. You can attribute just so much of it to the shock of Harold's death. I didn't think Fishl's character was so fragile. It was the old man who was trying to hit *you*. For God's sake, don't take Fishl seriously."

"I didn't, altogether. But in front of the box of ashes, it was a real zinger. He even quoted me Hamlet: 'You cannot call it love, for at your age/The heyday in the blood is tame . . .'"

"Damn unfair of him—even sneaky, Uncle Benn. He didn't acknowledge your grief. He was hogging it all. It now strikes me as a weird moment too. Only the two of you in that houseful of people were affected by Harold's death, and you two had to fight."

"I had no heart for fighting."

"I'll buy that. But your weakness is to consider any and all charges against you. That's the child side of you. With Fishl, a nut case, you should discount the damaging things he said—the sex attack."

"That's sound advice, but does it apply? You speak of my child side, as if I should still be working on my development. But no *Romeo and Juliet* has ever been written for lovers sixty years old. I have to admit that there's been a certain element of priming the pump in my behavior. Making a special effort. Unwillingness to accept the stages of life as people did in antiquity or the Middle Ages. (Though I don't trust historians altogether, either—their game is sometimes to intimidate their contemporaries.) But there is something buried under my extra tenacity about love. Not everybody has the gift for it. In that case we should sign off."

"It's because of your energy level, Uncle. You can't be productive at lower energy levels. Besides, most of the religious writers say that there is no old age of the soul."

"Episodes from past experience come back to me, Kenneth. I remember Della Bedell at the door, crying, 'What am I supposed to do with my sexuality?' Her time to love was already thirty years behind her. Our one sex act, in that case, was more like a memorial service."

I said, "Bear one thing in mind, Uncle—the insane have an extra talent for getting at you. But *you* they know nothing about. You're not what they take you for. You're not a regular instance of anything. It's scandalous how they abuse you. For instance, the Layamons, having no conception of what you're all about . . ."

"Dr. Layamon is crazy like the apparatus at Cape Canaveral for tracking objects in space. Besides, whatever I may have been, I don't seem to be *it* anymore."

"Don't you believe it, Benn. You've had a slip—a *glitch*, as astronomers say."

"You mean well, and I thank you for that. Everybody is entitled to a mistake. There is no perfect gift. But when you go against your deeper instinct you set off a train of cause and effect spreading in all directions. I drew on that damned azalea for weeks and got an illusion of feedback from it. Now everything has been adversely affected, so that I can't even believe myself when I say I did nothing to shorten Vilitzer's life."

I understood what he was talking about. At the center of his cause-and-effect network were Matilda's shoulders. His own prophetic soul had sent him a most special message. Avoid those wide shoulders. Next her breasts seemed too far apart, the eyeteeth boded no good. The prophetic soul, offended, led him to distort her beauty, so that her very loveliness repelled him. The case was built that there was a demiurge hidden just under the woman's skin—that while she was sleeping under her down-and-silk comforter, lying there like a sheaf of ferns (remember also the marvelous profile), there were exhalations of duplicity from that delicate, straight nose.

I said to Benn, "You mustn't let Fishl bamboozle you. You didn't deprive Vilitzer of anything. He was already outward bound on the fast track. Forget the Golden Age stuff; I'm sure Vilitzer loathed the very thought of it. When I restrained him his bones felt porous, like empty plastic-bubble stuff, like packing material. That's not how gold feels."

"Fishl said that I helped to destroy Uncle. I lined up with his enemies."

"Enemies? He left the enemies high and dry. He finessed them but good. He took all the tricks with the death trump. No Governor Stewart, no Amador Chetnik, no grand juries."

"I *said* something like that. But according to Fishl, that didn't excuse me. The big win is to cheat death. Hold it at bay. And if I didn't mean harm to Harold, I was a jinx nevertheless. Not even a jinx but a person from a different planet who had no business to meddle with normal human transactions."

The last, I instantly recognized, was a telling charge, for it was when Uncle had been installed as a member of the Layamon family, dressed in tailor-made tweeds; that plant observatory, his head, fixed up by a hairstylist; surrounded by illuminated cabinets of Royal Doulton or Rosenthal china—it was then that he felt like a spoiler, like a willful misrepresenter, like the odd man, the impostor, passing for a son-in-law, or a husband. Somehow he was persuaded that he had to make amends to the Layamons for this, as though he had placed *them* in a false position.

"Uncle," I said, "you listen to what I'm saying. What do you mean—normal transactions! If the planet is fucked up, *they're* the type that did it. People of that kind are nothing but instrumental. They are what the prevailing aim uses to shape its bad ends. They have no genuine initiatives; they're just utensils. Whereas a man like *you* . . ."

But he didn't want me to describe him in high terms. Thank you, no. He said, "Well, the service was starting, and Fishl and I were still having it out—arguing. Then he was sent for, to sit with the immediate family in the front row. I was in the back, listening to the Reform rabbi. He translated all the prayers into House of Lords English. I haven't been inside a synagogue of any kind in twenty-five years. But your grandfather *was* a Hebrew teacher, Kenneth—he never got used to your name, he thought it was a mistake for Kinnereth—therefore I didn't need translations. I never forgot anything. But when the rabbi began to chant the *El Malai Rachamim* at the conclusion, I lost control and started to sob, thinking whether the God of Mercy would ever receive the likes of Harold's soul. Or mine, for that matter. The Negro houseman came and took me by the elbow. He steered me out of Uncle Harold's villa and turned me loose in Bay Harbor Island to find my own way back to the spa."

"Christ, Uncle! All you need is a major bereavement like this! You never wanted to go to Brazil, but if I were in your shoes I'd be looking forward to it as a place to recover from all these shocks."

"That did cross my thoughts."

"Very different down there."

"Of course," he said, as if something else was on his mind. "It would be different in the next continent."

"And you're meeting Matilda at the airport tomorrow morning?"

"Later. Her plane lands at three P.M. and the flight to Brazil is two hours after. Plenty of time to get to the international terminal and make the connection."

"I hope you'll be able to unwind in Rio."

This was a terrible and false thing to say. Here was a man who had lost the privilege of vision, fallen into the opposite and brutal prevailing outlook, and I was telling him to relax in a city of Latin pleasures. He gave me a pass on this instead of getting sore. He seemed to understand that I was far away, disarmed, unable to offer support—repeating useless buzzwords: "unwind" and, even worse, "I hope." He was beyond hoping, certainly.

"What's the strange area code you gave me?" he said.

"I'm in Seattle."

"So that's where you've gone. You didn't want to disturb me. Having troubles of your own—getting your lumps from Treckie?"

"I'm flying home at five in the morning. Promise that you'll call me from Brazil. I don't even know where you can be reached down there, and you'll be gone for months."

"Of course. I'll do better than that—I'll telephone before taking off. What's your schedule tomorrow?"

"I give my Rozanov seminar—the Russian Sexual Mystics course. It ends at two. I can wait for your call at the dormitory."

"Better still, wait at my apartment. Just in case I've forgotten some item I may need. Besides, it'll be convenient to reverse charges, since I'll be calling on a public phone. And if Matilda gets in touch with you tomorrow, don't tell her anything. Nothing at all."

"I don't see how she'd find the time to call, or why she'd want to talk to me as she sets out for Brazil. I'd never discuss you with her anyway."

"About Vilitzer," said Uncle. "I prefer to break the news to her myself."

"Won't there be an item about him in the papers?"

"Not yet. The family, for some complicated business tactical reason, haven't announced the death. Dennis Vilitzer told me that."

"But reporters routinely check reports the doctors have to file. I mean, the death certificate."

"Ah, well, Dennis said that's been covered too. They've put out a release about a heart attack."

"What can they be up to? Fiddling funds around, monkeying with deposits, I suppose."

"So the papers will only announce that he's had a coronary."

"Enough said, Uncle Benn."

The early wake-up call was hardly necessary, since I slept very little. Repeated hot showers did not soften the knotted muscles of my neck, they only irritated the skin of my back and contributed to my insomnia. However, I sipped brandy from a silver flask given me by my father as a going-away present and I was alert, if not calmly wakeful. Beauty rest can't always be had in this era, described by an intelligent lady in a magazine as "post-human." Therefore crisis nights should be faced with maximum composure. You can't be worrying about haggard looks and rings under the eyes. You have to think, when so many supports and stabilities are removing themselves from you, about the possible advantages of removing yourself from *them*—the human being, preserving himself humanly, may find a channel which brings him to liberty. His reduced weight may defy the magnetic attraction of anarchy and allow him to float independently. Maybe I could educate my small daughter in this independence. Possibly I could transmit the perfected insight—*when* I perfected it—to Uncle Benn too. After all, when I came over from Paris to be with Uncle, I had already reduced the number of my significant relationships to two. For two, the ideal is to become one. That's what love is supposed to be about. Trying to transpose his magical powers from botany to love, my uncle had experimented (ignorantly, without illumination) with this fusion of two into one. I must remember to tell Uncle that. "It was an experiment, Uncle. You just didn't set it up right." I turned on the bedside lamp and made notes on the memo pad with the chained ballpoint. "It can't be done with fabricated persons," I wrote on Hotel Meany stationery. "Involved with fabricated persons, you can never preserve your magic, should you have any." Magic! Yes! Uncle certainly had that. If he hadn't had it, what was he suffering from this very day? "He gambled. He lost. What can he salvage now, or retrieve?"

I put out the light and went back to sipping from the flask in the dark. My father wouldn't have approved of the second-rate stuff I was drinking from his first-rate gift. But it was nevertheless helping me to put things together. I went back over my ground. Benn had had the privilege of vision. Made a daring—no, a foolhardy—experiment. Fell into the opposite, degraded view. Previously he could fly away and botanize (to some extent a pretext) in Indian forests, Chinese mountains, at the sources of the Nile. But now the faraway, the unvisited portions of the planet were nothing but the Third World, squalid, misgoverned by the kleptocrat military, scenes of famine, filth, AIDS, mass murder. And look—even Vilitzer in death had reduced himself by cremation to the ninety cents' worth of chemicals we so often hear mentioned. There's the brutal view for you—though I die leaving millions, my elements aren't even worth a buck.

The secret of our being still asks to be unfolded. Only now we understand that worrying at it and ragging it is no use.

The first step is to stop these oscillations of consciousness that are keeping me awake. Only, before you command the oscillations to stop, before you check out, you must maneuver yourself into a position in which metaphysical aid can approach.

With the prevailing winds behind us, we made the flight home in record time. I got back with an hour to spare before class and ate some Wisconsin Brie and saltines and then spent two hours at the seminar table explaining what I myself didn't understand about the sexual theories of that scoundrelly (yet somehow attractive) Rozanov—this Christian mystic who had envied the Jews their fertility cult (as he saw it) and believed their ritual bath to be a source of sexual potency. The kids wrote it all down. What, if anything, they make of it remains to be seen.

Afterwards I bought myself a delicatessen dinner and went to Uncle's apartment with my packages to wait for his call. I diverted myself with the journals and reprints on his coffee table—botanical stuff which didn't signify much to a Russian scholar. It was enough for me that it had engaged *his* attention. Most of the material had to do with lichens, and looking up technical terms would have been a bother. So I browsed instead through Aunt Lena's books, still kept in a separate bookcase—all those volumes of Balzac and Swedenborg and E.T.A. Hoffmann. In one of the Hoffmann volumes was a bookmark, undisturbed since she had left it there, and I opened it at that place and read: "Ludwig jumped up and, sighing deeply, took his friend's hand and pressed it to his bosom: 'Oh, Ferdinand, dearest, beloved friend!' he exclaimed, 'what will become of the arts in these rough, stormy times? Will they not wither like delicate plants that in vain turn their tender heads towards the dark clouds behind which the sun disappeared? . . . The children of Nature wallowed in lazy idleness, and the most beautiful gifts she offered them they trampled under foot in stupid wantonness. . . ." Well, I took this as a communication from my dead aunt. I wouldn't have admitted that to a police examiner, or in a sworn deposition, but I confess it freely to anybody who has taken the trouble to read my narrative. And affirm that I heard it in Lena's own voice.

I chatted awhile on the phone with Dita and told her that Treckie had decided to let me have Nancy for part of the year. "Starting out in marriage, she wants the kid out of her hair," I said.

"Sounds like a sensible interpretation. Be nice, having a kid around." Dita was offering assistance. I was not about to refuse it. A dear lady! "Are you free for dinner? Shall we go to a restaurant?" I said. "I bought delicatessen corned beef and pickles. I can't name a time because I'm waiting for an important call from my uncle. Any minute now. And I think I should hang up. He's just leaving for Brazil, you see."

But the phone remained silent far beyond the anticipated hour. I was becoming fretful by six o'clock, and I turned the bell to loud so that I would hear it if I was in the bathroom with the water running. The time in Miami was seven. Probably the flight had been delayed. I tried to guess what Benn and Matilda might be saying to each other in the Brazilian Airlines waiting room. Why would he want to withhold the news of Vilitzer's death? What was he trying to put over on her? When she and Dr. Layamon learned that Harold was gone, was there a Plan B they might put into effect? Sue the estate? On what evidence? Why should Amador Chetnik now testify that he had been suborned—or, if that wasn't the right word, had committed an impropriety? (What an exceptional term for such a common occurrence.) I wondered what comfort Uncle might be able to get from Matilda. Nothing could help short of recovering the powers he had lost. I thought, Brazil will be full of azaleas. How will he ever be able to face them?

It was just then that the phone rang.

I said, "Uncle! What's happened? The flight delayed?"

"Oh, no," he said, sounding (not vocally but mentally) distant.

"Will you tell me, please, what's happening down there? And why you didn't want Matilda to know that Vilitzer was dead?"

"It was to convince her that I couldn't leave Miami yet. Simple enough," said Uncle Benn. "Harold was still alive—feeble but conscious. That's what I said. Having a change of heart, I told her. Still a dim chance for us. In any case, I couldn't go away while my mother's brother was dying."

"Don't tell me she bought that. I'd never have thought it!"

"Yes, and I made sure that her luggage was checked through to Rio. As I told her mine was."

"Yours isn't?"

"You saw me carrying it with me."

"So you urged her to go on? She's in the air bound for Brazil?"

"I guess she's due in Rio tomorrow morning."

"Didn't she ask you for your claim checks, to pick up your bags?"

"I prepared an envelope with two slips of blank cardboard and we put that in with her own checks and ticket."

"Well, I can't imagine this," I said.

"The simple fact is—and it's the basic reason for this—that I couldn't face Brazil. Lecturing around the country in backwoods colleges. In return for which Matilda was still trying to arrange a diplomatic privilege so she could ship purchases for the furnishing of the Roanoke, duty-free."

"Knocking around that huge country would have drained whatever is left of your strength."

"Couldn't have done it, Kenneth. I would have died of it. You'll understand readily. You're the nearest thing to a son . . . less my nephew than my own child."

"Then are you coming back here?"

"At this moment I'm in another part of the airport and I've just bought a ticket for a different destination."

"Still another wrinkle? Not going home?"

"Matilda was reluctant to fly without me. Wanted to stay. Told me it was insane to hang around Vilitzer, nothing to be gotten out of it—never. Just my fetishism about family emotions. But I said that if I left I would feel the stain of it for the rest of my life. A spot I could never scrub away. God forgive me, I even told her that Fishl believed Uncle Harold might be willing to sign a last-minute codicil."

"I'd never have guessed there was so much deception in you," I said.

"Well, they all worked so hard to turn me around that I did turn around. At last I entered into it also. You'd better believe that I took counsel with myself and schemed this out. A pretty poor achievement, too. This stuff of theirs is zero-rudimentary. This once I've done it, and never again. But let me tell you what I've arranged. By the time she's landing in Brazil I should be well on my way to the North Pole. You see, they've assembled an international team of scientists for the purpose of special researches. And I signed on three days ago, to check out lichens from both poles, a comparative study, and work out certain morphological puzzles. Not acute puzzles. Matters of rather special interest. We're going to be based in northern Scandinavia, at the edge of Finland, actually. And beyond."

"With two or three hours of daylight? I can't see it at all for you."

"That has to be left to me," said Uncle. "And nothing but night and ice will help me now. Night so that I can't see myself. Ice as a corrective. Ice for the rigor. And also because there'll be no plants to see, except the lichens. Because if there's no rapport, if the rapport is dead, I'm better off in plant-free surroundings. This has been carefully felt through. Rather than thought out. It's a survival measure. I'm applying global masses of ice and hyperborean darkness. Thank God jet propulsion makes the remedy available, otherwise I'd have to go and drown myself right here, off Miami Beach."

"In that case, Uncle, even if mystified, I give your expedition my blessing."

"Well, then, I'm off within the hour. I've left an envelope for you with more complete information. You'll find it in the top left-hand drawer of my desk. I'm not absolutely certain of my Finnish mailing address. Which of course . . ."

"I won't give to Matilda. How long will you be gone?"

"I can't predict the time. As I feel now, it won't be soon. Maybe Matilda will go for an annulment, which shouldn't be hard to get, but that's a legal matter, and I'm no good at such things. I want nothing more to do with them, either."

"Would you like me to get you a lawyer to represent . . . if necessary?"

"It can never be necessary."

"You won't defend yourself?"

"Kenneth! What is there to defend! Was it my sister, or was it you, who said that I was a phoenix who runs with arsonists? Well, let's see what can be done, whether I can rise from these ashes. Right now it's about as likely as restoring Uncle Vilitzer from those cinders they sent home from the funeral parlor. Now I have to hang up. If I can pull myself together I'll send you a letter; I expect to be very busy the first few months. The Soviet Academy of Sciences is supposed to let us know whether they'll join the venture. You never can get a straight answer from those people."

"Did you tell me any more in the note you left?" I said, trying to keep him on the line.

"Just the fundamental, minimum information. I didn't have it in me to elaborate. Well, goodbye, kid. It's only you I'll miss."

The envelope contained, neatly printed in his scientific hand, the unfamiliar name of the research group and the addresses of a Finnish prof in Helsinki (home and office), plus the box number of an incomprehensible location in reindeer country, far out on the tundra. Probably near Novaya Zemlya. Even that was not remote enough.